SWORN
A WORLD WAR II NOVEL
ENEMY

SWORN

A WORLD WAR II NOVEL

ENEMY

A.L. Sowards

Covenant Communications, Inc.

Cover image: *WWII Beach Invasion* © Todd Headington. Courtesy iStockphoto.com.

Cover design copyright © 2013 by Covenant Communications, Inc.

Maps copyright © 2013 by Briana Shawcroft

Published by Covenant Communications, Inc.
American Fork, Utah

Printed in the United States of America
First Printing: April 2013

19 18 17 16 15 14 13   10 9 8 7 6 5 4 3 2 1

ISBN 978-1-62108-359-7

For Melanie
A wonderful sister, a smart test reader, a loyal fan, and a dear friend.

I've always wanted to write the type of books you love to read. When you picked out the Cambridge Five and Ultra clues, I knew this book had to be for you.

ACKNOWLEDGMENTS

I'M INDEBTED TO MANY PEOPLE for their assistance with this book. First, thanks goes to my wonderful test readers: Melanie, Laurie, and Teresa. And I am grateful to the other writers who looked over part or all of my manuscript: Linda White, Terri Ferran, Stephanie Fowers, Daron Fraley, Tod Ferran, and Marianna Richardson. Their constructive criticism and encouragement helped make this book better.

Thanks goes to Lela Machado for giving me access to an outstanding research library. Most of the books were informative and helpful, and I still laugh about that propaganda book written by Romanian Communists.

I also owe thanks to Briana Shawcroft for her maps. She did an excellent job helping me figure out what I wanted and then creating it.

The team at Covenant, especially my editor, Sam, also deserves a big thanks for all of their hard work on this and my previous book. I'm grateful to have such a talented group involved with my projects.

I am thankful for my husband and his patience and support. And for my young daughters, who usually napped at the same time so I could work while they slept.

I'd also like to express appreciation to all those readers who purchased *Espionage* and to those who shared their enthusiasm for it with others. Without their support, this book wouldn't have been accepted for publication. And I'm grateful for my first-time readers and their willingness to give my writing a chance.

Useful Terms

FFI—Forces Françaises de l'Interior. French Resistance group

Gefreiter—Soldier in the German Army, rank similar to a private in the US Army

Hauptmann—Officer in the German Army, rank similar to a captain in the US Army

Hauptsturmführer—Officer in the Gestapo, rank similar to a captain in the US Army

Korvettenkapitän—Officer in the German Navy, rank similar to a lieutenant commander in the US Navy

Kriegsmarine—German Navy

Luftwaffe—German Air Force

Maquis—French Resistance group

MI6—British Secret Intelligence Service, division responsible for foreign intelligence

Milice—Collaborationist French police during WWII

NKVD—Soviet secret police from 1934 to 1953, responsible for foreign and domestic espionage

Obersturmführer—Officer in the Gestapo, rank similar to a first lieutenant in the US Army

OSS—Office of Strategic Services. US intelligence and sabotage agency that operated from June 1942 to January 1946

Politruk—Junior political officer in the Soviet Red Army (Latinized form)

Rottenführer—Gestapo squad leader

SOE—Special Operations Executive. British intelligence and sabotage agency that operated from July 1940 to January 1946

Standartenführer—Officer in the Gestapo, rank similar to a colonel in the US Army

Sturmmann—Stormtrooper in the Gestapo

Unterfeldwebel—Junior-level noncommissioned officer in the German Army; squad leader

Wehrmacht—German Army

Major Baker's Team

Major Wesley Baker: British, MI6/SOE, special-ops veteran

Locotenent Constantin Condreanu: Romanian, SOE

Lieutenant Peter Eddy: American, OSS, combat and special-ops veteran

Sergeant Charles Logan: Irish, SOE, special-ops veteran

Sergeant G. Moretti: American, OSS, paratrooper, combat veteran

Corporal James Nelson: British, SOE, linguistic specialist, special-ops veteran

Kapral Krzysztof Zielinski: Polish, SOE, paratrooper, communications specialist, special-ops veteran

Private Daniel Fisher: British, SOE, paratrooper, sniper, combat veteran

Private David Mitchell: Canadian, SOE, paratrooper, sniper, combat veteran

Private Oliver Quill: British/Australian, SOE, paratrooper, forgery specialist

Private Richard Holmes (Sherlock): British, SOE, paratrooper, medic, combat veteran

Henry Lucaciu (Luke): American, OSS, civilian, demolitions specialist

Tiberiu Ionescu: Romanian, SOE, civilian, demolitions specialist, special-ops veteran

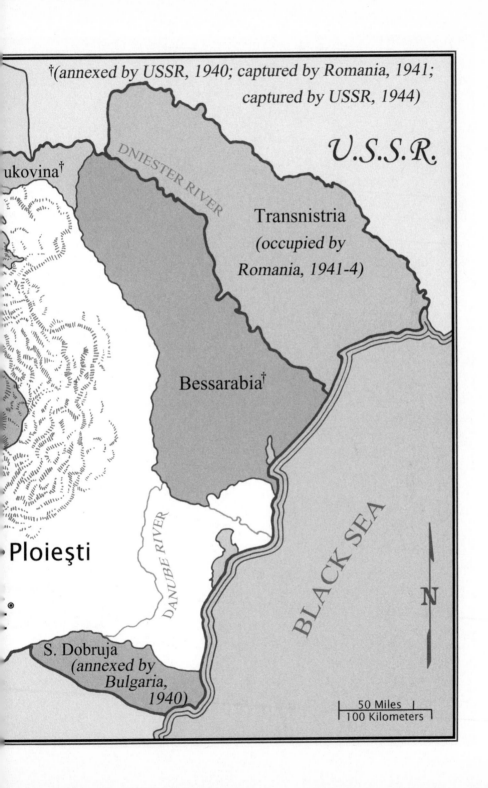

†*(annexed by USSR, 1940; captured by Romania, 1941;*
captured by USSR, 1944)

U.S.S.R.

ukovina†

DNIESTER RIVER

Transnistria
(occupied by
Romania, 1941-4)

Bessarabia†

Ploieşti

DANUBE RIVER

BLACK SEA

N

S. Dobruja
(annexed by
Bulgaria,
1940)

| 50 Miles |
| 100 Kilometers |

CHAPTER ONE

THE TRAP CLOSES

Friday, June 16, 1944
Near Basseneville, Normandy, France

GENEVIEVE WATCHED AS PETER POURED the last bucket of water into the trough. "You're going to spoil me," she said.

Even though it was dark, she knew he was smiling. She was glad she couldn't see it; she often had trouble breathing when she saw his smile and the way it lit up his eyes.

"I don't think you're in danger of being spoiled anytime soon. Not after I've dragged you halfway across France." He set the bucket on the ground and ran a hand through his thick brown hair. "To be honest, I've lost track of how far we've come."

"One hundred eighty kilometers by truck and cart from Calais to Rouen. One hundred kilometers on foot since then."

Peter nodded slowly. He was American and kept track of distances in miles. She guessed he was doing the conversions in his head. "I'd say the least I can do is get you a bath. I'd build you a fire, but that might attract too much attention."

Genevieve stared at the water and looked forward to being clean again. They'd been traveling on foot for a week, and she'd never felt so dusty, grimy, and sweaty. She'd complained about being dirty when the two of them arrived at the derelict barn a half hour ago, but she hadn't meant for Peter to wash the trough out and fill it for her. When she'd offered to help, he'd insisted on doing it himself.

"How are your blisters?" he asked.

"About the same."

"Hmm." Peter came over to where she was sitting and knelt down to look at her feet the best he could in the poor lighting. "Maybe it's time to steal another car."

Genevieve laughed. "The last time I was in a car with you, I barely made it out alive."

"Not because of my driving though, right?" Peter grinned at her again.

"No, not because of your driving."

Peter straightened. "I'm a completely safe driver when I'm not worried about getting shot or blown up. But stealing a car's probably a bad idea anyway. Some P-47 would see us driving along in a *Wehrmacht* jeep and shoot us to pieces. I guess we'll have to keep walking." Peter dug through a bag and handed her an old piece of bread. "Breakfast?"

Genevieve took the bread. "Aren't you going to eat?"

"I think I'll save it for a midpatrol snack."

"Peter, I haven't seen you eat your last two midpatrol snacks." Conversations like this were becoming a morning ritual. Peter always gave her a larger portion of the food they'd taken with them or scrounged along the way then put some of his back when he thought she wasn't looking. "You've walked just as far as I have—you need to eat something."

"But you've had a rough couple of weeks."

"So have you." She heard her voice crack as she remembered one recent event in particular. "And when your brother died, you didn't exactly take it easy."

Peter sat next to her and reached for her hand. "That was different. I wasn't there—just heard about it on the radio." Peter's older brother died at Pearl Harbor, and Peter had joined the US Army the next day. Genevieve's older brother had died eleven days ago. She'd witnessed his last breath, and then she'd left Calais with Peter, fleeing the Gestapo, trying to make it to the new front in Normandy. Peter ran his thumb over her fingers. "Besides, there aren't any recruiting stations around here. Not that they'd take you anyway."

"No, I doubt they're desperate enough to enlist skinny French girls."

"You could probably teach most new recruits a thing or two about making a bomb though." Peter reached for their bags. "Can I borrow your mirror?"

"Of course."

"Thanks. I'm going to backtrack to that creek we passed and try to get rid of this." He fingered his dark beard, scratching the skin underneath. "I wonder if the bruises will be gone when I get all the hair off."

Genevieve could pick out faded purple and yellow bruises all along Peter's arms, neck, and face. She was sure the bruises the Gestapo left on his cheeks and chin would be equally visible after he shaved.

Peter pulled out his razor, her mirror, and half of their soap, placing the items in his pocket. Then he reached for her Webley & Scott pistol and made sure it was still loaded. It had been her neighbor's weapon, brought to France as part of an SOE supply drop.

"I haven't emptied it, Peter."

She caught a hint of mischief on his face. "Good. A barn like this is bound to have a few rats in it somewhere. You can always shoot them if they start bothering you."

Genevieve shuddered as she looked around the old barn. She hated rodents, and the gaps between the barn's wooden boards were large enough to invite a small army of them to take up residence. The cracks in the wall were so wide she could make out the ruins of the home that had once stood nearby, likely destroyed at the beginning of the war. Her quick glance around the barn didn't reveal any animals, but she knew rodents weren't what Peter was really worried about. They were still in Nazi territory, and the Gestapo was tracking them.

Peter checked his pistol, a stolen German model, then slipped it back into its holster. He stood and opened the barn door. "See you at daybreak. Enjoy your bath."

"If I fall asleep before you get back, you *will* wake me at noon this time, won't you?" Since leaving Rouen, they'd traveled by night and slept during the day. While one slept, the other was on guard duty. Peter always gave her the first sleeping shift, and he never woke her at midday like he was supposed to. Yet he always made her promise to wake him the second the sun set so they could begin their nightly trek on time.

"Maybe."

That was Peter's way of saying he'd wake her if she was having a nightmare, which happened often enough—for both of them. It wasn't the answer she was looking for, but she was too tired to argue. Peter slid the barn door shut, leaving her alone with her bath. *I should have packed an alarm clock.* But even if she had, Peter would probably turn it off.

Three minutes into the bath, she caught herself singing an aria from *Carmen*. She stopped as soon as she realized what she was doing and chastised herself for being so careless. *Refugees fleeing the Gestapo are supposed to be invisible and silent.*

A smile replaced the song. Genevieve only sang when she was happy, and that morning, the singing had slipped out unconsciously, just as it had every day for the past week. Even though she was homeless and wanted by the Nazis, Genevieve was content. Being clean again was part of it, but she gave Peter most of the credit. It still surprised her, how he made her feel. She'd met him only a few weeks ago when he'd been assigned to work with her brother to investigate three suspicious intelligence sources for the Allies.

Peter hadn't been the first good-looking commando to work with Jacques, but he had been the first who'd offered to help with laundry.

Genevieve pulled herself out of the cold bathwater and used her blanket to dry her skin. When she was dressed, she strung a rope between several old posts and hung her blanket over it. Then she unpacked the extra clothing from their bags and washed it all in the bathwater. They planned to stay until nightfall, so the clothes would have time to dry. There was little soap, the water was cold, and the lack of light meant she couldn't see very well, but the promise of clean clothes was sufficient motivation for her to do what she could.

As she finished hanging Peter's spare pants, she caught herself singing again and stopped, shaking her head as if the motion might somehow get the tune out of her head. She heard someone outside and glanced through a hole in the east wall, assuming Peter was early. She expected to hear him call out to make sure she was dressed, but instead, she heard several pairs of footsteps.

Genevieve turned around as the barn door slid open. She felt her heart plummet and glanced at her pistol, still next to the trough. It was too far away.

"Bonjour, Mademoiselle Olivier; it's such a pleasure to see you again." The deep, menacing voice belonged to Standartenführer Tschirner, the Gestapo chief of Calais. He'd questioned her before, but she'd been using an alias then. She wasn't sure how he knew her real name but hoped it wasn't because he'd tortured her neighbors.

With Tschirner were four SS stormtroopers in shiny black boots and immaculate uniforms. One of them held a lantern, and in that light, Genevieve recognized two faces from her time in Gestapo prison, and from her nightmares. Sturmmann Weiss was tall and muscular, with suntanned skin and coarse blond hair. He stood at Tschirner's side with his arms folded and gave her an unpleasant grin. The second man, Sturmmann Siebert, was even larger. He walked to her side, towering over her petite frame, and grabbed her arm in a crushing grip.

Tschirner nodded his approval. "I must admit, mademoiselle, I am disappointed to find you all alone. Where is Lieutenant Eddy?"

Genevieve didn't answer. The standartenführer had a talent for scaring her tongue into immobility, but she was grateful for his question. If Tschirner was asking about Peter, it meant he and his men hadn't already found and killed him. Tschirner kicked over the two bags Genevieve and Peter were using and riffled through the contents. The bags held little—they were running out of food, and their extra clothes hung on the clothesline. Tschirner bent down, picked up the three framed pictures Genevieve had brought from home, and held them up to the light of the lantern. He spent only a second on her parents' wedding portrait and the family picture from almost nineteen years ago. But he studied the photograph of her brother and sister-in-law then showed it to Weiss.

Weiss nodded. "That's him."

"Where is this man?" Tschirner held the picture so Genevieve could see it, his finger pointing at the image of her brother.

Genevieve was still too frightened to speak. Tschirner glanced at her guard. "Sturmmann Siebert, I believe she needs her tongue loosened." Before the words registered, Genevieve found herself hurtling toward the wall. She put her hands up to shield her face just before she crashed into the weather-beaten wood boards and collapsed to the floor in pain. The graying boards were old, but they were still rough and hard. Her hands and arms stung where small splinters of wood pierced her skin. Her elbow, ribs, and hip throbbed from the impact.

Tschirner gazed down at her without emotion. She looked back at him, hoping the wet hair and bits of old hay sticking to her face obscured her fear. "Where is he?" he said, pointing again at the picture.

Her voice cracked as she answered—a combination of grief, pain, and fear. "He died."

"When?"

"June 5."

"What a shame. He didn't live to see the Allies make their pitiful invasion attempt," Tschirner said with a sneer. "Who is the woman with him?"

"His wife; she's also dead."

"When?"

"1941." The date was permanently engraved in Genevieve's mind, but she didn't think Tschirner needed to hear specifics.

"And these are your parents?" He pointed to the family picture. Genevieve nodded, feeling a new jolt of pain run through the left side of her body as she moved. That side had hit the wall the hardest. She held the bottom of her rib cage with her forearm to try to hold back the spread of pain. "And are they also dead, mademoiselle?"

"Yes." Her mother had died when she was three, her father when she was thirteen.

"Why, Mademoiselle Olivier, you appear to be completely alone in this world. How pathetic." Tschirner tossed all three pictures across the barn. The glass shattered, and Genevieve automatically moved to retrieve them. She moved only an inch before Siebert seized her arms and jerked her to her feet. She gasped in pain when the sudden movement triggered a new wave of physical agony.

Another SS guard handed a pile of papers to Tschirner. He leafed through them; they were the false identity papers Genevieve and Peter were carrying. "Mademoiselle Olivier, you are under arrest for traveling with forged papers and leaving Calais without permission. I could have you executed for such behavior." He stepped forward and studied her, his face within inches of her own. She was frightened, but she knew there were worse things than execution.

"I'll make a deal with you. Cooperate with me, and I'll have you assigned to a work camp instead of the gallows. Where is Lieutenant Eddy?" he asked.

"He left."

"Yes, but when will he return?" As Tschirner questioned her, he ran his fingers across her forehead, moving her hair so he could see her face better. She turned away, feeling suddenly nauseated as he touched her skin.

"He's not coming back." As she said it, part of her hoped it was true. Returning would mean capture, but for now, Peter was safe. Surely he'd see the lantern light through the cracks in the wall and escape. She would never see him again, but at least he would be free.

Tschirner laughed. His laughter reminded Genevieve of a sleet storm, icy and cold. "Don't lie to me, mademoiselle. I don't for one minute believe he has permanently abandoned you. Where did he go? To get more food? To make contact with the Resistance?"

"He's not coming back," she said again. "We split up, and we're to meet again later, in Basseneville."

Tschirner struck her with the back of his hand. Her cheek stung from the force behind it, and she again felt a burst of pain screaming up and down her body. "How many times will you make me repeat myself? No more lies, mademoiselle." Genevieve looked down, disappointed that he hadn't believed her. Through the cracks in the barn wall, she could see the top of the rising sun. She worried that the sunlight would hide the lantern's glow, Peter's only clue that something was wrong. He'd walk into a trap unless she quickly convinced Tschirner to leave and catch Peter somewhere else. "When is he coming back? Surely he is coming back, or you wouldn't have left wet clothes out to dry."

The clothes, of course. Genevieve changed her strategy. "Noon." She hoped Tschirner and his men would let their guard down if they thought they had until midday.

Tschirner struck the other side of her face with similar results. "I can see it in your eyes when you lie. When is he coming back?"

Genevieve knew she couldn't fool him, so she kept silent and braced herself for Tschirner's next strike. It never came. Instead, Siebert flung her into the wall so suddenly she didn't have time to move her feet or protect her head. She hit the wall face-first. Crumpled in a heap, miserable and dizzy, she looked up at Tschirner. *Will it hurt anything to tell the truth?* She gazed through the missing boards on the east side of the old barn and saw the sun through the cracks. "He's already late," she whispered.

* * *

Peter lay underneath a clump of dry bushes, watching the barn. He'd returned early from his bath but not in time to prevent the men from walking into the barn. He'd seen them encircle the dilapidated outbuilding, leaving one man hidden in the ruins of the nearby home and three others in the vegetation on the property's perimeter. In the dark, he'd been unable to identify any of the men, but he saw enough to suspect the Gestapo.

His initial plan had been to rush in and shoot as many men as possible before he was killed, but he quickly realized that following his instincts might prove his love for Genevieve but wouldn't secure her freedom. He watched the four sentries, keeping track of their positions, thinking he could take them out one by one. That would still leave five men inside, but Peter thought he might prevail if he had surprise on his side.

Peter headed for a Gestapo man hidden by a large tree to the north of the barn. As he drew closer, the sun broke over the horizon and he was forced to slow his pace. He'd just unsheathed his knife, yards away from the first sentry, when a dark figure stepped outside the barn, lifted his arm, and fired a single shot into the air. Peter paused, certain he'd heard a signal but unsure of what it meant. He waited a few tense moments then understood when he heard the sound of an automobile driving down the dirt road and recognized Tschirner's black Mercedes-Benz.

Three men left the barn, bringing Genevieve with them. Peter had counted five men entering the barn, and one had exited to signal the car, so he assumed they were leaving the last man as a guard. Three of them got into the car, forcing Genevieve in with them. A fourth began walking directly toward Peter. Peter wondered if he'd been spotted, but the sentry he'd been about to kill moved a few feet from the tree to meet the other Gestapo man.

"The American was supposed to be here at dawn. Tschirner wants us to wait another hour to see if he shows up then report back." Peter's limited German picked out the instructions. He watched the messenger move on to the next sentry, and he considered his options. He could wait and follow the five men Tschirner was leaving, or he could shoot the driver of the car and try to pick the remaining men off. There were plenty of shadows to hide in.

If he took the guard nearest him out with a knife and then shot the driver, he would have time to move before anyone closed in on the source of the single gunshot.

Peter was about to attempt the latter when he felt the distinct impression that he should wait. *Waiting* wasn't what he wanted to do, so he ignored the feeling and crept toward the guard. Then he felt it again. It had been a long time since he'd had an impression that strong.

Chapter Two

Nightmares

Genevieve's eyes fluttered open, and she tried to jerk into a sitting position. A handcuff binding her right wrist to a heavy four-poster bed halted her midway and jarred her sore body. She lay back down, trying to ignore the pain. Squeezing her eyes shut again, she attempted to clear the images from her head.

It was just a dream. But that wasn't entirely true. It had been a dream but also a collection of memories: Peter barely alive, covered in his own blood on the floor of a cold Gestapo prison cell. Prinz threatening her with his knife. Weiss sneering at them. Siebert dragging her away with the ugliest of intentions. Her brother, one bullet hole in his leg and another in his lungs. She took a few deep breaths, reminding herself that those images were in the past.

But she was a prisoner again. She was in a second-story bedroom of the Norman home Tschirner and three of his guards had commandeered that morning. The six men Tschirner had left at the barn had returned empty-handed. Now the ten of them guarded Genevieve, their bait.

A soft click caught her attention, and she glanced at the door as Siebert slipped into the room, leering at her and wearing a cruel smile on his lips. She'd woken up to a nightmare just as terrifying as the one she'd been dreaming.

"The more you struggle, the worse it will be for you," he said in German. Genevieve understood every word and panicked, tugging at her handcuff. It didn't do any good—the handcuffs and bed post were both solid. As Siebert walked toward the bed, Genevieve grabbed the table lamp and threw it at him. The cord caught and the lamp fell harmlessly at his feet. Siebert laughed at her attempt, crushing a few pieces of broken glass with his boots.

Genevieve tried to scream, but her throat constricted with terror. Screaming wouldn't help anyway. None of the other Gestapo guards would interfere.

As Siebert approached the bed where she lay, the door crashed open. Another Gestapo guard stood in the entrance, his eyes wide with concern. "Weiss, Kraus, Mullar, and Von Steuben are missing. Tschirner's put us all on high alert and wants to see you immediately." The guard was gone as quickly as he'd come, but Genevieve heard him giving the same information to someone in a room across the hall.

Four Gestapo guards missing? Genevieve wasn't sure what that meant beyond a reprieve from Siebert's attentions. He grabbed her face and glowered down at her then pushed her away with such force that her head cracked against the headboard. It hurt, leaving her dizzy and nauseated. Within seconds, Siebert was out the door, reporting to his standartenführer. Genevieve struggled to breathe as tears of relief slid down her cheeks.

A sudden thump startled her, and she saw a rock with thick string wrapped around it amid pieces of the broken lamp. Straining against the handcuff, she rolled the small stone toward her with her foot. As the stone turned, she saw the paper secured to the rock. She twisted to reach it with her unbound left hand and barely grasped it. She pulled the paper out and hid the rock behind a pillow. The rock wasn't her ideal weapon, but it was something for when Siebert returned. When she unfolded the paper, her heart momentarily skidded. The handwriting was Peter's.

Stay away from the windows if you can. Everything will be okay soon. Get rid of this paper.

After reading it twice, Genevieve tore the paper into shreds and pushed the scraps between the sheets and the mattress. Peter was here, somewhere, and four Gestapo guards were missing. Peter had come for her. The thought brought her hope but also fear. Tschirner wanted Peter to come for her; he was waiting for it. What if everything was unfolding exactly as Tschirner planned?

Genevieve twisted to see out the window. She saw Tschirner's Mercedes and the Opel Blitz most of his guards rode in. She couldn't see any of the guards, just the grounds around the house and the hedgerows. Based on the length of the shadows, it was early evening, which meant Peter was probably nearing twenty-four hours without sleep, because she couldn't imagine he would have lain down long enough to rest after he discovered she was gone. Peter was tougher and stronger than she was; sleep deprivation would affect him only a little, but that was one more advantage for Tschirner.

She listened to the distant thunder of artillery. The sound of battle had been growing louder the last few days, but they were still some distance from the front. Basseneville was in clear Nazi territory, where the Gestapo could act with impunity. After a while, Siebert and another guard walked between the vehicles and the house. Moments later, Genevieve heard the front door open and several loud voices boom. It was time to collect her weapon.

She held the rock in her left hand, hidden behind her back. Siebert came in, and as he unlocked her handcuff she brought her other hand around and aimed for the back of his head. Siebert's reflexes were sharp. Before she could hit him, his arm twisted around hers until her wrist was trapped under his armpit. With his arm wrapped around hers, he squeezed until she let the rock drop with a gasp of pain. His icy gray eyes glared at her through narrow slits. Her arm wasn't broken yet, but it would be if Siebert applied any additional pressure. Siebert called her a filthy name and brought his other hand around to the back of her neck for a sharp blow. Genevieve's world erupted in a burst of pain and then turned black.

She woke to see the bedroom door shutting behind her. Her view was skewed—she was hanging over Siebert's shoulder. "I can walk," she said. Siebert grunted but didn't put her down until they had reached the bottom of the stairs. Then he dropped her so quickly she didn't have time to catch herself.

"I said to hurry," Tschirner said darkly.

Genevieve pulled herself to her feet but was too dizzy to stand without the wall's support. Siebert grabbed her arm and pulled her outside. He shoved her toward another Gestapo guard, who snatched her and forced her to march with him toward the Mercedes.

There had been ten men at dawn. Then four went missing. Three additional guards seemed to have vanished since Genevieve first heard of Tschirner's problems. Tschirner climbed into the backseat, and the guard pushed Genevieve in next to him. He aimed his pistol at her to deter any escape attempt. The guard who'd just released her climbed behind the wheel, and Siebert took the front passenger seat with his handgun drawn.

"Where is Sturmmann Glick?" Tschirner hissed. Apparently, one of the guards had only recently disappeared. When no one answered, Tschirner ordered the driver to go, but the car wouldn't start. Genevieve immediately thought of Peter—immobilizing an automobile would be like child's play to him.

"Check the truck," Tschirner ordered. The driver jumped out and ran to the troop transport. He never made it. A bullet struck him in the head, and he fell halfway between the car and the truck. Genevieve didn't hear the shot until after the man had fallen, and that surprised her. Peter didn't have any long-range firearms, only a pistol and a knife.

Tschirner's normally pale skin was red with worry as he ordered her out of the car. Genevieve would have made a run for it, despite Tschirner's weapon, but Siebert was waiting for her. He wrapped his left arm around Genevieve's shoulders and held his pistol ready in his right hand. She could barely breathe inside his vicelike grip. The Gestapo men used her as a shield while they ran back to the home. Before they could get through the front door, they were distracted by the sounds of a scuffle on the other side of the house. Tschirner positioned himself between Siebert and the French home as they turned the corner.

A Gestapo guard lay facedown on the overgrown grass, with a knife in his back. Siebert brought Genevieve with him as he investigated. He unceremoniously flipped the body over with his boot. "Sturmmann Glick," he whispered. He didn't bother to close Glick's dead eyes, his attention now on another knife covered in bright red blood, five meters away on a stone path. Between the second knife and the kitchen door were four wet marks. As Siebert forced Genevieve to walk with him, she noticed each successive mark was longer and shaped more and more like a footprint. Her suspicions were confirmed by the last mark, a crimson shoe-print on the wooden step leading into the kitchen.

Siebert looked at Tschirner, who nodded. Siebert followed the bloody footsteps into the house. There were three more footprints inside, followed by an enormous red smear, as if whoever was making the footprints had collapsed. Stretching away from the smudge was a red streak, several inches wide, leading around the corner. They followed it through a hallway before it turned again. Siebert kept Genevieve in front of him as they peered around the final corner. The blood trail continued across the living room before stopping at a gash in Peter's left thigh.

Chapter Three
Leverage

Peter was on the floor at the foot of the stairs, his shoulders resting on the bottom step. As Genevieve took in the ghostly shade of his normally tan complexion and stared at the trail of blood he'd made pulling himself through the house, she was surprised he was still conscious. But there was determination in his eyes as he aimed his pistol at Siebert's head, about a foot and a half above Genevieve's.

Tschirner's pistol was aimed at Genevieve. "Put your weapon down or I'll shoot."

Peter's jaw hardened as he set his Luger next to his uninjured leg.

"Now slide the gun to me."

Peter obeyed, sliding the pistol a few feet away from him. Tschirner let his arm drop to his side.

Peter slowly picked up his belt, which lay on the floor next to him, and slid it under his wounded leg.

"Whatever are you doing, Lieutenant Eddy?"

"Trying to keep from bleeding to death. I don't suppose you'd send Genevieve over to help?" Peter's voice sounded soft and weak but not defeated. Genevieve wondered at that. Surely things weren't going according to his plans—not anymore.

"No, I don't suppose I will," Tschirner answered.

Peter didn't seem surprised. He tied his own tourniquet and gazed up at the three of them. "Where is Obersturmführer Prinz?" he asked.

Tschirner's face darkened.

"Dead, is he?" Peter continued. "That's strange."

"And why is that strange, Lieutenant Eddy?" Tschirner asked.

Peter smirked slightly. "I always thought you had to have a soul in order to die."

Tschirner's face colored. Prinz had been Tschirner's protégé until a grenade thrown by Genevieve's brother had killed him on June 4. Prinz, assisted by Weiss and Siebert, had been responsible for most of the torture Peter had endured in prison. "I'd forgotten how amusing I find our conversations, Lieutenant. But I am concerned you were less than honest with me when we last spoke." Their last communication had been in the basement prison of Calais's Gestapo headquarters, a rough interrogation about the cross-Channel invasion.

"Why do you say that?" Peter asked, his pale face showing surprise.

"You didn't mention any diversionary landings near Caen."

"They must have decided to move west from Le Havre," Peter said.

"Perhaps, but my superiors are beginning to doubt the information you gave me. Tell me, Lieutenant Eddy, are the landings in Normandy a diversion, or are they the real thing?"

"As I told you before, the main invasion will be in Calais. Feel free to move your troops to Normandy; it will make the real landing that much easier."

"And is the invasion of Calais still scheduled for July 4?" Tschirner asked.

"Last I heard," Peter said.

"I think I would know if tens of thousands of American troops were landing in England to prepare for a second invasion."

Peter smiled. "Yes, we know you'd know. That's why they aren't landing in England. They're sailing right to the French coast, and they should be nearly there by now."

"We would also know if tens of thousands of American troops were leaving the United States heading across the Atlantic."

"Would you? I'm sure you have your eyes on New York and Norfolk. But are you watching all of our port cities? You don't have many spies in, say, Galveston, do you?"

Tschirner frowned. He obviously didn't know. He looked at Genevieve. "Perhaps Mademoiselle Olivier will tell me what I want to know."

"She doesn't know anything about the invasion, and her brother was her only contact, so she won't lead you to any Resistance cells. You may as well let her go."

Tschirner laughed and turned to Genevieve with malice in his eyes. "I am certain Mademoiselle Olivier knows more about the invasion than you give her credit for." Genevieve swallowed, knowing Peter and Tschirner were both right. All she knew about the invasion of Normandy was what she'd heard from the radio, but she knew it was the real invasion. And she knew everything Peter had said in Gestapo prison was a lie—there were no plans for an invasion of Calais, and Peter had invented the date of the phony invasion. She assumed Peter's current conversation was a continuation of that story to help protect everyone involved in the real liberation taking place only a few kilometers away. Any Germans held back to defend the Pas-de-Calais couldn't move to the front in Normandy, giving the Allies a badly needed edge. A few wrong words from her could unravel all of Peter's previous efforts.

Tschirner looked back and forth between Peter and Genevieve. "If you persist in feeding me falsehoods, Lieutenant Eddy, I will have no choice but to give Sturmmann Siebert permission to interrogate Mademoiselle Olivier using whatever techniques he deems necessary. I'll get the information I want from her."

Genevieve felt the rough stubble of Siebert's cheek pressing into her neck and tried to pull away as his muscular arm wrapped around her waist, forcing her even closer to him, his intention clear.

"You won't live that long," Peter said in German so there would be no translation errors. Every muscle on his face had hardened, and his dark brown eyes were full of threat.

Tschirner chuckled, amused but not worried. Still, as he noticed Peter glancing at his weapon, Tschirner pointed his handgun at Genevieve's head again. "You won't make it, Lieutenant Eddy; your Luger is too far away. I'll shoot her before you have a chance to shoot Sturmmann Siebert."

Siebert was also amused, pleased his threats were getting such a strong reaction.

"Take your hands off her," Peter ordered. His voice lacked volume, but it didn't lack authority.

Siebert laughed, and Genevieve felt his hot, moist breath on her cheek. "All right, Eddy, I'll take my hands off her." She felt his grip loosen, but before she could run, Siebert threw her into the brick wall bordering the fireplace. She cried out as she crashed into it and collapsed to the floor. She pushed herself up and felt a sharp stab of pain that made it difficult to breathe. Then she heard gunshots and shattering windows and saw Tschirner and Siebert fall to the floor.

"Genevieve, are you all right?" Peter hadn't moved, and his pistol was still several feet away. "How badly are you hurt?"

Genevieve tried to be brave and tell him her injuries weren't nearly as bad as his knife wound looked, but as she inhaled, she felt that cutting pain in her ribs again. "I'm fine," she gasped. She had scores of questions she wanted to ask him, but that single phrase had hurt so much that she instead kept silent, wondering most of all who had shot the two Gestapo men. She glanced at Tschirner and Siebert. With enormous relief, she realized they were both dead. They wouldn't be able to hurt her or Peter ever again.

A tall, lanky man stepped through the window into the house. She took in his blue eyes and kind smile with surprise. He carried a Sten carbine in one hand and a rucksack with a Red Cross patch in the other. His trousers were tucked into a pair of jump boots. "A British paratrooper?" she uttered despite the pain.

"Richard Holmes, but everyone calls me Sherlock," he said, tipping his red beret. "Miss Olivier, I presume." She nodded, quickly getting over her surprise. A horrible knife wound might not have been in Peter's plan, but she was certain backup always had been. "Lieutenant Eddy, it looks as if you are in need of my medical services."

"Take care of her first," Peter replied.

"Peter, don't be ridiculous," Genevieve said. "You're the one bleeding to death. I can wait until you're stitched up."

"I am inclined to agree with Miss Olivier," Sherlock said.

"Take care of her first." Peter crossed his arms and set his jaw.

"Stubborn Yank." Sherlock sighed and knelt next to Genevieve. "How many times have you been thrown against a wall like that today?"

"Three." Genevieve resigned herself to quick cooperation so Sherlock could finish with her and get on to Peter sooner. "I think something is wrong with my rib."

Sherlock nodded and motioned for her to lie flat. "Take a deep breath." She obeyed, but the pain was so intense she had to blink back tears. "Hmm," Sherlock said, carefully feeling her rib cage. She gasped in pain when he found the injured one. "Well, at least it doesn't need to be set; you are skinny enough that I'd feel any sharp edges." He helped her sit up again. "Now look out the window toward the sun." Genevieve obeyed, and then as Sherlock instructed, she followed his finger with her eyes. "Cracked rib and a mild concussion. No driving or shooting machine guns for a few days."

Genevieve had never driven before or shot anything more dangerous than a semiautomatic rifle, so she found the restrictions more humorous than bothersome.

The medic turned his attention to Peter and frowned. "You look a bit peaky." Sherlock brought his bag over but couldn't find what he was looking for. He walked past Genevieve into the kitchen, where she could hear him exploring the cupboards. "Is there any liquor in this house?"

"Upstairs, in the room on the right." Genevieve had spent most of the day in the room on the left and had heard the men across the hall drinking. She stood to fetch whatever she could find for the medic but had to stop when her head spun so badly that she nearly fell over. Sherlock returned in time to offer her a steadying arm and help her move to Peter, then he ran upstairs.

"I think with a cracked rib and a concussion, you're supposed to avoid unnecessary movement," Peter said with a tired smile.

"I think with a gash in your leg and a few pints of your blood staining the floor, you're supposed to avoid getting into mind games with Gestapo officers."

"I suppose neither of us is acting very intelligently today. Will you hand me my pistol? I don't like being unarmed." She leaned over, grabbed his Luger, and handed it to him. Her brother had felt that way too—like he was incomplete without a weapon. Thinking of her brother made her remember the thigh wound Jacques had suffered just before he died. "It will be okay, Genevieve," Peter said as if sensing her fear. "We're close to the front now, but almost everyone is focused on Caen, so if we stay off the main roads and avoid the bridges everyone will be trying to hold, we can sneak around to the north and then loop west—"

"Peter," Genevieve interrupted. "I know crossing the front line will be tricky, but right now, I'm much more worried about you."

He grinned mischievously with the same half-crooked smile that had caught her attention the day she'd met him. "I've been through worse."

She knew he was right, but that didn't calm her concern.

Sherlock returned with a bottle of alcohol. He cleaned a needle with the liquid then threaded the needle with precision.

"You might want to drink some of this, sir. It will help with the pain," Sherlock suggested.

Peter's religion discouraged drinking, so Genevieve wasn't surprised when he shook his head.

Sherlock shrugged. "Stubborn Yank. Still, you did a good job with this tourniquet." Sherlock ripped Peter's pant leg so he could get at the cut better and used the liquor to clean it. Peter's head jerked back as the alcohol soaked his wound, then he clenched his jaw and exhaled through his nose. "If you happen to get stabbed again, you should leave the knife in the wound. Taking the knife out makes the bleeding worse."

Genevieve could tell Peter wasn't paying attention to the paratrooper. His eyes studied her face, and she knew he was searching for something to help him ignore his leg, which Sherlock had begun stitching up.

"Tell me, Genevieve, what would you have rather done today?" Peter asked.

Genevieve forced a smile. *His leg must really be bothering him if that's the best distraction he can come up with.* "Playing baseball," she said, willing to help him take his mind off his leg and knowing baseball was his favorite pasttime.

"Baseball?"

"Yes. Which position did you play?"

"Shortstop or second base. It depended on who was pitching."

Neither position meant anything to Genevieve. "Did your brother play baseball?" She watched Sherlock make a stitch then looked back at Peter.

"Yeah, he was a catcher but not quite as obsessed as I was."

"Do your sisters play?"

"Ruby did, but just with us. Pearl never; Opal rarely." Peter clenched his teeth as Sherlock started another stitch.

"What did they do instead?"

"Dolls." Peter gasped. He was losing his battle to ignore the pain as Sherlock pulled his stitches snug. The muscles on Peter's face were tense from his chin all the way up to his temples.

"Just a few more," Sherlock reported.

"Where are Fisher and Grey?" Peter asked.

"They'll both move slowly with sprained ankles," Sherlock said.

"More paratroopers?" Genevieve asked.

"Yes." Sherlock's eyes never left his work. "We were dropped exceedingly far off course. Fisher and Grey twisted their ankles when they landed. Grey landed in a tree; Fisher landed on a roof, and his parachute stuck. He had to cut himself out and had a fifteen-foot drop to the ground."

"Closer to a twenty-foot drop, I'd say," a new voice said. Genevieve turned around to see a redheaded paratrooper limping into the house. He was about Peter's height, just under six feet, with freckles and an infectious grin. He used a walking stick to support his injured ankle and had a rifle with a scope slung across his shoulder.

"Where's Corporal Grey?" Peter asked between stitches.

"'E's dead," Fisher answered, all mirth in his voice gone.

Peter looked upset. "My first time in charge, and I've got twenty-five percent fatalities."

"Sir," Sherlock broke in, "we were outnumbered significantly, and our enemies were all killed or captured. I think overall, we can count this a success."

Peter still looked miserable, and Genevieve knew it wasn't just his leg bothering him.

The second paratrooper glanced at the medical procedure then sat next to Genevieve and extended his hand. "Daniel Fisher. I'm the sniper."

"Pleased to meet you." Genevieve took his hand. "Genevieve Olivier."

"Lieutenant Eddy 'ere told us you were an important source for General Eisenhower. 'E forgot to mention that you're also an astonishing beauty."

Genevieve felt her face go hot. She didn't consider herself beautiful, especially with her hair a mess and scrapes from splinters running up the side of her face. Nor did she think anyone on Eisenhower's staff would be remotely interested in questioning her.

Peter grunted. "We'll have to liberate Calais eventually. She knows the area quite well."

"Better than our reconnaissance aircraft?" Fisher asked, not impressed.

"Yes," Peter said with finality. "Reconnaissance aircraft can't see inside buildings."

Fisher shrugged. "Well, miss, I was 'appy to finally shoot that tall SS bloke. I almost got 'im upstairs. 'Ad 'e moved a foot closer to you, it would 'ave been a clear shot. I was rather put out when that other guard interrupted 'im, though I expect you were relieved."

Fisher's words sank in. Peter hadn't forgotten what Siebert had wanted to do in Calais. He'd planned for it and set a sniper outside her window to protect her. Genevieve met Peter's eyes and gave him a smile of gratitude.

"It was brilliant to try to smack 'im with that rock," Fisher continued. "But next time, instead of bringing it around in an arch, you should go for a quick jab, straight from your shoulder into 'is nose, giving 'im less time to react. I would be 'appy to teach you a little self-defense."

"She has an injured rib and a concussion," Sherlock said. "No self-defense lessons for a few weeks at least. And the stitches are finished."

Peter sighed with relief. "How many?"

"In the neighborhood of twenty."

"I shouldn't have asked," Peter said. "How many prisoners do we have?"

"Your three, plus one Sherlock captured, so four total," Fisher said. "I can change that if you'd like."

"We don't need to execute our prisoners," Peter said. "Make sure they're completely unarmed and immobilized and throw them in the back of the truck. Someone will want to question them eventually."

Fisher saluted and obeyed.

"Would you like me to assist him, sir?" Sherlock asked. Peter nodded. "I'll come back to help you out when we have the prisoners loaded."

Peter's eyes followed Sherlock out the door. "There were more than a dozen of them, plus a pilot and crew, when they took off from England. Now there are only two."

Genevieve brushed her fingers over Peter's hand. "And if the Nazis had been expecting them, they would all be dead," she said, trying to remind Peter of how much his earlier mission had helped the Allied cause by making the Germans expect an invasion in the Pas-de-Calais instead of in Normandy. "How did they get here?"

"Their pilot was off course then ran into flack and veered even farther to the east to avoid it. Most of their platoon didn't even make it off the plane before it exploded—more flack. Fisher hurt himself when he landed; Grey broke his arm and twisted his ankle. The three of them ran into a member of the Resistance. He hid them in his barn while they waited for their army to catch up with them. They didn't realize how far they were from the drop zone and kept expecting the front to come to them. Yesterday they set out on foot, despite their injuries. They stopped to rest not far from here and fell asleep."

"How did you find them?"

Peter turned his attention from the paratroopers back to Genevieve. "I didn't. A few of Tschirner's guards did, and I decided to intervene. I took two guards as they were roughing up Fisher. Turns out, I'm the only Allied officer these paratroopers have seen since they bailed out of their plane. They might not have believed I was on their side if I hadn't just knocked two Gestapo guards unconscious, but all that British discipline seemed to kick in pretty quickly."

Peter moved his leg into a different position. Genevieve knew it was hurting him, but he kept his face even. "Grey and I took Weiss prisoner as we were getting Fisher set up in his position. After that, I sent Grey and Sherlock to round up Tschirner's second patrol. We knew how many we were up against, and I told them to come back and cover the house after they got their targets."

"I'm sorry I didn't stay away from the windows," Genevieve said, remembering the warning tied to the rock.

"The note was a precaution. Fisher's a good sniper; he was just concerned his rifle would be off after his rough landing. I remember how strong Siebert is. If he wanted you to be in front of a window, how could you resist?"

Genevieve nodded and took Peter's hand. "How did get stabbed?"

"I was trying to take another guard prisoner—the one Grey missed. I should have just killed him: he ended up dead anyway." Peter clenched his teeth again. Genevieve admired Peter's reluctance to kill even his enemy, so different from how her brother had been.

"What are you thinking about?" Peter's voice was quiet, tired.

Genevieve realized she'd been staring off into space. She looked back at Peter. "Jacques . . . and you. In some ways, you're so alike. In other ways, you're very different."

Peter looked thoughtful. "I managed to collect a few things after Tschirner arrested you." He reached into the inside pocket of his coat and pulled out three thick pieces of paper. "The frames weren't salvageable, and a few of the corners are torn." They were Genevieve's pictures: Jacques and his wife, Mireille; Genevieve's parents on their wedding day; and a family portrait from when Genevieve was a baby.

"Thank you, Peter." Genevieve could feel tears forming in her eyes. "These pictures are all I have left."

CHAPTER FOUR

WHISPERS AND GIFTS

PETER'S HEAD LOLLED BACK AND forth on the hard truck bed. The road they drove along was unpaved, and the truck lurched up and down violently, each bump aggravating the ache in Genevieve's side. Sharing the back of the truck with Genevieve and Peter were the four prisoners. Fisher had stripped each of the Gestapo guards down to their underwear and wrapped them in ropes like mummies. They all had handkerchiefs packed into their mouths, and Fisher had used their dress shirts to cover their faces and secure their mouths. Genevieve was guarding them with Peter's pistol—but she only had to bang on the back of the cab and Sherlock and Fisher would stop the truck and assist her. None of the Gestapo men were moving, but Genevieve suspected they were awake since none of their heads were bouncing around like Peter's was.

She slipped closer to Peter, putting his head on her lap to cushion it. Then she ran her fingers through his thick hair. It was getting long enough to curl a bit at the ends. She studied his face, though she'd long ago memorized all of its features, including the scars. Peter's nose was slightly crooked: Prinz had broken it almost two weeks ago. Now that the swelling was gone, it looked almost normal, and Genevieve decided she liked the slight angle that remained. She ran her fingers over his cheeks and across his lips and found herself humming *Carmen* again.

Peter groaned softly and opened his eyes. He glanced up at Genevieve then looked around, taking in their surroundings. "Is Sherlock driving?" he asked. His voice was quiet and slurred, still weak from his injury.

"Yes, and he and Fisher are keeping a good lookout so you can rest."

Peter relaxed a little and shut his eyes. Genevieve thought he would go back to sleep, but he kept talking. "If it weren't for my leg, I might mistake this for heaven."

Genevieve smiled, assuming the truck bed itself couldn't be mistaken for anything angelic. "Heaven?" she asked, thinking of their frequent religious conversations. "Don't you believe in three heavens? Which one looks like the inside of a troop transport?"

A crooked smile crossed Peter's face, but he kept his eyes closed. "If you were there, it would be the right heaven. And if you were there, I wouldn't be paying attention to anything else." He opened his eyes in time to see her blush. He reached over and took her hand. "I'm sorry, Genevieve."

"Sorry? For what?"

"For leaving you alone and for not rescuing you sooner. I arrived just after they did this morning, in time to see Tschirner position his men and go inside. I almost followed, but I knew they'd kill me before I could help you. Not that my death would be the end of the world, but I knew I'd have another chance."

Your death would be the end of my world, Genevieve thought. Rather than say those words out loud, she concentrated on the second part of his sentence. "How did you know you'd have another chance?"

"It's hard to explain."

"We have time."

He didn't answer right away. He studied her carefully, his gaze so intense that she almost forgot what she'd asked him. "It was a feeling—clear, strong, and contrary to all of my instincts, but I knew I could trust it."

Genevieve didn't completely understand him, but she believed him. She squeezed his hand to let him know that all was well. Then she brought her head down and gently kissed his forehead.

Peter smiled at her. "You know, Fisher is right; you are astonishingly beautiful."

"Peter," she started in protest, "I'm just an ordinary girl, scrawnier and less fashionable than most—"

"No, you're beautiful. *Un beau canari.*"

Beautiful canary. "My brother and sister-in-law used to call me their canary. How did you know?"

"Jacques told me," Peter said. "Do you mind the nickname?"

"No, but you're using the wrong adjective."

"No, I'm sure it's the right one. Today's not the first time I've noticed how pretty you are. I wanted to tell you before. I'm sorry I didn't, but it wasn't exactly easy to be alone with you for so long and still behave like a gentleman."

"Peter, you haven't even kissed me since we left Calais."

"Do you miss it?" he asked with his crooked smile.

She did but didn't say so. "That's not the type of question a good Mormon boy should ask a good Catholic girl," she said, pretending to be shocked.

"Sorry." She could tell he didn't mean it. His smile was unchanged, his eyes closed again.

"Do *you* miss it?" she asked him.

"I thought we weren't asking questions like that."

"You're impossible." She sighed in frustration.

"Yes."

"Yes what?" she asked.

"Yes, I can be impossibly stubborn. And yes, I've wanted to kiss you so many times these last ten days that I've lost track. I'd probably kiss you now if several of our prisoners weren't straining to hear every word we say and if you didn't have a cracked rib. Am I hurting you now, leaning on you like this?" He opened his eyes, looking at her with concern.

"It aches all the time. You aren't making it any worse."

"I'm so sorry I let him hurt you like that—"

She placed a finger on his lips. "It's not your fault, Peter. Siebert is responsible for his own actions. Nor is it your fault Corporal Grey was killed." She traced his eyebrows with her fingers, trying to ease away some of the pain she saw in his eyes. "Please believe me." He looked away and was quiet for a while. "Peter?" she finally asked.

He turned back to her and gave her half a smile before closing his eyes again. "I'll miss seeing you every day when we get to England."

"Won't we still see each other?" she asked, surprised. All of their planning had focused on their escape to England; she'd given little thought to what would occur when they arrived.

"I'm not sure what will happen. The war's not over. Once my leg heals, there may be more work for me to do. But I'll try to see you as often as I can—if you'll see me after everything I've put you through."

The thought of not seeing him every day was depressing, but she knew she had to be brave. "I'll still want to see you."

"Will you want to return to France once it's liberated?"

She ran her hand through his hair again. "I'm not sure. It's not really home without my family. But I don't know if I'm ready to say good-bye and never return."

"What will you do in the meantime? Before you decide where you want to be?"

"I think I'd like to become a nurse." Genevieve was tired of feeling so helpless around the wounded—first when her brother was injured then while Peter bled.

"You'll be good at it, although I fear all of your patients will fall in love with you."

"I doubt that." She felt a blush warm her cheeks again. She was glad Peter's eyes were closed so he couldn't see.

"It happened to this one."

He'd spoken so softly Genevieve didn't know if she'd correctly understood the phrase over the sound of the truck and its abrasive progress. "What did you say?"

"Never mind." He formed a soft curve with his lips, and after a few minutes, he drifted off to sleep again.

* * *

Peter sat on a bench at a convalescence hospital in Southampton and shifted his leg, hoping it would reduce the pain. It didn't. He gritted his teeth and reminded himself he'd given up swearing. He was still a little surprised that he'd slept through their entry into Allied territory three days before, but he'd been dizzy and worn out. That hadn't changed much.

Fisher and Sherlock had followed Peter's plan, avoiding the main roads and bridges and crossing into territory controlled by the British 6th Airborne division shortly after nightfall. Sherlock had pulled the car to the side of the road and walked until he found a checkpoint; then he'd brought a few British soldiers back to the truck to take custody of the German prisoners. Peter, Genevieve, and Fisher were inspected in a field hospital and spent the night in the French village of Ranville. Sherlock had been redeployed the next morning; there was a constant need for healthy medics on the front line. The rest of them had been sent to Arromanches with a group of wounded men from the front. From there, they'd sailed to England.

Peter glanced across the garden to where Genevieve spoke with SOE Colonel McDougall, the man who'd sent Peter to France. McDougall was also an old friend of the Olivier family, but as Peter watched the colonel debrief Genevieve, he felt a little uneasy. He knew McDougall was loyal to the British Empire, and his past schemes were no doubt helping the Normandy invasion succeed. McDougall was willing to sacrifice much to defeat the Nazis—but most of his sacrifices involved the lives of his subordinates.

The colonel was taking a long time to debrief Genevieve—almost as long as he'd taken with Peter. A thorough debriefing would give McDougall a better understanding of what had happened in France and would offer invaluable intelligence about the German forces still holding Calais. But Peter was afraid McDougall wasn't just debriefing Genevieve; he was worried McDougall was recruiting her. Peter wasn't sure which was worse: worrying about Genevieve joining SOE or replaying what had happened in Basseneville to figure out what he could have done to prevent Corporal Grey's death.

Peter was relieved when McDougall finished his conversation with Genevieve and moved on to questioning Fisher.

Peter watched a breeze blow through her brown hair as she walked over. She sat next to him and took his hand. "How's your leg?"

"More manageable now that you're here. How are your ribs?"

"Better than yesterday."

The bench they sat on faced west, so Genevieve watched the sunset, and Peter watched the way the fading sunlight changed the color of her face and played with the glimmer of gold in her brown eyes.

"What did McDougall want?" Peter asked after the sun slid beneath the horizon.

"Just details about the mission. He was hoping I knew some of my brother's contacts—but I don't. Jacques was their only link to SOE, so I don't know what will happen to them. Maybe they can go back to their normal lives and wait for the war to end." She brushed a stray strand of hair behind her ear. "They discharged me while you were being debriefed. McDougall's arranged for me to stay with someone who lives nearby until my rib's healed."

"He's not trying to employ you, is he?"

"Don't turn into my brother, Peter."

"Your brother asked me to look after you. I don't think I'll be honoring his wishes very well if I let you join SOE." And it wasn't just his promise to Jacques. The thought of Genevieve going back into occupied territory made Peter sick.

She leaned closer and whispered in his ear. "He did offer me a job, but I told him I'm going to nursing school, and I was very firm."

Peter sighed with relief, put his arm around her, and kissed her gently on the temple. "Thank you," he whispered. She put her head on his shoulder and began humming a song that sounded vaguely familiar. Eventually, a nurse came around and reminded Genevieve that visiting hours were almost over.

Peter tried not to glare at the departing nurse. "I almost forgot; I was going to give you this earlier." He pulled an envelope out of his pocket and handed it to her.

"What's this?"

"Part of my back pay."

"I can't take your money, Peter." She glanced into the envelope. "Especially not this much of it."

"Why not?"

"Because it's yours."

"Well, I want you to have it. How else will you buy food or pay rent or apply for nursing school?"

"I'll figure something out." Genevieve tried to hand the envelope back.

Peter locked his hands together and put them behind his head, leaning back so she couldn't hand him the money. "Yeah, you'll figure something out. And that will help you."

"McDougall said he was happy to help out. My brother never received a salary or anything, but some agents did, so—"

"Please don't take any money from him, Genevieve. It might have strings attached."

She studied him carefully. "And your money won't?"

"No. You can consider it a substitute for all the gifts your boyfriend would like to purchase for you but can't since the nurses won't let him leave the property. They wouldn't even let me go to church yesterday. They're regular prison wardens," he muttered under his breath.

"Maybe if your church wasn't so far away. Or if you hadn't almost been killed last Friday."

"You aren't taking their side, are you?"

"You have been a little cranky with them." She gave him an amused smile.

"Maybe I'd be nicer if the head nurse didn't insist on waking me before six every morning. It's not like there's any reason for me to be up that early. They won't let you visit until eight. I finally get to sleep after my three a.m. nightmare and there she is—turning on all the lights and pushing her squeaky cart and wishing us all a cheery good morning. Most mornings, I'd like to smother her with my pillow."

Genevieve pulled one of his hands down and laced her fingers through his. "I'm sorry about your nightmares, Peter. But you should probably keep your pillow to yourself. And your money too." She tried to give the envelope back to him again, but he refused to take it.

"Look, the army will feed me and clothe me and give me somewhere to sleep. And pay the nurses to wake me up at the crack of dawn. I don't need the money. And I promised Jacques I'd look after you. If you don't take it, I'll worry about you all the time."

Genevieve hesitated. "I know you won't give up easily, so I'll accept half." She opened the envelope to sort through the British pounds, but Peter cupped both his hands over hers and held them firmly to prevent her from handing any of the money back to him.

"Stop being so stubborn," he whispered.

"You're the one who's being stubborn," she whispered back.

Peter grinned and put one of his arms around her waist, bringing his face to within inches of hers. "Please take it." Then he gently ran a finger along her jaw, tilting her chin up until their lips met.

Genevieve accepted the kiss with a sigh.

"Was that a yes?" Peter asked, kissing her again before she could reply.

"That's not fair." Her hands were on his chest, but she didn't push him away. "You're trying to distract me."

"Is it working?" Peter brushed his lips along her cheek.

"Maybe."

"Good. Then take my gift and come visit me tomorrow." Peter followed his request with another kiss. Not long after, the same nurse came through again, informing them it was now past visiting hours. "*Au revoir, beau canari.*"

* * *

A week and a half later, Genevieve arrived at the convalescence home, but Peter was gone, and so was Daniel Fisher. Genevieve stared at the stranger sleeping in Peter's old bed until one of the nurses came over to her.

"Some major came by late last night and picked those two up, he did. He showed up, and not five minutes later, they were gone. But the lieutenant left you this." She handed Genevieve Peter's Book of Mormon with a letter poking out of the top.

Dear Genevieve,

I'm sorry I couldn't say good-bye in person. I have to leave in a few minutes, but I wanted to give you something that was more personal than a few British pounds and less violent than my weapons. This is all I can think of. I have two copies—my old copy was in my back pocket when my tank exploded in Sicily, so it has a few bloodstains. I can still read everything, but my mom was horrified and sent me this second copy. I'd like you to have it. I'll send another letter soon. You can write me care of Major W. W. Baker, Dravot Manor, Croxley Green, Hertfordshire.

Peter

Genevieve walked slowly back to the home where she was boarding, holding Peter's gift and trying not to cry. She'd known Peter would leave the hospital soon, but she'd thought she'd have a chance to say good-bye.

Feeling very alone, Genevieve ran her fingers along the top of the book, remembering the way she'd seen Peter study it with a look of concentration, his lips moving slightly as he'd read. She figured the book was less than a year old, but it looked older. The side of the book away from the binding felt thicker, and several of the corners were bent, either from frequent use or from spending too much time jammed in Peter's pocket. She felt a smile form as she realized how much the book meant to him.

He was right; it was a better gift than a stolen German pistol.

She knew what she'd do next: McDougall had arranged employment for her as a nurse's aide in a London hospital. It wasn't her dream job, but it would give her experience while she tried to get into nursing school. And London was closer to Croxley Green and to Peter than Southampton was.

CHAPTER FIVE

PARATROOPERS ARE INSANE

0030 Hours, Friday, July 14

PETER TOOK THE LETTER FROM Kapral Krzysztof Zielinski's hand and opened it. It was addressed to Zielinski's father. Peter glanced at it before stamping *censored* on the envelope with black ink.

"I didn't know Americans were so lax with their censoring," Fisher said.

Peter flipped the letter over so Fisher could see the series of random letters and numbers written with Zielinski's precise hand. "I'm not worried about a mole in the British postal system getting anything out of this. Nor is Major Baker."

Fisher took the letter and studied it, turning it upside down, then right side up. "Is that some kind of code?"

"Yes," Zielinski said. "Just a hobby."

"Interesting 'obby. Been at it long?"

"Since I was four."

Fisher handed the letter back to Zielinski. "Do many people in Poland write letters in code?"

"Just sons of mathematics professors."

Peter initialed the envelope and gave it to the lanky, somber-faced paratrooper. "One of these days I'll figure out what your dad does." Peter knew Zielinski's father did something highly classified at Bletchley Park. What went on there was top secret, and Zielinski was quiet in general and completely mute on what his father did. Still, Peter knew it was something to do with codes and code breaking.

"When you find out, let me know," Zielinski said.

"Don't you know?" Peter asked.

Zielinski shrugged. "I have my guesses, but I know better than to ask for a confirmation."

"Right, I think it's about time to get our gear on board," Peter said.

Zielinski saluted and went to grab his equipment. As the team's communications man, he had to care for the radio in addition to his weapons and gear. Despite the extra weight, no one on the team ever heard him complain.

"I think that's the most words I've ever 'eard 'im say at one time," Fisher said.

Peter nodded. "Did you get your rifle sighted in?"

"Yes, sir."

"All right, load up."

Peter was the last to board the C-47 that would take the team to its final destination. He had a T5 parachute attached to his back and an A4 emergency chute fastened to his chest. Also strapped to him were the usual things one brought into battle: a few knives—a small one for cutting himself free from his parachute, a larger one for close combat—his Colt M1911 pistol, an M1A1 rifle, two hundred rounds, and thirty pounds of explosives. Peter wasn't technically a paratrooper, but he was about to lead five men on a jump. When they hit the ground, their assignment was to destroy a bridge before anyone discovered they had dropped from the sky.

Peter settled in near the front of the plane's cargo bay, next to Moretti and Luke, who were already deep in conversation.

"So who's crazier, kid, the Spartans at Thermopylae, or the 82nd at Sainte-Mère-Église?" Moretti asked.

Luke hesitated. "I don't know, Sarge; those Spartans were pretty tough."

Moretti laughed then gave Luke a serious look, his dark eyes under his thick eyebrows conveying disappointment. "Wrong answer, kid. I'll let you try again. Who's crazier, defenders of the Alamo, or the 82nd at Salerno?"

Luke shook his head and shrugged.

"I'll give you a clue, Luke," Peter broke in as the plane barreled down the runway and into the sky. "If Moretti's asking the question, the answer's always going to be the 82nd."

"But is that really the right answer?" Luke grinned, his blue eyes sparkling behind a pair of round glasses.

Peter tilted his helmet back and shrugged. He was certain all paratroopers—including the ones in the US 82nd Airborne—were insane. Though he was grateful for their help and impressed with how the British 6th Airborne had fought in France, the fate of Fisher's strung-out, disorganized platoon was still fresh on his mind. "I think anyone who would voluntarily jump out of an airplane into enemy territory with an extra hundred pounds strapped to them should have their head examined."

"That's a heck of a conclusion to come to before we even reach altitude, sir," Moretti said.

Peter grinned. "I came to that conclusion long before we boarded."

Like many OSS recruits, Moretti was a first-generation American, raised by parents who taught him fluent Italian and fierce American loyalty. Peter suspected Moretti's background of growing up in a rough New York City neighborhood had taught him his initial fighting skills. He was tall and muscular, with dark eyes and curly dark hair. Moretti was tough, friendly, and competitive. Peter had liked him instantly upon meeting him.

"Does my opinion about paratroopers make you any less eager to follow me out of the plane when we reach the drop zone?" Peter asked.

Moretti shook his head. "No, sir. As long as you know we're both crazy, we'll get along just fine."

"And you, Luke?"

"No, sir. You've just confirmed all my theories." Luke, whose full name was Henry Lucaciu, was the team's demolitions expert. Luke's parents had immigrated to the United States from Romania. Despite a worldwide depression, Luke's father had done well in business and had sent his only son to a top university. OSS had snapped the younger Lucaciu up right after he'd graduated from Yale with degrees in chemistry and physics. After two years of training, Luke was one of the best explosive experts in any of the Allied armies. At age twenty-four, he wasn't the youngest on the team—he was several years older than Peter. But he was the team's most recent arrival to Europe and didn't complain that Moretti kept calling him *kid*.

"Nervous about the jump, Lieutenant?" Moretti asked, breaking Peter's concentration.

"No," Peter lied. "But if I freeze up, feel free to give me a push."

"It wouldn't be the first time I pushed someone out of a plane," Moretti said with a grin. "Trust me, the way some of these pilots fly, it would be worse to stay in the plane for the landing." Peter believed Moretti's first statement but doubted the second.

"How many times have you jumped?" Peter had never been on an airplane before, let alone jumped from one.

Moretti thought for a few seconds. "Couple dozen training jumps. And, of course, Sicily, Salerno, and Normandy."

"I missed Salerno," Peter said. "Drove a tank in North African and Sicily. Heard about the landings in Normandy from behind enemy lines."

"Tanks, huh?"

"Yeah. Sure beats jumping out of an airplane."

"Until your tank gets hit."

"Yeah, that's why I missed Salerno." Peter's tank had been hit by a German shell, and he'd been lucky to live through the resulting explosion. Though he was nervous, Peter reminded himself that jumping out of a plane was better than being stuck in a hospital.

"How 'bout you, Luke? Nervous?" Moretti asked.

Luke grinned. "If I was, I wouldn't admit it to a partially insane former pathfinder from the 82nd."

Moretti laughed, his deep voice briefly drowning out the sound of the engines. "You know, kid, Eddy and I might make a decent commando outta you yet."

As Moretti continued quizzing Luke on the history of the 82nd Airborne Division, Peter went to check on the rest of his men. He could see them all from where he sat, but the engine noise made communication difficult with anyone farther away than Luke.

As Peter approached, Zielinski looked up from the code book he was studying. "Everything set?" Peter asked.

"Yes, sir."

Peter nodded. Zielinski was as quiet as he was competent.

The last two members of the team, Privates Daniel Fisher and Oliver Quill, were playing a card game. Fisher's sniping abilities had impressed McDougall, and Major Baker had read McDougall's report. Fisher had always wanted to be a commando, but his working-class background and lack of higher education meant he'd been previously overlooked. When Baker had offered Fisher a change of assignment to SOE, he'd accepted immediately.

"How's the game going?" Peter asked.

Fisher frowned, making Peter think Fisher's poker skills weren't as developed as his marksmanship. "I'm glad I left most of my money at the manor."

Quill grinned as he slapped down a pair of kings. "We could keep playing anyhow and you can pay up when we get back." Though he'd lived in England almost a decade, Quill's Australian childhood was still apparent in his speech.

Fisher shook his head. "I may not 'ave taken first in my airborne training like you did, but I'm smart enough to know when to quit."

Quill put away the cards and popped a few of his knuckles. "All right, then, Fish, you were going to show me how to sight in a sniper scope."

Peter thought Quill's desire to master new skills was his biggest asset. That, and his talent for forgery. Quill had no combat experience, and he was young, but Peter didn't think he would let the rest of the team down.

Peter walked back to his spot by the door the team would soon exit. They'd been thrown together a week ago and had spent nearly every waking moment together since. As a group, his men had the ability to sabotage transportation lines, kidnap enemy leaders, gather intelligence for military or political purposes, blend in with the local population, and survive in occupied territory for as long as they needed to. They were extraordinary men, and Peter felt keenly his responsibility for their safety.

A red light turned on in the back of the plane as they neared the drop zone. "All right, stand up and hook up," Peter ordered.

Each of the men hooked a line from their parachutes to the anchor line running down the middle of the plane. As they jumped, the line would yank the parachutes from their packs, and the blast from the plane's engines would open them. In theory, it would be an easy, gentle drop from that point on. Moretti helped Peter open the door they would fall from. Peter would be the first out.

The light turned green. Peter held his breath as he stepped out of the C-47 into the dark summer night. For a second or two, the wind and the wash from the plane pulled him horizontally, then his parachute filled with air and arrested his movement with a sudden jerk. Jumping out of an airplane was a noisy sensation—at least at first. But then, as the plane flew away, the night grew quiet. Peter drifted toward the ground, rocking back and forth at the end of his parachute line. There was no light from the ground, a combination of the early hour and blackout curtains on every window below. Above and to the west, Peter could make out one other parachute. The rest of his team was invisible.

As he hit the ground, Peter felt a slight twinge in his injured left thigh, a reminder that he still wasn't in peak physical condition. He'd landed in a field, barely disturbing the sleeping cattle a few yards away. The smell of grass and cows filled his nostrils as he checked his rifle. He spotted Moretti and Fisher farther down the field and pulled off his parachute, balling it up so he could hide it.

"That was my best landing ever," Fisher whispered as he approached Peter.

"Yeah, mine too," Peter said.

Fisher smiled. "Your only landing, isn't it, sir?"

"First and best. Have you seen anyone besides us and Moretti?" Peter asked.

"No, sir."

Moretti joined them, and they ditched their parachutes in a haystack before heading east. There was supposed to be a church steeple to the east of the drop zone, and beyond that was their bridge. Peter couldn't see the church steeple, despite the promise at their briefing that it stood out for miles. *Yet another less-than-accurate briefing?*

They found Quill five minutes later. He'd landed in a tree, but by the time they arrived, he'd freed himself. Five minutes later, they found the church steeple and Zielinski.

"Has anyone seen Luke?"

"Not since we left the plane," Quill said. "I saw him jump."

Peter looked around, hoping Luke would suddenly appear, but he didn't. All the men were carrying enough explosives to blow out a pylon, and Peter and Luke each carried enough to knock out the bridge on their own. Peter could destroy the bridge without Luke, but it would take twice as long. "Quill, Moretti." Peter paired the least experienced man with the most experienced man on the team. "Swing south of the church; see if you can find him. Zielinski, Fisher, swing north of the road. Remember to be invisible. Better to avoid our opponents until we've completed our task than to alert them we're here. If you have to engage them, use your knives. I want everyone at the bridge in ten minutes."

The men split up seamlessly, blending into the night as if they were ghosts rather than mortals packing half their weight in gear. Peter stayed just south of the road that wound through a sleepy village and across the bridge they were assigned to destroy. He saw no one, not even a civilian. Since he had the most direct route, Peter was the first to arrive at the target, an average-looking bridge that crossed a tiny creek. Infantry would be able to cross the stream without getting their knees wet, and civilians would be inconvenienced only a little. But the surrounding embankment was steep enough to stop a tank or a truck.

Peter's men were at the bridge within eight minutes. He was pleased with their speed, but there was still no sign of Luke. Peter almost swore but caught himself. If he wanted to ensure the bridge was properly destroyed, Luke was the best man to do it. But Quill was good at just about everything and had spent several days the past week working with Luke, absorbing as much as he could about demolishing bridges. Quill still hadn't outgrown his boyhood enthusiasm for lighting things on fire and blowing them up. Peter decided to give him the extra practice.

"Fish, cover this side of the bridge. Zielinski, Moretti—down the ravine and cover the other side. Quill, you're with me—we'll wire the six supports and blow it all at once."

It would have been quicker with Luke, but Peter and Quill managed. It was a two-lane bridge supported by six pylons, and the four supports on either end of the bridge were low enough that they could reach them from ground level. The two in the center were more difficult. After Peter checked

Quill's earlier work and was confident Quill could do it correctly, Peter had him stand on his shoulders to do the wiring in the middle. Everything was wired together then fed to a push-down detonator on Moretti's side of the bridge. The back of Peter's shirt was wet from Quill's shoes, but as they finished, Peter felt a smile of accomplishment pull at the corners of his mouth.

"Give the signal," Peter said.

Quill let out a bird call. It wasn't very lifelike, but it would warn the team to move away from the bridge so they wouldn't be injured when it exploded.

Seconds later, huge floodlights glared through the night and settled on Peter and Quill. A dark-haired junior officer who looked like he belonged on a recruiting poster appeared. "Hands up," he said in slightly accented English, pointing his rifle at Peter. Quill obeyed. Peter took a half second to calculate—he knew he could blow the bridge before the other man's finger pulled the trigger. So Peter slammed the lever down as hard as he could.

CHAPTER SIX

THE OTHER HALF OF THE TEAM

NOTHING HAPPENED. QUILL AND PETER had done their wiring correctly, but they'd used ordinary wax candles instead of dynamite.

"Well done, Lieutenant Eddy," Luke's voice said. Peter looked past the glare of the spotlight and could make out his shape. Luke stepped into the light, and Peter could see his hands tied behind his back and the two men guarding him. Luke was relaxed, and his calm manner didn't surprise Peter. Two days ago, Luke had been playing poker with the men who now guarded him: Private David Mitchell and Tiberiu Ionescu.

"All right, exercise over," an authoritative voice said. Quill put his hands down, and Mitchell cut Luke's shackles. The voice belonged to Major Wesley Baker. He was British, on loan to SOE from MI6 since 1940. He'd served SOE in Italy for nearly a year, operating a large spy ring before returning to England in early June. Baker was soft spoken, direct, and determined to mold his new team into a stealthy, lethal unit greater than the sum of its parts.

Two days ago, they'd been divided into two six-man teams. Peter's team from the airplane—Moretti, Luke, Zielinski, Quill, and Fisher—had worked well together in preparation for their assignment at the bridge. Technically, they had accomplished the task of demolishing their target, though they would have suffered casualties had this been more than an exercise.

Locotenent Constantin Condreanu still had his rifle aimed at Peter. He was in charge of the second half of Baker's team. Condreanu was a Romanian aristocrat and, like Baker, a member of SOE. He addressed Baker with confidence. "Major Baker, I will concede that Eddy's team got the bridge—barely. But we've captured half his team, and the barn and the train station are still completely unharmed."

"Yeah, but we got all your NCOs," Moretti's voice rang out. The rough Italian-American paratrooper had little patience for Condreanu's upperclass airs, one of the more obvious difficulties Baker was having as he tried to get his team to cooperate. Moretti and Zielinski walked into the glow of the floodlight with Corporal James Nelson and Sergeant Charlie Logan. Logan in particular was a competent soldier. Peter was surprised Moretti and Zielinski had captured him before he'd nabbed them.

The brilliant James Nelson—Jamie to his friends—had served with Baker in Italy. He knew more than a dozen languages, and while he might not pass for a native in a handful of European countries, few things a native said would get past him. He had blond hair and blue eyes, and he could have been Condreanu's handsome sidekick in a Hollywood movie. Nelson and Condreanu were alike in many ways: good looks, rich families, and contempt for those of lesser birth. The two aristocrats, both Cambridge men, tolerated the rest of the team. Nelson's presence gave the team four Romanian speakers: Nelson, Condreanu, Luke, and Ionescu. Most of the team predicted their final target would lie somewhere between Germany and the Black Sea, but Baker wasn't giving his men any confirmations.

"Make that three captured," Fisher shouted from halfway across the bridge.

With Fisher was the last of Baker's men: Sherlock, the medic who'd patched Peter up in Normandy. He'd been retrieved from a field camp in Normandy one week ago.

Condreanu frowned. "They left two targets standing."

"I ordered you to protect three targets. I ordered them to destroy one," Baker said. "Ionescu, check out the wiring." Ionescu went to inspect the work on the bridge. He wasn't quite as talented as Luke when it came to explosives, but he was close.

"Sir, it seems my team's assignment was a bit lopsided," Condreanu protested.

"Do you plan on complaining to the Nazis about the general unfairness of life should your next assignment also be lopsided?"

Condreanu looked at Baker then looked away. "No, sir."

A black car drove up and screeched to a halt in the center of the floodlit area. The local constable got out. "What is going on 'ere?" he roared.

Baker walked toward the constable. "Just a training exercise, sir. I have the paperwork giving us the necessary permissions in my pocket." Baker had genuine papers and an identical forgery Quill had made two days ago. Peter wondered which set Baker would hand the constable. "Give me an hour and it will be as though we were never here."

"Do you 'ave my bridge wired to explode?" The constable looked at the box in front of Peter, still upset.

"It would have blown sky-high too if Eddy and Quill had used real dynamite," Ionescu said in heavily accented English. Peter wasn't surprised with his analysis. Quill and Peter knew enough to blow a bridge successfully, but, like amateurs, they'd erred on the side of using too much explosive.

"You 'ave dynamite on my bridge? There are civilians within an 'undred meters of that bridge. You could 'ave killed women and children!"

Ionescu threw a bundle of the wax candles they'd strapped to the bridge's pylons at the constable. "Relax, sir, it's just a candle."

The constable's face was red. "And where did you get the lights?"

"We were just borrowing them," Nelson said.

"Borrowing them from my station?"

"Just for the night. We thought they would have been better secured if they were off-limits." Nelson grinned. According to rumor, Nelson's smile had charmed women all over Europe, but it didn't seem to charm the constable. As Peter watched, the constable's face turned purple.

"Jamie," Baker said quietly. "Do not insult the man's security."

"Sorry, Wesley," Nelson replied, no sign of remorse in his voice or his face.

Baker turned to the constable. "My men will put them back exactly as they found them. In an hour, the wires and the candles will be off the bridge. All equipment, including parachutes, will disappear by dawn."

"And who will reimburse the local farmers for their missing chickens?"

Baker's face tightened in anger as he turned toward Condreanu's team. "You had rations."

"Surely you didn't expect us to eat those 'orrible things if we're not in actual combat? They're worse than British cookin'." Logan's Irish accent brimmed with humor. His piercing blue eyes and short-cut curly blond hair gave him a youthful look, tempered by the long scar running down the right side of his face.

"How many chickens are missing?" Baker asked.

"Three," the constable reported.

"Send me the bill. I will make sure my men pay it." Baker handed the constable a piece of paper with his address.

The constable nodded. "If anything else is missing or if my equipment is not back where it belongs when I return to work, I will complain to the war department."

The war department was unlikely to care, but Baker nodded. The constable got in his car and drove away. "All right, men, good job on the bridge. Well done using what resources you could find, even if they did belong to the local constable." Baker paused, his voice lower and fiercer as he continued. "I know it's hard to be serious during an exercise after being in the field. But I would expect each of you to be smart enough not to steal food during an extended operation. Missing food would tip off the Gestapo just as easily as it tipped off this constable. Who took the chickens?"

Ionescu spoke up first. "Logan and I liberated two of them, sir."

"Liberated?"

"Yes, sir." Logan looked up from his sketchbook, where he was lampooning the recently departed constable. "They were so skinny we figured they 'ad to be POWs."

Luke laughed. Baker gave the three of them a look that immediately silenced them. "And the other chicken?"

Sherlock and Mitchell raised their hands. "We shared one, sir," Mitchell confessed, his jaw working on a piece of gum. He was a Canadian paratrooper, raised on a farm in Saskatchewan, and like Fisher, a gifted sniper. He could hit targets most of the team could barely even see.

Baker nodded, thinking. "At least you're honest with me. Don't let it happen again, not to English farmers. Out in the field, it's different. Here it's just plain theft. All of you will pay the fines, even if the constable overcharges you. Eddy's group—get your gear. Sherlock, Ionescu—clear the bridge. The rest of you take the lights back. I expect all of you to do your tasks without being seen."

The team broke up, completed their assignments, and returned to the bridge. Condreanu's group was the last to arrive.

"Did the constable know you were there?" Baker asked.

"No," Nelson said.

"Good, then I won't cancel your leave. It is currently Friday morning. In eight hours, a driver will take anyone who wishes to go to London. Stay out of trouble, and be back by 1700 hours Sunday. If you still have a hangover come Sunday evening, I guarantee you'll regret it. In the meantime, enjoy your weekend."

CHAPTER SEVEN

ALMOST LIKE PEACETIME

As she finished her shift and left Hammersmith Hospital, Genevieve glanced at the four men sitting on the short brick wall out front. Two wore civilian clothing; two wore uniforms. It wasn't until one of the uniformed men stood that she looked more closely.

"Peter?"

"*Bonsoir, beau canari.*"

She ran to him and threw her arms around him. "Why didn't you tell me you were coming to London?" Genevieve was sure her hair looked like it had just finished a twelve-hour shift, but Peter looked terrific. It was the first time she'd seen him in full uniform. She could still pick out some of his scars, but the bruises had disappeared. She studied him from head to foot, smiling as she took in his good health. Her eyes caught on his shoulder insignia. "I thought you were a second lieutenant?"

He shrugged. "I got promoted."

"Congratulations, *First* Lieutenant."

"Thanks. How are your ribs?"

"Fine. I haven't seen you in ages, Peter." It had been two weeks and a day since she'd last seen him, but it felt much longer. "I was starting to get worried about you." She'd been afraid he was off on another assignment or that she'd misread his affection for her.

"Didn't you get my letters?"

"Just the one you left with the nurses. Were there others?"

Peter nodded, looking surprised. "About a dozen."

"Well, that's the army for you: boxes of soap when you need bullets, wool uniforms for tropical assignments, months between leave, and plenty of lost mail." Genevieve looked past Peter's shoulders and noticed Daniel Fisher.

"Daniel?" Genevieve gave him a hug. "How's your ankle?"

"All better now," Fisher said.

"Genevieve, you already know Fish, but I should introduce you to Luke and Ionescu. Fish's mum lives a few blocks from the hospital and offered to let us stay for a few days."

Fisher smiled. "I thought she'd like to thank Lieutenant Eddy for keeping me out of a POW camp. And she's never yet complained when I bring 'ome stray Yankees."

"Stray Yankees?" Peter seemed amused by the expression.

"And a few stray Romanians like Ionescu 'ere too."

"It's good to meet you both." Genevieve nodded at the two men in suits. "Well, now that I've said 'ello, I think it's time for me to be on my way."

Fisher, Luke, and Ionescu said their good-byes and left.

"Are you doing anything tonight?" Peter asked.

She shook her head. "Nothing that can't be postponed."

"Would you care to spend the evening with me?"

"I'd love to." She let him take her hand and lead her away from the hospital.

"And tomorrow?"

"I have to work another shift, seven to seven." She frowned, knowing it was too late to switch her schedule.

"After that?"

"Nothing planned." She shifted closer to Peter to make room for passing pedestrians.

"Then I'll be here tomorrow night. What about Sunday morning?"

"I have Sunday off. I'm going to church with one of the hospital volunteers. You'll come with us, won't you, Peter?"

He seemed to hesitate before answering. "Yeah, I'll come with you."

"How long is your leave?" she asked as they crossed a busy street.

"I need to head back Sunday afternoon. Sorry I couldn't give you any warning. Leave was granted last minute. I think the only reason we're getting it is that Major Baker has a meeting with some big general."

"I'm glad you could come."

"Me too." Peter paused on the sidewalk and brushed Genevieve's cheek with his fingertips. The motion was so affectionate and tender that she almost forgot to breathe. "I missed you."

It took her a few moments to find her voice. "I missed you too, Peter. I hadn't realized how good we had it back in France when I could see you every day."

Peter's mouth pulled into a half grin as he looked around to make sure no one was within earshot. "Being tracked by the Gestapo was good?"

"I said we had it good, not perfect."

Peter nodded. "How long can I keep you out tonight?"

"The landlady locks the doors at midnight, I'm afraid."

"Well, Cinderella, I'll make sure I get you back by then." Peter winked. "Or I'll help you pick the lock."

* * *

After a stop at her boardinghouse, Peter took Genevieve to a pub Fisher had recommended for dinner. Then they took a cab to Hyde Park. As Peter took Genevieve's hand to help her out of the car, he heard a familiar laugh. He turned around, recognizing James Nelson and Constantin Condreanu. They were exiting a nightclub, their arms around ladies in evening gowns.

"Prayer Boy has a girl? I am astounded," Nelson said loudly, his words slightly slurred. Peter ignored the jibe, wishing he'd stayed at the pub a little longer. There wasn't a way to ignore them without being rude, so Peter and Genevieve waited the few seconds it took the group to reach them.

"Good evening," Peter said.

"Introduce us to your girl, Eddy," Nelson said briskly.

"Genevieve, this is Locotenent Condreanu and Corporal Nelson."

"Pleased to meet you," Genevieve said.

Nelson wasn't so drunk that he missed her distinctive accent. He replied in her language. "You are French? Pleased to meet you, mademoiselle. What part of France are you from?"

"Calais."

"Have you been in London long?"

"No, not long."

Nelson tilted his head to the side, probably trying to figure out how someone from Calais could be a recent arrival to the United Kingdom. Calais, after all, was still occupied by the Nazis.

Nelson's escort was an elegant woman with auburn hair and green eyes glazed over with alcohol. She was wearing a low-cut black dress and diamond jewelry. When she spoke, her voice revealed she was British and well-educated. "Are we still attending the opera?"

"Yes, of course." Nelson gave his date his attention for a moment before eying Genevieve again.

"Yes, we have boxed seats," Condreanu said. "Privilege of birth and all that. Not that we'd expect a farm boy from the United States to understand."

Nelson laughed, taking his cue from Condreanu. "America . . . I am not sure how they have survived so long without us. No nobility, no sense of tradition. But perhaps we are better off having lost them. Indeed, 'I do desire we may be better strangers' with the entire country." Nelson had a habit of peppering his speech with Shakespearean quotations. Peter could always pick them out because Nelson's voice would change, booming out as if he were onstage. "Mademoiselle, we are meeting a friend at the opera, an officer in the Royal Navy. He is handsome, intelligent, and rich, and his uncle is a duke. His date canceled at the last minute, so there is still room for one more in our box," he said, looking straight at Genevieve in obvious invitation.

"Well, in France, we beheaded most of our nobility. I'm afraid I don't understand dukes and their nephews any better than Peter does."

Condreanu narrowed his eyes at Genevieve's flippant reply. Nelson laughed harder. "Mademoiselle, you are quite charming. Are you sure you wouldn't like to attend the opera with us? Eddy is unlikely to buy you anything stronger to drink than a strawberry soda."

"I like soda," Genevieve said sweetly. "It was a pleasure to meet you. Enjoy your show."

They left then. Condreanu seemed irritated that his social status had failed to impress, and Nelson seemed amused by the same thing. Peter was happy to see them go.

"Wasn't your sister-in-law some type of aristocrat?" he asked.

Genevieve shrugged.

"So, um, do you want that strawberry soda now?"

Genevieve smiled and turned toward him. "No, I'm not thirsty."

He held her at arm's length, studying her. "Do you dance, Genevieve?"

"A little."

"I also dance a little, and there's a USO dance somewhere around here. Shall we try it out?"

Genevieve nodded her agreement, and ten minutes later they found themselves in a club crowded with US servicemen and local women.

Peter considered a dance successful if he met two requisites: not bumping into other couples and not stepping on his partner's toes. At first he had to focus all of his attention on meeting those two requirements, but after a few songs, he allowed himself to pay less attention to his feet and more attention to Genevieve, who followed him easily and seemed to find his awkwardness amusing.

"Why did those soldiers call you 'prayer boy'?" Genevieve asked.

Peter shrugged and pulled her a little closer. She came willingly. "Condreanu's my roommate. One night he came in while I was praying. He didn't hear anything, but he and Nelson thought it amusing to walk by and see me on my knees. They aren't very religious."

"Don't let them get to you. Sooner or later, they'll respect your beliefs."

Peter thought any respect would come later rather than sooner. "I don't know. They're having an awful lot of fun hating me."

Genevieve looked thoughtful. "Nelson's voice carried hatred but not his eyes."

Peter hadn't noticed, but he nodded, trusting her judgment.

There was a six-member jazz band accompanying a female singer. The singer had ebony skin, a blue sequined dress, and a silky voice. When Peter recognized the song, he leaned in next to Genevieve's ear and softly sang along. Genevieve seemed to enjoy it, and Peter liked the excuse to brush his lips across her cheek and inhale the hint of perfume she was wearing.

As the clock crept past 2330, Peter caught Genevieve yawning. "I should get you home," Peter said with a hint of regret.

"Mm, one more dance."

They finished the song then danced the next one. Peter knew the lyrics, so he whispered them into Genevieve's ear and watched the curve of her smiling lips. When the song ended, he was tempted to ask for another dance but instead led Genevieve toward the door.

Outside, Peter hailed a cab and opened the door for Genevieve. She gave the driver her address, and they settled into the backseat together. Peter put his arm around her shoulders and she leaned into his chest, softly humming the band's last song: "How High the Moon." By the time they reached the boarding home, she was nearly asleep. Peter paid the driver and helped Genevieve from the car.

"You've had a long day." He felt selfish for keeping her out so long when she'd just worked one long shift and had another in seven hours.

"Long, but good."

"But you'll be exhausted at work tomorrow."

She squeezed his hand. "I'll be okay. I loved dancing with you, Peter. I wish we could have danced until dawn." When they reached the door, she gazed up at Peter with a smile.

"What are you thinking about?" he asked.

"Whether or not you're going to kiss me good night."

"I'm considering it," Peter said.

"Oh? And which way are you leaning?"

"I'd already be kissing you if your landlady weren't watching us through the window."

Genevieve spun around. The landlady had disappeared, but the curtain was still swinging. "That old cow. She drives me crazy."

"Hmm. You know who drives me crazy?"

"Who?" Genevieve turned back to Peter.

"You do. But in a good way." Peter gave her the good night kiss she'd asked about. He'd missed her lips, missed the way it felt to hold her in his arms, missed the way her fingers played with his hair. He didn't want the kiss—or the evening—to ever end.

CHAPTER EIGHT
MEN ARE LIKE SHOES

Saturday, July 15

PETER SPENT THE NEXT DAY with Fisher, Luke, and Ionescu seeing the sights of London. Fisher had grown up there, and Peter had seen most of the city before, but London was new to Luke and Ionescu. Fisher spent the morning picking positions he'd take as a sniper. The two demolition experts bounced ideas around on how they could best destroy each landmark—strictly a mental exercise, of course. Luke had more training, Ionescu more experience. Ionescu had escaped Romania a year before when a sabotage project targeting an oil refinery went awry. His last assignment, dropping into France before D-day to help the Resistance destroy German petroleum supplies, had been carried out with incendiary success. When Luke and Ionescu weren't planning theoretical explosions, they traded stories about Romania.

As the afternoon progressed, Peter excused himself and bought some sandwiches before meeting Genevieve at the end of her shift. He walked her back to her boarding home so she could change.

They were about to leave when Genevieve's landlady interrupted them. "You 'ad best watch yourself, missy. These young Yanks are only after one thing. Supposed to be fighting the Jerries, but they seem more interested in conquering the local female population. We ought to send the lot of 'em back 'ome."

Peter felt his face turn hot. He had no intention of seducing Genevieve, but he'd laughed when Fisher and Luke had suggested he take Genevieve to a dark, deserted bomb shelter. He knew it was difficult for civilians to find housing in London and didn't want to cause trouble for Genevieve, so he stepped toward the door. Nelson and Condreanu had given him plenty of practice at ignoring insults; he could ignore one more. "Come on, Genevieve. Let's go."

Genevieve's eyes had narrowed, and she placed her hands on her hips. "You're speaking of things you know nothing about. Peter is a perfect gentleman. And if you'd rather not have American help, perhaps a quick trip across the Channel where they're dying by the thousands will change your mind. I ask that you never insult Peter again."

The landlady stood there, looking at Genevieve in slight awe. Peter too was surprised by Genevieve's force. Surprised, impressed, and grateful. After a minute, the landlady nodded her head toward him and uttered a quiet apology.

"No hard feelings, ma'am," he said. The landlady excused herself and left through the back door.

Genevieve threaded her arm through Peter's and led him outside, where a cool, refreshing breeze met them, clearing Peter's mind.

"Thanks for sticking up for me."

"I couldn't let her malign you like that." Genevieve shook her head in frustration. "She wasn't being fair."

"Fair or not, it's a common enough sentiment. I don't want you to get evicted because of me."

Genevieve grinned. "She won't evict me. She's scared of Colonel McDougall."

"Why?"

"He knows the man in charge of signing draft waivers for railroad workers. Her son works on the railroad, and I think few things scare her more than losing her son to the army. That's why she was cranky tonight—her son. She's glad the Americans are sending boys over so her Godfrey can stay in London and come home to her every night, but she's also jealous for his sake. I've told him I have a boyfriend, but he still asks me to dinner most nights. And I keep turning him down."

Peter studied Genevieve's face, looking for clues about her new suitor. "This Godfrey sounds like a persistent fellow. Should I be worried?"

"No. Godfrey can take his handsome face elsewhere. I'm not interested."

"But he's handsome? I bet he doesn't have a crooked nose or scars everywhere." *And he's not responsible for all the horrible things you've been through the last few months*, Peter thought.

"Honestly, Peter, your nose is hardly crooked at all now the swelling's gone away. I like your nose." She tapped it lightly with one of her fingers. "And I like the rest of you, scars and all."

"Thanks. And thanks for defending me."

"Someone has to stick up for you, and I knew you were too nice to do it yourself."

Peter laughed. "Me? Nice? I guess Tschirner wasn't the only one I fooled in France."

"Oh, Peter, I know all about you."

Peter stopped walking and turned to study her expression. "And just what dirty little secrets do you know about me, Mademoiselle Olivier?"

Genevieve smiled and kept him waiting for a few seconds before she began. "I know exactly which muscles along your jaw tighten when you're trying to keep from saying something you think you shouldn't and which ones tense when you're in pain. I know you normally snore for about thirty seconds when you first fall asleep. Then you sleep silently until you wake—unless you have nightmares, which you often do. Then you start mumbling and shaking your head back and forth."

"Better not let your landlady hear such talk. She'll think her accusations are spot on."

Genevieve smiled, but her voice was more serious when she continued. "I also know you're very good and trying to be even better. I know you'd rather suffer yourself than hurt anyone else. And I know somehow you helped Jacques find his way again. Thank you. To have him turn to God again—it makes everything else okay."

"I can't take credit for Jacques." Genevieve's brother had changed the week before he died, but Peter doubted he was responsible.

Genevieve was quiet for a moment. "Peter, I've known Jacques my entire life. I watched him slowly change as the war dragged on—and there wasn't anything I could do or say to stop it. Believe me, I tried. Something about you helped him, Peter. Maybe it was something you said, maybe it was something you did, or maybe it was just the way you lived your life. The last day—it was like the old Jacques was back, and it was because of you."

Peter looked away, unconvinced. "I'd like to believe that."

"Then believe it." She cupped his jaw in her hand and brought his face back around until he was looking into her eyes, seeing a firmness there he couldn't ignore.

"Because of me, Jacques is dead."

Genevieve looked down then looked back at Peter and slid her hand from his chin to his chest, resting it there, next to his heart. "We all made a few mistakes in Calais, didn't we? My brother never planned to live to the end of the war. Thanks to you, his soul wasn't lost when he died."

Still focused on her dark brown eyes, Peter brought his hand up and brushed a stray strand of Genevieve's hair behind her ear. "You can be kind of stubborn. You know that, right?"

She smiled. "So can you, remember? Peter, let's not talk about my brother's death. I only have a few hours with you before you go back to training, and I don't want to spend it feeling guilty about the past. Can you please accept that I don't blame you for any of my recent hardships, nor for any of my brother's?"

He nodded. Peter thought she was wrong not to blame him but believed her when she said she didn't. They walked to the grassy area of Wormwood Scrubs, near the hospital, and had a picnic.

"Let's play piquet," Genevieve said when they finished the sandwiches Peter had bought earlier. "The winner can ask the loser any question they like—and the loser must answer honestly."

Genevieve dealt, and Peter won the first game.

"How handsome do you find this Godfrey fellow?" He was lying on his stomach, his head propped up with his left hand.

"Oh, Peter, I told you not to worry about that, didn't I?"

"You made the rules; you have to answer honestly."

Genevieve sighed. "Well, let's put it this way: men are like shoes."

"Oh, of course," Peter agreed. "We're meant to be walked all over."

"That's not what I meant," she said with a laugh. She was sitting on the blanket Peter had borrowed from Mrs. Fisher, her legs extended and crossed at the ankles, one arm supporting her. "The point is a good pair of shoes needs to fit and be comfortable and be attractive. A cute shoe won't do a girl any good if it's the wrong size or if it fits but gives her blisters. Godfrey is like a good-looking pair of shoes, but I can tell he'd be a bad fit without even trying him on."

"Hmm." Peter considered her analogy. "And what type of shoe am I?"

"You're not a pair of shoes; you're a man."

"But if you were to compare me to a pair of shoes, what type would I be?" He put his left arm down and propped his head up with his right arm instead.

Genevieve paused before answering. "Well, not the shoes I'm wearing now."

Peter looked at her feet—she was wearing a pair of brown oxfords.

"I mean these are comfortable and everything but not very attractive. I only bought them because they were the sole practical pair in my size. And the shoes I borrowed from a housemate yesterday were gorgeous, but they gave me blisters, so you're not like a pair of heels either." She tilted her head to the side and thought a little longer. "I can't say, Peter. I've never found a pair of shoes that I like anywhere near as much as I like you. I don't think such shoes exist."

Peter dealt the cards for the next round, and this time he lost.

"Have you ever been in love before?" Genevieve asked.

"Before when?" He avoided her eyes, focusing on the discarded pile of cards instead.

Genevieve thought for a moment. "How about before May of this year?"

"No, not *before* May." He'd met Genevieve at the end of May but hadn't fallen in love with her until June.

"What about *since* May?"

Peter could feel the corners of his lips turning up into a smile. He knew exactly what she was asking but couldn't resist teasing her. "I only have to answer one question per loss."

"I answered more than one question last round!"

"Not my fault. You didn't have to."

Genevieve tried to frown but laughed instead. "Then I had better win the next round."

She didn't, and by the time they were done, it was too dark to play anymore. With the sun down and all artificial light hidden behind blackout curtains, the middle of London felt completely secluded. Peter helped Genevieve to her feet but didn't release her hand.

"I love you," he whispered. He watched the smile form on her face as he ran his fingers over her perfectly smooth cheek. When he met her lips, Genevieve's response was immediate, avid, and satisfying.

* * *

Peter waited for Genevieve on the street outside the boardinghouse Sunday morning, ready to attend church with her as he'd promised. He'd been hesitant to accept her invitation on Friday because he'd wanted to attend his own church services. He hadn't been since May, because he was either on assignment, in the hospital, or unable to get leave, but he knew where the London branch met. Yet he hadn't been able to say no when Genevieve asked him to join her. Mass, Peter justified, might be spiritually renewing, and if not, it would at least be culturally enriching.

Genevieve slipped out the front door and smiled when she saw him. She wore a blue dress, and she looked beautiful.

"Good morning, *beau canari*." Peter kissed her cheek and took her arm. "Which cathedral are we going to?"

"We're not going to Mass, Peter; we're going to sacrament meeting."

Genevieve's answer surprised him. "A Mormon sacrament meeting?"

"A lady at the hospital asked me to go with her last week, and I enjoyed it. And I thought you'd prefer a Mormon service over a Catholic one. But if you'd rather go to Mass, I'm sure we can find one . . ." Genevieve trailed off, teasing him.

"Sacrament meeting would be wonderful."

The rented building where the London branch met was familiar to Peter, and so were many of the faces. A member of the branch presidency greeted them as they arrived, and Peter remembered him from when he'd attended the branch the previous winter.

"Welcome back, young man," Brother Lind said, shaking Peter's hand. "I remember your face, but you'll have to remind me of your name."

"Peter Eddy."

"Brother Eddy, would you be willing to help bless the sacrament today?"

"I'd be honored." It felt good to be in church again, almost like touching a bit of home.

* * *

After the meeting, Peter and Genevieve said good-bye at the nearest tube station.

"How long do you have?" Genevieve asked.

"Before the train? Maybe four minutes."

"That's not what I meant."

"I know," Peter said. "I'm not sure when we'll ship out. I don't think the team's ready yet, but depending on our objective, it might not matter."

"Do you think you'll have leave again?" He could hear emotion sneaking into her voice, like she was about to cry.

Peter took her hand. "Don't know. But I'll keep writing to you." He paused, looking past her for a moment at the trickle of other passengers. He suddenly wanted to beg her to wait for him, but he didn't think that would be fair. He'd yet to hear of a mission thought up by OSS or SOE that wasn't at least slightly suicidal. He didn't want Genevieve to be haunted by promises made to a ghost if he never returned, so he stayed silent.

"Will you do me a favor, Peter?"

"What can I do for you, *beau canari*?"

Her fingers found the scar on his left temple, then with her other hand, she gently touched the scar on the opposite ear and felt for the scar running down his chin. "If you want a souvenir, collect something other than a scar on your next mission." Her mouth was smiling playfully, but her eyes were serious.

"I'll do my best," Peter promised. He reached into his pocket and pulled out a Purple Heart, putting the medallion and ribbon into one of her hands.

He'd planned to say something about leaving his heart with her, but he looked into her eyes and knew she understood.

Despite the small crowd waiting for the train, Peter leaned in and kissed her, feeling adoration mingled with fear. He held her tightly, hoping he would see her again soon but knowing he might never see her again at all.

He kissed her until the train arrived, and then he looked back as he boarded and found Genevieve's face. He saw the glint of tears in the corners of her eyes, saw how her cheeks were beginning to color, and noticed the faint lines appearing between her eyebrows and around her lips. He knew that face. Genevieve was worried.

CHAPTER NINE
DISTANCE AND TIME

Sunday, July 16

BACK AT DRAVOT MANOR, THE team spent the evening—Sunday evening, Peter realized with chagrin—learning twenty-two ways to kill someone with a knife. A middle-aged Scottish sergeant taught twenty of the techniques. Nelson taught the final two.

The supper chatter was divided between discussion of the class and of leave.

"What did you do during leave, Zielinski?" Luke was sitting between Peter and the Polish kapral.

"Visited my family."

Luke adjusted his glasses. "I'm a little jealous. It was nice to visit Fish's mother and all, but it kind of made me miss my own mom."

"You barely saw my mum." Fisher was across the table from them.

"Ate some pretty good scones she made though. Zielinski, did your mom cook you anything special when you went home?"

"No, but my sister did."

"I miss my sister. And my parents," Luke said.

Moretti was sitting next to Fisher. "Give it some time, kid. The homesickness will pass."

"I know, it's just that Fish got to see his mom, and Zielinski got to see his whole family." Luke shrugged. "I'm fine. Tomorrow I won't even care."

Peter noticed a sad look cross Zielinski's face, so he asked, "You didn't see your whole family, did you?"

Zielinski glanced at Peter. "No."

"I thought you went to stay with your parents. And your sister cooked for you," Luke said.

"My father had to work. And I have three sisters. Two are still in Poland— if they're alive."

Luke's face softened. "How long has it been since you've heard from them?"

"Five years." Zielinski played with his food for a few more minutes but didn't eat anything else. He excused himself as Moretti tried to shift the conversation to some of the techniques they'd learned earlier.

When the meal was finished, Nelson wandered over to Luke and handed him a glass of milk.

"What's this for?" Luke frowned at the glass.

"'Tears, then, for babes—blows and revenge for me!' And milk for a homesick American ninny."

"Leave him alone," Peter said.

"Of course. Please accept my apology, Mr. Lucaciu." Nelson turned from Luke and smiled at Peter. "I am sure you have never been homesick, Eddy. What is there to miss about a poverty-ridden farm in the middle of Idaho?"

Nelson turned his back and went outside to join Condreanu for a cigarette. Peter clenched his teeth together to keep from saying something he knew he'd regret.

* * *

Krzysztof Zielinski heard footsteps in the hallway and turned as Logan entered the room.

"Quill's organizin' a poker tourney, if you're interested."

Krzysztof felt himself smiling. Poker was a popular pastime at Dravot Manor. "I need to write a letter."

"That's what Eddy said." Nelson's laughter drifted in through the cracked window, and Logan's smile turned to a scowl, making the long scar on his face more prominent. "One o' these days, I'll 'ave to practice 'and-to-'and combat with that arrogant sod and smash 'is pretty British nose."

Krzysztof knew there were several members of the team who felt the same way. Nelson was an enigma to Krzysztof. Three weeks ago, Baker's team had consisted of only two men: Krzysztof Zielinski and James Nelson. At first, Nelson had been polite and friendly. He even spoke decent Polish, and Krzysztof had enjoyed their exchanges in his native language. Nelson had spent his early days at Dravot Manor reading Shakespeare plays and telling Krzysztof about his past.

Nelson had lived most of his youth in southeastern Europe, piloting his father's yacht up and down the Danube. Nelson's father was a smuggler, and since Hitler's rise to power, people had become the most commonly smuggled cargo. Nelson had interacted with a variety of people fleeing the Third Reich:

Jews, God-fearing clergymen, Communists, and anti-Nazi politicians. His father's business, combined with Nelson's first-class education, left Nelson confident and easy to converse with. Yet as the team assembled, his confident nature had turned arrogant.

Now Nelson showed nothing but contempt for Americans in general and Lieutenant Eddy in particular. Eddy was tolerating it stoically, but Krzysztof had heard the jokes Logan told about Nelson and the rest of the British Empire and had seen a few of his scathing drawings. Krzysztof also noticed the dagger looks Moretti shot at Nelson's back. Nelson and Baker were close friends; Krzysztof wondered why Baker didn't insist on cooperation and why Nelson didn't give it.

"Want me to bring you up a pint o' somethin'?" Logan asked.

Krzysztof shook his head. "Thanks for the offer. Did you have a good leave?"

Logan shrugged.

"London?"

"No, I stayed 'ere. I've never cared for London," Logan said then nodded his farewell.

Krzysztof sat at a desk and stared at the blank sheet in front of him. He knew what he wanted to write to his father but also knew he wouldn't write it. He leaned over the desk and pushed the window open wider then lit a cigarette and placed it in the ashtray. Krzysztof didn't smoke, yet he always carried matches and a package of cigarettes because he never wanted to be without an excuse to carry matches should he need to burn pieces of codes, and the stench of the tobacco covered the smell of burnt paper. Krzysztof didn't have anything to hide from his teammates, but he wouldn't allow himself to skip a step that might be vital in the field.

Krzysztof heard Nelson's laughter again and picked out another object from his package of cigarettes. It looked like a cigarette, but it was stiffer. Krzysztof gently drew the faux cigarette apart and pulled out the scroll of paper inside, unrolling it with great care to reveal the five hundred sixty five-digit cipher groups, each representing a word or phrase. Then he picked out the groups he wanted.

Krzysztof had turned eighteen the day the Germans invaded his homeland. By then, his family had been in London for two weeks. They'd left Poland despite his father's prestigious and satisfying job as a mathematics professor at Jagiellonian University, despite their comfortable home, and despite the large extended family who lived nearby. And they had left without Krzysztof's two older sisters. One had been expecting a baby and hadn't wanted to travel so far under the circumstances. The other had decided to stay with her husband, and he'd refused to leave. Krzysztof knew it was for his sake his father had dragged the incomplete family away. His father wasn't opposed to Krzysztof fighting the Nazis, but he wanted him to fight when he could win.

So Krzysztof's letter was short, summarizing his excellent training, reporting the weekend spent with his mother and younger sister. He didn't tell his father he missed him—his father would already know. And he didn't ask about his father's work. Even in code, Krzysztof's father would never go into detail about what he did at the Government Code and Cypher School at Bletchley Park. Krzysztof's father had been involved in breaking German codes before the family left Poland, and Krzysztof suspected that was still what his father did. But the codes his father spent twelve to twenty hours a day cracking were too important for a mere kapral to inquire about.

Krzysztof finished the first draft of his letter then began transposing the coded numbers into a second set of digits. Krzysztof didn't need a key for the secondary encoding method. He and his father rotated through three memorized formulas. He could remember which he had used last as easily as he could remember the color of his sisters' eyes.

He paused, wondering if he would still be able to tell his two older sisters apart. They were identical twins, but Ania's eyes had always seemed a half-shade darker. She had dark blue eyes, just as Krzysztof did. He wondered if she'd given birth to a boy or to a girl. Somewhere in Poland, he might have a niece or a nephew. He thought of Ania's husband, the teacher, and doubted he was still alive. The Nazi regime had set a goal to eliminate all Poles capable of leadership. After nearly five years of occupation, Krzysztof guessed they were close to achieving their aim. Or would the bright young teacher have listened to his father-in-law's parting advice and pretended to be an illiterate farmer? Krzysztof's other brother-in-law, a baker, wouldn't have been as much of a target because of his trade, but Krzysztof couldn't picture the stubborn Slavomir meekly submitting to occupation.

Krzysztof shook his head, thinking no longer of the family that might be dead and focusing instead on the numbers and letters of his code. It was one of the things he loved about his work. The numbers were simple. There was a pattern. And as long as he found the key, the answer was clear.

Krzysztof put the cigarette with the scroll back inside his cigarette pack and placed the pack in his pocket. The scroll inside was meant to be used as a one-time pad. When used only once, one-time ciphers were almost impossible to break, but Krzysztof and his father had used this cipher twice before, so it was no longer infallible. Krzysztof had started a new one during leave, but he hadn't been able to complete it.

Krzysztof lit the first draft of his letter and placed the burning sheet on the ashtray. Then he looked out at the stars. It was a clear night. He wondered if the weather in Poland was similar and if his sisters were still alive to look at the same stars and remember him.

CHAPTER TEN

HOW FAR

Monday, July 17

BY MONDAY, SPY SCHOOL WAS in full swing again. After morning calisthenics and breakfast, the team met in the manor's formal dining hall. The room's long table had been replaced with several rows of chairs, a chalkboard, and a slide projector. Three crystal chandeliers still hung from the ceiling, a reminder of the room's former elegance. The morning's subject was interrogation, the teacher a British Army colonel. Colonel Poole encouraged student participation, and several of the men had feedback for him.

"If your target is a woman, you should make her think you are seducing her rather than interrogating her," Nelson said.

Poole looked amused. "Has that worked for you in the past?"

Nelson nodded with a knowing smile. "Yes, and it was much more enjoyable than beating the information out of someone."

"All right, if you are as charming as Corporal Nelson, you can woo the information out of your target. But for those of us who are not so handsome, let's discuss another method Nelson mentioned: physical pain as a lever."

The class continued the discussion for nearly an hour. Everyone but Peter, Baker, and Logan had something to say. Logan was normally more talkative or at least busy drawing something; Peter wondered about his reticence. Peter was intimately acquainted with several interrogation techniques, but he'd always been the recipient of those methods, not the one applying them.

"Lieutenant Eddy." Peter looked up to see Poole's hazel eyes staring at him. "You have been completely mute throughout our discussion."

"I'm paying attention, sir. But I've never interrogated anyone."

Out of the corner of his eye, Peter could see Nelson lean over to Condreanu. "Farmers," he whispered derisively, just loud enough for Peter to hear.

"Lieutenant Eddy, I was hoping you could help me transition into the next part of our discussion. You are the only one here who has been questioned by both the *Wehrmacht* and the *Geheime Staatspolizei*. Instead of breaking, you successfully misled your captors. You are more of an expert on getting through interrogations than I am."

Fisher looked from Poole to Peter, startled. "You did look like someone 'ad used you as a punching bag the first time I saw you."

Condreanu stared at Peter, surprise replacing his contempt. Peter realized the entire class was looking at him. "I thought those incidents were classified, sir."

"The details from your debriefing are classified, but your techniques are not and would be useful to other members of the class." Poole wasn't going to let him off the hook.

Peter thought about the experiences, wishing everyone would stop looking at him. He wasn't normally so self-conscious, but thinking about his time in Gestapo prison always brought back hints of the pain and despair he'd felt there. He shoved his feelings aside and tried to answer objectively. "I think the most successful technique was pretending to break and giving them false information. With the Gestapo, I built on an existing disinformation campaign. With the army, I made something up. You have to tell them something plausible, of course. It's a mistake to underestimate their intelligence."

Poole picked up the lecture from there. "Lieutenant Eddy is rather remarkable in his ability to come up with a convincing lie while under extreme physical and emotional distress. I suggest no one in this classroom assume they will spontaneously have the same talent. That is why preparation and a good cover story are so key. Know beforehand what you will say if you get caught. Say you are arrested with all your demolition gear. Your orders are to blow up a bridge before the German Army can retreat across it. What would you tell your captors if you were caught, Mr. Lucaciu?"

Luke adjusted his glasses as he thought. "I was taking the explosives to a resistance contact, and they were planning to sabotage a railroad."

"Not bad," Poole said. "But where were you meeting your contact?" Before Luke could answer, Poole asked another question. "What is your contact's name? Which rail was he planning to destroy? Why that rail and not a different one? Why not blow the rail yourself? Who are your other contacts? And don't forget, all the techniques we discussed earlier are now being used against you."

"What about the Geneva conventions, sir?" Quill asked, popping his knuckles. "If we're captured in uniform, they have to treat us civilly."

Poole seemed surprised by Quill's question. Quill was athletic, intelligent, and disciplined. He was also very young and had yet to come face-to-face with his enemy. "Have any of you heard of Hitler's commando order?" Poole asked.

No one raised their hand. "That doesn't surprise me. It was a secret order when issued. Most German Army generals haven't heard it either. Major Baker?"

"Any soldier behind enemy lines, in uniform or out, is considered a commando. Commandos are to be slaughtered."

"Yes, slaughtered," Poole repeated. "After they are broken and as much information is extracted from them as possible. Lieutenant Eddy, when you were in Gestapo prison, did you notice any Red Cross personnel?"

"No, sir," Peter said.

"Afternoon tea service?"

"No, sir."

"Brutal beatings?"

Peter still didn't want to talk about what had happened in prison, but Poole was waiting for his answer. "Yes, sir." Peter tried to keep his tone even, but the volume of his voice dropped.

"I am sure you can all use your imaginations. The best plan is to stay out of enemy hands. But always be prepared for the worst. When you come up with a cover story, think of the questions you would ask if you were the one in charge of the questioning. And stick to your story. Every time you change a detail, you create suspicion." Poole continued on for some time but didn't request any additional comments from Peter. At about noon, the colonel wound up his lecture and the class was dismissed.

"Be at the firing range at 1300 hours," Baker ordered. "I borrowed a few schmeissers, and I'd like you to become familiar with them." Baker wanted his men to be skilled with any weapon they might come across in the field; he'd collected an impressive variety. "And prepare for a little run at 1600 hours." A "little run" would be five miles, minimum, with at least fifty pounds of gear strapped to their backs. "Eddy, stay behind for a minute."

Everyone else left, a few of them with raised eyebrows. Peter wasn't sure what to expect, so Baker's statement caught him off guard: "It can be hard to be a good spy. It can also be hard to be a good man. Sometimes I think being both at once is nearly impossible." Baker pulled a chair around and sat facing Peter.

"I don't remember anyone saying it was supposed to be easy, sir."

Baker sighed, his face kind. "You didn't enjoy class today." Peter stared at the floor. "There's no need for embarrassment, Lieutenant. Colonel Poole and I were the only ones who noticed."

"I think my perspective on interrogation is different from the rest of the men."

"Yes, you see yourself as the one being questioned. They see themselves as the ones doing the questioning. Frankly, I hope none of us will have to be on either end of an interrogation during our upcoming mission. But we have to prepare for that possibility. I want you on my team, Eddy, but I need to know how far you're willing to go."

Peter studied his commanding officer. Wesley Baker was tall, with solid muscles and a soft voice. He was a good leader and a good man. Baker wouldn't enjoy inflicting pain on a prisoner any more than Peter would. Peter looked into Baker's intelligent, penetrating eyes and knew the man would do whatever it took to complete his mission. "Meaning how much am I willing to hurt someone?"

Baker nodded. "If we needed information, what would you be willing to do to get it?"

It was a fair question, but Peter didn't know the answer. "It would depend on the scenario, sir." Peter couldn't think of anything that would justify abusing a woman or a child. A soldier was in another category, a Gestapo officer in yet another. "If it was important and if there was no other way, I wouldn't interfere."

"And if the mission or a member of the team was at stake and you had to perform the interrogation?"

Peter didn't ever want to interrogate anyone, not with the methods they were talking about. To act like the men who'd tortured him would make him a little like them, wouldn't it? And Peter didn't want to be like Prinz, Tschirner, Siebert, or Weiss.

In his mind, Peter rephrased Baker's question. What would he do if it were Genevieve's life in danger and the information that could save her was locked in his prisoner's brain? The answer scared him: he would do anything.

Peter met Baker's eyes. "I would be a good spy, sir, even if that meant shooting out someone's kneecaps. But I hope it never comes to that."

"So do I." Baker looked relieved. "You are a religious man, Lieutenant. Pray we will never find ourselves in such desperate circumstances. See you on the firing range in fifty minutes."

* * *

The evening run ended up being six miles with sixty pounds of equipment. Like most of the team, Peter stayed with the group and allowed Quill to set a reasonable pace. Mitchell and Moretti stayed with the group the first half of the run then began pushing each other farther and farther out in front. Mitchell was a former collegiate runner, and Moretti just liked to race. The two of them were laughing at one another when the rest of the team finished. Moretti was doubled over, massaging his thigh.

"Who won?" Luke slid his pack off and looked at Moretti.

"Our northern neighbor, kid. But only because my leg cramped up."

Nelson began humming "Rule, Britannia" as he walked by and let his pack slip to the ground.

Moretti shook his head. "Mitchell is Canadian, not British. If you wanna celebrate his three-second victory, you should be humming 'O, Canada.' Ain't that right, Mitchell?"

Mitchell grinned and nodded, wiping the sweat off his forehead and putting a piece of gum into his mouth. But as Nelson walked by, Condreanu in tow, the smile slid off his face.

"What?" Moretti asked.

Mitchell waited until most of the team had moved on. Moretti and Peter were the only ones nearby. "If looks could kill, I'd be dead."

"I don't know how Baker survived working with that stuck-up snob in Italy for as long as he did." Then Moretti called Nelson an unpleasant name.

"You may not be too far off," Mitchell said.

Moretti raised his eyebrows. "Oh? You think he's illegitimate?"

"You know that girl I told you about—Sally? The one I met a few weeks before D-day?"

Moretti nodded. Peter remembered censoring a letter Mitchell had sent her.

"Nelson's in line to inherit a huge estate from his maternal grandfather, Lord Tinley. Tinley had two daughters. One of them, Mary, ran off with Nelson's father. The other one's an old maid, and Sally's her cook, so she hears most of the family gossip. Mary died a few years after marrying Nelson's father. Henry Nelson came back then to pay his respects to Mary's family, but he didn't mention anything about having a son. Five years later, Henry came to visit again. This time he had a little boy with him. Our very own Corporal James Nelson. Only little Jamie was small for his age and not very bright for a five-year-old. Little Jamie's aunt still isn't convinced that her nephew is, in fact, her sister's son."

"Why would someone pass off . . . never mind. The estate," Moretti said.

"Yeah, Nelson's father wants his son to inherit," Mitchell said. "But if James was born before Mary died, Henry Nelson would have mentioned him when he came to pay his respects."

"And the aunt?" Moretti asked as he lit a cigarette.

"The aunt's been overridden. Lord Tinley wants Nelson to be his grandson. He's perfect: male, Cambridge graduate, handsome, brilliant—even if he was a late bloomer. Everything an aristocrat should be."

"Everything an aristocrat should be, minus firm parentage," Moretti finished with an amused smile. "Why were you wasting time with your girl talking about Nelson?"

Mitchell shrugged, chewing his gum. "I was telling her about the team. She met Nelson back before he and Baker shipped off to Italy. Only last time Nelson visited his aunt, he was wearing a lieutenant's uniform."

Moretti laughed. "I bet he got busted down to a corporal. I wonder what he did . . ."

"Hey, don't say anything—Nelson's aunt is a real stickler about upholding the family honor. I don't want to get Sally in trouble."

"Oh, I'll keep quiet," Moretti said. "But it will give me something to think about next time he looks down his superior nose at me."

Chapter Eleven

Promises

Sunday, July 30

Genevieve put Peter's Book of Mormon down when the girls across the hall began playing their music. She grabbed her sweater and walked to the alley behind the boardinghouse. It wasn't dark yet, but the light was fading, and the evening air was refreshing. Genevieve liked this section of London. It was old but tidy, if one ignored the buildings that had been bombed into rubble.

Genevieve found herself thinking about Peter's religion more and more as the summer progressed. As she walked, she thought about the story she'd just read. A group of people had been taught the gospel and joined the Christian church. Not wanting to go back to their bloodthirsty ways, they buried their weapons and refused to pick them up again, even when attacked. Her thoughts gradually shifted from the Ammonites to her brother, Jacques. A few tears crept down her cheeks, and she wiped them away.

Jacques had been a caring brother to her. He had also played the role of parent after their father died, and she knew he had worked hard to provide for and protect her. And he had been a wonderful husband to Mireille. But as the war dragged on, her good brother had become vengeful—and bloodthirsty. He had been like the people of Ammon before they'd heard the gospel and buried their swords. Yet before he died, Jacques told her he'd made his peace with God. Genevieve wasn't sure exactly what that meant, but Jacques had been different that day. He'd been gentle again and merciful. She wondered if he, like the Ammonites, had buried his sword. And she wondered if the Lord had taken him then out of mercy, before he had a chance to dig his sword up and backtrack into ruthlessness.

So many thoughts and questions swam through her head. The Book of Mormon—she still thought of it as Peter's book—confused her. Before meeting Peter, she'd been a good, faithful Catholic, never questioning what she was told. She knew it seemed naive to believe everything a priest told her, but after living through the death of both of her parents and then facing Nazi occupation for four long years, clinging to religion seemed the best way to control something in her life. She hadn't always known what would happen next week or next year, but at least she'd known what to expect in the next life.

Then Peter suggested her priest might be wrong about something and even had a scripture in his book to back it up. The more she read the little book, the more it seemed right, even though she'd never heard of it before meeting Peter. On their ten-day trek from her family's farmhouse to the front lines of Normandy, religion had been a common topic. She'd asked question after question about what Peter believed, and he had patiently satisfied her curiosity. Only it hadn't just been curiosity. The things he told her—even things that differed from what she'd previously been taught—felt exactly right. *Or do you just want them to be true? Do you just want prophets and apostles, eternal families, and an atonement that unconditionally saves little children?* Genevieve wasn't sure if she was drawn to Peter's religion because it was true or if she was drawn to it because she *wanted* it to be true.

Then there was the other complication: Peter himself. She loved him. She loved everything about him and sometimes wondered if his religion was just another characteristic that appealed to her, like his eyes or his laugh or the way he kissed her. She wanted to trust her heart when it came to the Book of Mormon, but she'd given her heart to Peter. She needed to take Peter out of her decision, so she needed something more than just her heart to tell her if the Mormon Church was true.

Genevieve continued to wander, trying to determine how she could really know. She remembered the first time she'd seen the book. Peter had pointed out a section to her near the end of the book. She'd read his recommendation then the pages that followed. In the last pages, the author had promised if she asked God whether the book was true, God would tell her.

All right, Genevieve thought, *I'll finish the book and then I'll ask*. But then another thought came to her. *Why not ask now?* Sunlight had disappeared, and the streets were quiet and empty. She came to an arched doorway, sheltered from the street, and stopped. Genevieve had prayed before. She had even prayed out loud before—but always with memorized prayers. She felt she should say this prayer out loud, but as she knelt down, she wasn't sure what words to use.

She knelt and wondered what she should say until her knees began to hurt. Finally, she began. "God, is the Mormon Church the only true church on the earth, like Peter says? And is the Book of Mormon true?" She paused then quickly ended her prayer. "Please help me to know. Amen."

What happened as she ended her prayer was hard to describe. She felt at peace, but the feeling was so strong that *peaceful* didn't seem an adequate description. Tears came to her eyes, but she wasn't sad. Her throat felt slightly constricted, but she wasn't scared. She simply knew. She stayed on her knees, awed that she could know something so completely and amazed that her Father in Heaven cared about her enough to answer her simple prayer.

* * *

After work the next day, Genevieve took the Underground across London to visit her friends from France, Marcel and Hélène Papineau. Their niece had married Genevieve's brother, and they were the closest thing she had to family. She usually made the trip once a week, but she was a few days late for this visit.

Their flat was small, and it had been built many years ago. They'd fled France in May and had left behind a comfortable home with a beautiful yard. Like Genevieve, they'd come to England with almost no worldly possessions, and their apartment was still largely bare.

Hélène gave Genevieve a hug and pulled her through the door. "It's been too long, Genevieve."

"I'm sorry. I meant to come earlier, but work is busy." She sat on a chair next to Hélène, who handed her a pair of trousers and a seam ripper.

"Will you take the hem out, dear? I have difficulty with black on black at night."

Genevieve nodded and began removing the threads.

"You're lucky to have a job so quickly." Marcel had only recently found work translating for the British War Department. Hélène was still looking for employment, taking in other people's mending while she waited.

"Yes," Genevieve agreed. "The Lord has been very good to me."

Marcel muttered something under his breath. Neither of the Papineaus had adjusted to life in London, and over the last month, Genevieve had noticed Marcel taking his frustration with life out on everyone else. "The Lord would have done better to keep you safe in France with a brother to look after you and a home to live in."

"Everything happens for a reason," Genevieve said.

"When did you become philosophical?" Hélène asked. She also missed France.

Genevieve shrugged. "I haven't really gained an interest in philosophy, just religion. I'm planning to join a new church."

Both Marcel and Hélène stopped what they were doing and stared at her in shock. "But you've been Catholic your entire life—your parents were Catholic, your grandparents were Catholic, their parents were Catholic. Why would you even consider turning your back on centuries of religious tradition?" Marcel asked.

"I believe the Mormon Church is the only completely true church on earth. How can I not join myself to it?" She tried to convey the depth of her feelings and how happy she was with her new knowledge, but Marcel's face hardened at the mention of the Church's nickname.

"Genevieve, who's been teaching you about that heretical religion?"

Genevieve was dismayed by Marcel's anger. "I've been reading their scriptures and listening to their speakers in church. And Peter is a member, and he's taught me a little."

"Who's Peter?" Marcel asked.

"Lieutenant Eddy—he helped rescue you from the Gestapo the night you left France. Surely your remember him." Genevieve went back to her work on the black fabric, hoping the conversation would soon turn to another topic.

Hélène put her hand on Genevieve's shoulder. "What is this man to you?"

"Peter?" Genevieve asked.

Hélène nodded, taking a pile of mending off her lap and putting it on a worn-out table beside her.

Genevieve looked down at the trousers in her lap and felt herself blush. "I suppose he's my best friend now, and I'm in love with him."

"So you're joining this church for him?" Marcel said.

She looked up. "No, I'm joining it because I believe it's true."

"And if you had never met Peter, would you still be joining it?" Hélène asked.

"If I'd never met Peter, I doubt I would have heard of his church, but the fact that I'm in love with the person who introduced me to the gospel doesn't make the gospel any less true."

Marcel and Hélène looked skeptical.

"How old is this church?" Marcel asked.

"I'm not sure . . . About a hundred years, I think."

Marcel let out a scornful huff. "And how many members are there?"

Genevieve looked at the hemline she was undoing, but she'd already stopped removing the threads. "I don't know that either."

"Do they practice Lent?" Marcel continued.

"I don't think so."

"What is their belief on transubstantiation, the Trinity, and proper succession of leadership?"

"I don't know."

"You don't know anything about this new church!" Marcel was almost shouting.

"I know enough," Genevieve said firmly, looking up again.

"I think you've been deceived," Hélène said. "Look, Genevieve, I do remember Lieutenant Eddy. He was kind and brave. I imagine after Jacques died, it was natural to turn to him, but you should think of his friendship as just a temporary thing. After the war, things will settle down again, you can go back to France with us, and you can meet a nice French boy, a nice Catholic French boy."

Genevieve shook her head in disbelief and frustration. "This isn't about Peter; it's about following the Lord—why are you being so doubtful? I know what I felt, and I know what the Lord wants me to do. I thought you'd be happy for me—"

"Genevieve," Marcel interrupted, "we're skeptical because we care about you and we think you're making a bad decision, likely the result of desperation and a very influential young man."

"If you'd just learn a little more, I'm sure you'd come to agree with me," Genevieve pleaded.

"Study heresy?" Marcel asked.

"It's not heresy," Genevieve said, her voice a little sharper than it needed to be. She took a few deep breaths to calm herself. "The Church the Savior set up on the earth apostatized long ago. The Mormon Church is the restoration of His Church. It's complete, without centuries of corruption from men and governments. I know it's true because I prayed to ask if it was, and I received an answer."

Marcel and Hélène stared at her. "Did you see an angel, Genevieve?" Marcel asked.

"No, it was just an incredible feeling—and I've never been so sure about anything before, not in my entire life."

Marcel walked to the door and opened it. "Good night, Genevieve. I hope you'll change your mind."

Genevieve stared at him in astonishment. She had known Marcel her entire nineteen and a half years. He had never kicked her out of his home before. Marcel's eyes were cold, like he was a different man than the one she'd known in France. Genevieve looked at Hélène, who turned away and refused to meet her gaze. In stunned silence, Genevieve left their apartment, fighting back tears.

* * *

Genevieve arrived at the boarding home in a melancholy mood. She walked through the lobby, picked up the Bible buried under a pile of British magazines, and went to her room.

She remembered a passage in the New Testament of Paul bearing witness to Festus and Agrippa. She found the story in Acts chapter twenty-six. Genevieve had never read it in English before, but she studied it carefully that night. She felt a new kinship with the apostle Paul. She thought she better understood now what he must have gone through, bearing testimony to people who didn't want to hear it.

She put the Bible away and pondered her situation. The Papineaus' disapproval hurt. She trusted them, and that night, they'd dismissed everything she had wanted to share with them. Then they'd dismissed her. Genevieve didn't want to lose their friendship—they were the oldest friends she had—but she couldn't deny what she'd felt when she prayed to know if The Church of Jesus Christ of Latter-day Saints was true. She hadn't told anyone other than the Papineaus yet, but she wanted to be baptized. She just hadn't expected her decision to require such a large sacrifice.

* * *

Genevieve had the most extraordinary dream that night. It was vivid, almost real—unlike any dream she'd had before. She saw her brother. Jacques was dressed in clean clothing, the type he'd worn most days, and seemed happy to see her. Unlike the last time she'd seen him, he was whole and healthy, and he was smiling.

"I've missed you, Jacques."

"I know," he said. "But you're doing fine without me. I'm proud of you."

"So much has changed—I keep wanting your advice, but you're gone."

"You rarely took my advice when I was alive. I suppose it took dying for that to change." He smiled at her, quiet, like he always had been when deciding what to say. "I'm here now. And you're about to join a new church, but something is troubling you?"

"Hélène and Marcel are upset."

"They'll come around," Jacques predicted. "Besides, you really shouldn't let anyone but you make a decision about your soul."

"Am I making the right choice?" Despite Jacques's earlier assertion, Genevieve had sought his advice her entire life. Even when unsolicited, she normally followed his suggestions, and her current decision seemed so much more monumental than any of her other inquiries.

"My good, sweet little sister." Jacques put his hands on her shoulders. "You already know the answer to that question."

Genevieve nodded. Jacques was right. She knew the Church was true. And since it was true, she needed—and wanted—to join it.

"Do something for me, please," Jacques said.

"What can I do for you now? You're dead—this is just a dream." Even as she dreamed, Genevieve knew her time with Jacques would end again.

"I only had two-and-a-half years with Mireille." Jacques smiled wistfully. "You can give us an eternity together."

Genevieve woke the next morning sure of what she was going to do. It didn't matter what Hélène and Marcel thought. It didn't matter what her parents or Jacques or even Peter thought. What mattered was what her Father in Heaven thought. Whether what happened was a dream or a vision or a visit from beyond the grave, it was exactly what she had needed. She grabbed a sheet of paper.

Dear Peter,

Do you think you'll have leave soon? I'd like you to baptize me.

CHAPTER TWELVE

THE ASSIGNMENT

Tuesday, August 1

FROM THE AMMO BOX ACTING as third base, Peter watched Sherlock's pitch hit the grass at Moretti's feet.

"Strike two," Condreanu said.

"Are you blind?" Moretti glared at Condreanu, who was catcher and umpire.

"Not one of my better pitches, I'm afraid," Sherlock said. "I didn't want to give away another triple."

"The pitch was fine." Condreanu tossed the baseball back to Sherlock. "The sergeant is just a poor loser."

Moretti swore. "Even your pitcher admits it wasn't a strike!"

"Would someone please remind me why we are playing this imbecile game?" Nelson was manning third base.

"Because Major Baker thought our eight-mile run wasn't sufficient activity for the night, and everyone from North America wanted to play baseball," Peter said. The team had switched to night training a week ago.

"We should have played rugby instead. It would have kept more of us active." Nelson crossed his arms.

"We've been *active* all night long," Moretti said. "And I think we've all got enough bruises from that hand-to-hand combat class last night without us tackling each other."

Nelson rolled his eyes. "Football, then."

"We've played soccer the last five nights." Peter turned to the pitcher. "Sherlock, how about we keep the count one and one?"

Sherlock nodded, but Condreanu shook his head. "It was a strike—"

A sharp whistle cut off his words. Everyone looked toward the manor, where Baker was waving them in. Next to him, the probable source of the schedule change, was a British colonel. When the team arrived, Baker dismissed everyone except the lieutenants.

Peter and Condreanu waited outside the library, Baker's office. They both saluted when the colonel followed Baker inside. Baker didn't shut the door.

"Our time line has changed," the colonel began. "You need to pack today."

Baker swore. "Colonel Gibson, you told me I would have eight weeks to train my men. I've had only half that. They aren't ready yet."

"Major Baker, we gave you every man you requested. Some we pulled from the middle of battle for you. They were ready from day one. We do not have the luxury of more time. You and your men will be at the staging area at 1900 hours tonight," Gibson ordered. "The status quo in your target area is changing, and your team is to ensure it changes in our favor. We want you on the ground within seventy-two hours."

"Yes, sir," Baker said. Gibson left, ignoring the salutes he received from the lieutenants.

"Eddy, Condreanu, get in here," Baker said. "You heard the colonel. We're leaving sooner than expected. Get the men ready and the equipment packed. I'm going home to let my wife know she no longer needs to plan on me for supper—tonight or for the next several weeks. You two are dismissed."

* * *

As the men arrived at Grantham air base that evening and unloaded their equipment, Peter noticed a telegraph office not far from the entrance. When they finished with the equipment well before the scheduled briefing, Peter sought out Major Baker. "Sir, may I send a quick telegram?"

Baker folded his arms, bringing one hand up to play with his chin. "To whom?"

Peter hesitated, but he knew Baker was a fair man. "My girlfriend, sir. I'd like to tell her good-bye."

Baker smiled then nodded. "Keep it short, and don't be late."

Peter jogged to the telegraph office and was surprised to see Nelson in line ahead of him. When Peter finally stepped to the window, the telegraph officer turned his back.

"Excuse me, I'd like to send a telegram."

The man glanced at him. "Sorry, sir. I'm on break."

"I promise I'll only take a minute—and I doubt I'll have a chance later. Could you delay your break? Please?"

The man shrugged, looked at the clock, and disappeared behind a door labeled "water closet." Peter waited impatiently for the man to return. When he finally did, Peter almost wished he hadn't. First the man pretended he couldn't understand Peter's English, then he gave him the wrong form. For fifteen minutes, Peter pleaded, argued, and cajoled the man into letting him send off a short, eight-word telegram to Hammersmith Hospital in London. Peter suspected the man had suffered a serious head injury sometime during his life. His age seemed to fit the generation that would have fought in the trenches from 1914–1918. *Did mustard gas cause brain damage?* Completely exasperated, Peter shook his head and decided to give up. He should have used his time to write a letter instead—he could have written a love ballad several pages long by now.

As he turned away, his eyes caught sight of a paper the telegraph officer had recently uncovered while looking for the proper form. Peter recognized the bold handwriting as Nelson's. *Delay the American*, it read. Under the form, Peter could see the corner of a ten pound note.

"Are you allowed to accept bribes?" Peter asked the clerk, pointing to Nelson's note.

The man looked at the paper, and the color drained from his face.

"If you give me the correct form in the next ten seconds and give me the correct change before I've finished filling it out, I won't report you."

Moments later, Peter had the correct form. A few minutes after that, he was finished. He shook his head at the man, not even saying thank you as he glanced at his watch and realized he'd wasted forty minutes.

Peter arrived in the briefing room at 1845. He was there fifteen minutes before the scheduled briefing, but everyone else had been there since 1830, and that meant Peter was late.

Colonel Gibson stood at the head of the room, pacing. When Peter entered, red spots formed on Gibson's cheeks, and his eyes narrowed into a glare. "Lieutenant Eddy, did you misplace your watch? Or do you not feel my briefing is important?"

"I'm sorry, sir."

"Everyone else managed to arrive on time. Is your personal schedule more important than the rest of the war?"

"No, sir! I apologize." Out of the corner of his eye, Peter saw Nelson wink at Condreanu.

"Why weren't you with the rest of the group, Lieutenant?"

"I wanted to send a telegram, sir," Peter said.

"A telegram?" Gibson's voice rose in anger.

"A personal matter, sir. I was saying good-bye to someone."

Nelson laughed. "Let me guess, someone with long eyelashes and a French accent."

Peter felt his face grow warm and wanted to kick Nelson. Instead, he stood as tall as he could and looked over the top of Gibson's head. He might have fallen into Nelson and Condreanu's trap, but he wasn't going to give them the satisfaction of seeing him grovel.

"I was ready to begin the briefing seven minutes ago. That is four hundred twenty seconds. Give me four hundred twenty push-ups, and then I will begin the briefing. Corporal Nelson, since you find Lieutenant Eddy's tardiness so amusing, you can count for him. Out loud please."

Peter dropped to the floor and began his punishment. He knew he wouldn't make it to four hundred twenty. He doubted he could make it to one hundred but told himself to concentrate on doing one at a time. Nelson counted evenly, and his voice and Peter's breathing were the only sounds in the room.

"Forty-nine, fifty, fifty-one . . ."

"Colonel Gibson, sir?" Baker broke in.

"Fifty-four, fifty-five . . ."

"What is it, Major?"

"Fifty-seven, fifty-eight . . ."

"I don't wish to question your instructions, sir. However, I'm the one who will be leading this team, and I'd prefer to have everyone in top condition when we hit our target. If you insist on Lieutenant Eddy completing his entire punishment now, he will be less effective when we're inserted. That will be dangerous for him and for the rest of my men."

"Sixty-three, sixty-four, sixty-five . . ."

"What do you suggest then, Major?"

"Sixty-seven . . ."

"Postpone the rest of the push-ups until after the mission."

"Seventy, seventy-one, seventy-two, seventy-three . . ."

"Fine, Lieutenant Eddy, you may stop." Peter sank to the floor in relief. His arms and face felt like they were on fire, but he didn't allow himself to rest long. Within seconds, he found his seat, feigning interest in the blank chalkboard positioned in the front of the briefing room, and tried to control his heavy breathing. He was extremely grateful to Baker: not only had he understood Peter's desire to tell Genevieve good-bye, but he'd also prevented the inevitable humiliation that would have come when Peter's arms stopped working.

The briefing confirmed what Peter and the rest of Baker's team already suspected: they were going to Romania. Specifically, they were to be dropped in the Carpathian Mountains north of the Prahova Valley, near the village of

Scorțeni. Gibson gave them a rough outline of what to expect. They would be met by a few sympathetic Romanians and receive assignments as a need for their work arose.

After a brief introduction, Gibson turned the briefing over to the bookish Captain Wolsey. He was British, and he was missing the bottom half of his left leg.

"Before you chaps drop in, it may do you some good to know the history of the area. Six years ago, Romania was closely allied with France, as were Czechoslovakia, Poland, and Yugoslavia. Together, France and her allies surrounded Germany neatly." Wolsey unrolled a map of Europe and had Luke and Quill tack it to the wall for him. "At least until Hitler took over most of Europe." As he spoke, Wolsey used a pointer to tap Hitler's conquests, one by one.

"Four years ago, Stalin took the Romanian provinces of Bessarabia and Bukovina. The Romanians still had a defensive agreement with France and Great Britain, but by then, most of France was occupied, and it looked like England herself would soon fall. With the Soviets ready to take more territory and Hungary eying Transylvania, the Romanians turned to the only country that could prevent further dismemberment: Nazi Germany. It was a costly decision. Axis arbitration gave most of Transylvania to Hungary and a few southern areas to Bulgaria. The decision was so unpopular in Romania that King Carol lost his throne. He made his teenage son a figurehead monarch but transferred dictatorial power to General Antonescu, who invited the Nazi Army in as an ally."

Wolsey handed a new map to Luke and Quill, this one of Romania. "The arrangement with Antonescu worked well for Hitler's plan to invade the Soviet Union. In addition to its strategic value for an invasion of Soviet Ukraine, Romania is rich in oil, with the largest concentration of refineries in the Ploiești area." Wolsey pointed to the map, showing a circle of refineries in the Prahova Valley. "Romania is Hitler's largest source of oil. Destroy Ploiești and the Nazi Army will soon grind to a halt."

Wolsey continued the briefing for nearly an hour, describing the area's geography, local population, and German guests. He detailed the American air campaign to destroy its oilfields and the rapidly advancing front with the Red Army.

"Should we anticipate any collaboration with the Russians?" Nelson asked.

"That depends on how the situation unfolds. For now, avoid all contact with our Soviet allies. We'd prefer your presence in the country remain secret."

"Yes, I imagine you would. I believe they consider Romania their turf," Nelson said.

* * *

After the briefing, they were given an hour to eat in the mess hall before boarding a plane for Bari, Italy. They were to spend the next day in Bari and, weather permitting, drop into Romania the day after. Peter didn't go straight to supper, wanting a few minutes to process the briefing. He was watching the clouds float past the moon when he heard the door to the briefing room open and glanced behind him to see Baker and Nelson.

"You are taking your orders too literally, Wesley. I think you are making a mistake this time." Nelson looked at Peter, no expression on his face, and walked toward the mess hall.

Baker sighed as he approached Peter.

"Good evening, sir."

"Good evening, Eddy. What did you think of the briefing?"

Peter chose his words carefully. "It's not what I expected."

"And?" Baker prompted.

"Why me, sir?"

"I'm not sure what you mean by that."

"I understand why everyone else is on the team. Luke and Zielinski are brilliant in their fields. Nelson speaks so many languages that even if that were his only qualification he'd be an asset. All the paratroopers have the right experience. Logan too. And Condreanu has all his contacts there. But I don't speak Romanian, and I'd never even jumped out of a plane until you put me on the team. I'm a jack-of-all-trades at best."

Baker smiled. "You are on this team because I want you on this team. In your past assignments, you were able to adapt to changing circumstances. I need that quick thinking—it's not my strength. Sometimes those off-the-wall OSS schemes are exactly what the situation calls for. And I know you'll stay out of trouble."

"Won't everyone?"

Baker looked thoughtful, his hand stroking his chin, his mouth pulling to the left. "Maybe. Do you know why SOE recruited Private Quill?"

"He can forge just about anything and was best in his training group in all the skills they normally teach. I assumed that made him stand out."

Baker smiled. He had a smile that took ten years off his face. "Yes, Quill was top of his class until his commanding officer discovered the forged passes to London he was creating and selling. He was nearly court-marshaled.

Then someone from SOE decided to channel his skills into something more productive for the war effort."

Peter grinned as he imagined Quill selling phony passes to his fellow paratroopers. "I'm sure he wouldn't do anything like that on a mission."

Baker watched an airplane speed along the runway. "True, but I'd never have to worry about you doing something like that on a mission or during training. Did you hear much about my mission with Jamie in Italy?"

"Just that you ran a huge spy ring then left this summer."

"Did you hear why we left?"

"No. I assumed your area was liberated."

Baker shook his head. "I wish that was what happened. Jamie is brilliant, but he can be stubborn and tactless. He suspects a few of his former classmates working for SOE. Thinks they're Communists. We were supposed to pass our information to one of them, and Jamie refused. During the debacle, our cover was blown and we were recalled. We would have been caught if a local man working for OSS hadn't warned us when he did. Jamie was severely reprimanded."

"And his former classmate?" Peter asked.

"There was no evidence against him. Jamie's instinct notwithstanding, he is still widely respected."

"Has Nelson ever disobeyed your orders?"

Baker smiled. "Yes."

"So much for rigid British discipline."

"There's more to it than that," Baker said. "I owe Jamie a lot. He has saved my life on more than one occasion. And three years ago, he introduced me to his cousin—one on the middle-class side of his family. Now she's my wife. Jamie was my best man." That explained why Baker and Nelson always called each other by their first names.

Peter hesitated before bringing up his next question. "And the fact that some of the men on the team hate me? Doesn't that make you nervous?"

Baker looked at Peter, surprised. "Most of the men admire you. There are perhaps two exceptions. Jamie will straighten out in the field, and he seems to be the ringleader. Whatever his personal feelings, he wouldn't do anything to jeopardize the mission. I spoke to him about the prank at the telegraph office. He promised it will be last time he insults you."

Peter nodded. "Can I be frank, sir?"

"I hope you always will be. That's why you're on the team."

"Our objective is unclear. From what Captain Wolsey said, the air raids are finally starting to slow production at the refineries. The Russians are about to overrun the county anyhow, and I'm sure they'll deny Hitler his oil. I don't see why we're going."

Baker studied Peter's face. "What you say is true. Captain Wolsey's briefing was informative, but it wasn't meant to detail our objective, because our objective is largely unknown. SOE wants a team in place in case something changes and we're needed. Do you remember what Gibson told me this morning?"

"He said the situation on the ground is changing, and he wants you there to ensure it changes in our favor. I still expected a solid objective. You're saying he wants us there and he'll figure out why after we're inserted?"

Baker nodded. "Which is another reason I'm happy to have a jack-of-all-trades along. I'm still not sure what I'll need once we get there."

"Doesn't that make you uneasy?"

Baker raised one eyebrow. "Yes, it does. Trying to plan for every possible contingency has kept me up more nights this last month . . . I wonder how the generals manage. But regardless, we have a flight to catch in fifty-five minutes, and I heard Private Fisher telling Sergeant Moretti we're being served ice cream for dessert."

"A sumptuous last meal?"

"Nonsense, Lieutenant. It won't be our last meal. They'll feed us in Italy."

Peter laughed. "You know, it's been awhile since I've had ice cream."

Chapter Thirteen

Unhappy Reception

Thursday, August 3
Near the Prahova Valley, Romania

PETER LISTENED TO THE RUMBLE of the airplane engines and hoped his last letter to Genevieve would make it past the censors. He was about to enter Nazi Romania, and he was nervous, just as he'd been before going into combat with his armored division or sneaking into France on his previous OSS missions. Over and over again, the reason the team was jumping near Scorţeni instead of Ploieşti, some thirteen miles to the south, went through Peter's mind. With the exceptions of Berlin and Vienna, Ploieşti was the most heavily defended target in the Nazi realm.

The light in the back of the airplane turned red.

"Stand up and hook up." This time, Baker was giving the order and leading the jump. Peter was to be the last one out. When the light changed from red to green, he watched everyone else leave the airplane: Baker, Ionescu, Zielinski, Mitchell, Quill, Condreanu, Nelson, Fisher, Logan, Luke, Sherlock, and Moretti. Peter was alone on the plane for less than a second before he followed the rest of the team out into the night lit by an almost-full moon. Looking down, he could make out three small lights forming a triangle. It was their drop zone, marked by two anti-Nazi locals.

Peter barely missed the trunk of a tall evergreen, crashing into some of its outer branches before he hit the ground solidly with his feet and collapsed onto his rear. He was untangling himself from his parachute when Moretti approached him.

"How did you ditch your chute so fast?" Peter asked.

Moretti grinned. "Experience. And I didn't have a tree slowing me down and leaving scratches all up the side of my face."

Peter put his hand to his cheek. The tree's needles had left marks, but he'd received worse cuts shaving. He put the landing out of his head as he wadded up his parachute and stuffed it into the hole Moretti had dug nearby. The two had landed just outside the drop zone but easily found the rest of the team assembled with the two local Romanians. Baker nodded when they arrived. So far, the mission was going well. Everyone had landed without injury, and there was no sign of the Nazis.

"You may proceed," Baker told Zielinski. The Polish paratrooper already had his radio out, and he began signaling the plane that everyone had arrived without problem.

Baker questioned one of the locals, a tall, dark-haired women. Peter guessed she was in her midtwenties. She spoke adequate English, briefing Baker on the local German presence. The Nazis were still around Ploieşti in force, but they were concentrated in the valley. Baker's team had landed in the mountains.

"Iuliana?" Ionescu asked. She turned toward him and stared. Recognition and then anger crossed her face as she walked over to him, said something in Romanian, and slapped him.

Peter stood five yards away, covering Zielinski while he put his radio away. "What's going on?" Peter asked Luke, who was on the other side of Zielinski.

"She called him a filthy traitor."

Iuliana was about to slap Ionescu again, but this time, he grabbed her wrist and questioned her in Romanian. Her reply was abrupt, and though Peter couldn't understand her words, they seemed icy.

"He asked where his brother is. She said he's dead."

Ionescu dropped his hand, looking like he'd been punched in the stomach. Whatever his history with his brother was, he hadn't been expecting that answer. He asked another question, more quietly, and she answered back in her same icy tone.

Peter looked at Luke in inquiry.

"He asked about Anatolie, and she said Anatolie doesn't associate with cowards."

Peter studied Ionescu's face. Ionescu wasn't a coward, but Peter was beginning to think there was more to his past than a narrow escape from his homeland.

"I apologize, Major Baker," Iuliana said. "If I were you, I wouldn't trust Tiberiu."

"And why is that, Miss . . . What is your name?"

"Mrs. Ionescu. I was Tiberiu's sister-in-law until my husband was murdered last year."

"What happened to Vasile?" Ionescu asked.

"The police came looking for you. You were gone, so they took him instead. He was shot while trying to escape."

They looked at each other for several long seconds—Iuliana's face full of loathing, Ionescu's showing a mix of grief and guilt.

If Baker was surprised to learn of Tiberiu Ionescu's past, he hid it well. "Thank you for the warning," he said politely.

Iuliana nodded, giving Ionescu one final glare before leaving with the other Romanian, an older man who didn't speak English. Everyone on the team watched them go. As Peter glanced around, he saw curiosity on most of his teammates' faces. Ionescu's face, however, showed raw hatred.

"All right, men," Baker said. "Time to move out." The landing site was two miles from where Baker planned to establish headquarters—only two miles away, but in the dark, through mountainous terrain, carrying heavy packs of equipment. They still had several hours until dawn, but getting to the safe house was only the beginning of their night's work.

The men moved quickly and silently, their training kicking in. They covered the distance in less than an hour, arriving at the safe house Baker had been told to expect. It was a small two-room cabin, abandoned early in the war. The forest around it was thick and concealing.

The cabin seemed secure, but Baker had the men divide the explosives, food, and other equipment into three portions. Most of the items stayed at their headquarters. Two smaller shares were put aside for secondary safe houses.

"Locotenent Condreanu," Baker said.

"Yes, sir," Condreanu answered.

"I want you to organize a perimeter sweep. Use Nelson and Sherlock. I'll need the three of you back before dawn. Be careful and thorough, but stay within a mile."

"As you wish, sir."

"Sergeant Logan, Sergeant Moretti."

"Yes, sir," both men answered.

"Take Luke and Quill. Find somewhere safe and defensible for this bit." Baker pointed to one of the piles. "If this site is compromised, I want us to have a fall-back location. Go east. Find a location and secure it. Stay and observe from your location today and return tonight. I'll expect a full report at midnight."

Logan and Moretti took their men and supplies and disappeared.

"Lieutenant Eddy."

"Yes, sir."

"I want you to do the same thing, but go west. Take Mitchell, Fisher, and Ionescu. This way, if anyone is captured, there will be at least one location they can't reveal."

Peter saluted and gathered his team and their gear. Just before leaving, he heard Baker's last order.

"Kapral Zielinski?"

"Yes, sir."

"Get some rest. This next week may be a busy one for you."

* * *

Iuliana Ionescu was still angry when she reached the gates of the estate owned by Cosmina Ionescu, Vasile and Tiberiu's wealthy cousin. *Haven't you learned anything?* She couldn't believe she'd been tricked into helping Tiberiu—that she had committed acts of treason to help the man who'd ruined her life.

The estate was quiet as she entered. She went to the room next to hers and found her almost-three-year-old son sleeping with Sabina and Sabina's infant son. Like Iuliana, Sabina was a refugee from Bucharest. Both had left the city to escape the air raids. The two women were similar in age and often helped one another with the children, but Iuliana hadn't meant for Sabina to tend Anatolie all night.

Iuliana lifted Anatolie and turned to go back to her own room.

"Did you have fun, Iuliana?" Sabina yawned.

Iuliana didn't answer right away, confused by the question. Tromping through the woods holding up flashlights for her brother-in-law's commando team hadn't been fun, but Sabina didn't know what she'd been doing.

"I've seen the way that colonel looks at you. And I heard him ask you to dinner. Out with him, weren't you?"

Colonel Eliade was perhaps the one man on earth Iuliana detested more intensely than Tiberiu Ionescu. She didn't want the entire estate to think she was having an affair with the colonel, nor did she want them to know what she'd really been doing. She couldn't decide which was worse: staying out all night with a man she wasn't married to or treason. She hesitated and almost set Sabina straight, but there were no legal penalties should a young widow decide she was lonely and give in to a handsome war hero's advances. Cosmina would think less of her, but few others would care. The penalty for treason, however, was death, and what would happen to her son if she were executed? So rather than correct Sabina's false assumption, Iuliana remained silent. She thought it would be better for Anatolie that way.

"I'll keep it quiet," Sabina said after awhile.

"Thank you. And thank you for watching Anatolie." Iuliana took her son back to their room, hoping she hadn't made yet another mistake by not telling Sabina the truth.

CHAPTER FOURTEEN

PICKING AT THE PAST

Friday, August 4
London, England

GENEVIEVE FINGERED THE TELEGRAM IN her pocket as she walked home from work. It was short, and she'd had it several days now, so she could recite it from memory.

LEAVE CANCELED STOP I LOVE YOU STOP PETER

The message was bittersweet. Peter loved her. Peter was leaving. She'd received the telegraph at work on Tuesday evening, the same day she'd written and mailed her letter to Peter, telling him about her desire to be baptized. He couldn't have received the letter before he'd left, and she wasn't sure what to do. She didn't want to postpone her baptism indefinitely, but giving up the sweet, beautiful vision of Peter baptizing her was difficult.

A dark car pulled up next to the sidewalk in front of her, interrupting her thoughts. A British Army lieutenant with thick glasses stepped out and addressed her as she walked by.

"Miss Olivier?"

Genevieve stopped, startled. "Yes?"

"Colonel McDougall would like to speak with you. I've been instructed to drive you to his office."

Genevieve hesitated. The lieutenant sounded British, and she was in London, but getting into a car with a stranger seemed foolhardy. "Can I take the tube instead?"

The lieutenant smiled. "Colonel McDougall would rather not wait that long. He thought you might hesitate to come with me—given your recent arrival from occupied Europe. He asked me to remind you of your favorite demigod when you were twelve, Perseus; of your last location in France, Arromanches; and of the last guest to sleep in the compartment under the stairs of your Calais home, Lieutenant Eddy."

Genevieve smiled at the mention of Peter's name. McDougall had chosen his clues carefully. She didn't think anyone else living knew the combination of those three facts. "All right, Lieutenant, I'll come with you."

He drove her to an old warehouse. She could smell the river when he opened the car door. The lieutenant guided her to McDougall's office, but he didn't follow her in. The office was dusty and lit by a single lightbulb hanging uncovered from the ceiling.

McDougall sat behind an old table in front of walls lined with floor-to-ceiling cabinets, but he stood as she entered. "Genevieve, welcome! I was afraid you wouldn't let Lieutenant Hatch drive you." McDougall pulled a chair out for her, and she sat.

"Having a stranger address me by name did surprise me," she admitted.

"Flashbacks of the Gestapo?"

"They never offered me a ride, professor."

McDougall sat across the table from her. "Genevieve, I need your help."

Wary, Genevieve tilted her chin to the side. "What do you need?"

"I need you to go into France and help with a mission I am organizing. It's a simple mission but urgent. I need a good agent on the ground immediately."

Genevieve sat back in her chair, surprised at his directness. "Surely you have access to hundreds of French speakers. Why do you need me? I already told you I don't want to work for you."

McDougall leaned forward. "Yes, Genevieve, I have access to trainloads of British girls who speak a little French, and they sound like British girls who speak a little French. And I have access to boatloads of French girls who sound like French girls, but the Nazis are leaving agents behind as they retreat. I don't trust any of the new French volunteers. I do trust you."

Genevieve didn't want to go back to France, not while the war was raging there. "Professor, I'm trying to start nursing school. I want to help people—I don't want to lie and carry a gun. You always encouraged me in my education."

"I am not asking you to give up your schooling, just to postpone it. Besides, you have yet to receive an acceptance. I think it will be difficult while all of your school records are in France behind the front line."

Genevieve sighed in frustration. McDougall was right. Her quest to get into nursing school was not going well.

"Genevieve, do this for me, for France, for the Allied cause—and I will make sure you are accepted to any school in the United Kingdom."

"And if I wanted to go to school in the United States? Could you assist with that?"

McDougall looked confused. "Why would you want to go to the United States?"

Genevieve felt herself blush. "That's . . . that's where Peter's from."

He studied her face before speaking. "Lieutenant Eddy?"

Genevieve nodded.

"Oh, Genevieve." McDougall shook his head. "Didn't your brother warn you not to fall in love with commandos?"

"Jacques approved of my choice."

McDougall paused again, silent for a time before speaking again. "I cannot guarantee a nursing school in the United States, but I am working with an American colonel, and perhaps he can. Here is what I can guarantee: a US visa. And after your return from France, I can send you to wherever Lieutenant Eddy ends up when he is done with his current assignment."

"Can you tell me where he is?"

"No, but I can get you to him within a week of his return."

Genevieve looked down at her hands. McDougall was manipulating her, that she knew. But part of her felt guilty that he had to manipulate her. She did want to help the war effort—though picking up where her brother had left off wasn't what she had in mind. She was sick of being used as leverage or bait by the Gestapo, and this was a chance for something more useful. But working for McDougall scared her.

"Genevieve, if you want to save lives, postpone your schooling and help me end the war. If you begin school now, you will still be a student when the war ends. If you do this job, you can help us shorten the war. Think of how many lives you can save if you cut a month or two off this war."

"I don't think I'd be a very good spy," Genevieve said, thinking of how easy it had been for Tschirner to read her thoughts.

"Spying is in your blood. We will train you, and you will learn. I suspect in two days you can pick up what it would take the average person a week to learn."

"Just because my brother had an extraordinary gift doesn't mean I'll magically develop the same abilities . . ."

McDougall smiled. "Your brother and your father were both skilled in espionage. Part of their abilities came from hard work, but they also had a great deal of natural talent."

"My father?" Genevieve asked, confused. "He was a cheese maker, not a spy."

"Your father, Julian Olivier, worked with me from 1915 to 1918. Most of that time, he was in Berlin, working as a manservant to a rather loose-lipped member of the Kaiser's government. I handled the transportation of his information across enemy lines to where it could be of use. Your father was a hero and a spy."

"I've never heard about any of that." Genevieve wasn't sure she believed the Scottish colonel.

"Yes, you were still young when he died. Too young for buried family secrets to have surfaced."

"Did Jacques know?"

McDougall nodded. "Yes, I told your brother the details of your father's early life after your father passed away. Your brother elected not to tell you. At first, he preferred to wait until you were older. When the war started, he feared it might encourage you to do something dangerous."

"Your claims are somewhat unexpected, professor." *Surely Jacques would have said something if it was true*, she thought.

"Unexpected perhaps, but I doubt they are very surprising. I knew your father well. I imagine if you thought hard enough, you could remember things he taught you that would prepare you for what I am asking you to do. Your languages, for example. He thought it was important that you spoke English and German."

Genevieve's father had died six-and-a-half years ago, but she remembered him clearly. He had insisted on language lessons and language practice, but that didn't prove McDougall's assertion. "Being trilingual has application in life beyond its use in espionage."

"He taught you to be a respectable markswoman with a rifle or a pistol, am I correct?" McDougall prompted her.

"Firearms were just a hobby of his."

"He also made sure you were very observant, did he not?" McDougall continued.

"Yes." Her mind flashed back to dozens of conversations.

Genevieve, how high was the tide today? Describe what the priest did at Mass yesterday, Genevieve—every detail. Genevieve, could you find your way back to the home we visited today, even if it was dark? Genevieve, if you wanted to convince someone you were wealthy, what would you say and how would you act? Genevieve, talk to the lady at the bakery and find out which bachelor she prefers, the bookseller's son or the new teacher. But don't make her suspicious.

"My father asked questions, but that was just a game of his. He wanted to make sure we were paying attention." But then another memory came to mind, making McDougall's assertions no longer seem so far-fetched.

"You remember something else?" McDougall asked.

"Yes, his codes." She had been eleven. Her father had written her a letter. *But, Papa, I can't read this; it's all numbers.* Then he had shown her how. The first numeral was the page number to a book they owned. The second number indicated the line, the third number the word. She had pieced it together over a few hours, and her father had been pleased with her success. Then he'd asked her to write a letter back to him, using the same system.

McDougall opened a folder and removed a weathered piece of paper. He turned it and set it before her. She looked at the writing, then up at McDougall, shocked.

"One of your father's reports. Few people would be able to read it. Can you?"

Genevieve nodded. "Yes. But it would be easier with a mirror." Genevieve's father had the unique ability to write backward, and he'd taught his children. Jacques had been able to write backward only while looking in a mirror, but Genevieve had developed a talent for it. Her father had called her his little Da Vinci. "You worked with my father?"

"Yes, we were partners for many years. We had to depend on each other for our lives."

"Then why didn't I meet you until he was sick?"

McDougall paused, looking at his hands. "Your father and I had a bit of a falling-out after the war ended. I took him to a party and introduced him to a girl I was very much in love with. She was also a spy of sorts, keeping tabs on suspected German agents in Paris, informing the right people who they were meeting with. Your father fell in love with her too, and she chose Julian."

"My mother was a spy?"

McDougall nodded. "You look very much like her, except she had green eyes. Will you help me end the war, Genevieve?"

Genevieve was dizzy with all of the information she'd just received. "Can I think about it for a while?"

McDougall frowned while he considered it. "Will you attend church on Sunday?"

"Yes," Genevieve answered, surprised he knew not only how her school applications were going but also that she attended church. "Do you have someone tailing me?"

McDougall ignored her query. "I will see you Sunday after your church meeting. Look for me and give me your answer then."

She nodded and stood to leave. "It's the man with curly blond hair and a red necktie, isn't it?" she said, remembering the man she'd seen several times in unrelated places.

"Yes. You see, Genevieve, you will make a good spy. You may be interested to know that he spoke to your landlady and, among other questions, asked her if you receive any regular correspondence. She said no, but he thinks she was lying."

* * *

Shock wasn't the right word for it. To be told both her parents had been spies left Genevieve reeling. She wished her brother had told her, had at least hinted. But Jacques had always been protective; hiding the past was exactly in line with his other habits.

Genevieve didn't believe McDougall's promise that the assignment wasn't dangerous. He'd told Peter and her brother the same thing before their mission that spring. Peter had barely survived, and Jacques was dead.

She thought of her father, her brother, and the mother she'd barely known. When they were needed, each of them had risked their lives for their country. Could she do any less? She wanted to continue with her school applications and wait for the war and Peter's role in it to be done. But what would her parents think if she simply stood on the sidelines, letting others take the risks of war so she could enjoy the blessings of peace?

Genevieve was still distracted with her thoughts when she returned home. As she came inside, she saw her landlady lock her ground-floor office and walk out the back door.

She thought back to McDougall's claim that the woman had lied about the mail Genevieve was receiving. Were her ill feelings for Peter strong enough to make her hide or destroy letters? Genevieve had yet to receive any mail, despite Peter's promise that he wrote her often. If the landlady had lied, saying Genevieve had received no mail, then surely there was mail for Genevieve somewhere. And who would write to her other than Peter? She took his medal from her pocket and rubbed her thumb over the heart with Washington's silhouette.

Genevieve returned the Purple Heart to her pocket and thought back to her exodus from France, when they'd rested in an attic in Rouen. She could still picture Peter amusing himself by flicking bits of old grain at the mice to keep them away from her. The attic had been full of odds and ends, and in one box, there were a dozen old doorknobs of varying sizes and types. After Peter had scared the mice away, he'd shown Genevieve how to use her hairpins to unlock each of the doorknobs. She remembered how his strong hands had gently guided hers, could almost feel his breath on her cheek as he leaned over her shoulder to watch her progress, could almost hear his soft, easy laughter with each setback and each triumph.

Genevieve hesitated. She still wasn't sure she wanted to accept McDougall's assignment. The office doorknob, however, would be a good test of her skills, and if she had mail from Peter, she thought the risk worthwhile. Genevieve slowly removed two of her hairpins, bent them into the tools she needed, and went to work.

It was a five-pin cylinder lock, and it took her several minutes. Had she still been in the attic in Rouen, Peter would have told her something encouraging then would have made her try it again until she could do it in one-tenth the time. Genevieve glanced around the empty lobby and went into the office. Trying to ignore a rising sense of guilt, she looked under piles of paper and searched through the slots the landlady used to sort mail for her tenants. Genevieve finally found a pile of twenty-eight letters, all addressed to her, all from Peter. They were in a desk drawer under a pile of utility statements. The envelopes were still unopened.

She fingered her letters and instinctively drew them next to her chest, thinking about Peter's good-bye in the tube station. She hadn't realized it until later, but his last kiss had been different. Usually Peter's kisses were tender, almost gentle. His last kiss had been more powerful, more ardent. *Was it different because he thought it was the last kiss we'd share?* She held the letters a little tighter, wondering if they were the last she would ever have of Peter.

A shadow fell across the desk in front of her. "Genevieve?"

She looked up and cleared her throat to keep her emotions from choking her voice. "Hello, Godfrey."

"Did my mum let you in? She doesn't usually let tenants in her office."

"No, Godfrey, I broke in." She watched his face as she spoke. He thought she was joking. She stood and walked past him, heading toward her room. Then, in a moment of clarity, she knew exactly what to do: she would complete McDougall's assignment, because like her parents and her brother, Genevieve was going to do her part to oppose evil.

There was another decision to make too. Would she wait for Peter, not knowing when or if he'd ever return, or would she be baptized at once? She pondered that question all evening as she read Peter's letters. He wouldn't hesitate to do what he knew was right, would he? As she lay in bed that night, trying to fall asleep, another thought crossed her mind: McDougall's missions were dangerous. If Genevieve wasn't baptized before she returned to France, she might never have another chance.

* * *

Genevieve expected McDougall's vehicle to be waiting for her when she left the building the branch rented for Sunday meetings. She saw it immediately, parked across the street, but she hesitated. The morning had been the embodiment of the new life she wanted. A deep, peaceful feeling had filled her when Brother Lind baptized her and confirmed her a member of the Church. That was what she wanted: a peaceful, religious life . . . with Peter. She sighed. The biggest obstacle to her dream was a madman named Adolf Hitler. The sooner he was gone and his armies defeated, the sooner she could get on with her life.

Hatch stepped from the car as she approached. He gave her a nod of recognition and opened the rear door for her. She slid in and sat next to McDougall. "I'm in."

McDougall smiled but didn't say anything.

"How soon will I leave?" Genevieve asked as Hatch started the car and pulled into the street.

"Tomorrow."

Genevieve had been looking out the window, but she spun to face the colonel. "Tomorrow? What about the training you promised?"

"You will do fine, Genevieve. You speak the language. You know how to build a bomb. You know how to blend in with a crowd. A contact in France will handle all communications between you and headquarters, so you won't need to worry about that. We will supply all of your equipment, and you can practice using your new handgun tonight."

"But who will teach me how to lie convincingly in one day's time?"

McDougall handed her a sheet of paper. "Start with this. It is your legend. Memorize it. Hatch is taking us to your boarding home now. You can retrieve your things, and I will see that they are properly stored."

"Is there an address I can have my mail forwarded to?" She'd found a letter from Peter for each day they'd been apart. The last was dated July 31. If he'd left the first of August, the date of his telegraph, there might not be any more letters. But if there were, she didn't want them to end up in a drawer in her landlady's desk.

McDougall looked at her before nodding. "I will send Lieutenant Hatch weekly to collect anything that comes for you."

Genevieve nodded and read through the paper McDougall had handed her. Her new name was Colette Bertrand. "Where am I headed?"

"Marseilles. What do you know of it?"

Genevieve shrugged. "It's the second largest city in France and a major port along the Mediterranean. My sister-in-law's family owned a summer home there, but that was before the war. What am I to do in Marseilles?"

"That depends. Eisenhower and Churchill are still debating the next step. If Eisenhower has his way, there will be an invasion somewhere along the French Riviera within the month. Marseilles will be one of the primary targets. You will be providing information for the military—location of antiaircraft guns, movement of German commanders. An agent already in place will give you more specific assignments."

"And if Churchill has his way?" Genevieve asked.

"Then you will be sabotaging any German supplies that come through Marseilles on their way to a different front. Do you understand now why I need you? I have to prepare for two different possibilities. Who else can I trust with either task?"

CHAPTER FIFTEEN

THE MARSEILLES SPYMASTER

Saturday, August 12
Marseilles, France

GENEVIEVE INHALED THE SEA AIR as she walked along the rue de l'Arbre in Marseilles, France, toward the night club where she would meet her contact. She was overwhelmed by all that had happened since McDougall's assistant offered her a ride one week ago. There had been a last-minute change the day she'd left England: her assignment was switched from an SOE operation run by Colonel McDougall to an OSS operation run by one of his American associates, a colonel she hadn't yet met. One week she was employed by Hammersmith Hospital, the next by OSS.

She'd been paired with an experienced agent, a Frenchman known as Henri, and put on a flight to Lisbon with him. The two had taken a train from Lisbon to the foot of the Pyrenees in Spain then crossed into France through the heavily monitored forbidden zone the Nazis maintained along the border. A Basque guide had helped them avoid enemy patrols. Carefully forged paperwork and plenty of OSS cash had allowed them to purchase train tickets in Toulouse. Genevieve's ticket was to Marseilles. Henri's was to Toulon.

Completely alone, with only a small bag filled with clothing, papers, and a hidden handgun, Genevieve entered the club. Henri had done his best to help her overcome the telltale signs that revealed when she was nervous, frightened, or lying. She hoped his crash course had made as much of a difference as he claimed. Could someone really change how they reacted to the world in six days' time? Genevieve suspected her life would soon depend on the answer to that question.

A man dressed in a waiter's uniform raised an eyebrow as she approached. It was early—well before the usual supper hour.

"Pardon, I'm supposed to meet someone here," she said.

"Oh, when is your meeting planned?"

Genevieve ducked her head, pretending embarrassment. "Ten minutes ago." That was the phrase she'd been told to repeat.

"Ten? Someone was looking for a young woman twenty minutes ago." The waiter gave her the prearranged counterphrase. "He went for a walk along the rue Longue des Capucins. I suggest you look for him there." The waiter pointed her in the proper direction then lowered his voice to a whisper. "A gray Renault is parked in front of a tobacco shop. Get in the backseat."

"Thank you, monsieur." Genevieve found the street, the shop, and the car without a problem. She climbed into the backseat of the Renault as casually as she could.

A man was seated behind the steering wheel, his head tilted back, his eyes shaded with a hat. He glanced at her but didn't give up his show of taking a late siesta. Under the hat, she could make out his dark hair, but his face was smooth, like a school boy's. "Your name?" he asked.

"Colette Bertrand."

"Welcome to Marseilles, Colette." The young man stretched and righted his hat. "I hope you won't mind, but you'll be blindfolded for the next stage of your trip. July was brutal, so Arnaud is taking every precaution." He started the car. "You'll find a black sash on the seat next to you. When I say, please blindfold yourself and duck to the car floor."

Genevieve nodded. She hated being at the mercy of someone she didn't know but had little choice except to obey. McDougall had hinted at the recent devastation wrought by the Gestapo against local resistance groups. She understood their caution.

They drove five minutes before the man turned into a narrow alley. "Now, mademoiselle."

Genevieve dutifully blindfolded herself and felt her way to the floor of the car. She felt the bump as the car left the alley but didn't see anything for what she guessed was the next fifteen minutes.

When they stopped, the man opened the door, helped her to her feet, and kept hold of her hand. "If you don't mind, mademoiselle, leave your bag in the car. I'll lead you inside before removing your blindfold."

She felt lightheaded and slightly nauseated after the twisting drive, so she was glad to let the man guide her. She heard noise from a few distant cars, but the area was otherwise quiet. Before long her head stabilized, and she heard a door shut behind her and then felt her blindfold loosen. She looked around, taking in the chairs that lined two of the room's walls. An empty desk stood in the center of the room, and beyond that was another door. If she hadn't known any better, she would have said she was in a physician's waiting room.

"Have a seat, please." The young man slouched into a chair and set his hat on the next chair over.

Genevieve obeyed, remembering what McDougall had told her about Arnaud, the spymaster: *He is a seedy character, just as likely to sell an assassin's services to a mobster as to sell Nazi secrets to us. He has no love for the Nazis— my understanding is they police Marseilles more effectively than the French police did before the war. They are hurting his business. Still, he knows how to stay hidden, and he knows how to get the information we need.* She stared at the door to Arnaud's office, not sure if she was ready to meet him.

The room was quiet other than the sound of muted voices coming from the other room and the ticking of a clock that hung on the wall behind the desk. She watched the clock's second hand make seven revolutions before the door opened.

She was surprised to recognize the first man who walked out of the office. Agent Browning of SOE had stayed at her home for several weeks one January, working with her brother to set up a network that had helped crashed airmen return to England. He was twenty-five years her senior, tough and intelligent, and fluent in French.

He noticed her at once. "The woman I see before me reminds me of a girl I met in 1942. You have certainly blossomed, mademoiselle. Whatever are you doing in Marseilles?"

"Assisting Arnaud. I'm sure you don't remember my name. It's Colette." In fact, she was sure Browning did remember her name, but she preferred Arnaud and his assistant know only her cover name.

"Ah yes. And in Marseilles, I am known as Gerard. Tell me, Colette, how is your brother?"

Genevieve couldn't maintain eye contact. Despite all the practice she'd had the last week at hiding her emotions, she found herself fighting tears. "He's dead."

Browning stepped toward her and put a sympathetic hand on her shoulder. "I'm very sorry. Your brother was the best agent I ever worked with. He earned my complete respect, something few others have ever managed."

"I hope I've also made your selective list." The man who spoke had a bass voice. He was well dressed and had a cigar in one hand. He was a large man— tall and rounded. His face looked padded, but his eyes were shrewd as he looked Genevieve over from the top of her head to the well-worn shoes on her feet.

"I have met no one else, Arnaud, who has your talent for staying alive while maintaining such an extensive network of intelligence sources. You are on a list of one." Browning strolled across the room and took a seat. When the driver picked up his hat, Browning held out his hand. "No need, Jean-Luc; I'll save you a trip. I can wait until Arnaud is finished with Colette."

When Jean-Luc looked to Arnaud for instructions, the big man nodded his approval. "Mademoiselle Colette, please join me in my office."

Like the waiting room, the office had no windows, and the air was stale and tasted of cigar smoke. Arnaud shut the door behind him and motioned for Genevieve to sit in a leather armchair. He sat in a similar chair across from hers.

"Jean-Luc will take you to your apartment this evening. You'll find it ready for you—a little food, a small wardrobe, some ration cards. I trust OSS sent you with a generous amount of currency?"

Genevieve nodded.

"Are you familiar with the rationing system?"

"Yes, I lived in Calais until June."

"Good. That should help you fit in." He took a paper out of his pocket. "Travel papers. Vizeadmiral Wever died yesterday. He was in command of German naval forces along the southern coast of France. Headquarters are in Aix-en-Provence. I want you to find out who's replacing him. Be on the train tomorrow morning. It leaves at seven thirty. When you arrive in Aix, go to the parish Church of Saint-Jean-de-Malte. Use the main entrance and advance three pews. Look for a gray-haired woman about five feet tall sitting to the left of the aisle. She cooks for most of the *Kriegsmarine* officers at headquarters. Ask her what she's heard about Wever's replacement. Are you Catholic?"

Genevieve smiled. "I've attended most of my life. I'll blend in with the other worshipers."

Arnaud nodded. "Good. Your source is there Sunday mornings. Ask if her grandson is walking yet. She should reply that he prefers crawling and climbing. Find a place to talk; get the information. Take the train back to Marseilles tomorrow evening so we can radio it in."

"How will I get the information back to you?" Genevieve asked.

"Jean-Luc will be at the train station. Have a newspaper, and put your report inside. A quick brush pass."

"How would you like the report?"

Arnaud raised one eyebrow. "Can you encode it on the train?"

Genevieve nodded. "It won't be unbreakable, but it will help. Use a mirror to read it."

* * *

When the meeting was done, Arnaud opened the door for her.

Browning stood as she entered and shook his head as she walked across the room. "What would your brother think?"

Genevieve could guess what Jacques would say about her involvement and what he would have done if McDougall had asked him instead. "He would do the same thing were he in my shoes."

Browning shook his head again and clicked his tongue. "If you get into trouble, call me." He handed her a scrap of paper with a phone number. "Memorize that, then burn it. Leave a message for me. *Please tell Pierre his pants are hemmed.* Then go to the Hotel du Quinzième, and I will meet you in the lobby. For your brother's sake, eh?" Browning turned toward the young man with the Renault. "Jean-Luc, I believe we are ready for our blindfolds."

CHAPTER SIXTEEN
THE TRAIN TO AIX

Sunday, August 13
Aix-en-Provence, France

STANDING IN THE STREET OUTSIDE the Church of Saint-Jean-de-Malte, Genevieve found her eyes rising heavenward, following the tallest spire. She admired the rose window above the entrance before walking into the church, reverently stepping along the central nave. She walked past two rows of chairs before turning left in front of the third. She knelt down not far from a woman who fit Arnaud's description.

"This church is beautiful, isn't it, my friend?" the woman whispered with a kind smile.

Genevieve looked at the arched ceiling and then forward to the stained glass casting a warm glow over the chapel. "It is." Genevieve had been hesitant to enter the church, afraid the saints might somehow express their displeasure at her recent conversion to another faith. Instead, she felt at peace. The building was dedicated to worshiping the Lord, and she didn't feel out of place there. "It must give you great joy to worship here."

The woman nodded. "The only thing that approaches it is my dear family."

"Children?"

"Three."

"And grandchildren?"

The woman glanced at the other worshipers. "One grandson. About a year old."

"One year. Is he walking yet?" Genevieve whispered.

"Not much. Why walk when crawling is quicker? He's found his way into cupboards and up the stairs. Such a climber. He will be ready for the Alps before he turns ten." The woman paused, making the sign of the cross and bowing her head. Her voice was barely audible when she spoke again. "When I stand, I will stumble. Perhaps you could offer me assistance?"

Genevieve nodded. Acting feeble would play out perfectly with the woman's deep wrinkles and slight frame. Several minutes later, the woman stood and stubbed her toe on one of the chairs. Genevieve rose and offered the woman her arm, and the two left the chapel together.

They'd walked to the Cours Mirabeau before Genevieve felt they were completely alone. "Vizeadmiral Wever is dead?"

"Yes." The woman paused under a tree. The road was lined with them, and the shade was refreshing.

"Do you know who his replacement is?"

"Yes, Ernst Scheurlen, but he's not here yet." The woman took out a handkerchief and wiped a hint of perspiration from her forehead.

Genevieve pretended to admire the building across the street as a pair of German soldiers strolled past them. She waited until they turned a corner. "Who's in charge until Scheurlen arrives?"

"Admiral Südküste."

Genevieve nodded. She didn't recognize any of the names, but until a few days ago, German naval command along the French Riviera had seemed unimportant to her. "Do you know anything about Scheurlen? When's he supposed to arrive?"

"This week sometime. His specialty is coastal artillery. That's about all that's left of the German Navy around here, I gather."

"You cook meals for them?"

The woman nodded.

"And they tell you things?"

"No." The woman smiled. "But they don't know I speak German."

* * *

Genevieve waited to write her report until the train was nearing Marseilles. She didn't want to carry incriminating notes longer than she had to. The train was crowded, but she found a seat near a window and used her newspaper to shield her succinct note from prying eyes.

Admiral Südküste in command until Ernst Scheurlen, artillery specialist, arrives later this week.

As the train slowed, she tucked the note into the paper and folded it as Arnaud had suggested. Jean-Luc was to fold his the same way. She looked at the platform, scanning the French Milice and the German patrolmen. Most of the Germans were very young or very old; more age-appropriate units had been pulled north to face the British and American armies pushing out from Normandy, or to the east to stop the advancing swarm of Soviet troops.

Several Milice officers were checking paperwork as the passengers left the train. She didn't think much of it until her papers were returned to her and she spotted Jean-Luc fifteen meters away. His paper was folded correctly, but the Milice had slowed the progress of the other disembarking passengers. There was no crowd, just a line of passengers waiting for their papers to be checked and a few civilians, like Genevieve, who'd already been cleared and were strung sparsely along the platform. In an area with so few persons, what excuse could there be for bumping into a stranger?

Genevieve glanced at Jean-Luc. He showed every indication that he was planning the brush pass, just as he would in a crowd. *What is he thinking?* She could see a Milice officer watching her. Knowing Jean-Luc would give both of them away if he continued, Genevieve did the first thing that came to her mind: she fell. She tripped over an imaginary obstacle and caught herself with her knee and both hands. Drawing attention to herself wasn't ideal, but as the passenger who'd been behind her in line helped her to her feet, Jean-Luc picked up the newspaper she'd dropped and handed her his in exchange.

"Are you all right, mademoiselle?"

Genevieve turned away from Jean-Luc and smiled at the man who'd helped her to her feet. "Yes, thank you for your help."

"You've a few cuts on your hands," the man pointed out. He offered her his handkerchief, and she meekly followed him to the nearest sink, letting him take her right arm as she tucked the newspaper under her left arm. Within seconds, Jean-Luc had disappeared. Her good Samaritan might think she was clumsy, but at least no one had seen her connection with Jean-Luc.

Genevieve waited until she was in her apartment to search Jean-Luc's newspaper. She rubbed her bruised knee as she read the note telling her to await her next assignment at a new cover job. She was to report to the specified bakery Monday morning at six. Something told her a bruised knee and early work hours were only the beginning of her work in Marseilles.

Chapter Seventeen

Unnecessary Risk

Friday, August 18
Prahova Valley, Romania

"Wake up, Fish." Peter tapped his friend's shoulder and glanced at Ionescu, who was already awake. "I think we're finally in the right place at the right time."

Baker's team had been in Romania for more than two weeks. For the most part, the men had stayed in the mountains near Scorţeni, watching for troop movements and trying to remain invisible. For the most part, the team was bored to tears.

There were a few exceptions: Krzysztof Zielinski reported by radio to their SOE contacts in Cairo almost daily. And twice now, Baker had sent Constantin Condreanu and James Nelson into Ploieşti. Since they both spoke the local language, they were the natural choices. That left everyone else with patrol duty and not much else to occupy the time.

Yesterday Baker had sent a team to monitor the Romano Americana refinery. And he had decided not to wait until Nelson and Condreanu returned from their most recent trip to Ploieşti. Peter, Daniel Fisher, and Tiberiu Ionescu had been delighted to spend the night hiking south to the refinery instead of monitoring the same square mile of forest-covered mountain. They had left the rest of the team in Scorţeni, most of them jealous that they couldn't tag along.

Peter had spent the morning observing while Fisher and Ionescu slept. It wasn't time to switch yet, but Peter thought they'd want to see the massive air raid coming in over the refinery. Peter's first clue that an air raid was approaching had come when the Ploieşti defenders had lit large smoke pots, creating thick, dark smoke to obscure the plane's targets. Now the planes themselves approached through the black haze.

"B-24s?" Fisher asked.

Peter nodded. They flew at a high altitude, still some distance from the refineries, but he could make out the distinctive tails. In awe, they watched the first wave come in and drop their bombs on one of the more distant refineries. The earth shook with each explosion. And antiaircraft guns all along the valley sent up an angry chorus of flak in answer. Most of the 88 millimeter cannons were aimed skyward, and the shells they spewed had timed fuses, making them explode into a wide sphere of flak at just the right altitude to rip through airplanes.

The next wave of planes targeted the refineries directly south of Peter's position. Before the lead plane had dropped its first bomb, an 88 emerged from a haystack and filled the air with flack. The German-made 88 was versatile. In addition to its antiaircraft use, it could be mounted on a tiger tank, used as traditional artillery, or used as an antitank weapon. It was probably an 88 that had destroyed Peter's tank in Sicily, and he'd had an intense loathing for the gun ever since.

Almost immediately, one of the detestable weapons hit an American bomber. Dark smoke streamed from one of the plane's engines for a few seconds, and then the smoke stopped. Peter supposed the pilot had simply cut the fuel to that engine. Antiaircraft weapons surrounded the refineries, all of them firing on the B-24s, but the one that had just emerged from the haystack was the gun nearest their position.

"How far away do you suppose that 88 is? A mile?" Peter asked.

"About that," Ionescu answered.

"Fish, how close would you need to be to hit the gunners?"

Fisher watched the branches of the nearby trees, judging the strength of the wind. "Where the trees thin out, that should be close enough."

Peter nodded. That was about halfway between their current position and the 88. "All right, let's take it out before it downs one of our planes." The three left the bulk of their supplies behind, moving through the forest just as they had during training. Peter covered the other two while they advanced, then they covered him while he came up to join them and moved closer to the target. They advanced quickly, knowing they'd be difficult to see among all of the fir and pine trees. They also knew the 88 might shoot down a plane any second.

When they reached the edge of the forest, they moved along the border until Fisher could see the two men operating the gun. Peter estimated the 88 was a thousand yards away. He wouldn't have trusted himself to hit its operators at that range, even with a specialized rifle, but he wasn't Fisher. The British sniper looked up at Peter, who nodded. Fisher, lying in the dirt, held his Lee-Enfield sniper's rifle perfectly still and depressed the trigger. Then he loaded the next round and fired again, only seconds elapsing between the two shots. The 88 fell silent.

"Well done, Fish. Cover us." He motioned for Ionescu to follow, and the two of them moved toward the gun. They moved quickly, staying under the sparse tree cover as best they could. The valley was full of antiaircraft guns, so destroying the one they were heading for wouldn't make much of a difference to the overall war effort. Yet, after two weeks of nothing but patrol duty, Peter was ready to strike a blow against the Nazis, even if it was a minor one. Besides, B-24s carried up to ten crew members. Preventing even one from being shot down would be worth the risk.

When they reached the gun, Peter brought out an explosive roughly the size of a chocolate bar. He attached a pencil detonator to it and pinched the detonator, then strapped it to the base of the gun's barrel. The acid inside would eat through the detonator's metal wall in approximately five minutes, and when that happened, no one would be using the 88 for anything other than scrap metal. One of the gun operators was still alive. The man, only a boy really, had been shot through the jaw, and Peter could see his chest move as he struggled for breath. Ionescu had already turned away from the gun but looked back when Peter called him.

Peter handed him his rifle. "Take this."

Ionescu raised an eyebrow as if he was questioning Peter's sanity, but he obeyed. Peter picked up the surviving gunner, who was barely conscious, and ran as fast as he could under his burden toward the forest. The Romanian weighed less than Peter, but carrying him was strenuous, making Peter's legs and lungs burn and his shoulders ache. He didn't bother staying near the trees: he made a straight line for Private Fisher.

Ionescu had reached the thicker forest by the time the 88 exploded, and Peter wasn't far behind. The explosion was one of dozens sounding across the valley, joining the massive blasts from the B-24s' bombs and the frequent shells spewed from the 88s. As the last wave of American planes dropped their bombs, Peter sprinkled sulfa powder on the unconscious teenager's wound and wrapped a bandage around the boy's face. By then, it seemed the air raid and any future production at the Romano Americana refinery were finished. The air was full of smoke from the bombs and the burning oil fires. It made Peter's eyes sting and his lungs itch. He stood next to a tree and tried to clear his throat.

"I'm surprised I missed," Fisher said, his face tense as he looked at the bandaged gunner.

"So am I, but I'm not sorry you did." Peter tried to decide if Fisher was upset because he'd missed or because an enemy was still alive.

"And when 'e recovers enough to return to 'is post?"

Fisher had a good point, but with the Red Army massing on the Romanian border, Peter thought it unlikely the man he'd saved would return to the fight against American airmen. "I don't think he'll be back in action anytime soon."

"Well, Lieutenant, you're the officer." Something in the way Fisher spoke was more distant than usual. "If you consider it worth the risk to run in the open to save your enemy, I won't question you."

Peter had an angry retort on the tip of his tongue, but he clenched his jaw and suppressed it. He hadn't kept his temper intact all through training whenever Nelson or Condreanu insulted him only to lose it now with his friend. "Fish, come on. I doubt one in a hundred snipers could have taken that shot as well as you. And he's just a kid."

"So were my nephews, but that didn't stop the Luftwaffe from killing them and my sister, did it? I suppose with your family safe in America, you can afford a little reckless mercy."

Peter had seen pictures of Fisher's sister and her family while he'd been in London. He hadn't known they were dead. Peter began second-guessing himself. He'd been so eager for action that he'd jumped into a quick, unplanned sabotage assignment then accentuated the risk by dragging the wounded gunner back with him, all for a mission of questionable worth. And he hadn't risked just his own life—he'd risked the lives of Daniel Fisher and Tiberiu Ionescu as well. Good officers didn't risk their men's lives on a whim.

Peter knew Fisher wasn't upset about his recklessness in destroying the 88, just about saving the young gunner, but Peter thought he probably should have avoided both. What if Fisher or Ionescu had gotten killed? Peter was still haunted by his decision to send the wounded Corporal Grey to his death outside of Basseneville. He didn't want to be responsible for stripping Mrs. Fisher of her one remaining child.

Fisher shook his head. "In case you've forgotten, the Nazis are the bad guys."

"I'm sorry about your family, Fish. When the Japanese killed my brother, there was nothing I wanted to do more than take out the entire Japanese Navy and the Japanese Army too. If it had been the Luftwaffe instead, I imagine I would've wanted to kill Germans pretty badly."

Fisher looked away.

"He's Romanian, not German." Peter wondered if it would matter and was grateful when Ionescu joined the conversation.

"If he's anything like the rest of my countrymen, he's still hoping the Germans will somehow beat the Russians and then the British will beat the Germans."

Fisher smiled. "That doesn't seem very likely now, does it? The first part, anyhow. Is that 'ow you feel?"

Ionescu shrugged. "I have no love for the Russians or the Germans. During the last war, the Germans pillaged us as enemies. The Russians did the same thing, only they pretended to be our allies."

"I suppose that's 'ow Condreanu feels too?"

"Condreanu doesn't confide in me, but most aristocrats have a soft spot for the Western democracies," Ionescu said.

"And your sister-in-law?" Fisher asked.

Ionescu's face hardened at the mention of his brother's wife. "I doubt Iuliana is a Nazi, but she is the worst mistake my brother ever made."

"Why?" Fisher asked.

Ionescu shook his head, refusing to go into detail about his family's past.

"All right, Lieutenant Eddy, sir, what are your orders?" Fisher seemed back to his usual self, and Peter was glad.

"First we'll get our gear. Then we'll find out as much as we can about the damage to the refineries. When the sun goes down, we head back to Scorțeni." *And I won't risk either of your lives again without a compelling reason*, Peter added to himself.

CHAPTER EIGHTEEN
LIPSTICK ESPIONAGE

Marseilles, France

GENEVIEVE NOW WORKED FOR SOME of Arnaud's less reputable associates, two bakers who kept a job open for anyone Arnaud sent not out of sympathy for the Resistance but by threat of blackmail. They were cool toward her at first, but when they discovered Genevieve could bake, they became friendlier and began sharing information heard on an illegal radio tuned to the BBC.

On Tuesday, she'd heard the first rumors: the Allies were dropping strips of aluminum nearby, certainly with the intention of clogging German radar. Genevieve had noted German couriers on motorcycles frequenting the street in front of the bakery all week. They seemed to be the enemy's main method of communication, and they were busy. Something big was happening.

Then came the official news via the radio. An Allied Army, made mostly of American and French troops, had landed near Saint-Tropez, roughly one hundred kilometers from Marseilles. The new invasion was on, the Allies were advancing, and the *Wehrmacht* lacked adequate troops to stop them.

Genevieve received no word from Arnaud for five days, despite the recent developments. Friday afternoon, she looked up from the pile of dough she was kneading when a man walked into the bakery. "Can I help you?" she asked.

The man looked around, ignoring her. Genevieve watched him for a few seconds before turning back to her dough.

She wasn't looking at the man when he finally spoke, his voice deep and gravelly. "I'm looking for someone. I was supposed to meet them ten minutes ago."

Genevieve's hands froze in the middle of the dough. "Ten minutes ago? Someone came in twenty minutes ago looking for a man of your description."

The two were alone, but the man came closer and whispered. "There are rumors the German Army is withdrawing to a more defensible position. Find out if they're leaving Marseilles or if they plan to stay and fight."

Genevieve didn't reply right away. She'd heard the invasion was going well but hadn't known it was going that well. She waited for further instructions, but the man turned to leave. "How am I supposed to find out what they're doing?"

The man looked back at her and addressed her like she was a child. "Put some lipstick on, unbutton a few of those buttons on your blouse, and bat your eyelashes at a German officer. Hope he knows something." The man turned and left.

Genevieve stared at the lump of dough on the counter. Just what did Arnaud think she was capable of?

* * *

Partially following the advice from Arnaud's messenger, Genevieve changed into her most flattering clothing, pinned her hair up, and put on some lipstick. She tried unbuttoning two of the buttons on her off-white blouse but refastened the lower one after glancing in the mirror. The hem on her gray skirt hit her legs just below the knees. She'd always thought her legs skinny and unattractive but hoped a talkative German officer would disagree.

Genevieve strolled toward the harbor, smiling at every German soldier she saw. She earned a few catcalls in return but mostly from enlisted men. She doubted they'd have useful information. When the street she was walking along neared the waterfront and German patrols increased, she stopped at a café. She wasn't sure what to order when the waiter arrived. Alcohol and war-time imitation coffee both seemed like normal choices, but if she didn't drink what she ordered, it would look suspicious.

"I'll take one of your pastries."

The service was quick. She would have preferred it to be inefficient because she was trying to waste time. Genevieve ate slowly, looking between the sea and the yellow rose sitting in a vase at the table's center.

"Dessert first?"

Genevieve hadn't heard the man approach. She turned to look behind her and smiled at the korvettenkapitän glancing down at her with an amused expression on his face. "When it's available."

"Is it any good?"

"The best I've had all summer."

The man pulled his lips into a warm smile. "Do you mind if I join you? Perhaps eating dessert first is not such a bad idea."

Genevieve nodded her consent. The man looked every bit the naval officer. He was tall with broad shoulders, brown hair turning gray at his temples, and a hint of wrinkles around his eyes and his mouth when he smiled.

He sat down with easy confidence, signaling the waiter and ordering the same thing Genevieve had. "Thank you, mademoiselle. My name is Gerd."

"I'm Madeleine," Genevieve said. It was an alias she'd used before but not in Marseilles.

"Charmed to meet you, Madeleine."

Gerd was friendly and talkative. Genevieve did her best to encourage him, and soon she knew what had to be close to his entire life history up until 1939. She rested her head on her hand and leaned forward, pretending to absorb each word with interest. He ordered a white wine for both of them, and Genevieve acted like she was sipping hers. She poured most of it into the vase in the center of the table when he wasn't paying attention. Despite her questions, he was reticent about his war experience, and Genevieve began to fear she'd overplayed her interest.

"Madeleine, I'm on my way to supper with some associates." He glanced at his watch. "Several of them have French girlfriends, and I would be most pleased if you'd join me."

* * *

The food served at supper was the best she'd eaten in years. The korvettenkapitän's friends were also naval officers: four of them all together, two with escorts. The men switched between French and German, unaware Genevieve understood both languages. She pretended not to mind when Gerd put his arm around her and gave him her warmest smile when he laughed and touched his forehead to hers. She put up with it because the conversation between the officers included a long string of complaints about recent developments, especially about the army commander's recent order to convert most of the naval personnel in Marseilles into infantrymen to boost the city's defenses. It seemed the Germans wouldn't be abandoning Marseilles without a fight.

Genevieve grew restless as most of the men became too intoxicated for useful conversation. Gerd was still sober enough to notice. "Do you like German music?"

"Of course," she said.

"Beethoven?"

Genevieve sang a few lines from the final movement of Beethoven's Ninth Symphony.

"Madeleine, your voice is like an angel's. Perhaps we can go to my apartment and listen to my records?" His invitation included a sloppy kiss on her cheekbone. She knew if she went to his apartment, there would probably be music playing, but listening to it would not be the primary activity.

"Sounds wonderful." Genevieve batted her eyelashes. "Would you excuse me for a moment? I'd like to freshen up before we leave."

Gerd nodded his agreement. As she walked toward the ladies' room, she looked back and noticed Gerd following her with his eyes, a confident smile on his face. A tall man in an SS uniform approached the table, another reason she wouldn't be returning. She would get no additional information from the korvettenkapitän, not tonight.

Genevieve said a quick prayer of gratitude when she saw a window in the bathroom. It wasn't large, but it was big enough for her to slip through. She pulled the garbage can over and used it as a stepstool to get through the window, dropping a foot or so before hitting the alley in back of the restaurant.

She froze when she heard someone clearing his throat.

"I heard the prices in there are monstrous. Are you avoiding a bill or an unpleasant date?"

Genevieve slowly turned around. The man who'd spoken was German and wore an unterfeldwebel's uniform, but his French was almost perfect. He looked at her closely, a rifle gripped in his hands, not pointed at her but positioned so it could be within a second or so.

"The latter," she replied.

"Well, I'm all in favor of getting out while you can." The man loosened his grip on his rifle, turned, and walked toward the main road.

"What do you mean?" Genevieve followed him, wanting to be done with her night's assignment but sensing there was something she could learn from the young German sergeant.

The man paused and turned back. It was dark, but she could make out the fear lining his boyish face. "You seem harmless enough."

Genevieve wasn't sure how to respond. "Of course, I'm just a civilian."

"Not a maquisard?"

Genevieve shook her head, though he wasn't far from the truth.

The unterfeldwebel studied her while he pulled a cigarette from his pocket. His hand trembled as he lit the match. He finally succeeded in lighting his smoke and seemed to relax when he drew his first puff. He closed his eyes for a second and leaned against a brick wall.

"Are you all right?"

He shook his head. "I led a patrol today—out to the countryside. Six men. All of them dead except me."

Genevieve tried to keep all emotion except sympathy from her face. "The Allied armies?" *Could they be so close already?*

The unterfeldwebel shook his head again. "No, maquis. They're everywhere. They aren't strong enough to take Marseilles, but they're strong enough to keep us in. I only escaped because another group came and they started fighting each other." He inhaled through his cigarette. "I'm supposed to lead another patrol tomorrow with more *ost* troops, but I just want to go home."

Genevieve took a hesitant step toward him. She had seen some of the *ost* troops—men forced into the Red Army, captured by the Germans, then organized into battalions with German officers and NCOs. They were treated little better than slaves, but they were given more to eat than the average Soviet POW. "Where are you from?"

"Passau, in Bavaria."

"It must be beautiful. I hope you'll see it again soon."

He took another puff on his cigarette. "We're supposed to hold Marseilles at all costs, but we don't have the men or the supplies." He lowered his voice and looked into her eyes. "I won't leave Marseilles alive."

"Don't give up hope." Despite his uniform, Genevieve felt sorry for him. She wondered if the rest of the German Army was as demoralized as he was.

"Madeleine?" Gerd's voice called from the street, but it sounded like his were not the only footsteps.

The unterfeldwebel looked toward the street then back to her. "Is that the man you're trying to avoid?"

Genevieve nodded.

"If you keep walking down this alley, there's a blue door on the right near the end. The building is unoccupied. You can cut through it and make it to the main road."

"Thank you." Genevieve smiled at the young man's kindness. "I hope you make it home again."

"Get out while you can," he whispered.

CHAPTER NINETEEN

MAJOR SCHROEDER

Saturday, August 19

GENEVIEVE WAITED FOR ARNAUD'S MESSENGER to collect her report while she was in the bakery Saturday morning, but she didn't see the condescending man with the gravelly voice again. She was confident Arnaud would find a way to contact her soon, so she left as scheduled and went to the market to purchase food for the rest of the weekend. She was about to buy some cheese when a shadow fell across the table in front of her.

"Mademoiselle Bertrand?" a husky voice whispered.

Genevieve turned around. Two large men looked down at her. They wore civilian clothing, but the material making up their suits was too fine for French civilians. She suspected they were members of the Gestapo, but she forced a smile. "Yes, may I help you?"

As the second man spoke, Genevieve's suspicions were confirmed. His French was good, but his accent was unmistakably German. "Your presence is requested by one of my superiors. Will you follow us, please?"

If she didn't go voluntarily, they were capable of making her join them, so she allowed them to escort her to their car. One of the men opened the back door for her and followed her inside. A third man waited in the backseat, so Genevieve was sandwiched between the two of them. The other Gestapo agent drove. Genevieve spent the next ten minutes focused on her breathing. She felt like her chest was being squeezed between two boards, and she had trouble filling her lungs with air. She knew she had to appear calm, so she used all of her willpower to keep from hyperventilating.

The driver pulled to a stop outside the main administrative offices of Marseilles. A young gefreiter opened Genevieve's door for her, and the man on her left exited so she could do the same.

"Mademoiselle Bertrand, please follow me," the gefreiter said.

Genevieve thought it a bad sign that someone was waiting for her. The man's invitation was polite, but she had only two choices—follow or run. There was a steady flow of soldiers coming in and out of the building. Running would be a guilty plea; she wouldn't get far. She followed the gefreiter into the main building, down a narrow hallway, and into a busy office.

"Mademoiselle Bertrand to see Major Schroeder," the young soldier announced to a secretary wearing bright red lipstick. She picked up a phone and announced Genevieve's presence to someone in another office.

"Show her in."

When she entered Schroeder's office he was standing with his back to her. "Sit down, please." His voice was calming—but that only made her wary. Nevertheless, Genevieve obeyed his order and sat down in the antique chair facing his desk. The young gefreiter left the office and closed the door behind him. Schroeder continued with his original task for a few minutes. Genevieve did her best to breathe normally.

Finally, Schroeder finished his work and turned to face her. He was tall, with blue eyes, a narrow face, and thick blond hair. He had a pleasant smile and actually looked like a kind, decent man. His uniform put him in the army rather than the SS or the Gestapo.

"Thank you for coming to see me," he said. "I hope your escorts behaved themselves."

"Yes, of course, sir." The original two were intimidating, but that was because of their size and their employer. They'd been otherwise polite.

"Please tell me about yourself, mademoiselle." He dragged his right leg as if it was injured and sat across from her.

"What would you like to know, sir?"

"Begin with your birth."

She launched into her cover story. "I was born in Calais." A careful ear would know that anyway, so McDougall hadn't switched her birthplace. "I had a typical childhood. When the war began, my father wished to live in unoccupied France, so we moved here. My father was an admirer of Marshal Philippe Pétain until he died last year." That was half true. Genevieve's father had admired Pétain, but that had been before Pétain's collaboration with the Nazis. Since then, Genevieve and her brother had cursed Pétain's name, and Genevieve was sure her father would have joined them had he not died when Genevieve was thirteen.

"How did your father die?"

"He fell ill," Genevieve said, a remark that fit her cover story and her real history.

"And your passions?"

"Anything but politics." Genevieve forced a smile. "This year I enjoy baking and hope the war and the rationing that accompanies it will soon be over."

"Yes, you work at a bakery now, don't you?"

"Yes, sir, you seem to know quite a bit about me already."

"May I see your papers, mademoiselle? Standard procedure, nothing more." Genevieve handed them over, and he studied them. "There seems to be a problem with your papers, mademoiselle."

Genevieve was surprised. OSS had done a good job forging them. "What's wrong with them, Major?"

"It says you've lived in Marseilles for almost four years, and I've only now made your acquaintance."

Genevieve concentrated on keeping her face even, her smile intact. "I'm glad we were able to meet today and fix that problem."

He nodded, deep in thought. "Yes, I suppose I should let you get on with your activities now."

"Thank you, sir." She stood.

"One more minute of your time, mademoiselle."

Genevieve sat, worried, but doing her best to hide it.

"It's rather silly. I happened to look over a file this morning that caught my eye. There was a description of an agent who could have been your twin."

"I'm sure at least a quarter of the young women in Marseilles could be described as thin brunettes with brown eyes."

"Yes, but this description was much more detailed. You'll forgive me if I indulge myself and read it to you?"

Genevieve nodded—what else could she do?

"Brown hair falling midway down her back, straight. Brown eyes, dark, immaculate eyebrows and thick eye lashes. Petite nose, mouth, and ears. Nineteen years of age, five feet, three inches high, approximately forty-five kilograms. Known to use the alias Madeleine Petit. May have two small scars on the back of her neck and has a round birthmark on her left shoulder blade. Fond of Bizet's *Carmen*. A native of Calais, last seen in the countryside near Basseneville, Normandy, in June of this year. She traveled with an American agent and appeared to be in a romantic relationship with him."

"That is a detailed description." Genevieve wished she had dyed and permed her hair, or at the very least cut it. She had no idea how Schroeder knew of her birthmark—no one outside her immediate family had ever seen it, not that she could recall, and they were all dead. She put the mystery aside and concentrated on keeping her face calm despite the panic that had grown inside her with each additional description Schroeder had read. "Do you have the agent's name?"

Schroeder looked up from his file and watched her. She was prepared for his answer, so she managed not to flinch when he said her name. "Genevieve Olivier."

Genevieve carefully tilted her head to the side. "Well, it sounds like Mademoiselle Olivier could indeed be my twin. But my name is Colette Bertrand, I've never been to Normandy, and I turn twenty-one today." She hoped she was convincing as she spoke. Genevieve's birthday was really in November, and she would turn twenty instead of twenty-one, but the papers Schroeder held in his hand stated Colette Bertrand had been born exactly twenty-one years ago.

"Well, mademoiselle, since it's your birthday, I shall arrange for a special toast." Before Genevieve could protest, Schroeder picked up his phone and asked his secretary for a bottle of champagne and two champagne flutes.

"Sir, that's very kind of you but hardly necessary."

"It's not every afternoon that I'm able to meet such a charming young French woman on her birthday."

Genevieve smiled as the secretary brought the glasses and the champagne in but stopped him before he poured a glass for her. "I appreciate your gesture, sir, but I've given up alcohol."

"Why?"

"Why what, sir?"

"Why do you not drink?"

"I gave it up for Lent," Genevieve lied. "And I found I had fewer headaches when I avoided alcohol."

Schroeder mulled over her response for a few seconds. "How interesting. The American agent traveling with Olivier belonged to an obscure religion that also frowned upon alcohol."

Genevieve was shocked that Schroeder knew of Peter's religion but did her best to hide her surprise. "What an interesting coincidence." She forced her shoulders to relax, forced an unconcerned smile to form on her lips. Genevieve was certain she was about to be arrested.

Schroeder returned her smile. "Well, Mademoiselle Bertrand, it was lovely to meet you. I hope to see you again someday."

"Thank you, sir." She tried to hide her relief as she stood and reached for her papers. She knew he could still arrest her any minute.

When she opened the door, Schroeder bid farewell again. "Good-bye, Genevieve."

"It's Colette, sir," she said without turning around.

"My apologies, Colette."

"Apology accepted, Major Schroeder." She left his office, thinking he would surely arrest her now, even though she hadn't fallen for his last attempt to trip her. She walked past his secretary and the other women typing and answering phones, down the hallway, and out into the sunshine without anyone calling her back.

Schroeder knew who she was, that was clear. *But why did he release me?* Genevieve pondered that question briefly before coming to the obvious conclusion: he had more important targets, and he wanted to use her to get to them. Schroeder had tried to make her panic in his office, and it hadn't worked. It would be natural for her to now seek help from her contacts. That was what Schroeder would expect her to do, and it would lead him right to the people he sought.

Genevieve suspected she was being tailed, but it took her ten minutes to pick the man out—he was good at blending in. She had an unpleasant suspicion that even if she was able to slip the man following her from half a block away, there might be someone else watching her movements, someone she hadn't yet identified in the crowd.

Genevieve needed to get information to Arnaud, and she needed to do it without Schroeder's men observing her. The problem was, she didn't know who would come for her report. She expected Schroeder to arrest her soon. It was her duty to ensure she was the only one who slipped into his net and to make sure her report made it out before Schroeder came for her, but she wasn't sure how she could manage both.

* * *

Schroeder leaned back in his seat and propped up his right leg. The Mediterranean climate was an improvement over his previous post outside Leningrad, but his knee still ached more often than it didn't. The Soviet shrapnel that had torn through his leg in 1941 had damaged the nerve endings, and they had never healed properly.

His phone rang. "Rottenführer Weiss to see you, sir."

"Send him in," he told his secretary.

Weiss entered the room seconds later. He was tall, proud, and dressed in an immaculate SS uniform. He took a seat without Schroeder offering one.

"Your men are tailing her?" Weiss asked.

"Yes, two of my best. Another should be finished searching her apartment by now. He's taken over the apartment across the road so he can monitor her entry."

"I think we should arrest her at once."

"Yes, you've expressed that opinion before. Did you see her leave?" Schroeder had told Weiss to watch Olivier's exit, giving him another chance to confirm her identity.

"I'm certain it's her." Weiss leaned forward. "I recognized her voice last night and her profile."

Schroeder eased his leg off the stool. "Yes, the physical description is a perfect fit, what I was able to see."

"Did you check her neck and shoulder?"

"I am not in the habit of forcibly unclothing young women in my office."

Weiss stood, his nostrils flaring. "The birthmark would prove it was her! You asked for proof and didn't check it?"

Schroeder held out his hand. "I'm convinced it's her without examining her shoulder." Cooperating with the Gestapo was bad enough; Schroeder didn't want to stoop to using evidence discovered during torture. When Weiss returned to his seat, Schroeder continued. "Her response to my questions was different from what you predicted. She was calm the entire interview. I think she was surprised by some of your information, but she hid it well."

"Perhaps her associate has been tutoring her. That man could convince me paratroopers were landing in Frankfurt tomorrow."

"The American?"

Weiss nodded.

"You seem eager to catch this American, yet you keep suggesting we arrest Olivier at once."

"If she's arrested, he'll come find her," Weiss said.

"And if he isn't in Marseilles?"

"Then we can at least eliminate the pawn. Partial punishment is better than complete impunity." Weiss's words confirmed what Schroeder already suspected: Weiss had a personal vendetta against Peter Eddy, the American agent who'd captured him in Normandy. He was more concerned with revenge than with successfully defeating the French Resistance. In Schroeder's mind, that made Weiss not only a fool but a danger to the overall situation in Marseilles.

"I prefer to follow her until we can arrest her associates. That technique has worked well for us this summer." July had been a good month for the German forces occupying Marseilles. They'd arrested dozens of top Resistance members, but there were scores of them still operating.

"May I assist with the surveillance? I could recognize Eddy if he's here."

Schroeder shook his head. "No, Olivier might see you. Let my men do their work. They have experience with this sort of thing." Schroeder didn't add that his men knew Marseilles much better than Weiss did. Weiss was a newcomer to Marseilles, and though Schroeder hadn't confirmed it, he suspected Weiss had come to Marseilles primarily because it had been far from the front line at the time. Despite Weiss's recent escape from a British POW cage and his subsequent promotion, Schroeder was certain the man had never been in battle. As Weiss turned to leave, Schroeder shook his head again, wishing he had the authority to transfer him to Saint-Tropez, where, according to the spotty reports Schroeder received, the Americans were having a great deal of success securing a beachhead.

Schroeder put his file on Genevieve Olivier away. He would leave her to the three men he'd assigned to tail her. The new invasion meant he had other, more important matters to attend to. Marseilles would undoubtedly become an Allied target soon. Schroeder began working on his plans to defend the city. Weiss's obsession was just that: an obsession. Schroeder would not let it distract him or his men from more vital matters.

* * *

Genevieve searched her small flat. There was nothing useful there, nothing she could use effectively as a disguise. *Anyone searching my home would know this isn't a permanent dwelling: it's too empty.*

She heard the sound of her neighbor's two small boys running up the stairs and slamming the door behind them. She hadn't spoken much with her neighbors, but surely their apartment would have more items to peruse than hers did.

Genevieve made sure her curtains were shut in case Schroeder's tail was positioned where he could see into the third-story window and quietly opened her door. The hallway was empty, so she cautiously approached her neighbor's door.

Genevieve heard the thin, overworked woman yelling at her children to be quiet. The apartment fell silent when Genevieve knocked.

"Hello?" The young mother opened the door only a foot.

"Hello, I was wondering if I could borrow something—or make a trade?"

The woman's eyes narrowed. "What do you want to borrow?"

Genevieve looked beyond the woman. Nothing she could see in the small flat caught her eyes. "I'm not sure yet. Do you have any hydrogen peroxide?"

The woman shook her head. One of the boys followed a marble across the floor of the room, and when she saw the toy, Genevieve had a sudden idea.

"Could I borrow one of your marbles? And a hat? Or exchange something for them? I have cash and ration cards."

* * *

Genevieve spent the few hours until dusk changing her appearance the best she could. She ignored the day's sweltering temperature and put on extra clothing, trying to make herself look heavier. She tried to bleach her hair, but the resulting change was small. Finally, she cut half her hair off and hid what remained under the ugly hat she'd traded all her remaining ration coupons for. She placed the marble, which she'd purchased from the boys, in her shoe, where it would force her to walk with a limp.

Her room had no telephone, but she found one in the hall on the building's bottom floor. She asked the operator to connect her with the number she'd memorized the week before in Arnaud's office. She was relieved when someone answered. It wasn't Browning, but Genevieve assumed the woman who answered would give him her alert.

"I would like to leave a message, please. Tell Pierre his pants are hemmed."

* * *

The Hotel du Quinzième was two kilometers from Genevieve's apartment, but she walked five kilometers to get there. First she slipped out of her apartment building through a different exit from the one she normally used. The street was well trafficked but not crowded. She couldn't tell if anyone followed her, so after limping along two blocks, she took three right turns in succession. She couldn't detect a tail, so she walked a few more blocks and disappeared into a building. When she emerged again from a different exit, she had on a different blouse and no longer walked with a marble-induced limp. She did the same thing again as she approached the hotel—emerging from the second building with yet another shirt and without a hat.

A few blocks from the hotel, Genevieve bought a newspaper and wound her way around the same block she'd just circumnavigated. She was sure she hadn't been followed this far but was still nervous when she entered the hotel lobby. She didn't recognize anyone there, so she found a seat and did her best to hide behind the newspaper. Every time someone in uniform entered the hotel, she feared they were there to arrest her. As time passed, members of the staff began giving her curious looks. It was one of the longest hours of her life, but she stayed where she was, hoping Schroeder's man or men were still watching her abandoned apartment.

A woman walked behind the sofa and bent down to adjust her shoe. "A mutual friend suggests you try the sixth door on the left, second floor. The room is not locked, nor is the window. He's waiting in the alley."

Genevieve nodded slightly. She wasn't sure who the woman was, wasn't sure she was really Browning's friend, but decided to follow the instructions. She waited for the woman to leave the lobby then folded her newspaper and walked to the nearest stairs.

When she reached the correct door, it was unlocked, as promised. The room was quiet—no one was inside, and Genevieve didn't linger. The window was already cracked. As she climbed out, she saw a tiny blue Simca parked in the alley and heard the engine start as she crawled down the fire escape. She walked to the passenger's side of the car and recognized Browning immediately.

"Get in the backseat."

Genevieve complied. The backseat was tiny, but Genevieve was petite.

"Duck down and pull that blanket over you."

Genevieve obeyed, despite the August heat.

Browning drove several minutes in silence. Genevieve was too scared and too relieved to interrupt. "All right, Genevieve Olivier, tell me all about it." His voice was calming, comforting, like a father asking his daughter to tell him all about her bad day.

Genevieve began with her latest assignment and ended with Schroeder's interview.

"Were you followed?"

"I noticed someone following me after I left Schroeder's office, but no one since then. I think I lost them at my apartment. I'm sure no one followed me all the way to the hotel."

The car pulled to a stop. "Well, you are safe now. Go ahead and pull that blanket off your head."

Genevieve pushed the blanket away, letting it slide to the floor, her damp hair stuck to her neck and forehead. She hadn't realized how hot it was under the blanket until she felt the fresh air against her skin.

Browning turned and stared at her for an uncomfortably long time.

"What?" she asked.

"I am trying to imagine what you will look like when your hair is blonde and curly. That will be our second project tonight. I don't know how to make contact with Arnaud, but I have my own radio, so I can send your information in, and that will be our first project. Until we manage to find Arnaud, perhaps you could assist me with my work."

Genevieve nodded. "What are you working on?"

"What is it about Marseilles that makes it a target for the Allies and a defend-at-all-costs garrison for the Germans?"

"The port." Genevieve didn't even have to think about it.

"And if you were the German Army and knew you were going to lose Marseilles, what would you be doing to all its port facilities?"

"Wiring them for demolition."

Browning nodded. "I am unwiring them. If you are even half as good as your brother was, I could use your help."

Genevieve smiled. "I think you've found yourself a new assistant."

CHAPTER TWENTY
A CHANGE OF SCHEDULE

Sunday, August 20
Prahova Valley, Romania

KRZYSZTOF ZIELINSKI SHIFTED THE RADIO on his back, wondering if it had somehow grown heavier over the last two weeks. SOE was demanding frequent reports. It took most of the night to find a suitable location, set up his radio, make contact, and then evade patrols as he returned to headquarters. Then he had to decode the new message from the SOE base in Cairo and code Baker's reply. At least the messages from Cairo were consistent: continue monitoring, report any troop movements, report again in twenty-four hours.

Krzysztof was never alone—Baker always sent someone to assist him, but his escorts were rotated. Most of the men on the team, including Moretti, his current escort, were eager for real action. Not Krzysztof. He was exhausted, but pride prevented him from complaining.

Krzysztof felt his foot sliding as he walked down a steep embankment. He paused, reminding himself that Romanian patrols weren't going to cut him any slack just because he was feeling overworked. At least it was night. The darkness was his unfailing ally.

"I can carry that for you," Moretti said.

"That's not necessary."

"Maybe not, but this is the way I figure it. You're what, six foot one, six foot two?"

"Somewhere in between."

"As am I." Moretti held out his hand to take the radio. "But I'm about thirty pounds heavier than you, and you've made this trek how many times in the last two and a half weeks?"

Krzysztof handed over the pack. "You are large for a paratrooper."

"Yeah, a nice fat target."

Krzysztof smiled at Moretti's response. The extra weight was all muscle, but Moretti's brawny frame would be easier to hit than Krzysztof's slim form.

The two went to one of Krzysztof's favorite locations for calling Cairo: a small shed near the Scorțeni post office, twenty meters from German headquarters.

"Are you trying to prove something?" Moretti asked, his whisper barely audible. "Or are you just suicidal?"

"Neither. This close, our signal will mix with theirs and make it impossible for them to triangulate our position."

Moretti let out a soft, slow whistle. They spent an hour approaching the shed, passing through several small homes and behind a butcher's shop. It took Krzysztof only seconds to unpack his radio and tune it to the proper frequencies, the result of intensive training and extensive experience.

Krzysztof gave his coded report: *little movement, nothing new observed.* He was expecting the reply to contain what it always did. Instead, Cairo sent a long message, long enough that Krzysztof couldn't decode it in his head.

"Something new." Krzysztof packed his radio away, eager to get back to base to decode the message. He looked at Moretti and watched a huge grin spread across the sergeant's face.

* * *

Peter could tell something was different when Moretti and Zielinski returned. The excitement was written in Moretti's face, hinted at in Zielinski's eyes. Peter was impressed with how quickly Zielinski used his decoding skills even with Moretti and Luke looking over one shoulder, Quill popping his knuckles and watching over the other shoulder, and Baker pacing only yards away.

When he finished, Krzysztof Zielinski handed the paper to Baker. While most of the men were salivating for action, Baker remained calm, responsibility for his men's safety tempering any relief at a change in schedule. "A new shipment of barrage balloons is scheduled to arrive by train. We've been asked to destroy it before the balloons are deployed and used to bring down Allied bombers."

"What's left to protect?" Peter asked, thinking of his trip to Ploiești with Fisher and Ionescu. They'd returned yesterday morning. He remembered the drastic damage to the Romano Americana structures, and the other refineries were similarly incapacitated.

Baker shrugged. "The Romanians have rebuilt before. They'll be under pressure to rebuild again. Regardless, we have our orders. I shall take a small team. Five of us should be enough." Baker unfolded a detailed map of the valley and spread it on the table. Most of the team watched him, though Logan and Fisher were on patrol and Sherlock, Condreanu, and Mitchell were sleeping.

"Do you plan to destroy the shipment before it arrives or after it's been unloaded?" Luke asked.

"I'm not sure yet."

Luke pointed to a spot on the map. "Is that a tunnel?"

Baker nodded.

"How long would it take us to get there?" Luke pointed to a train station on the other side of the tunnel. "And how accurate is our timeline?"

"We know as much as the Germans," Zielinski said. "The trains in Marshal Antonescu's Romania are normally punctual."

"Are you suggesting a Casey Jones?" Ionescu asked Luke, who nodded.

"What's a Casey Jones?" Quill asked.

"It's a light-sensing detonator. We could plant it on the train when it stops at the last station before the tunnel. When it enters the tunnel, it'll explode, accomplishing our assignment with the added bonus that it takes longer to clear a disabled train from the track when the wreck is stuck in a tunnel. And the Nazis won't know where or when the train was initially sabotaged," Luke explained.

"What if someone sees it?" Quill asked.

"Hold that thought." Luke walked over to a box of equipment and removed the device in question. "Do you read German?"

Quill shrugged. "Mostly."

"If you were a lowly German—or Romanian—patrolman, would you take this off a train car?"

Quill looked at the sticker on the object and read it out loud, slowly translating into English: "'This is a Car Movement Control Device. Removal or tampering is strictly forbidden under heaviest penalties by the Third Reich Railroad Consortium. Heil Hitler.' No, I wouldn't dare touch it." He handed the Casey Jones back to Luke.

"Nor would I," Luke said.

"Ionescu, are you familiar with this area?" Baker asked.

"Yes, my brother and I went there nearly every spring to bid on horses."

"How long will it take us to get there?"

"On foot?"

Baker nodded.

Ionescu thought while he studied the map. "We usually rode or took the train. If we left at sundown we could probably arrive by dawn. It depends on how heavily patrolled our route is. When does the train pass through?"

"It's scheduled for Ploiești at 1300 hours tomorrow," Zielinski said.

"We could arrive there in time, but we'd have to work in the daylight," Ionescu predicted.

"Or we could wait for it to arrive in Ploiești and hit it there." Luke looked back at the equipment box as if it might hold more alternatives.

"Yes," Baker said. "But Ploiești is better protected—which is why we're here in the mountains instead of there in the valley. I'll take Sherlock, Luke, Ionescu, and Quill with me. Change into civilian clothing; we leave at noon. I prefer the risk of daylight here to daylight in our target zone. Luke, oversee the preparations. Zielinski, when is your next contact with Cairo?"

"Twenty-two hundred hours tomorrow, sir." It was a longer-than-usual break in communications, perhaps because of their increased responsibilities.

"What is the patrol schedule?" Baker asked Peter.

"Logan and Fish are out now," Peter said. "At nightfall, Mitchell and Sherlock were to replace them. I can take Sherlock's patrol since he'll be with you. I planned to send Nelson and Moretti in the morning. Tomorrow evening, I suppose I'll send Mitchell with Zielinski and have Logan and Fish patrol again."

Baker nodded. "Carry on. You'll be in command during my absence."

Nelson made a small cough and moved toward the door. Baker glanced at him and gave a few final instructions before joining Nelson outside.

"I can guess exactly what that louse is saying," Moretti said. "*I must protest being left subservient to such a common officer. He's not even British. My noble blood chafes at the very thought of it.* If he gives you too much trouble while Baker is gone, let me know, and I'll box his ears for you. I placed third in the 82nd Airborne's boxing competition this spring. Normally, I wouldn't brag about a third-place finish, but I'll wager it's good enough to beat him."

Peter laughed, as did Luke, who had overheard. "Not a bad impersonation, Sarge. I'll be sorry to miss a boxing match like that if it happens while I'm gone."

"You'd be more sorry to miss that big explosion, kid."

"I won't see it," Luke reminded him. "The train won't explode until it enters the tunnel."

Nelson and Baker returned, Nelson looking decidedly unhappy. He glowered at Baker as the major carefully unloaded, dismantled, cleaned, and then reassembled his Webley & Scott 1907 pistol, testing the trigger before reloading it.

* * *

That evening Peter walked with Mitchell to brief Logan on the new situation.

"And the rest o' us are stuck 'ere?" Logan asked when Peter finished.

Peter nodded.

"Too bad Baker didn't take you with him," Mitchell said to Logan. "You could have sketched the explosion. Then the rest of us could at least see a picture."

Logan smiled, making his long scar more prominent.

"Gum?" Mitchell offered them both a stick. Logan declined, but Peter accepted, hoping it would help him stay alert.

Logan headed back to headquarters, and Peter went to relieve Fisher.

"Lieutenant?" Fisher spotted Peter before Peter saw him. "I was expecting Sherlock."

"We finally have an assignment. Baker took Sherlock, Luke, Quill, and Ionescu on a little trip to blow up a train."

"Drat. I would 'ave liked to go with them."

"Maybe next time."

"Have a good patrol, sir."

"Get some rest," Peter said. "I'll need you again tomorrow night."

"Missing out on all the fun and extra patrol duty? We are a lucky bunch."

Peter laughed. "We did get one trip to Ploieşti."

"Yes, but blowing up a train sounds more exciting than blowing up an 88."

CHAPTER TWENTY-ONE

THE SEARCH FOR PRIVATE MITCHELL

Monday, August 21

PETER THOUGHT HE MIGHT RUN into Mitchell, the team's other patrolman, sometime during the night, but he didn't. Nor did he see any German or Romanian action. Peter kept moving and chewing his gum to stay awake. He hadn't slept as much as he would have liked to prepare for an all-night patrol, but he told himself he could sleep as soon as dawn came and Nelson relieved him.

Peter returned to the designated rendezvous when the sun broke over the horizon. But Nelson didn't appear. At first Peter assumed it was Nelson's usual snobbery, yet as the sun continued to climb, Peter began to worry. Staying at the rendezvous would provide poor security for their headquarters, but if he left, Peter wasn't sure Nelson would find him. After waiting an hour, Peter left to check all the major roadways again.

Another hour passed. Peter peered through his binoculars at the military convoy approaching Scorțeni from the south. It was nearly a mile from where he was hidden in the foothills, but he could see the trucks and the tank that escorted them and could just pick out the individual soldiers marching to the side. He counted the trucks and the soldiers, but it was too far away for him to distinguish if the men were German or Romanian. He spent over an hour watching the convoy arrive and unload its supplies. As the activity ceased, he slithered into thicker coverage and pushed himself to his feet. He'd been up for over twenty-four hours and was irritated that Nelson hadn't relieved him.

His irritation grew when he found the switch-off point still deserted. He decided to head back to headquarters. James Nelson didn't have to like that Peter was in charge, but he did need to complete his assignments. Peter also needed to give details about the convoy to Zielinski so he could encode it for that evening's message to Cairo. Peter knew his effectiveness as a patrolman was dwindling with his lengthening lack of sleep, and he was hungry.

When he arrived at headquarters, Condreanu greeted him with surprise. "Lieutenant Eddy, didn't Sergeant Logan find you?"

"No, I didn't run into Sergeant Logan. Was he going to explain why I wasn't relieved by Corporal Nelson at dawn this morning?"

"Corporal Nelson has fallen ill," Condreanu explained.

Peter strode to the back room of the cabin, assuming Nelson's illness would be something minor. In his head, Peter prepared a stern lecture. He expected to find a few of his teammates resting in the other room, but when he opened the door, the room was empty except for a sleeping Nelson.

"Where is everyone?" he asked Condreanu.

"Mitchell never returned from his patrol. I sent Zielinski and Fisher out to investigate."

"How long have they been looking?"

Condreanu looked at his watch. "About three hours."

Peter guessed they'd left in a hurry. Half-empty cups of coffee littered the table, the ammunition boxes were out of place, and Zielinski's radio was unpacked. Zielinski usually put it away when it wasn't in use to protect it from accident and prepare it in case he needed to tote it off in a hurry. "Did Moretti say anything?"

Condreanu shrugged. "I haven't heard back from anyone."

Peter nodded, wondering what had gone wrong. "And what's wrong with Corporal Nelson?" Peter walked to the cot where Nelson still slept, despite the conversation between Peter and Condreanu. Nelson's normally handsome face was pink, beaded with sweat, and stuck in a grimace of pain. His uniform was soaked in sweat around his neck and under his arms, and he was breathing rapidly. Peter wrinkled his nose at the nearby puddle of vomit. "How long has he been like this?"

"Since I came to wake him for his patrol. He seemed fine when he went to sleep."

Nelson groaned and shifted in his sleep. His eyes fluttered open for an instant, but he wasn't cognizant enough to know what was going on.

"I suppose we should have brought more than one medic," Peter said. Sherlock was the team's only man trained in medicine, and he'd left with Baker.

"Should we try to find someone local?"

Peter hesitated. Nelson would probably benefit from a doctor's care, but Peter wasn't ready to look for one in Scorțeni. "I'll consider it, but it would be risky, especially while we're undermanned."

"Well, Eddy, Baker left you in charge. What shall we do?"

Peter thought for a moment, feeling his responsibility a little more heavily than usual. "I'm going to look for Mitchell or at least find the others to see how the search is going. Stay with Nelson; he looks pretty bad. And clean up that mess." Peter didn't even take pleasure in assigning Condreanu the unpleasant task of clearing away the vomit. "I'll send someone back to help patrol the perimeter. We have to consider the possibility that Mitchell was captured. If he was, we may have company soon."

* * *

It took Peter an hour to find anyone. His patrol route the previous night had been to the east of their headquarters, Mitchell's to the west. Peter searched Mitchell's territory, carefully watching the roads and wondering what he should do about Nelson. On a previous mission, he'd had bad luck when he sought help from local doctors. *At least I left Nelson in the care of the one man on the team he's never insulted.*

Peter heard the crunch of dry twigs and turned to find Logan only yards behind him.

"Rough mornin', sir?" Logan asked.

"I'll say. Have you been in contact with anyone on the search party? Or found Mitchell?"

Logan shook his head, and just then, Peter heard the same artificial bird call his half of the team had used as a signal during training. Not long after, Fisher ran through the trees. "Any news?" he asked, slightly out of breath.

"No," Peter and Logan both said.

"Have you seen Moretti?" Peter asked.

Fisher nodded. "Mitchell never made it to their rendezvous this morning. Moretti thought 'e might 'ave just gone back to 'eadquarters without meeting 'im until we confirmed Mitchell never showed up. Lieutenant Eddy, do you think 'e may 'ave been captured?"

"It's possible."

"Sir, I volunteer to go into town and see if 'e is being 'eld in the local jail," Fisher said.

"By yourself?"

"I can go with 'im, sir," Logan said.

Peter nodded. "Give me some time to think about it. I'd like more evidence that he's been captured before I let either of you go. With Baker's group gone, Nelson down, and Mitchell missing, we're low on manpower. And if I remember correctly, Zielinski has to call in tonight."

Fisher nodded, subdued.

"I promised Condreanu I'd send help back. Logan, go back to HQ, fill him in, and then patrol the eastern end of our zone."

"Yes, sir," Logan replied then left.

"I wish I knew what was wrong with Nelson," Peter said to Fisher. "If Mitchell's in the same condition, he could be in a coma in a ditch and we'd have to practically step on him to find him. I'm going back to the rendezvous—that's the last place he was seen."

Fisher came along. Still a quarter mile away, they heard another signal. "I think that was Moretti," Fisher said.

Within minutes, they found Moretti kneeling next to their Canadian teammate. Private Mitchell was dead.

CHAPTER TWENTY-TWO

DARK THOUGHTS
AND DARK ALLEYS

"HE WAS KILLED WITH A knife," Moretti said, squatting next to Mitchell's body as Peter and Fisher approached. "Someone hid his body in the bushes—I only found him 'cause his shoelace was sticking out from under a leaf." As he spoke, Zielinski approached from another direction.

"Dead?" Zielinski asked, his face almost as white as the corpse's.

Moretti nodded.

"Fish, go back to headquarters and get the picks and shovels," Peter ordered softly. He felt as though he'd just been punched in the stomach. One of the men Baker left him in charge of was dead. He watched Fisher leave and forced himself to stay focused on the team's assignments. "Zielinski, I wrote this down earlier. Might be worth radioing in along with an update on our team: Mitchell dead, Nelson ill. Go ahead and get back to HQ. We'll follow when he's buried."

"Would you like me to help bury him?"

"I don't think you have time, Kapral."

Zielinski looked at Peter's notes then glanced at the sun. "I think you're right, sir."

Peter nodded, and Zielinski turned to leave.

"Help me move him," Peter said to Moretti. They pulled the stiff corpse out into the open. None of his equipment had been stolen, and he still had a pack of gum in his shirt pocket. Peter looked over the body, undressing it and detecting no bruises or other injuries—no sign of a struggle. He knew the Germans had talented agents and assumed the Romanians did too, but why would one of them be in the mountains around Scorțeni? And why would an enemy operative kill Mitchell and leave the rest of the team alone? "What do you make of an assassin taking Mitchell out and not approaching the safe house?"

Moretti shrugged. "Maybe he went back for reinforcements."

Peter nodded. If Moretti was right, they needed to move—the team was low on numbers and would have difficulty defending themselves. "How do you suppose they knew to look up here for us?"

"Could of been a random patrolman."

"A random patrolman talented enough to surprise Mitchell that completely?" Peter thought it was possible but not likely. "You don't suppose Mitchell fell asleep?"

"Doubt that, sir. He started the patrol rested, and I can't see him getting sloppy like that."

The more Peter thought about it, the more he agreed with Moretti. Mitchell had been a skilled, well-disciplined soldier, not the type to fall asleep on duty.

The knife was still sticking into Mitchell's side, angled up through his ribs into his lungs. Peter studied the handle. It looked like an ordinary knife. The handle was made of smooth wood, stained now with Mitchell's blood. Peter grunted as he pulled it from the body. The blade was six inches long with no distinguishing marks. "Any thoughts on the knife?"

Moretti took the knife and shook his head. "Looks common enough. Could of come from the kitchen of a local home. Could of come from one of our mess kits."

Peter had started clothing the corpse again, but he turned at Moretti's statement, a grim suspicion forming in his head. "You've cooked more meals than I have. When you get back to headquarters, see if we're missing a kitchen knife."

"You don't think someone on our team killed him?" Moretti asked, shocked.

"I don't know," Peter said. "But it would take an extraordinary assassin to get close enough to Mitchell to stab him in the ribs—unless he was a friend."

"Who?"

Peter didn't know. The thought that one of the men Peter had trained with and trusted his life to might have turned on Mitchell was bitter but suddenly persistent in his mind. "I wish I knew. Don't say anything to anyone else yet—I don't want to put the killer on his guard. And I'm still hoping to be wrong."

"Don't trust anyone?"

"Something like that," Peter replied.

"Glad you still trust me, sir."

"If you killed him at the beginning of your patrol, I don't think rigor mortis would have set in yet. Although I suppose you could have sneaked out and killed him last night. Did you notice anyone leaving the safe house overnight?"

Moretti shook his head. "No, but I was asleep most of last night, sir, and the men on this team are quiet enough to get out without waking me. You and Mitchell left, Fish and Logan came back. Didn't notice anything odd until Mitchell didn't meet me this morning."

Fisher returned with two shovels and two picks. Peter removed one of Mitchell's dog tags, then the three of them dug a grave and laid the quiet farm boy from Saskatchewan at the bottom of it.

"Should we say something before we cover 'im?" Fisher asked.

"Something religious, probably," Moretti suggested.

Peter had his pocket-sized Book of Mormon, the one with a bloodstain through the first dozen pages. He flipped through it until he found something appropriate. "'Wherefore, may God raise you from death by the power of the resurrection, and also from everlasting death by the power of the atonement, that ye may be received into the eternal kingdom of God, that ye may praise him through grace divine.' Rest in peace, Private Mitchell."

"Amen," Fisher said.

"Rest in peace, David," Moretti said.

They filled the grave and covered it with leaves and brush to make sure the ground looked undisturbed.

"You'll have to stay on patrol awhile longer, Moretti," Peter said. "With Mitchell dead and Nelson sick, I can't guarantee you'll be relieved at sundown. If not then, expect someone at midnight."

Moretti nodded.

Fisher and Peter took the tools and went back to headquarters. As they walked, Peter's mind churned. *Could I have done something to prevent Mitchell's death?* Worse than the fear that he'd done something wrong was the fear that whoever killed Mitchell was only getting started.

Of all the members on the team, Peter was the one who'd had the best opportunity to kill Mitchell. They'd both been on patrol for twelve hours, and it wouldn't have been unusual to run into each other even when assigned different areas. But he hadn't killed Mitchell. Fisher had also had the chance. He'd been relieved and could have made a detour on his return to headquarters, killing Mitchell and hiding the body. But Peter didn't think it could be Fisher. Fisher was his friend. He'd trusted Fisher with Genevieve's life. Surely he wasn't capable of turning against his teammates. And what possible motive could he have? As hard as it was, Peter had to consider every possibility. But as he looked at Fisher, all he could think was, *Not you, please, not you.*

"Fish, I want you to tell me everything that happened after you returned to headquarters last night. Anything you can remember."

Fisher nodded. "After I arrived, Logan and I 'ad dinner."

"Did you arrive before or after him?"

"After, but only by a few minutes, I think. Nelson and Condreanu were playing cards, and the rest of us went to sleep. Sometime in the middle of the night, Nelson and Condreanu woke Zielinski and 'ad 'im keep an eye on things until a bit before dawn. I suppose 'e woke Condreanu first, maybe Moretti too. Condreanu brought tea with 'im when 'e woke Nelson and me up, so 'e must have been up long enough to brew it."

"Did you see Nelson when he woke up?" Peter adjusted the shovels he was carrying across his shoulder.

"No, I took my tea into the other room and ate breakfast with Moretti and Zielinski. After Moretti left, Condreanu came out and said Nelson was sick. I asked Condreanu if someone else should relieve you and 'e said we'd wait a bit and see if Nelson improved. Then when Mitchell didn't show up, Condreanu sent Logan to update you and sent Zielinski and me to go check the west patrol."

Peter nodded. "Did anyone leave during the night?"

"Not for longer than it would take to go to the outhouse and back." Fisher paused, looking around to make sure they were alone. "Lieutenant Eddy, there's something bothering me. I spent 'ours this morning searching the area. There's no sign of a struggle. Mitchell never was one to miss much. 'E would have spotted someone trying to kill 'im, I'm sure of it. Quite frankly, I'd feel better if 'e'd been shot or if there was evidence of a fight. I've killed a few soldiers with a knife in my time, so I know 'ow it's done. If someone managed to sneak up on Mitchell, why did they stab 'im like that? Why not slit 'is throat or stab 'im in the back? And why kill Mitchell and leave the rest of us alone?"

"I agree," Peter said. "Do you have any theories?"

Fisher hesitated. "What if it was someone on our team?"

"Go on," Peter prompted.

"All of us can use a knife lethally, and any one of us could get close to Mitchell—if not by stealth, then because 'e wouldn't be on 'is guard with a teammate. And everyone 'ad an opportunity. You could 'ave stabbed 'im during your patrol. Logan or I could have stabbed 'im on our way back to 'eadquarters last night. Moretti could have done it when they met at the beginning of 'is shift. Condreanu and Nelson could 'ave done it while the rest of us were sleeping. And Zielinski could 'ave done it while 'e was on watch alone."

Fisher had just confirmed all of Peter's thoughts, and Peter doubted Fisher was guilty if he was pointing out all the evidence. Besides, Peter knew Fisher. He might execute a German prisoner, but he wouldn't turn on his Canadian teammate. "You're right, Fish, everything points to an inside job. But why? Why would anyone kill Mitchell?" That was the question troubling Peter the most. "Maybe if we find out *why*, we can find out *who*. When we get back to headquarters, keep your thoughts to yourself. If you're right, whoever killed Mitchell could target anyone who gets too suspicious. Leave out the details on how he was stabbed too. Moretti and I discussed the possibility that it's someone on the team earlier, so you can talk to him. And see if we're missing any kitchen knives."

Fisher nodded, his eyebrows furrowed, and his jaw tense.

When they arrived at headquarters, Logan was on the eastern patrol. Nelson was still sick, although his sleep looked more relaxed than it had that morning. After checking on Nelson, Peter sat at the table next to Zielinski, across from Condreanu. He could see Fisher making sandwiches, and assumed he was also counting the number of knives in their supplies.

"When do you need to leave?" Peter asked Zielinski.

"Within the hour."

Peter nodded. He needed to send someone to cover Zielinski but wasn't sure who.

"I can go with him," Condreanu said.

Peter hesitated. He didn't like the Romanian, but if Condreanu had been with Nelson all night, it seemed unlikely he was the one playing a double game. Peter nodded his consent. Condreanu was, after all, the most rested man on the team.

"Look, Eddy," Condreanu said. "How long have you been awake?"

Peter shrugged. "Awhile."

"Why don't you get some rest. You too, Fisher. Let Logan and Moretti stay out a little longer and relieve them when you've had a chance to sleep. We can give them an update on our way out."

Peter nodded again. It seemed like a good plan.

* * *

Krzysztof moved the dials on his radio into the correct position. He usually left the dials on their lowest setting. They hadn't been there when he took the radio out, and he couldn't remember moving them, but he shrugged it off. A lot had happened since he last radioed in.

"We're late—will they still be listening?" Condreanu asked. The two of them were transmitting from a butcher's attic in Scorțeni on the same street as German headquarters.

"Only one way to find out, sir." Krzysztof's words were terse. Condreanu had taken too much time finding and updating Logan and Moretti and then had been overly cautious on their trip in. Krzysztof wasn't reckless, but the darkness should have masked and shortened their journey rather than lengthening it.

"Did you hear that?"

Krzysztof looked around. "No, sir. What did you hear?"

"I'm not sure, but I think I'll reconnoiter."

Krzysztof peered out the small attic window. The street below was quiet, but he nodded. "I'll try to make contact in the meantime."

Krzysztof was midway through his transmission when Condreanu returned. His finger paused for a half second. "Anything?"

Condreanu shook his head. "I must be hearing things."

Krzysztof finished the transmission, waited for the reply, then moved the dials to the left and put his radio away. He looked around the room to make sure there was no evidence of their visit.

Condreanu checked the street from the window. "We're clear."

They descended the stairs silently. Krzysztof had his radio on his back and a handgun at his side. He preferred his rifle, but the smaller weapon was easier to carry. He felt the wind blow through his hair as he left the butcher's shop. The breeze was refreshing; the attic hadn't yet cooled from the day's heat. He listened carefully, expecting silence and hearing it. He edged along the back of the shop, Condreanu tailing him, and inched his head around the corner.

"Surrender!" Someone was waiting in the shadows, his rifle pointed at Krzysztof.

Krzysztof brought his pistol up, but a second man appeared from nowhere and grabbed his wrist, throwing his aim off. The man who'd ordered his surrender plunged his rifle butt into Krzysztof's gut, and he doubled over in pain. Something hard hit the back of his head, and Krzysztof fell to the ground as a dozen men converged around him. He couldn't see Condreanu, couldn't identify the uniforms of the men who surrounded him, couldn't see the stars. The initial order had been in English, but the few communications that followed weren't in any of the languages Krzysztof spoke. He didn't understand their words as they took his weapon and his radio, dragged him to his feet, and pushed him toward the road.

CHAPTER TWENTY-THREE

INTO THE DARKNESS

Tuesday, August 22

"LIEUTENANT EDDY?"

Peter woke with a start, wondering how long he'd slept. "Nelson? Glad to see you up. How are you feeling?"

"Horrible. But that can wait. Where is Condreanu?"

"Covering Zielinski."

Nelson seemed upset. "But that was Mitchell's assignment. How long have I been ill?"

"Coming up on a day," Peter said. "Mitchell was stabbed during his patrol last night. He's dead."

"Private Mitchell is dead?" Peter heard the shock in Nelson's voice but couldn't see his face very well in the dim light. "How long ago did Condreanu and Zielinski leave?"

"What time is it?"

"Oh one hundred hours."

Peter got out of bed. "They should be back anytime now."

Nelson cursed. Peter wasn't sure why Nelson was so upset that Condreanu was gone, but Peter was concerned that he and Fisher had overslept, leaving Moretti and Logan out on patrol for too long. He walked to the front room; Nelson hobbled along behind him. Fisher was asleep near the door, where he'd be easily woken if someone tried to enter.

"Fish," Peter said. Fisher woke immediately and jumped to his feet.

"Lieutenant Eddy, when was Private Mitchell killed?" Nelson asked.

"Sometime during his patrol. He was missing when Moretti went to relieve him."

"How can that be? Killed last night? Are you sure?" Nelson asked.

Peter glanced at Nelson. "Yes, we're sure it was last night. Fish, get ready to relieve Logan. Didn't the alarm go off?"

"No, sir, I never 'eard it."

Peter believed him. Fisher was disciplined, and he wasn't a heavy sleeper.

Nelson picked up the alarm clock and played with a few of its parts. "This clock has been disabled."

"Why would someone—" Fisher stopped himself midsentence, looking at Nelson and quickly looking away.

"What were you going to ask?" Nelson said.

"Why would someone be so careless with our equipment?" Fisher said, but Peter knew that wasn't the original question.

Nelson raised an eyebrow, clearly doubting Fisher's cover. He looked from Fisher to Peter, giving them both careful scrutiny. Peter considered telling Nelson about their suspicions but decided against it.

After leaving the cabin, Peter motioned for Fisher to walk with him instead of going directly to find Logan. "Why would someone want us to be late? Is that what you were going to ask?"

Fisher nodded.

"Or was confusion the goal?" Peter realized he'd hardly had time to think the last twenty-four hours. Little time to think and little energy to think clearly.

"Well, if Nelson is in on Mitchell's death, I've tipped 'im off. I apologize, sir."

Peter considered the possibility of Nelson's guilt as they continued on a few paces. "I'm positive Nelson wasn't faking his illness. It seems like too much of a coincidence that he fell sick within a shift of Mitchell's death. Mitchell dead, Nelson almost dead. And the rest of the team overworked and sleepy."

"Maybe someone is 'oping we'll be too busy and too exhausted to notice 'is mistakes."

"Or hoping we'll make mistakes of our own," Peter said. "What am I overlooking?"

Fisher shook his head, looking as bewildered as Peter felt. "I don't know, sir, but be careful. We're missing more than one knife. And Baker left you in charge, so if confusion is the goal, you could be the next target."

Peter was surprised by Fisher's suggestion. Mitchell was only a private. If Nelson was also a victim, that meant the bad apple in their group wasn't targeting officers. Not yet, anyway. "We've got to figure out who's behind this— whether it's the Nazis or an inside job. Meet me at the western rendezvous at oh four hundred hours. Maybe we'll have thought of something by then."

* * *

Krzysztof winced as he felt the raised bump on the back of his head. At least it had stopped bleeding. He remembered little of his arrest and initial imprisonment. He'd been too dizzy, everyone and everything around him foggy.

They'd left him alone in a room—it wasn't a proper jail, but there were no windows, and he could hear a guard pacing in the corridor outside the room's only door. A small table held a basin of water. He drank some of it then wet his handkerchief and wiped away the worst of the mess on the back of his head.

He'd been in the room for several hours. He was tired, and it was dark, but he couldn't sleep. He'd never been captured before, not on any of his previous assignments. He thought of the discussion on interrogation Colonel Poole had led back at Dravot Manor and felt sick to his stomach, wondering what to expect. He didn't know where Condreanu was. He hadn't seen the locotenent since the arrest and wondered if their captors were busy questioning him. The men who'd led Krzysztof to his cell hadn't been unduly rough with him, not since they arrested him outside the butcher shop, but that didn't mean they weren't currently torturing Condreanu.

He tried the doorknob and wasn't surprised to find it locked, just as it had been the previous times he'd tested it. He knocked on the door, mostly out of curiosity. He was pleasantly surprised when the guard stopped his pacing and opened the door a few inches.

"Do you speak English?" Krzysztof asked. "Or Polish? Or German?" he asked in the respective languages.

The guard spoke a smattering of German.

"Can you get me a bandage for my head?" Krzysztof motioned toward his injury.

The guard wanted to see the wound and pushed the door in a little farther. As the guard stuck his head through the door for a quick look, Krzysztof shoved the door shut, smashing the guard's head between the door and the doorframe. The guard was too stunned to resist when Krzysztof grabbed the man's collar and brought his knee up, slamming it into the guard's face. Krzysztof let him fall to the floor and dragged him the rest of the way into the room. He immobilized his prisoner, using the guard's shirt as a rope and his handkerchief as a gag.

Armed with the guard's rifle and set of five keys, Krzysztof left his prison and set out to look for Condreanu. He spent what he guessed was the next twenty minutes exploring the building, hiding from patrols, and unlocking doors only to find empty rooms. He was squandering his escape time but couldn't leave without trying to find Condreanu. Personal differences aside, Condreanu was one of his teammates. He hadn't seen him since they'd left the butcher shop, but he hadn't heard any weapons other than his pistol discharge during the arrest, so he assumed Condreanu was still alive.

Krzysztof followed a thin sliver of light through an otherwise dark office and found the source: a cracked door. He heard voices and peered through the crack. There, seated before a grand mahogany desk, sat Condreanu. Opposite him, behind the desk, sat a Romanian colonel and a German hauptmann. He could see the back of Condreanu's head and the faces of the other officers.

Krzysztof recognized his radio on the table. He wanted it back but knew it would help the Nazis little. Only Krzysztof and Baker knew the proper codes to send at the beginning of the transmission. Even if someone guessed the correct frequency, any information transmitted without the correct codes as prologue would be suspect.

Changing positions, Krzysztof noticed one Romanian soldier standing by the door he was looking through and a second guard standing near the room's other entrance. Both stood at attention, but the guard at the other entrance looked bored. Krzysztof couldn't see the face of the man near his door.

The three men at the table spoke Romanian; Krzysztof couldn't understand their conversation, but Krzysztof could see Condreanu's scowl when he turned to the side, and it didn't look as if he'd been tortured. The German spoke little, and the Romanian colonel seemed to carry the conversation. The man had dark, thick hair and a face reminiscent of a Renaissance sculpture. At his neck, Krzysztof could make out a medal: a cross with flourishes at the end of each equal-length branch.

Four men against me, Krzysztof thought, *but I'll have them by surprise, and Condreanu can grab one of their weapons to make it two against four.*

Then the situation changed. The building seemed to awaken, filled with the sounds of boots rushing through the hallways, bells ringing, and dogs barking. A messenger came to the door on the far side of the room and spoke to the officers inside. The German hauptmann spoke to the Romanian colonel, who stood and directed the messenger.

Sprinkled amid the myriad orders, Krzysztof caught a phrase Condreanu spoke in German to the hauptmann: "I told you not to underestimate the men I dropped in with."

From the moment the alarm sounded, Krzysztof suspected his escape was discovered. Condreanu's sneer confirmed it. Doubting he could mount a rescue now, Krzysztof left the building through the nearest window. He couldn't see anyone nearby, but he could hear several dozen men searching for him. He took one final look at the building that held his officer, and then he ran.

CHAPTER TWENTY-FOUR

LOGAN'S SCAR

PETER GOT TO HIS FEET. He'd taken a break from his patrol to say a long, heartfelt prayer, pleading for wisdom and safety for each of his men and for himself. He'd been left in charge of seven men, and he'd already lost one. *Please don't let me lose any more*, he prayed.

Peter moved higher on the mountain, getting a clearer view of the valley below. The night showed no signs of civilization. Like the rest of Europe, Scorțeni was under blackout every night. Nazi patrol cars might use headlights, however, so Peter kept his eyes moving, looking for anything out of the ordinary in the valley below and on the roads leading into the forested mountains. He noticed a dim light and suspected it was a cigarette. But whose?

Peter crept toward the small light. He'd expected a Romanian soldier but recognized Logan as he drew near. He watched for a few minutes. Logan had been late from patrols in the past, taking time to draw the landscape, but it was too dark for that tonight. Peter didn't want to jump to the wrong conclusion, but he did want to find out why Logan hadn't returned to the safe house after Fisher relieved him.

"You should probably put that smoke out," Peter said quietly. "I don't think anyone in Scorțeni would pick it out, but I saw it from three hundred yards away."

Logan dropped his cigarette and smothered it underneath his boot. "I thought you might see that." He stepped toward Peter. "Why is it you don't smoke, sir?"

"Religious reasons. And I don't think my girlfriend likes the smell."

Logan chuckled. "Based on what I've 'eard, she seems like she's worth keepin' 'appy."

"Yeah, she's more than a guy like me deserves." Usually talking about Genevieve or his religion made Peter smile, but tonight's conversation made him feel physically ill. "Why didn't you go back to the safe house?"

"I wanted to speak with you, away from the rest o' the team."

"Go ahead, then."

"I 'ave some concerns about Mitchell's death," Logan began, taking another step toward Peter.

"Who doesn't? What concerns do you have?"

Logan was only an arm's length away. "Why didn't whoever killed 'im bring reinforcements and take the safe 'ouse?"

"They may still plan to." Peter wasn't feeling any better. Something wasn't right. "But you could have said that at headquarters."

Logan nodded. "I suppose I no longer trust everyone on the team. Mitchell knifed, Nelson poisoned."

"Poisoned?" It was a new thought, but it fit with Nelson's sudden, severe symptoms. Peter was about to ask Logan how he knew it was poison when Logan brought his arm up. Instinctively, Peter lifted his left arm, knocking Logan's arm and sending the knife he was holding flying. With his right hand, Peter grabbed his Colt M1911 and pointed it at Logan's head. "I wouldn't try your handgun or your rifle, Sergeant. Fish would hear it. He knows someone on the team killed Mitchell, and he's a better shot than you." Then Peter remembered who had relieved Logan from his patrol. "Or was Fish another of your victims?"

Logan slowly raised his hands in front of his chest, where Peter could see them. "I do not kill for fun. I've not received orders to kill Private Fisher, and so 'e is still alive."

Peter took Logan's rifle and pistol then stepped back, giving himself a few feet of space in case Logan decided to lunge at him. "And whose orders are you following?"

Logan sneered. "That's my secret, isn't it now?"

"I really think you'd better tell me."

"Or what?" Logan asked. "You'll torture it out o' me? I remember our training, and frankly, I'm not concerned."

Peter was quiet, his pistol still pointed at Logan's head. "Moretti and Mitchell were close friends. Perhaps I'll ask Moretti to find out what he can from you. I'll continue my patrol—and stay far enough away that I won't have to hear anything."

Logan was silent.

"Will you at least tell me why?" Peter asked. "Money? Or have you found something to admire in Adolf Hitler?"

Logan let out what could almost be described as a laugh. "Hitler is a madman. 'E's destroying Germany and most o' Europe with it. I don't trust 'im or 'is Romanian underlings, but I'd cooperate with the devil 'imself if 'e was promisin' to take down the British Empire."

"Your file says you're a Protestant from Belfast. I thought the Protestants wanted to stay with the United Kingdom? Joining Ireland would turn them into a minority."

"I lied."

"I see. Catholic?"

Logan nodded. "A prolonged war with Nazi Germany is just the thing to leave the British Empire too weak to stop another Irish revolt."

"And you're willing to kill your teammates for that?"

"Ever heard of the Black 'n' Tans?"

Peter shook his head.

"They were a group of irregulars, 'ired by the British to suppress the Irish revolt. They came lookin' for my father, but they were drunk, and arrestin' an IRA supporter wasn't enough for 'em. You know 'ow I got this scar? Tryin' to protect my mother. But I was only nine, so I couldn't stop them. Nor could I stop them from giving matchin' scars to all my sisters. But I'm older now, so yes, anything I can do to weaken the British Empire, I'll do it." Logan pointed to the long scar running down his face. "Every time I look in the mirror, I'm reminded why."

Peter felt his initial determination waver. How would he have felt if he'd watched British troops assault his mother and cut up his sisters? Perhaps that explained why Logan had been so quiet during their class on interrogation. Like Peter, he'd been reliving torture from his past. Remembering Mitchell, Peter pushed his sympathy aside. "How does murdering a Canadian and an American weaken the British Empire?"

"Don't be deceived. Baker's mission is to look out for British interests. Mitchell was in the wrong place at the wrong time, easy prey to cause confusion. And you . . . I 'ave orders to kill you specifically. Would 'ave got you this mornin' if Fisher 'adn't shown up and complicated things."

"Why me?"

Logan let a small smile form on his lips. "Nothin' personal, sir. While everyone was on leave, I went through your letters, so I know your family and your girlfriend would miss you, but I'm only followin' orders. Decapitate the team, leave everyone confused and scared."

Logan had read Peter's letters? Peter felt a surge of anger but ignored it. Reading other people's mail was the least of Logan's crimes.

"Believe me," Logan continued. "I'd rather kill the Englishmen on the team, and you o' all people should understand or at least sympathize. Your Mormon ancestors were persecuted because o' their religious beliefs. And your country too was once under the thumb o' the British Empire. You fought for independence, accepting aid from the French, who gave it primarily to 'urt the British. Hitler is a poor substitute for Lafayette, but we 'aven't anyone better."

Peter grew quiet again. He did understand, a little. A desire to maintain his country's freedom was among the reasons Peter had enlisted. Surely a yearning to earn that freedom would be just as strong. "You have my sympathy, but you're still under arrest. Back to the safe house. Walk in front of me and keep your hands on your head."

CHAPTER TWENTY-FIVE

SHADES OF GRAY

DAWN WAS APPROACHING, THE WORLD changing from black to gray. Krzysztof's head was pounding. He'd been evading patrols for hours, and he was exhausted and dizzy. Every time he thought he could make a break for the mountains, a patrol would cut off his route, almost as if they knew where he was trying to go. Forced away from his goal, Krzysztof worked his way out of town but toward the south, away from the mountains. As the pain in his head worsened, he realized he needed rest, soon, before he slipped up and stumbled into a patrol.

A fresh dizzy spell convinced him to climb the wall of a large estate to search for a hiding place. He dropped to the other side and hid in some nearby bushes, hoping to rest for at least a few minutes.

He watched an early riser walk past him toward a well and didn't recognize her at first—she was too far away, and the light was too dim. Yet something about her seemed familiar. It took him a few moments to pinpoint it—her walk. There was too much side-to-side motion for complete efficiency of movement. After the figure drew her water and turned back toward him, Krzysztof was sure: it was Tiberiu Ionescu's sister-in-law, Iuliana. He remembered the bad blood between the two of them. Yet she had helped the team land, and he needed assistance. He let her draw level with his hiding spot before he spoke.

"Iuliana, can you hide me?"

She looked down toward him, her dark eyes meeting his. "Who are you?"

"I came with Major Baker's team."

She stared at him for a few seconds and then nodded. "You were the one with the radio. What's your name?"

"Krzysztof."

"And who are you hiding from?"

"The Romanian police and the German Army."

She fell silent.

"Mama?" a child's voice called. It was in Romanian, but Krzysztof could understand a word as simple as that.

Iuliana called back to the child, her voice sweet and calming. Then she looked back at Krzysztof. "Do they know you're here?"

"Not yet."

"Then I'll help you. Wait here—I'll be right back."

Krzysztof waited, hoping she wasn't retrieving the police.

She returned, still alone. "Come before someone sees you. In another hour, everyone will be awake." She led him into the large home.

"Is this your home?" he asked.

"No, the estate belongs to one of Vasile's cousins. I've been a guest since the Americans started bombing Bucharest."

"The Americans are bombing Bucharest?"

"Yes, since April. I never thought we'd go to war against the Americans . . . perhaps if they had a better taste in allies."

Krzysztof almost laughed but managed to change it into a cough.

Iuliana smiled. "I can guess what you're thinking, and you're right. Romania's taste in allies is just as bad. Antonescu is Hitler's lackey, and the king is either powerless or indifferent. Who do you suppose is the most evil? Stalin, Hitler, Satan himself?" She didn't wait for a reply. "We weren't given much of a choice when we had to choose sides. We could be Germany's ally, or we could be invaded. I don't blame the British for cozying up to Stalin. His army is massive, and he doesn't share a border with you."

"I'm not British," Krzysztof said.

Iuliana looked at him more carefully. "You aren't? I thought all of Baker's team was British except Tiberiu."

"No, I'm from Poland."

"I'm sorry," Iuliana said, leading him down an unlit flight of stairs.

"I'm not ashamed to be a Pole."

"No, that's not what I meant. I'm sorry about what happened to your country—about what's happening to your country right now." They had reached a small, windowless cellar. There were two partially opened doorways leading into darkened rooms. "You probably understand better than Major Baker what a poor ally the Soviet Union is."

Before Krzysztof could reply, they heard movement above them.

"Anatolie and I are not the only guests on the estate. It's a lot of work to feed all the refugees, and I usually help in the kitchen. I'd better go before I'm missed. If someone comes, hide." She pushed open the door to her left and pointed to one of the back corners. "We rarely fetch anything from over there." Then she left.

* * *

Logan had been completely silent since Peter tied him to a chair in the safe house. Peter had sent Moretti to find Fisher and tell him to shift his route inward—they were down to a one-man patrol. Nelson was sleeping, winning the battle against the poison but still weak. Condreanu and Zielinski hadn't returned, and that concerned Peter. They could have been delayed or been forced to hide on their way back. But even with a delay, they should have returned by now.

Peter and Moretti had tried to reason with Logan. Moretti had even made some serious-sounding threats before going to relieve Fisher at dawn. Still, Logan remained mute, ignoring Fisher when he returned and only glaring at Peter when he asked questions. Peter knew how to inflict pain, but every time he contemplated anything beyond questions, flashbacks of the Gestapo jail in Calais flooded his mind. He didn't want to be like Prinz or Weiss or Siebert. And he had *liked* Logan. He'd laughed at Logan's jokes and swapped cigarettes for chocolate bars with him when they got their rations. Peter flipped through Logan's sketchbook, the less-than-flattering drawings of Nelson the only clue to Logan's political philosophy.

Shortly after sunrise, the door swung open and Condreanu walked in. He looked pale as he glanced around the room and set Zielinski's radio on the floor.

"We expected you hours ago. Where's Zielinski?" Peter asked.

"He's not here?" Condreanu asked.

"No."

"We were captured. I managed to escape, but I couldn't find him. I looked for hours—thought maybe he made it back somehow. Why is Sergeant Logan tied up?"

"Because he poisoned Nelson and stabbed Mitchell."

"What! Why?" Condreanu staggered backward.

"Something about the British Empire and his desire to see it crumble. What happened at the call-in?"

Condreanu blinked a few times, looking at Logan before focusing on Peter's question. "We made contact. As we were leaving, the Romanian police surrounded us and we were separated. I tried to find Zielinski but couldn't."

"Sir?" Fisher was looking at Peter.

"Go ahead, Fish."

"I'm willing to volunteer for a rescue mission. By myself if need be."

"Alone? On two hours of sleep?" But Peter understood Fisher's desire. "Make a plan. Tonight. After sunset. I'll go with you."

"Has Logan told you anything useful?" Condreanu asked.

Peter shook his head and looked at Logan. "No, but I've given him lots of time to change his mind."

"Mind if I ask him some questions?" Condreanu said.

"No, not at all. I'll go update Moretti." Peter had been postponing Logan's interrogation for hours and was grateful Condreanu seemed willing to step in.

As Peter looked for Moretti, he wondered if he was doing the right thing. He doubted Condreanu's methods would be gentle. Though relieved that he didn't have to do the rough questioning, he wondered how much guilt would still rightly be his. He wished Logan would just cooperate and leave no need for Condreanu to apply harsh techniques.

Moretti's bird call drew Peter in.

"I didn't think anybody would relieve me this quick, sir." Moretti dropped the end of his cigarette and stomped it out. "Saw Condreanu show up solo. What's happening?"

"They were both captured after the radio transmission. Condreanu escaped. Fish and I might see if we can find Zielinski, but we'll wait until dark."

"I think our Polish radio man is about as tough as they come. Wouldn't want to lose him, would we, sir?"

"No." Peter did not want to lose Zielinski. He'd already lost Mitchell.

"Want me to come along?" Moretti's voice suggested he was willing.

"Maybe. But unless Baker gets back, we'll need you here. I think it's time to switch safe houses, though that should probably wait until dark too." Peter shook his head in frustration. "I'm really making a mess of things, aren't I?"

"I've seen lots of officers do worse, sir. You letting Condreanu do the interrogation?"

Peter nodded. "It probably should be me, but I don't want to do it. I don't even want to hear it."

"That's what I like about you, sir. You're tough, but you got that good-boy Bible streak in you. That's why I'd follow you all the way to Berlin."

"Even after all this?"

Moretti nodded. "You're doing all right, sir, especially for an ex–tank driver."

Peter shook his head and smiled. "Carry on, Sergeant. I'll send someone to update you if anything changes."

As Peter approached the cabin, he was relieved to hear no cries of intense human suffering. *This guy killed Mitchell, poisoned Nelson, and tried to kill me*, he reminded himself. Everything appeared calm when he opened the door. Logan was still tied to his chair; Condreanu sat next to him, playing with a trench knife. They were both silent as Peter entered. No one else was in the room, so Peter assumed Nelson and Fisher were sleeping.

"Is Logan cooperating?" Peter asked.

Condreanu nodded, though the expression on Logan's face suggested otherwise. "Oh, he's about to. He didn't answer your questions?"

"No, not most of them," Peter said.

"Well, I think I'm making progress," Condreanu reported. "I'd like to continue my work. I'll guard him if you want to rest up before your rescue mission tonight."

Peter fell asleep quickly but didn't sleep long. He checked his watch when he woke. He'd only slept a few hours, but something felt wrong. He looked around the room and saw Fisher and Nelson still sleeping. He didn't hear anything from the front room but decided to check the interrogation anyway. Condreanu was asleep, sitting in a chair with his feet propped up on a bench. Logan was dead, a trench knife sticking out of his chest.

"Why is Logan dead?" Peter's hands balled up into fists.

"I grew tired of his Irish propaganda," Condreanu replied with a yawn. He shifted in his seat and closed his eyes again, like he was going back to sleep. "He was bad for morale—mine and everyone else's. Quick justice has its merits."

"That's not a decision you should have made on your own." Peter's voice was significantly louder than it needed to be.

Condreanu looked surprised and sat up. "I suppose you're right. I'm sorry. I'm at the point now where I hardly remember when I last slept for more than a few minutes. I shouldn't have let him get to me."

Peter clenched his teeth, unsure if he was more irritated with Condreanu for acting so rashly or with himself for allowing Condreanu to become exhausted past the point of common sense. Peter counted to ten in his head and forced his fists to relax. "Did he talk?"

"Yes, he was completely cooperative in the end, between his anti-British rants."

"How was he contacting his associates?" Peter asked as Fisher and Nelson appeared at the doorway.

"In person, during his patrols. He used a mirror to make signals during the day and a cigarette during the night."

"Did he have any other plans?"

"Just to kill you." Condreanu looked genuinely repentant as he spoke. "I'm sorry. I let my temper get out of control. I should have consulted with you first."

Peter walked to the body. Even though Logan had tried to kill him, Peter felt grief, not anger. "What else did he tell you?"

"Nothing worth hearing. I'll bury him," Condreanu offered.

Peter nodded and sent Fisher to help. He sat down, buried his face in his hands, and wondered when he had lost control of the situation. It had been less than two days since Baker left him in command of seven men. Of the seven, two were dead, one was missing, and one was recovering from poison.

Peter had been sitting there a long time when Nelson sat across the table from him. "Lieutenant Eddy, are you absolutely certain Logan was working with the Nazis?"

Peter looked at Nelson, surprised by the question. "Yes, Corporal Nelson. I am *sure*." Peter stressed the last word. "He confessed to it after trying to stab me."

Nelson nodded. "Well, given the circumstances, I will take your judgment as accurate," he said as Moretti and Condreanu opened the door and walked into the room. It was difficult to say which of them seemed more surprised by Nelson's sudden civility. Nelson laughed softly, covering his earlier statement with an insult. "Listening to a poorly educated, backwoods Yankee farm boy takes some getting used to." Nelson stood and joined Condreanu. Moretti sat in his place.

"I think I liked him better when he was sick," Moretti mumbled under his breath.

"Did you see anything on patrol?"

"Other than another funeral, sir? No. Fish offered to give me a little break. And I took him up on it, sir, because I would've been willing to put a little pressure on Mitchell's killer, if you know what I mean, but it ain't right to kill him without consulting nobody else."

"It's not how I would have handled it."

Moretti shifted in his seat. He'd been speaking quietly enough that no one but Peter could hear him, but he lowered his voice even more. "And what are you gonna to do about it, sir?"

Peter glanced at Condreanu. "Keep a close eye on him."

CHAPTER TWENTY-SIX

IULIANA

IULIANA TAPPED ON THE DOOR before opening it. "It's me." When her eyes adjusted to the dim lighting in the storage room, she found Krzysztof not in the corner she'd recommended but behind her, where he could have escaped or attacked had she been someone he didn't know.

She handed him a bowl of stew and a thick slice of black bread. Then she took a squat candle from her apron pocket and lit it with a match, shutting the door behind her. "I'm sorry the food's only lukewarm. Some patrols came by and asked questions. They suspect you're hiding here, and I didn't want to stir up suspicion by disappearing during the noon meal."

"Thank you for bringing it. It smells good." He sat down to eat. "Will they search the estate?"

Iuliana sat on the floor next to him, placing the candle in front of them. He'd been through a rough night, and it showed on his face. Even in the dim light, she could see his eyes were bloodshot and his eyelids droopy. "I'm not sure. Hauptmann Bloch wants to. He came by this morning with a patrol, and my host turned him away."

"He obeyed her?"

She noted the surprise in his voice. "Cosmina Ionescu has always cooperated with the Germans and takes it as a personal insult that Bloch wishes to search her home. She doesn't think she has anything to hide, but she's stubborn. She told him to produce evidence that her household was harboring fugitives, and he said he'd return with his superior. Technically, Romania is still a sovereign country, so Bloch will have to involve the Romanian authorities."

"Then I should leave now," Krzysztof said. "I was arrested by Romanians, so Bloch will get the cooperation he needs."

"No. Bloch left several men patrolling the roads nearby. They'd see you if you left, and you'd be caught. Besides, you look tired. Didn't you sleep at all this morning?"

"Not much."

"Because you didn't feel safe?"

He shrugged. "I'll leave tonight when it's dark."

Iuliana nodded. "Cosmina would be horrified if they found you here. She's spent years trying to not antagonize the Germans."

"You approve of her acquiescence?"

Iuliana thought for a moment before answering. "It's protected her and her household. I think she's been wise."

"Then why did you mark our drop zone?" Krzysztof asked.

Iuliana paused before she answered. Romanian public opinion had been volatile the last decade, seeming to change as quickly as the seasons. Iuliana's political feelings were complex, but she knew why she'd helped the team. "Because of my late husband."

"Did he work against the Nazis?"

"I think so. After he helped Tiberiu leave and before he was arrested, Vasile told me if I ever saw a man wearing a green sash and walking a dog near the garden, I was to offer him my help. For a year, nothing happened. I almost forgot about it when I left Bucharest, but Vasile must have planned it for Scorțeni too. Eight hours before you dropped in, I saw the man. His sash was ridiculous—I suppose he wanted it to be visible from a mile away. And he had with him a mangy, half-starved mutt. I offered my help, and he told me to meet him in the foothills at twilight. I didn't know what I was helping with until you arrived. When I recognized my brother-in-law, I knew it had been planned before Tiberiu left."

Krzysztof put the empty bowl on the floor. His eyes focused on the candle. "You speak your brother-in-law's name like it's a poison. I haven't known Tiberiu long, but I find it difficult to believe he could inspire such hatred. He wouldn't ask for his brother to die in his place."

"No, he didn't ask, but Vasile gave because Vasile would give anything for his brother," she said bitterly.

"You don't approve?"

"It's not that simple. I understand fraternal love: I had a brother until he died outside Odessa, and I would have done much for him. But I think Vasile should have been more concerned with his wife and his son and left Tiberiu to clean up his own messes. When Vasile told me of the signal, he must have suspected he'd be arrested. True to form, he made sure Tiberiu would have help if he returned. Couldn't he see how dangerous it would be for me? For Anatolie? The family of a man accused of treason?" She shook her head in frustration. "And now I'm a traitor. Right or wrong, my county is allied with Germany.

Who would take care of Anatolie if I'm executed for treason?" She shook her head again. The world was about to change once more, and she feared what that would mean for her little boy.

"Did you love your husband?" Krzysztof asked.

"Very much. Why else would I honor his request even after his death?"

"How did you meet?"

Krzysztof was giving her the chance to talk about something less political, and she took it. Iuliana clearly remembered the day she'd first met Vasile. It had been June 27, 1940, the day Romania gave in to the Soviet Union's ultimatum and abandoned the provinces of Bessarabia and Bukovina. The morning's radio announcement had informed them that the Red Army would be arriving that afternoon, and like most of the ethnic Romanians in her village, Iuliana and her family had fled. "We met during the evacuation of Bessarabia. Vasile was in the army, stationed near the border with the Soviet Union."

"You're from Bessarabia?"

Iuliana nodded. "My father settled there after the Great War. When the Tsar fell, Romania took a little of his territory. Romanians make up the majority of both provinces, but that didn't stop the Soviets from wanting them back twenty-some years later. And as we left, sizable minorities were happy to see us go. They stole our car, so my father, my brother, and I set out for the train station on foot."

"Who stole your car?" Krzysztof asked.

"Probably the same people who threw garbage at us. Communists and Jews."

"Ah." Krzysztof nodded in understanding. "The Communists were glad to join the Soviet Union, and the Jews were glad to escape King Carol's anti-Semitic legislation."

"That's what Vasile said when we took the territories back and he argued for forgiveness. During the evacuation, I was separated from my family. I took a wrong turn and ended up in a gang of them. At first they just called out insults, then they took my suitcase. Some of them left after that, looking for other targets to rob. Some of them stayed. They pulled my hair, shoved me into the wall. Then Vasile came and stopped them."

Krzysztof smiled. "Your knight in shining armor? Or handsome officer in immaculate, freshly pressed uniform?"

Iuliana returned his smile. "Closer to the latter, but his uniform was far from tidy. He'd been fighting all morning. Similar gangs had torn the collar patches and shoulder bars from his uniform—I had no idea of his rank. He was bareheaded, his hair a mess, his front tooth chipped, and his right eyelid swollen. But he protected me and helped me find my family."

Iuliana would never forget her first sight of Vasile Ionescu. The morning had been warm. His temper had been hot. Despite being outnumbered four to one, he'd knocked two of her assailants unconscious with his fists then sent the other two running with broken noses and cracked ribs. "My father was a doctor, so he set up practice in Bucharest until he rejoined the army in 1941. Vasile escaped Bessarabia in one piece, but a month later, he dislocated his shoulder while duck hunting. He went to see my father. They recognized each other, and my father brought him home for dinner."

"And how soon were you married?" Krzysztof asked, finishing his bread.

"Two months after that. Anatolie was born a year later."

"It was a happy marriage?"

Iuliana hesitated. "It began that way."

"But it didn't end that way?"

Iuliana shrugged. "I was sick while expecting Anatolie, at least at first. Vasile was wonderful. He did the cooking; he did the cleaning. Then I started to feel better, and I gained a little weight, and one day he just turned cold. I hoped things would be different when I gave him a son, but little changed."

"What happened?"

Iuliana was crying. She hadn't meant to cry in front of Krzysztof, but she couldn't help it. She had loved Vasile, and his sudden change had broken her heart. The mystery behind it still haunted her. She wiped the tears from her eyes and held back a sob. "I don't know what happened, but Tiberiu was visiting the day Vasile changed, and I think he was involved."

Krzysztof didn't speak for a while. When he did, his voice was quiet. "So you helped mark our landing zone to respect a husband who may or may not have loved you, who has been dead for over a year, and who was more concerned with your brother-in-law than with you or your son?"

Iuliana nodded, feeling warm tears run down her cheeks.

"And why are you helping me now? Is that also for him?"

"I don't know why." Iuliana looked away, studying a crack in the floor. She was not so brazen a liar that she could look Krzysztof in the eye while she withheld information. In truth, she knew exactly why she was helping. The wounded, worn-out Polish soldier reminded her of how Vasile had looked the day they met. But there was more to it than that. She saw in Krzysztof the same idealism she had so admired in her husband. Vasile's idealism, she also suspected, was what had always kept her second or third place in his heart.

* * *

Iuliana spent most of the afternoon in the cellar with Krzysztof. She hadn't meant to disappear for four hours, but she liked Krzysztof. He wasn't as much like Vasile as she first thought. Vasile had been hot tempered and passionate, and when things were good, he'd made her laugh. Krzysztof, on the other hand, was logical, gentle, and he'd already elicited more tears than she'd cried since her husband's death.

It wasn't that Krzysztof was mean—nothing could be further from the truth. But the questions he asked were so direct, cutting right to the core of the bitterness she'd held inside since Tiberiu had fled and Vasile had gone to jail. Others had tried to help her work through her grief, but they'd focused on the external events: the uneasy alliance with Germany, the losses on the battlefield, the fact that her husband, father, and brother were all dead.

Krzysztof was different. He didn't condemn Romania—or Iuliana—for siding with the Germans, but he held a quiet pride in Poland's resistance and in its suffering. Poland had been ripped apart by armies from Germany and the Soviet Union, and Krzysztof's concern for the part of his family still in Poland seemed etched in his face as he spoke of them. Now it looked as though the Soviet Union would control both countries at the war's end, but Poland would have no shameful Nazi alliance in its past. Krzysztof hadn't said so, but she could tell he wouldn't trade his country's honor for anything. The two of them were not unlike their countries. Krzysztof would follow his conscience, even if it led to martyrdom. Iuliana, like her country, had chosen survival.

Vasile and Tiberiu had understood, just as Krzysztof did. They had seen the evil in Stalin's empire. And though they'd been eager to use the German Army to take back what the Soviet Union had stolen from Romania, Vasile and Tiberiu had also seen the evil in fascism and worked to undermine the Nazi empire, beginning with the regime at home. Iuliana had been so focused on survival that she hadn't seen the beauty of the brothers' struggle. Not, that is, until she'd spent the afternoon with Krzysztof.

Iuliana went to the well and drew some water. She washed her face, drying it on her apron, hoping the cool water would reduce the swelling around her eyes.

She checked on her son, who was with Sabina. "Is it all right if Anatolie stays with you awhile longer? I have some work I need to do."

Sabina nodded. "Of course. He's entertaining my baby while I sew."

Iuliana was on her way to the kitchen when Vasile's cousin placed a hand on her arm. "Where have you been all afternoon?" Cosmina was twice Iuliana's age, with elegant gray hair and a regal presence.

"I'm sorry, did you need me?"

Cosmina shook her head. "No, you haven't been shirking your work. I'm just curious where you were."

Iuliana looked at the ground, wondering what she should say.

"If you've been hiding the fugitive Bloch is seeking somewhere on this estate, you had better bring him to me now. If we turn him over to the authorities quickly, perhaps we'll be forgiven."

"But Cosmina—"

Cosmina cut her off. "If Bloch returns and finds anything amiss, I will turn you in. I won't risk the safety of everyone who lives here, not even for Vasile's widow. Bring him to me now. Bloch will be back any minute."

Cosmina stepped away.

"Wait, Cosmina."

Cosmina paused and turned back.

"He's not on the estate. I've been helping him, but he's not here; he's in the woods."

"For your sake, he'd better not be here, not when Bloch arrives." Cosmina turned sharply and left.

Iuliana stood there for a moment, her hands shaking. She'd never lied to Cosmina before. *What are you doing? Just turn Krzysztof over to the authorities and concentrate on keeping Anatolie safe.* She forced herself to move. She couldn't help anyone if she stayed frozen outside the kitchen door. She passed a window and saw a car pull up in front of the house. Hauptmann Bloch and Colonel Eliade climbed from the rear seats, and two lower-ranking men climbed from the front. Eliade's eyes scanned the house and paused when he saw her through the window. She shuddered at his gaze and hurried past the window. She'd known Eliade since shortly after her marriage, and she'd never enjoyed any of their previous interactions.

Iuliana ran to the cellar and knocked as she opened the door to the storage room. She spoke at once, not seeing Krzysztof but assuming he was still there. "I'm so sorry, Krzysztof. They're here—I should have let you leave earlier."

"If the roads were being watched, you had good reason to suggest I stay." Iuliana followed his voice to a corner of the room and could barely discern his outline. "Will they search the estate?"

"Yes. Cosmina suspects you're here—she noticed my absence, and I didn't think quickly enough to reassure her. She isn't willing to help." Iuliana found it hard to breathe as panic set in. There was nothing she could do to prevent the search, and it was far too late to move Krzysztof.

"How many are there?"

"Four, plus the men Bloch left earlier."

"What will happen if one of the men searching the estate ends up dead?"

Iuliana hesitated, but she'd told enough lies for the day. "They'll arrest everyone who lives here. They'll release most of us eventually. But in the meantime, they'll call reinforcements and search until they find you."

"And if I'm found? I can say I found my own way to the cellar."

"If you're found, Cosmina will know I lied to her." Iuliana fought to keep her voice even. "She won't protect me; I'll never see my son again."

Krzysztof was quiet for a few moments. "And if I surrender? Or if you turn me over to the police?"

Iuliana didn't have time to answer. She saw a light in the stairwell, heard the footsteps as someone descended the staircase. She reached for a jar of oil on a nearby shelf and shut the door behind her, hoping Krzysztof would stay where he was, hoping that somehow, whoever searched the room wouldn't see him.

She'd taken only a few steps when Eliade arrived at the bottom of the stairs, a lantern in his hand.

"Iuliana, what a pleasant surprise."

She nodded at him then stepped to the side of the hallway to let him pass.

"What are you doing in the cellar?" He stopped walking and stood, inches away.

She looked at the jar of olive oil in her hand. "I'm gathering supplies for our evening meal."

His face was calm. "Without a light?"

The basement had no electricity. Some light drifted in from the window at the top of the stairs, but the two underground rooms were nearly black. "I know where the oil is kept. I don't need a light."

Eliade glanced at the jar in her hands then at her face. "Your late husband's family has made you their slave, then? And you're worked so hard that you've become intimate with the estate's food stores?"

"I'm happy to help."

"Come with me." Eliade opened the door to the room across from the one Krzysztof was hiding in. It contained unused furniture. All the spare rooms of Cosmina's estate had been converted into sleeping chambers. The tables, chairs, chests, and vases that had once furnished the rooms were in the basement, their place in the grand home now occupied by mattresses. Eliade handed her the lantern and walked through the room, searching every shadow, lifting the white cloths that protected the furniture from dust to make sure no one was hiding underneath.

"Colonel, what are you doing here?" Iuliana asked as he finished his search and motioned for her to follow him into the other room, the room where Krzysztof hid.

"Protecting you by searching for a dangerous fugitive."

"But what are you doing in Scorţeni?" She followed him into the room, keeping the lantern low, where its light would be less illuminating.

Eliade turned to her. He was so close she could see every detail of his handsome face and the cold eyes that seemed to look right through her. "I followed you."

She wasn't sure he was telling the truth. He'd come from Bucharest to Scorţeni only a few weeks after her, but she'd hoped it was just coincidence.

"My offer still stands, Iuliana."

He reached for her face, and she stepped away. "Colonel, if you want a mistress, I'm sure you can find one younger and more beautiful than me."

Eliade stepped toward her again, and this time her foot hit the wall when she tried to back away. She let his fingers caress her hair. She wanted to slap him, wanted to throw the lantern at him and run, but a new thought had formed when her foot hit the wall. Distracting Eliade would be good for Krzysztof and for her.

"You're the only woman I want," Eliade whispered.

He'd told her the same thing only months after her marriage. She'd been shocked—Valise's superior officer had tried to seduce her. She'd turned him down, despite Eliade's threat to deny Căpitan Ionescu the promotion he'd just earned. Vasile hadn't received his promotion, and Iuliana had never told him her part in Eliade's decision. Eliade had threatened to send Vasile away to the front with a hazardous assignment if she mentioned anything.

Since Vasile's death, Eliade's attentions had increased. Rarely a week went by that he didn't offer her his protection, his home, and his bed. Coming to Scorţeni had given her only a brief respite. She shuddered and turned away as his hands moved from her hair to her cheek.

"Someday, when you and that little brat of yours are starving, you'll change your mind. Continue to cross me and Anatolie will suffer." With that warning, Eliade tore the lantern from her hand and left the basement without searching the dark corner where Iuliana had last seen Krzysztof.

Eliade had never threatened Anatolie before. With her savings nearly exhausted, her family dead, and Cosmina's faith in her shaken, she worried Eliade's prediction might prove prophetic. She'd managed to keep food on the table in Bucharest by tutoring English students. But each month there were fewer and fewer pupils interested in language classes, and work was growing scarce. In time, she'd have no other option but to seek Eliade's help. Iuliana fell to her knees. Her entire body felt cold, as if all hope and all warmth had suddenly been sucked out of the basement and out of Romania. Everything felt cold except part of her shoulder, where Krzysztof's hand was softly resting.

CHAPTER TWENTY-SEVEN

CONFESSIONS

PETER ADDED A FEW STICKS of dynamite to his pack, thinking he probably wouldn't need them. He and Fisher had outlined their preliminary plan and gathered their supplies. Now they waited for darkness.

"Perhaps I should go instead," Condreanu said. "I speak the language. And I know where Zielinski was captured and where I was being held."

"Aren't you likely to be recognized?" Peter organized the explosives as he waited, preparing for the move to their secondary headquarters.

"Not in the dark."

"I would like to go with him," Nelson said.

Peter turned in surprise. "I thought you were sick. Isn't that why Moretti's still out on patrol instead of you?"

"I won't have a chance to fall asleep in Scorțeni. Patrol might be different."

"I appreciate everyone's willingness to go into harm's way, but I'd rather stick with the plan Fish and I've drawn up." Peter didn't add that he no longer trusted Condreanu's judgment.

"Come now, Lieutenant, I think you should give it more thought." Condreanu walked to Peter and knelt next to him. "What will you do if someone tries to talk to you? Pretend to be French?"

"I don't plan on anyone seeing us. Fish and I have worked together before— we know how to disappear in the dark. If Zielinski's still in Scorțeni, we'll find him."

"And if they've moved him?" Condreanu asked.

"Then we'll be in the same situation you'd be in if you went."

"Not quite," Condreanu said. "If I run out of luck, I can ask for directions. I got information out of Logan—I think I can get information from just about anyone. Besides, Baker left you in charge. What will we do if you run into trouble?"

"Major Baker should be returning soon."

"And if he doesn't?" Condreanu put his hand on the pack Peter was about to swing onto his back.

"Then you'll be in charge, won't you?" Peter said.

"Let me go. I'll take Fisher. I should have found Zielinski yesterday, and I need to redeem myself."

Peter hesitated. His gut told him he should be the one to go. *Or is it my pride speaking?* He understood Condreanu's desire to make right what had gone wrong on his watch, but Peter dreaded another night of waiting.

"Sir?"

Peter couldn't remember James Nelson ever addressing him as *sir* before. "You still want to go along?" Peter asked.

"Yes, but first I would like a word with you outside."

Peter motioned toward the door and followed Nelson, gratitude for a reason to postpone his decision outweighing annoyance at the two Cambridge graduates.

Nelson opened the door and laughed. "We were just arguing about which of us was to have the honor of rescuing you." Nelson stood to the side, revealing Krzysztof Zielinski and Iuliana Ionescu in the doorway.

"What happened?" Condreanu asked.

"I was arrested. I escaped. I was pursued until I recognized Iuliana. She hid me until twilight."

"What's she doing here?" Condreanu asked.

"I was hoping to speak with Tiberiu. Is he here?" her voice was hesitant, as if she was a little scared of Tiberiu Ionescu.

Condreanu shook his head.

"Do you know when he'll return?" she asked.

"No." Condreanu's voice was cold.

"I should get back, then, before I make anyone else suspicious. Perhaps I can see him another time." Iuliana turned toward the door.

"Would you like me to see you back?" Zielinski asked. "At least past that last patrol? They seemed like competent woodsmen."

"I think your friends would prefer you stay." Iuliana smiled. "But if you run into trouble again, I'm sure I can find a place for you to hide."

"Thank you for everything." Zielinski opened the door for her.

"Good-bye, Krzysztof." She closed the door gently behind her.

"You two seem to be on friendly terms," Condreanu noted.

Zielinski's only response was an almost imperceptible upturn of his lips.

"Why did you bring her here?"

"She wanted to patch things up with her brother-in-law."

Condreanu snorted. "Ionescu doesn't think we should trust her."

Zielinski scowled at him. "I would be in jail if she wished us ill."

Condreanu opened his mouth to argue, but Peter interrupted him. "Come sit down, Zielinski. I want to hear details. Fish, Nelson, get everything packed. We're moving in fifteen minutes."

* * *

They moved to their secondary safe house, the one Peter had set up with Fisher, Mitchell, and Ionescu the night they arrived. Peter and Mitchell had dug a hole into the side of the mountain while Fisher and Ionescu had made a set of two concentric trenches. Then they'd covered everything with tree branches and woven a roof of sorts for the main safe house. Even with their earlier efforts, it was a significant downgrade from the cabin they'd left.

"Aren't we glad we brought along a Boy Scout?" Nelson mumbled to Condreanu.

"Get some sleep, Corporal Nelson," Peter said. "Unless Major Baker shows up with a well-rested team, you'll be relieving Fish in a few hours."

Nelson raised his eyebrows but didn't voice any additional complaints about their primitive sleeping quarters.

"There's an old lookout post a half mile west. We'll keep an eye on it tomorrow, see if it's abandoned or not." Peter thought it might be more comfortable, but it was also more exposed to enemy observation.

He checked to see that all the equipment was properly stored. Despite Peter's suggestion, Nelson hadn't gone to bed, launching instead into a Shakespearean quote about insomnia. "'O sleep, O gentle sleep, nature's soft nurse, how have I frighted thee, that thou no more wilt weigh my eyelids down, and steep my senses in forgetfulness?'" Or at least that's what he'd said until Condreanu went to lie down. Nelson suddenly started yawning then. Peter bit his tongue to hold back a rude comment and walked to the outer trench. Within a few minutes, Moretti joined him.

"Don't you think you should get some sleep, sir?"

"Probably." Peter glanced at Moretti then back into the forest. "But it seems like every time I fall asleep, something bad happens."

"We got Zielinski back. And Nelson seems to have returned to his healthy, arrogant self. He and Condreanu." Moretti shook his head and chuckled. "I think most married couples give each other more space."

Peter felt himself smiling.

"Fish said you didn't get any sleep on your little trip to Ploieşti. And you ain't had much since then. Why don't you take a few hours, sir? I'll wake you if anything changes."

Peter fought a yawn. "So you and Fish are both worried about my lack of sleep, huh?"

"Fish and I think you're too busy worrying about everybody else to worry about yourself. A good officer, which you are, takes care of his men. And a good NCO, which I'm trying to be, takes care of his officer." Moretti smiled. "You gonna take my suggestion, sir?"

Peter nodded but didn't go back up to the safe house. If anything happened, he wanted to be able to react within seconds. He settled into the bottom of the trench and tipped his helmet over his face.

* * *

"You blow your train up, kid?"

Peter heard Moretti's voice and pulled himself to his feet. He blinked a few times before recognizing Luke.

Luke grinned. "Yeah. We didn't see it, but we got everything set right."

Baker walked into view next with Tiberiu and Iuliana Ionescu. The latter two didn't look at all happy to be with one another. Peter glanced at his watch. He'd been asleep an hour.

"Easy, Ionescu. Remember, you're a gentleman," Baker said as Ionescu pushed Iuliana toward the trench.

Peter had thought Zielinski was asleep, but he appeared as Baker and the Ionescus rejoined the group. Peter was still uncertain about Iuliana. Ionescu had painted a dark picture of her, but Zielinski's account left Peter wondering.

"Where are Quill and Sherlock?" Moretti asked Luke.

"Went to the other safe house. We ran into Fish on our way in, but that was after they'd headed east."

Baker looked around. "Is everyone else at the other safe house?"

Peter looked down before meeting Baker's eyes. "Fish is on patrol. Nelson and Condreanu are asleep. Mitchell and Logan are dead."

"What?" Baker sounded shocked.

Luke's jaw dropped.

"You should also know that Nelson is recovering from a nearly fatal bout of poisoning, and at the last radio call-in, Condreanu and Zielinski were both arrested, but they have since made their separate escapes."

Baker sat down on the ground, his legs dangling in the trench. "I need details."

Peter updated Baker on all that had happened since he left, and Luke and Ionescu paid close attention. Ionescu was standing next to his sister-in-law, like he was guarding a dangerous prisoner. Zielinski was near her too, but his posture was more friendly than threatening.

"So you've at least learned not to lie when people who can prove you wrong are within a few hundred yards," Ionescu said after Peter explained Iuliana's role in Zielinski's escape.

Iuliana's face colored as her temper flared. She glared at her brother-in-law then forced herself to calm down, inhaling deeply and exhaling slowly. "I told you I was on my way back to your cousin's estate; I just got delayed waiting for a patrolman to leave. Why didn't you believe me?"

"I have my reasons."

"I apologize for what happened when you landed." Iuliana's hands had been balled into fists. With obvious effort, she unclenched her hands. "It was wrong of me to question your courage. That was never lacking."

Ionescu let out a cross between a laugh and a huff. "Don't flatter yourself. An insult from you? Why would I care?"

"Then what? What have I done, Tiberiu? What have I done to justify such loathing?"

Iuliana's voice was growing louder. Peter worried the two might attract the attention of a Romanian patrol, but when he looked at Baker to see if he shared Peter's concern, Baker's face was phlegmatic, his fingers resting on his chin, his eyes locked on the Ionescus.

"You broke my brother's heart!" Ionescu hissed.

"I loved your brother! I gave him everything, including a son. You poisoned him against me. You ruined both of our lives, and Vasile is dead because of your recklessness. What did you think, that Antonescu's clemency for political rivals would extend to a reckless, unconnected oil saboteur?"

Ionescu maintained an even tone. "I may have trusted the wrong person, but I wasn't reckless. If Vasile stopped loving you, it's because he was never sure who Anatolie's father was."

"What?" Ionescu's last statement left Iuliana looking like she'd been physically struck.

Ionescu glared at her. "You heard me. Whether Vasile stopped loving you or not, I don't know, but when he stopped trusting your fidelity, that was the end of your marriage. Maybe if you'd been faithful, he wouldn't have been so willing to trade a dishonorable marriage for a prison sentence."

Iuliana clenched her fists again. "How dare you, Tiberiu! I have always been completely faithful to my marriage vows. For you to spread lies about me to Vasile—"

"Vasile told me," Ionescu interrupted. "Don't try to cover your own disgrace by accusing me of deceit."

"I did not break my marriage vows!" Iuliana said. "Why would Vasile have believed such a lie?" She looked bewildered, desperate, and ill.

Ionescu folded his arms and turned away from her. "He wouldn't have believed it without reason. Deny it if you wish; you won't bring Vasile back or convince me of your innocence."

She held out her hand as if she didn't dare touch him but still wanted to stop him from walking away. Her earlier anger had vanished, replaced by grief. "Tiberiu—wait, please. I swear I was never unfaithful to Vasile. Come with me and see Anatolie. You'll know instantly who his father is: he has Vasile's nose, Vasile's smile, Vasile's hairline."

"Even if Vasile was Anatolie's father, it doesn't prove you were faithful."

"Then what will?" she pleaded.

"Tell me, Iuliana, why was Vasile transferred to Germany?"

"I don't know." Her dark eyes were wide, worry causing lines to form between her eyebrows.

"Were such transfers customary at the time?"

"No, rare."

Ionescu shook his head. "You can't even tell me the truth about his death."

She stared at him, shaking her head slowly, her mouth slightly open, tears spilling onto her eyelashes.

"Iuliana?" Zielinski was standing at her side. "Maybe it's time for you to go." The words themselves seemed hard, but his voice and his face were soft, leaving Peter to conclude that Zielinski's opinion of her remained unchanged.

She glanced at Zielinski's face and nodded. Then she took an envelope from her pocket and handed it to Ionescu. "Vasile left this for you." He looked at the paper then glowered at her, keeping his arms crossed and refusing to reach for it. She let the envelope fall into the trench. No one picked it up. She turned and walked down the mountainside.

Zielinski followed her for a few yards. "Would you like me to see you safely back to Scorțeni?"

"No, thank you, Kapral." She didn't look back, not at her former brother-in-law, not at the man she'd spent the day hiding.

Peter noted she'd addressed him by his title, though earlier that night they'd been using each other's first names.

Zielinski didn't follow her any farther. He watched her walk away, a slight frown on his otherwise expressionless face.

Everyone was silent until Baker got back to business. "What were you planning to do next?" he asked Peter.

Peter pulled his eyes away from Iuliana and the Polish kapral who was watching her leave with more than casual concern. "I was going to have Nelson relieve Fish at dawn. Zielinski's supposed to contact headquarters about then. I planned to send Moretti with him and have them stay in the mountains, regardless of the triangulation risks. I thought I'd let Fish take it easy for a few hours while Condreanu and I went to investigate a lookout post not far from here. It might be more defensible." Peter felt one corner of his mouth pull wearily into a half smile. "Now that you're back, sir, I'm happy to turn things over to you again."

Baker nodded. "Jamie," he called. "Wake up."

Nelson appeared a few seconds later. "I am awake, Wesley. I doubt anyone within half a mile slept through that family feud."

"Take a walk with me."

While the two were gone, Quill and Sherlock found the team. Fisher had spotted them and directed them to the western safe house. Peter found himself filling them in on all of the misfortunes that had plagued the team while he was in command. When Baker returned, he told Peter to get some sleep. Peter complied, hoping that with Baker back, he could close his eyes without waking up to disaster.

Glancing back, Peter saw Nelson and Baker conferring again. He couldn't hear what Nelson said, but he heard the catch in Baker's voice. "What have I done?"

CHAPTER TWENTY-EIGHT

THE BUSINESS END OF THE PISTOL

Wednesday, August 23

THE NEXT MORNING BAKER ACCOMPANIED Zielinski on the radio run, Ionescu and Quill were sent on patrol, and the three Americans—Peter, Moretti, and Luke—went to investigate the lookout post.

Peter watched Moretti walk along the post's weather-stained wooden floor, open the trap door, and stick his head into the small cellar. "It's dry. Empty." Then he prodded the wooden roof with the butt of his rifle. "The roof's all right, sir."

"I'd rather store our explosives here than down the hill. Seems more weather-proof." It didn't surprise Peter that Luke was thinking primarily of the explosives.

"It was real nice having a roof over our heads, sir," Moretti said. "Wouldn't mind having one again."

Peter nodded. "It's not a bad safe house. Big enough we could all lie down and sleep at the same time—not that we would. The equipment would stay dry. The walls are thick enough to stop a bullet." Peter ran his hands along the concrete bricks and crumbling mortar. "And the windows would provide an excellent view of anyone driving a jeep or a tank right up to our door."

Luke's face fell. "I didn't think about that. I guess it's a bad idea to settle in right next to the only road for a good mile." The post sat along a narrow track with the mountains rising steeply on either side. Behind the post, the road continued through a thin pass, broadened with dynamite to little more than the width of a car.

Peter smiled. "Most locations have at least a couple of drawbacks. Truth is, we need a fallback location. With a little work, this one might do."

Peter and Moretti spent the morning digging trenches and building up earth banks in front of the blockhouse, where the mountain smoothed into a wider, less abrupt slope. They also dragged tree trunks across the road in several locations. Summer mornings at that altitude were mild, but Peter and Moretti were still soaked in sweat. Luke brought his equipment with him, and Peter gave him free rein to do as he wanted. As the sun passed its zenith, the three of them began working together on the last trench only a few yards in front of the post.

"How long do you think we could hold out here?" Luke asked.

Moretti laughed. "That depends on what's being thrown at us and what kind of troops are doing the throwing, kid. Might also depend a little on how well your booby traps work."

"They'll work."

"They better, kid."

Peter interrupted them. "We're not anticipating an attack anyway. Zielinski was never questioned. They might be looking for him still, but they don't know where he is or who he's with. And Condreanu . . ." Peter broke off, his shovel full of dirt.

"What is it, sir?" Moretti asked.

Peter shook his head and emptied his shovel onto the mound in front of the trench. "I'm not sure. Zielinski saw him being questioned by a Romanian colonel and a German captain. But Condreanu never mentioned an interrogation. Could have just slipped his mind."

"He did have a lot of important things to do, like stab Logan." Moretti had one eyebrow raised.

Peter hesitated with his next query. It was a new thought, and he hadn't had time to fully process it, but he wanted Moretti's opinion. "There's something else. Condreanu said he looked for Zielinski after he freed himself, but according to Krzysztof, someone interrupted Condreanu's questioning with news of the escape. Why try to rescue someone when you know he's already left? And why haul a radio around while doing it?"

Moretti stuck his shovel in the dirt and folded his hands across the handle. "That's a good question, isn't it, sir? What do you make of it?"

Peter began digging again. "I'm not sure. Their stories don't quite match up. I guess he might have thought Zielinski got recaptured. Maybe I just don't like Condreanu, so I'm making a big deal out of something insignificant. I don't trust his judgment though, not since he killed Logan. Do you suppose he has family around here he's trying to protect?"

Moretti shrugged and picked up his shovel again. "Don't know what part of this country he's from. But he's a big shot somewhere."

"Transylvania," Luke said. "I remember 'cause that's where Dracula came from too."

Moretti smiled. "Well, none of us have seen Condreanu drinking blood, have we?"

Luke stiffened.

"Relax, kid, it's supposed to be a joke."

"What's wrong, Luke?" Peter asked.

Luke had stopped working, and he looked a little pale.

"Have either of you heard of the Legion of the Archangel Michael?" Luke asked.

Peter and Moretti both shook their heads.

"How about the Iron Guard?"

"Yeah," Peter said. "A group of Romanian Nazis, right? Antonescu turned on them a couple years back, and Hitler didn't seem to mind."

Luke nodded. "The Legion got into political trouble, so they regrouped with a new name—the Iron Guard." Luke paused, looking like he wasn't sure if he should continue. "I was born in America, but my parents kept a close eye on what was happening back in the old country. Some of it was pretty crazy—might not even be true. We heard some of the Legionnaires, the ones committed enough to kill someone if asked, drank a bit of blood from every other member of their nest."

"From the neck?" Moretti was leaning into Luke, one eyebrow raised.

"No, from the arm."

"So who's creepier, kid, Dracula or a Legionnaire?"

Luke shook his head, ignoring Moretti's question. "I'm sure it's nothing—just crazy rumors. Doubt it has anything to do with Condreanu. He's got a scar on his arm, but he has fewer scars than either of you do."

"Lieutenant Eddy and I have seen a bit more action than he has though."

"What else can you tell me about the Legion?" Peter asked.

Luke adjusted his glasses. "They claimed to be Christian but not the love-your-neighbor type. Hated the Jews and the other minorities, hated the Communists, hated the corrupt politicians. They were involved in a bunch of assassinations. While King Carol was still in power, he had their founder strangled. Antonescu worked with them for a while, but they started getting a little power hungry. He kicked the few of them in his government out, they took over some buildings in Bucharest, and Antonescu sent in the army to exterminate them. Berlin backed Antonescu, at least on the surface. Rumor has it that some of the Guard leadership got smuggled to Germany."

"Wait." Moretti stuck his shovel in the dirt again. "You're saying Hitler backed Antonescu over a Nazi movement?"

"When it comes to Romania, Hitler cares more about oil than ideology. Antonescu was more dependable," Luke said.

"We should get back. I want to talk with Major Baker." Peter climbed from the trench and looked at Luke. "Stay here and throw some branches across the front of this. I'll send some supplies over."

* * *

Krzysztof had hoped to see Iuliana again but hadn't expected it would be so soon. He saw her from a distance trudging up the mountain with Quill just after lunch. He walked down to meet the two of them.

"She wants to talk to you," Quill said when he approached.

Krzysztof nodded. Their last good-bye had been cool, making him think Iuliana was angry with him.

"I'll just get back to my patrol, then." Quill popped a knuckle and winked at Krzysztof.

Krzysztof waited until Quill was out of earshot. "Is everything all right? Did Colonel Eliade carry out his threats against your son?"

"Anatolie and I are fine. Eliade hasn't been back, and Cosmina is avoiding me, but she hasn't said anything." She walked toward him, her hips swaying as she picked her way through the underbrush. "The local constable's received some reinforcements. Artillery. I think they might start looking for you soon . . . and . . . and I didn't want your head to get blown off by a mortar shell." She spoke the last fragment very quickly, with her head down, her cheeks flushed.

Krzysztof smiled. "That would be ugly. Do you have time to give details to Major Baker?"

Iuliana nodded.

Krzysztof took her hand to help her up an embankment. "Thank you for the warning. We haven't seen anything."

"They unloaded early this morning, before dawn, put everything under camouflage netting. It might not be for you, but with the way the front's going, it has to be something important or it would be aimed against the Red Army."

When they reached the safe house, Condreanu glared at Iuliana. "What's she doing here again?"

"She saw some new artillery and came to warn us."

"Or lead a search party right to us," Condreanu said.

"Where did everyone go?" When Krzysztof left well under an hour ago, there had been five members of the team still at the safe house. Now Condreanu was the only one present.

"Nelson and Baker are making plans based on whatever you found out on the radio this morning. I sent Sherlock and Fisher to relieve Ionescu and Quill."

"Which direction did Baker go?"

Condreanu shrugged.

"Can you wait?" Krzysztof asked Iuliana.

"Yes." It was spoken sharply, but the sharpness was aimed at Condreanu, not at Krzysztof.

A few minutes later, Sherlock came running up the hill. Between gasps, he managed to get two words out: "Ionescu's dead."

Krzysztof managed to find his tongue first. "How?"

"Stabbed in the back. It's a recent wound."

Krzysztof watched Iuliana carefully. She seemed surprised then flinched when Condreanu turned to her.

"You killed him! You stabbed him in the back, and now you're leading the search party right to us!"

"No!" Iuliana protested. "I know Tiberiu and I were on bad terms, but I promise I didn't do anything to him. I'm just as surprised as you are."

Condreanu drew his pistol and aimed it at Iuliana. "I think I'll trust my instincts, and Tiberiu's."

Krzysztof had heard what happened to Logan. He stepped in front of Iuliana, shielding her from Condreanu. "Let's talk this through first."

Condreanu looked from Krzysztof to Iuliana and back again. He nodded. "I see how it is. Poor Kapral Zielinski. She's been working on you, has she? Don't you remember what Tiberiu said? She's an experienced seductress. She tricked her husband, and now she's trying to trick you. Step aside."

"You should think this through a little more, sir. Hold her for questioning if you like, but it's not your right to execute her."

Condreanu's pistol didn't waiver. "*Kapral* Zielinski, step aside."

"Sir, perhaps we should talk to Major Baker first," Sherlock said.

"I outrank both of you, and you will follow my orders. Kapral Zielinski, step aside."

Krzysztof didn't budge. He was staring at the business end of Condreanu's pistol and didn't like the view at all.

"You may outrank them, but you don't outrank me."

Krzysztof looked over when he heard Eddy's voice.

Moretti came into view behind him as Eddy continued. "I see no need to orphan a small child just because his mother and his uncle don't get along."

Condreanu lowered his weapon reluctantly. "I don't think you fully understand the situation, Eddy. Ionescu is dead. Sherlock went to relieve him and found him with a knife in his back."

Eddy looked at Sherlock, who nodded. "Then we'll keep her prisoner. But we're not going to shoot her. Zielinski, see that she doesn't leave without permission from me or Major Baker."

"Yes, sir." Krzysztof hadn't realized how tense he was. He forced himself to relax his shoulders, arms, and hands, then turned around to face Iuliana. Her face was white, and a few tears had fallen onto her black eyelashes. He put his hand on her arm and motioned toward the safe house.

Condreanu blocked their path. He was red faced and furious, his breathing hard, his voice elevated. "Zielinski will let her escape. She's experienced at manipulating men, and our radio man is her latest project. And he's guilty of insubordination."

Krzysztof turned to see what Eddy would do. The American lieutenant paused before answering. "Then Sergeant Moretti can guard both of them. Sherlock, find Fisher or Quill. Have them help you bury the body, then continue your patrol."

"I can't stand the sight of that woman a moment longer. I'll go with Sherlock and give Ionescu some of the respect his sister-in-law never gave him." Condreanu followed Sherlock, and Krzysztof moved Iuliana up the mountain toward the shelter, away from the Romanian officer.

"I think it's best if you stay, Condreanu. If you don't want to look at Mrs. Ionescu, you can wait in one of the trenches."

Krzysztof glanced over his shoulder, realizing Eddy didn't trust Condreanu any more than he did.

CHAPTER TWENTY-NINE
TRUST AND MISTRUST

IULIANA LOOKED DOWN, SEEING KRZYSZTOF's hand resting on hers. He had long fingers, each one ending with a neatly trimmed fingernail, except his index finger, where the nail had torn. As his fingers gently moved over hers, Iuliana felt herself calming down. Krzysztof was going to protect her. She was surprised to feel tears forming again. At first she thought they were simply tears of relief, but then she realized they were something more. After knowing her only a few days, Krzysztof trusted her. Vasile had been married to her; Tiberiu had known her for several years. For whatever reason, the Ionescu brothers hadn't trusted her, but Krzysztof did.

The sergeant assigned to guard them was lying across the front of the shelter, hands behind his head, legs crossed, eyes closed. He wasn't asleep. He opened his eyes whenever she shifted her weight and whenever Condreanu drew near. She watched him for a while. He was Krzysztof's height, with dark hair and a solid, wide build. *He's not guarding us so we don't escape,* she realized. *He's guarding us so Condreanu can't hurt us.*

Iuliana turned her hand over, grasping Krzysztof's. "Thank you." She heard the tremor in her voice, but until then, she hadn't been able to speak at all. "I thought he was going to shoot."

"So did I." His hand stopped moving, and Krzysztof reached up to gently touch her face. His eyes were kind, and a hint of a smile turned the corners of his lips.

As Iuliana leaned into his shoulder, she saw the large guard glance at them and light a cigarette, but he directed most of his attention outside, where the two lieutenants were still arguing.

* * *

Peter wasn't sure if Condreanu was more upset by his refusal to cooperate or by how Moretti and Sherlock had obeyed Peter despite Condreanu's counterorders. Peter had his binoculars out, looking for signs of the search party Iuliana had seen.

If she really saw anything. He wasn't ready to trust her, nor was he ready to see her executed. Peter looked over to see Condreanu still glaring at him and turned back to his watch. The men on patrol would have a better view, but staring through his binoculars gave him the opportunity to scan the entire area and keep an eye on Condreanu without looking obvious.

When Baker and Nelson returned, Baker surveyed his two lieutenants' faces but didn't ask why they were so obviously hostile. "Lieutenant Eddy, what did you think of the post?"

Peter put his binoculars down. "It has better line of sight than this does. It's right by a road, but we made a few adjustments, so I don't think any cars will be able to make it up. No tanks either. It's not a bad spot—we could defend it for a while if we were under attack."

"And Mrs. Ionescu? I see she is back?"

Condreanu shook his head. "She claims to have seen a small army getting ready to attack us. Ionescu is dead, and I don't doubt she had a hand in it."

"Ionescu is dead?" Baker's face fell.

"Stabbed by his sister-in-law, no doubt." Condreanu narrowed his eyes as he looked at Peter.

Baker sat down hard. "One more death on my hands."

Nelson looked grim. "You've done what you could today. 'Perseverance . . . keeps honor bright . . . Keep then on the path.' I can do it, Wesley."

Baker glanced at Nelson, studied him for a few seconds, then looked at Peter and Condreanu. "We received another assignment this morning. We're to evacuate a man in Scorţeni, a high government official. We have time on our side. I think the Romanians will hold off the most recent Red Army offensive for a few weeks at least."

Condreanu and Peter drew near so they could hear Baker's softly spoken instructions. "Locotenent Condreanu, I would like you and Jamie to find our contact. You can wait until nightfall if you wish, but as you both speak the language, you would blend in well enough to go during daylight if you switch into civilian clothing."

"And what will you do with our murderess?" Condreanu asked.

Baker glanced toward the earthen safe house. "Mrs. Ionescu, you mean? I suppose she has some questions to answer."

"Sir," Peter interrupted. "Could I have a few words with you? Alone?" Condreanu looked suspicious. Out of the corner of his eye, Peter could see Moretti straining to hear from his post. No one spoke above a whisper.

"I'm sure anything Eddy has to say can be said in front of us all." Condreanu wasn't sneering, not exactly, but neither was he being meek. "Isn't that right, Major Baker?"

Baker looked exhausted as he glanced at the men around him, each in turn. "Condreanu, I would give you the same privilege if you asked. Go with Jamie. He'll brief you."

Condreanu glared at Peter and somewhat reluctantly walked after Nelson.

Baker stretched his legs out and sighed before standing again. "Go ahead, Lieutenant, state what is on your mind."

"All right, sir. I think you should reconsider sending Condreanu into Scorţeni."

"And why is that, Lieutenant Eddy?"

"I don't trust his judgment. He executed Logan prematurely, and he almost shot Mrs. Ionescu—even if she is responsible for Ionescu's death, she deserves a trial before she's executed. He almost shot Zielinski too."

"I wouldn't have shot Zielinski." Condreanu had turned back in time to hear the last exchange. "As for my judgment, it's perfectly sound. If we're expressing doubts in each other, I'd like to file my serious reservations about Eddy's leadership abilities. While he was in charge, we had disaster after disaster. Deaths, poisonings, arrests. It's lucky you had a team to come back to."

Baker raised an eyebrow as Nelson came sliding down the hill behind Condreanu. "Done with your briefing already?"

Condreanu spoke before Nelson could offer an explanation. "I came back for my canteen. But if Eddy is going to accuse me of anything, I think I should be present to defend myself."

Baker sighed. "Fine. Do you have anything else you wish to discuss, Lieutenant Eddy?"

Peter looked at Condreanu, who was still glaring at him, and hesitated for only a moment. "There are discrepancies between the two accounts of what happened when he and Zielinski were arrested. I'd like to know what really happened before you trust him in Scorţeni. I'd also like to know why he had the patrols relieved hours earlier than originally planned this afternoon."

"Are you questioning my loyalty?" Condreanu's voice was louder than it needed to be.

Out of the corner of his eye, Peter saw Moretti. He looked as tense as Peter felt. "Right now I'm just questioning your judgment, but maybe we should look at that too."

"If anyone had an opportunity to kill Mitchell, it was you." Condreanu walked closer to Peter, circling him.

"Logan admitted he did it."

"But you were the only one who heard him make that confession, weren't you? You had your entire patrol to kill Mitchell. I also find it unsettling that on your previous two missions, you were the only one who made it back alive."

"That's not true." Peter glanced at Moretti, who was slowly, silently, walking down the slope toward them.

Condreanu sneered. "True enough. Your partners died in both your French missions. If you picked up Olivier's sister after arranging her brother's death, it only shows how well you can fool those closest to you." Condreanu stopped in front of Peter, his face inches away, oozing hatred.

"Wesley . . ." Nelson said quietly. Baker ignored him.

Peter had never had anyone doubt his loyalty before. He took a few deep breaths, reminding himself of the evidence against Condreanu before continuing. "How did you escape after you were arrested? And why did you go looking for Zielinski when you already knew he'd escaped?"

"How was I to know he'd gotten away?"

"He saw you talking with a pair of officers. He was attempting to rescue you when your meeting was interrupted and everyone in earshot was told the Polish prisoner was loose," Peter said.

Condreanu's eyes flashed, and he began circling again. "That's a lie. The Ionescu woman has it in for me, and she brainwashed Zielinski to make him tell you lies!"

Peter shook his head in disbelief, thinking that had to be the worst excuse he'd ever heard. "There's something else. On the morning of Mitchell's death, Zielinski's radio was unpacked. He never leaves his radio out. At the time, I didn't think much of it, but I doubt Mitchell being late from patrol would be enough of an emergency for him to leave it in the open. Were you using it?"

"Wesley?" Nelson was more urgent this time, one hand on Baker's shoulder, the other on his pistol.

Condreanu drew his Webley & Scott 1907 pistol, pointed it at Peter, and from two feet away, squeezed the trigger.

CHAPTER THIRTY

SECRETS

CONDREANU'S MOVE SET OFF A chain reaction. Moretti lunged at Condreanu and pulled him to the dirt. Nelson smashed his boot into Condreanu's neck. And Zielinski and Iuliana ran down the slope, Zielinski with his rifle in his hands.

Condreanu's pistol had failed to fire.

Baker shook his head at Nelson. "I told you not to worry, Jamie."

"It would have been a great deal more effective if you had told me you disabled his pistol!" Nelson yelled. A decibel or two lower, he continued. "I even asked you why you kept checking the trigger in your own pistol. Removed a spring and thought your weapons might get mixed up, did you?"

"You knew he was a Nazi?" Peter asked, slowly adjusting to the fact that he had come only a spring away from getting his head blown off. "Both of you knew?"

Baker nodded. "Condreanu, yes. He's a Nazi. We've been watching him for years."

"I owe you an apology, Lieutenant Eddy." Nelson moved his boot from Condreanu's neck and helped Moretti haul Condreanu to his feet and tie his hands behind his back. "Wesley told me to ingratiate myself with Condreanu. I found matching my behavior and attitude to his was the quickest way to do that. If he felt threatened by the fact that most of the men respected you far more than they respected him, I made sure I was his one loyal follower. The rumor that I lost my commission helped—it left me socially acceptable, but as only a corporal, I wasn't a rival. And if he found officers who received their commission based on performance instead of schooling and fancy pedigrees distasteful, I pretended I did as well and even led the persecution. Ironic really. Had he known the details of my parentage, he would have turned up his nose at me as well."

Moretti turned his laugh into a cough.

Nelson smiled. "Yes, I have heard my aunt's theories and that Mitchell repeated them to you. My aunt is only half right. I am not the son of my father's first wife. I am, in fact, the son of his second wife, whom he married one year *before* my birth. She died before I learned to crawl, and I was blissfully ignorant that I was not, in fact, a Tinley descendent until my sixteenth birthday. I found Mary Tinley's death certificate, and my father explained the entire history to me and told me to keep it secret. A month later, I felt guilty and went to visit my grandfather Tinley and confess my true origins. He told me to 'be a good lad and keep my trap shut' and then asked me what I thought of the latest Shakespeare play I had read—*King Lear*, if I remember correctly."

"Jamie's grandfather was instrumental in setting up MI6," Baker broke in. "His sources cover the empire. He knew the truth sixteen years before Jamie did."

"Yes, his contacts informed him of my father's second marriage within a month of its occurrence and of my birth within a week. He also told me that he himself suffered from a loveless arranged marriage to a silly woman who was highly susceptible to flattery and that he wasn't entirely sure that either of his daughters were biologically his. At least he knew who my father was."

"And Italy?" Peter asked. "Why did you leave?"

"The rumors about Italy are mostly true. I did indeed anger some of my superiors by accusing an old acquaintance of disloyalty without proof. As far as I know, he is currently serving quite honorably as an SOE-OSS liaison in Bari. I still trust my gut and therefore don't trust him. I refused to work with him in Italy and was recalled for insubordination when our cover was blown. I can thank my grandfather for that too. I was invited to be part of a semisecret Communist society in Cambridge, known as the Apostles. I wanted no part of it, but my grandfather, wiser than I, suggested I infiltrate. I know how the Communists think well enough to spot a Soviet sympathizer when I see one." Nelson looked over at Condreanu, who shifted uncomfortably. "Or a Nazi."

"Were you really demoted?" Peter asked.

"No. I am a civilian. I followed my grandfather's footsteps into MI6."

"Which should explain his lack of deference to his commanding officers," Baker broke in, directing his comments to Peter. "I should also apologize. Jamie asked me to brief you on Condreanu's past before we left England, but my orders were to keep it quiet. Jamie tried to convince me to disobey those orders before I left to sabotage the train. Had I listened to him, Mitchell and Ionescu might have been spared."

"And the real purpose of our mission?" Peter asked.

"To follow Condreanu and see who he contacted," Baker said. "Several local Romanian authorities have been making conciliatory gestures toward the British. It seems they're nervous about the proximity of the Red Army and might be willing to enter into a mutually beneficial relationship with British intelligence. SOE has been monitoring Condreanu's radio transmissions over the last nineteen months—oh yes, Constantin, we know all about your handler—everything but his name. By coming to the Prahova Valley, Jamie and I predicted we could pinpoint the Legionnaire spymaster, set up a ring of anti-Communist agents for our use postwar, and complete any tasks Colonel Gibson assigned."

"Gibson doesn't know why we're really here?" Peter asked.

Nelson snorted. "Gibson is exactly the sort of idiot pushing for more openness with our Soviet allies. Only the few of us and one very secretive general back in England know the real reason we are here."

"And Logan?" Peter asked.

Baker frowned. "Logan was a surprise. Tell me, Constantin, did you approach him, or did he approach you?" Baker asked.

"My contact knew of Logan's true loyalties. A little German agent passed the information along to him. Not that it matters. Eddy's blown open your entire charade. You'll have a difficult time discovering my contacts now I'm aware of your plans. Should you try to set up your spy ring, it's likely to have a Legionnaire in it, slipping you false information, recruiting double agents, and eliminating all your best sources. Poor Jamie, all your work for nothing thanks to a stupid American farm boy." Condreanu's face shone with defiance as he spoke. Being found out was a setback, but his Legion was not yet defeated.

Nelson looked at Condreanu and smiled. "What do you think I was doing when we went to Ploieşti? First you met with the grocer, Mr. Radu; there are the two men at the refineries: Mr. Popescu with Colombia Aquila and Mr. Diaconu with Astra Romania; a reporter for the local paper, Mr. Stancu; Mr. and Mrs. Farcas; and Pacurar, the police sergeant. I have also followed you on your half dozen *secret* trips into Scorţeni and watched whom you met there. All of your contacts are still members of the Legion, aren't they?"

Condreanu seethed with rage as Nelson recited the list. But when Nelson finished, a smile crept across Condreanu's face.

Nelson sighed in defeat. "Yes, you're right. We haven't located your superior, not yet. I suppose you met with him the time you knocked me unconscious and pretended it was a falling tree branch?"

Moretti whistled. "He knocked you unconscious and you still pretended to be his best buddy?"

"When I have a role to play, I can play it far better than any actor, even if it leads me to insult men I admire and fawn over men I detest. Knocking me unconscious was only the beginning. He also poisoned me. Fortunately, I knew he had smuggled some cyanide up from Ploiești, so I recognized the symptoms early on and expelled most of the poison from my system."

"None of that matters," Condreanu said. "If you haven't found my superior, your little spy ring will crumble. The men you've discovered are nothing—merely pawns."

Nelson twisted his mouth to one side. "Yes, I was hoping you would meet with him when we went into town to evacuate our refugee. We know your contact is a high-ranking military officer, currently in the Scorțeni commune, who works closely with a German officer. We will figure it out without your help."

"I doubt that. Scorțeni is full of military officers."

Peter smiled. "I think we might have a chance yet. A Romanian officer who works closely with a German officer? Nelson might not have seen you meeting with your contact, but I think Zielinski did."

Condreanu's face fell as he looked at Zielinski and saw him nod, but after a few seconds, he recovered. "You have a physical description, that's all. You still lack a name."

"Incorrect," Zielinski said. "There are a limited number of Romanian Army colonels in Scorțeni. Of those, few have been awarded the order of Michael the Brave, third class."

"Only one." Iuliana stood at Zielinski's side. "Colonel Dorin Eliade."

"I should have killed you," Condreanu hissed.

"You tried and failed," Zielinski replied. "Is that why you switched the patrol schedule? I suppose you saw her approaching then ran off and killed Ionescu, sending Sherlock on patrol right after so he'd discover the body while it could be blamed on Iuliana?"

Condreanu didn't deny Zielinski's accusations; he just glared at him. "It still doesn't matter," Condreanu snarled. "When I don't make contact again, the local authorities will attack. I've briefed them on our numbers, pointed our positions out on a map, and identified every weapon we have. They're already blocking all escape routes. You won't last an hour once the attack begins."

"In that case, I can transmit right now," Zielinksi said. "SOE will have Nelson's complete list with the addition of Colonel Eliade."

"And MI6 or SOE can put in another team to pick up where we left off," Nelson said.

"But you'll be dead." Condreanu glared at them with contempt.

"As will you be." Nelson lifted his pistol until it was only inches from Condreanu's skull. "'Turn thy false face, thou traitor, and pay the life thou ow'st me.'"

Baker put a hand on Nelson's arm. "Let's talk to Cairo first."

Zielinski managed to reach Cairo and provide the completed list and the name of the general it should be delivered to within five minutes. The SOE men in Cairo wanted the team to bring Condreanu back with them, so Moretti tied him more securely and left him in the bottom of the trench while they began planning for the attack.

"What type of artillery did you see?" Baker asked Iuliana.

She hesitated. "I'm not sure what it's called."

"Can you draw it?" Baker handed her a paper.

Peter watched from over her shoulder. "A pack howitzer. Looks like a Skoda, probably 75 mm. It breaks down into a half dozen–plus pieces, so they can strap it on mules and bring it right to us."

Baker frowned. "And the shells?"

Peter looked up from Iuliana's drawing. "Twelve to fifteen pounds each."

"That's what I thought. The new safe house you've established won't hold up against anything like that, will it?"

Peter shook his head. "Do you think we're really surrounded? Or was Condreanu bluffing?"

Quill returned from his patrol and saluted sharply. "Fisher and I have been around the east end of our area. We've spotted Romanian troops approaching, getting into position—a man every ten meters or so. Fish is continuing to check, but we thought I ought to inform you at once."

"Police or military?" Baker's hand reached up to stroke his chin.

"They look like mountain troops." Romanian Mountain Troops were some of the best-trained men in the Romanian Army.

"Did you spot any pack animals hauling up what could be pieces of a howitzer?" Peter asked.

Quill nodded. "I saw some mules . . . couldn't tell what was on their backs, but it was something big."

Nelson looked at Peter. "Can we last until nightfall at the blockhouse? We might be able to slip past them in the dark."

Peter looked at his watch. It was almost fourteen hundred hours. "Not if they assemble that artillery, but Luke's been working on some surprises, so if it's just us against the infantry, even their crack troops, we might have a chance. The way the blockhouse is situated, it will reduce the advantage their numbers give them."

"Like the pass at Thermopylae?" Nelson saw the irony in his comment and smiled.

Condreanu laughed from his spot in the bottom of the trench. "The lot of you are hardly Spartan warriors."

Nelson walked over to him and looked down. "No, we are much better armed."

Peter looked at Iuliana. She was still staring at her drawing.

"Mrs. Ionescu, thank you for your warning. I'm sorry you're now trapped with us," Baker said.

"If she went home now, wouldn't they let her through?" Quill looked like he was about to pop his knuckles, but he restrained himself.

Iuliana looked up. "If I left now, they would escort me straight to jail. I'd rather take my chances here."

Baker was calm. "Quill, Zielinski, Jamie. Grab as much equipment as you can carry and take it to our new safe house. Concentrate on the ammunition. We won't need our bedding or much food. Mrs. Ionescu, if you would like to assist them, your help would be appreciated."

Iuliana nodded.

"Sergeant Moretti?"

"Yes, sir."

"Bring Condreanu along." Baker walked over to the trench and looked at the prisoner. "But if you misbehave, you will find we can administer justice just as swiftly as you can, regardless of orders." Baker stepped into the trench and picked up a white envelope. He held it out to Iuliana. "Tiberiu won't be needing this now."

Iuliana nodded, putting the envelope in her pocket.

Peter walked over to join Baker. "Sir?"

"Yes?"

"Mind if I borrow Private Fisher?"

"What are you going to do with him?"

"I'm going to see about stopping that howitzer."

Chapter Thirty-One

Stopping a Howitzer

It took Peter a half hour to find Fisher, who was working his way back toward their old headquarters. A quick bird call made him change direction.

"I think we're surrounded, sir. And those troops look first-rate to me. Quill made it back to warn you, did 'e?"

Peter nodded. "We're going to try to hold out until nightfall then sneak away in the dark. Condreanu's a Nazi. He gave them all the information they needed—our location, our numbers, our capabilities."

Fisher cursed.

"My feelings exactly. But we've got to focus on staying alive until dark. We won't last long if they get their artillery set up. But if you manage to shoot the pack animals out from under the howitzer pieces . . ."

Fisher smiled. "That would give us a fighting chance."

"No one on this team is a better shot than you. But as soon as they figure out what we're up to, you'll be their number-one target. Are you ready for that?"

"Do you really 'ave to ask, sir?"

Peter grinned. "Have you seen any pack animals?"

Fisher nodded. "Mules. Eight of them. Down the slope a ways, working their way up, they were."

Fisher led Peter back to where he'd most recently seen the animals and their loads. A single soldier led the animals up a series of switchbacks, but other men were nearby, helping escort the caravan up the mountain.

When Peter spoke, it was barely audible. "Wait until they're about to cross that narrow stretch up there—should make the animals fall into a ditch, make it hard for them to retrieve the cargo. I'll go left. You go right. Shoot when you think the time is best, and I'll join in."

Peter situated himself above the animals, where he could aim his M1 rifle at their profiles. He didn't dare go too far away—he needed to make each shot count. He hoped Fisher, who had a finely honed talent and a better weapon for this sort of thing, was farther from their targets and the corresponding danger.

Poor defenseless mules. Peter didn't have much time to feel sorry for the animals. The lead mule stumbled—Peter had no doubt the cause was one of Fisher's bullets—and as it slid into a ditch below the trail, Peter shot the animal right behind it. He took another shot, and a total of five animals were down before the escorting soldiers found their rifles. Peter didn't think they could see him, but two of them ran his direction. As Peter retreated, Fisher managed to shoot one of his pursuers and two more animals.

Peter broke into a clearing and heard someone shouting at him in a language he didn't understand. He raced across the open area into the pine trees on the other side. He glanced behind him but didn't see anyone. When he looked forward again, a Romanian soldier was coming out of a patch of fir trees, moving right toward him. Peter dropped to the ground, ducking a bullet and firing his rifle at the newcomer, who fell to the ground.

Peter began advancing again, hoping Fisher was having better luck. Hearing someone coming through the brush, Peter hid behind a fir tree. When another Romanian soldier walked past him, he pummeled the back of the man's head with his rifle.

Squatting down, Peter peered past a tangle of wild strawberries. It was suddenly quiet, and Peter began to think he'd taken care of the men pursuing him. He continued uphill, eager to find Fisher or return to headquarters. Ten minutes later, he saw the line of mountain troops, fifteen yards between each man, stretching as far as he could see. *How did they get ahead of me?* It took him a few seconds to realize that though they were looking in all directions, they faced downhill toward him, not uphill, where Baker and the rest of the team waited. Peter paused, hidden in the underbrush, keeping his muscles still and his breathing quiet.

Going through the line would be difficult, but he might be able to go around it. He crept along silently, parallel to the Romanian troops, wishing he knew where the line ended. The men he passed weren't moving, but they were alert. Peter stayed where he could see at least two of them at a time but didn't try to make it past them.

It was nearly an hour until he regretted his decision.

Emerging from the woods in front of him was a second line of soldiers, perpendicular to the stationary line, moving slowly forward. The men of the second line were uniformly spaced, checking under fallen logs and looking up into the trees as they advanced. They were performing a very thorough, very professional manhunt.

Peter considered his options. The moving line was progressing slowly, but he'd have to give up his stealth if he wanted to outmaneuver them. He removed his pistol from its holster and set it down in front of him, where it was just visible, peeking out from under a bush. Then he moved downhill, away from his handgun.

When the line reached his Colt .45, they stopped. Several of the men in the line congregated on the weapon, just as Peter had hoped they would, creating a hole in the line that Peter thought was a large enough for him to move through. He started out slowly, coming even with the line, slithering on his belly past two of the soldiers, praying they wouldn't see him. He turned as they moved past him, keeping his eyes on the men and moving backward through the dirt and pine needles, going faster as the line moved farther away from him.

Then someone kicked the bottom of his boot. Peter jerked his head around to find his nose inches from the end of a bayonet. The man holding the bayonet, a Romanian soldier, reached down and took Peter's rifle from his hands then rammed the stock into the side of Peter's face. He shouted something in what Peter assumed was Romanian—and a dozen men surrounded Peter. He hadn't realized there was yet another line following the one he'd just breached.

* * *

They'd put Condreanu in the basement, gagged and immobilized from neck to toe with ropes. Krzysztof lowered himself into the hole and studied the locotenent briefly. On the opposite side of the room, Iuliana sat on the floor, her knees pulled to her chest. Krzysztof went to sit beside her, handing her some of the purple wildflowers he'd found growing near the trenches.

She smiled down at them. "Thank you."

"When the fighting starts, we'll close the trap door. It'll be dark, but it should be safer."

Iuliana nodded.

Krzysztof took her hand and squeezed it. "I'm sorry you're stuck here."

"It's not your fault. You aren't the one who betrayed your teammates." She glanced at Condreanu then back at Krzysztof. "What do you think our chances are?"

Krzysztof wasn't sure. Sherlock had returned and reported dozens of men forming a corridor around them. Quill had reported the same thing earlier— both reports coming from different directions. Eddy and Fisher hadn't returned yet, although the team at the blockhouse had heard a firefight. "We're in a good position. I think we can hold awhile if the artillery's been stalled."

"Can we last until nightfall?"

"I hope so."

"And if we make it that long, can we get out?"

Krzysztof studied her face. The lighting was poor, but he could make out the cupid's bow of her upper lip, the thick lashes that surrounded her eyes, and the worry lines that creased the skin between her eyebrows. He brought her hand up to his mouth, softly pressing the ends of her fingers into his lips. "We'll do our best." He motioned toward Condreanu. "I've got to get back. If things don't go well, shoot him before he can communicate with the army. Claim you were our prisoner. Do whatever you need to do to make it back to your son."

Iuliana nodded, wiping a tear from her eye.

Krzysztof left the basement. Baker was with Sherlock in the concrete-brick building, looking into the mountains through his field glasses.

"Do you see anything yet?" Krzysztof asked.

Baker shook his head.

Krzysztof went back to his assigned area. He walked past the first trench—it was empty. Luke and Quill occupied the next trench and were wiring dynamite to trip wires. Krzysztof walked past them to the outer trench, where Moretti and Nelson would join him as soon as they saw something. They were out on reconnaissance. Krzysztof knew he should be glad they hadn't seen anything yet, but he hated waiting.

* * *

Peter marched in front of his captors. His jaw—and a dozen other parts of his body—ached, mostly from being hit with the end of Romanian rifles. Overall, he couldn't complain about his treatment, not yet anyway. The bruises were annoying, but he was far more concerned about his captors using the other end of their rifles to put a bullet in the back of his head.

After he was captured, most of the Romanian troops had joined the group of men moving up the mountain, closing in on Baker's team. Three of them were escorting him downhill, he assumed toward whoever was leading the massive attack on Baker's team. Based on the number of men he'd seen, his teammates were outnumbered five to one. Peter thought the odds were probably worse because he doubted he'd seen the entire group of attackers.

Peter's hands were tied behind his back, making the mountainous terrain more challenging, but the mountain troops kept him moving at a brisk pace. Peter was surprised when one of them suddenly fell to the earth. When a second man fell backward, Peter suspected Fisher was still free somewhere within rifle range. His remaining captor hunched into the underbrush and pulled Peter down with him. From the ground, Peter could see the bullet hole in the first man's head.

"If you surrender to me, I'll make sure your life is spared," Peter said. The Romanian soldier looked at him but didn't reply. Peter tried again in French, then in German. Either the Romanian didn't speak any of those languages, or he wasn't prepared to surrender. The man pointed his rifle at Peter and motioned for him to continue downhill through a thicket of trees. Peter tried to stand, but the man wouldn't let him.

"Do you really expect me to crawl with my hands tied behind my back?"

The Romanian didn't answer. Peter sighed and made a meager effort to comply. He kept glancing back at his captor, and after fifteen minutes, when the man's attention was diverted by an artificial-sounding bird call, he jammed his boot into the man's face. As the soldier raised a hand to shield his face from another attack, Peter kicked the man's rifle from his other hand then lunged into the man's side, pinning him to the ground. Peter couldn't have held the man down for long, not without full use of his arms, but Fisher appeared and knocked the soldier unconscious.

Peter stood up, his back to Fisher, and held his arms out. Seconds later he felt the ropes fall away. Peter turned to face the British sniper. "Thanks."

Fisher had a huge grin on his face. "One rescue from Romanian Mountain Troops in exchange for one rescue from the Gestapo. I'm 'appy to repay the favor, sir."

Chapter Thirty-Two

Encirclement

Krzysztof took a lukewarm drink from his canteen as he looked behind his position, up the hill. He could make out the end of Sherlock's field glasses and Sherlock's hand shielding them from the sun so they wouldn't cause a reflection. Beyond that was the blockhouse. He thought of Iuliana as his eyes swept back to the trees and bushes and dirt below.

He raised his rifle the instant he saw movement below him then relaxed when he recognized Nelson. He was impressed with how quickly—and quietly— Nelson moved up the hill toward him.

Nelson waved Quill down from the other trench. "We have found Eddy and Fisher. They are headed this way, but there is a thick line of Romanian troops between us. We could use another man to help us arrange a breakout."

"I'll go," Krzysztof said.

Nelson nodded.

"I'm a better shot," Quill said.

Nelson looked at each of them. "'We few, we happy few, we band of brothers. For he today that sheds his blood with me shall be my brother.' Other than Logan, Wesley did a good job with this team. Not a coward among us. Quill, inform Baker of my plans then take Zielinski's spot in this trench. Kapral, grab a few grenades and follow me."

Quill looked disappointed but didn't argue. Krzysztof placed a half dozen grenades in a bag and followed Nelson down the slope.

"I hope they haven't tried anything desperate yet," Nelson said.

They covered a half mile quickly then slowed. Nelson stopped completely, straining to hear. All was quiet with the exception of the wind causing the tree branches to sway and rub against each other. The Romanian Mountain Troops had scared the wildlife into silence.

Krzysztof heard a soft crunch and spun around to see Moretti approaching them.

"Do you still know where they are?" Nelson asked when the three men had gathered.

"I have a good idea." Moretti pointed downhill, slightly to the west. "Last I saw, they were about twenty yards behind the line of troops. Then they disappeared again."

Nelson glanced downhill then back at Moretti. "What do you have in mind?"

Moretti smiled. "A diversion. I figure you two can start lobbing grenades at the line on either side of 'em. That should draw some of the men away. Chuck a few grenades, then book it back up to headquarters. I'll stay across from where I think they are and provide cover fire."

Nelson nodded. "You know the battle will begin then."

"The battle of Scorțeni. May it last until we can get our butts outta here."

* * *

Peter slithered closer to the soldier he was stalking. The mountain troops were methodically searching as they advanced up the hill. They didn't seem to be in a hurry. Peter wondered if they were waiting for their howitzer.

He forced himself to relax, slowly breathing in through his nose and out through his mouth. He and Fisher were about to kill two men. Peter didn't like it, but he had his team to think about.

Behind a tree, Peter unsheathed his knife, rose to his feet, and lunged at the man ahead of him. He clamped one hand over the man's mouth while the other guided his knife to a lethal spot in the man's lungs. Peter lowered the body to the ground, staying low himself. He looked to his left. Fisher had also knifed his man. The two corpses would be noticed in a matter of seconds.

Explosions boomed on either side of them. They were startled for only a few moments; then they ran through the hole they'd created, no longer as concerned with stealth. Peter heard an artificial bird call and ran toward it. He heard shouts and rifle shots as the Romanian troops reacted to the grenades exploding and the two men running through the middle of their line, but he didn't let the sounds distract him.

Peter and Fisher ran past a thick bunch of trees and spotted Moretti firing at someone behind them. The three of them retreated up the hill, moving quickly but taking time to lay down cover fire. They arrived at headquarters in time to see Nelson jump into the first trench, between Baker and Luke. Zielinski came running up just after them.

"Stirred up the hornet's nest, did you, Jamie?" Baker asked, shaking his head slightly.

Nelson smiled. "I think we have lost enough men, don't you? 'Cry "havoc!" and let slip the dogs of war.' 'O God of battles, steel my soldiers' hearts. Possess them not with fear. Take from them now the sense of reck'ning, ere th' opposèd numbers pluck their hearts from them.'"

"You're mixing your plays, Jamie," Baker said. "Lieutenant Eddy, what is the status on the howitzer?"

"At the bottom of a ditch, sir, buried under dead animals. It will take them awhile to get it out." Peter looked at the sun. "I'd be surprised if they managed it before nightfall."

Baker nodded. "Luke, is everything ready?"

"Yes, sir." Luke held up a box with wires trailing from it.

"What if they bring someone down the mountain on the road behind us?" Nelson asked.

"I've taken care of that," Luke said. "It's wired to explode—should cause a small avalanche and block the road completely. Iuliana offered to keep an eye on it."

Zielinski's head spun toward Luke. Seeing his worry, Luke continued. "She's just watching it for now—if we fall back to the post, we'll have her go back down in the cellar."

Zielinski nodded, but his face didn't relax.

"There they are." Baker peered through his binoculars. "Right below us."

Peter couldn't see them yet. He looked along the trench. Baker was in the center, with Nelson immediately to his left, then Luke, Sherlock, and Quill. Peter was to Baker's right. Moretti, Fisher, and Zielinski were between them. The men waited, their rifles pointing at the advancing line. The topography would force their opponents to consolidate and thicken as they approached.

Baker turned to Luke as the enemy came into view. "That log is the marker, correct?"

"Yes, sir."

"Reaching it now . . . let them get past it . . . Now, Luke."

Luke depressed the lever on his box. The ground shook. Blasts of exploding earth shot skyward, decimating the Romanian line. A significant number of the Romanians were now wounded or dead, but the disciplined troops reformed and continued their advance. Fisher was the first to begin firing. Peter and the others waited until the line was closer then began picking the men off one by one.

The Romanian troops abandoned their line and began using the terrain more to their advantage, sheltering behind trees and working in teams to provide cover fire for small advances from one defensible position to the next. They took their time, and Peter was grateful. Baker's men just had to outlast the sun.

"Welcome to the infantry, Lieutenant." Moretti reloaded his rifle. "I guess this is a little different than what you did in the armored division, eh?"

Peter shot one of the Romanians and glanced at Moretti. "Yeah, it's different. Not a new experience for you?"

Moretti grunted as he aimed and took down his target. "Naw, I'm a paratrooper. I'm used to being surrounded."

Bullets kicked up the dirt piled in front of the trench, and Peter watched as several of the Romanian troops brought up a tripod and set it on an elevated slab of rock, positioned above them on a slope. "Fish—machine gun, two o'clock."

Fisher began picking the men off.

Peter turned his attention back to the main line, but after several minutes, Fisher interrupted, his tone urgent. "Sir, more keep coming. If they get it set up, it'll be murder in this trench."

Peter ran along the back of the trench. "Luke, I need a bomb."

"How big?"

Peter pointed to the machine gun nest. "Big enough to crumble that rock up there."

"I've got something in the next trench." Together, Luke and Peter ran from the outer trench to the middle trench. Luke glanced at his supplies then picked up several sticks of dynamite that had been wired together. "Planning to throw it?"

Peter nodded. The rock jutted out from the mountainside. A big enough explosion would bring sediment down from the slope above, burying the position, or cause the rock to break away from the slope and slide to the valley floor.

"It's got a ten-second fuse. Should stay lit, even when you throw it. Don't give them ten seconds to disarm it though; hold it for about seven."

Peter nodded, feeling the weight of the bomb as he studied the terrain between him and the side of the mountain.

"I'll cover you, sir."

"Thanks, Luke. I'd appreciate that."

The Romanian troops were tough. Despite Fisher's precision and the corresponding pile of bodies, the machine gun was firing. A tree trunk and dead comrades partially shielded the man currently behind the gun. Peter watched as Fisher hit the man and another Romanian came up and took his place.

Luke kept the field ahead clear, but Peter still had to fight his way across a hundred yards of mountain ground, sometimes running from tree to rock, sometimes crawling in the underbrush. He climbed up the nearly vertical slope, ten yards from the nest. Peter struck a match, lit the fuse, and counted to seven before underhanding the bomb right into the machine gun's base. Peter rolled down the hill, stopping to cover his face just before the explosion.

The blast wasn't as big as Luke's earlier work, but Peter felt a few rocks pound into him, and his lungs itched with the smoke and dust. He glanced up. The machine gun nest was gone, a pile of earth in its place. Peter used the smoke as cover to make a quick return to the team.

As Luke and Peter approached the trenches, they saw the team abandoning the outer trench for the middle trench. Nelson was last to leave. As he stepped away, Peter saw him drop something. Less than a second later, flames shot upward and spread the length of the trench. The smoke masked their movement as the men backed across the more open ground and settled into the next trench.

"Where are Sherlock and Quill?" Peter asked when he and Luke joined the rest of the team.

"Quill got hit pretty bad," Moretti said over the noise of the submachine gun he was using. "Couple of rounds from that machine gun. Sherlock's taking him to the post. Think he's gonna bandage him up and then have him watch our rear."

Luke had more explosives wired from the second trench. The Romanian troops were more spread out now, so despite his craftsmanship, they weren't as effective as the earlier traps. The mountain troops kept advancing through the twilight, a seemingly endless reserve filling the gaps in the line as fast as Baker's men made them.

Baker spun around and cursed. He'd been hit in the upper arm. Nelson knelt next to him and examined the wound. "Passed clear through."

Peter turned to Zielinski. "Go send Sherlock back down. Make sure Mrs. Ionescu is in the cellar." Zielinski nodded and ran off.

Peter kept an eye on the sun as he helped defend the trench. It gradually dropped in the sky until it disappeared behind a ridge. As the Romanian troops drew closer, Peter put his M1 rifle down and grabbed a Sten 9mm machine pistol. Most of the men did the same thing, with the exception of Fisher, who preferred the precision of his Lee-Enfield, and Baker, who was using his good hand to put pressure on his wound.

Sherlock and Zielinski returned. Sherlock bandaged Baker's arm, and Baker began shooting again. But they couldn't defend the trench much longer.

"Do you have anything else, Luke?" Baker asked.

"Not here."

"All right, prepare to fall back."

As they retreated, they armed Luke's explosive devices positioned between the middle and inner trench. They were halfway to the last trench when one of the Romanians lobbed a grenade in their direction. Luke was closest, and he fell hard as the grenade exploded. With barely a pause, Moretti picked him up, threw him across his shoulder, and continued to their target trench.

When Peter followed them in, he could hear Luke moaning in pain. Moretti was covered in Luke's blood, and so was Luke, from his boots up to his glasses.

"Hang in there, kid." Moretti laid Luke flat. Most of the damage was to his right leg, but his left leg looked bad too. "Send Sherlock down here."

"Sherlock's dead," Zielinski said.

Moretti looked up in surprise.

"Hit in the neck."

Moretti cursed and started pulling the fabric from Luke's burned legs.

Luke was pale, his body trembling as he tried to keep from whimpering. "It's okay, kid. No shame in screaming a little."

Luke's voice was weak when he spoke. "Am I . . . Am I going to die?"

Moretti laughed. "Don't be silly, kid. In Salerno, we would of patched you up and had you back on the line in an hour or two." Moretti smiled but let the smile slip from his face the second his back was turned. He dug through the supplies, searching for sulfa powder.

Peter wanted to help, but with their numbers down, sparing Moretti was hardship enough. He aimed his weapon at anything moving below them. Then a huge explosion rocked through the air, causing the ground to vibrate.

"Guess they were trying to get around behind us," Fisher said.

"There goes our easiest escape route." Peter spoke quietly so only Fisher could hear him.

"At least the sun's down now."

Fisher was right. The sun was gone, but the attack hadn't slowed, not yet. The hearty Romanian troops continued to press forward. When Luke's traps injured them, others came up and took their place.

Moretti finished bandaging Luke and stood in the trench next to Peter.

"How is he?" Peter asked between shots.

Moretti looked to make sure Luke's attention was elsewhere. "I think there's gonna be permanent damage to that leg."

"But you aren't telling him that?"

"I'm hoping I'm wrong." Another explosion tore into the Romanian line. Moretti's expression and volume changed as he turned to Luke. "Hey, kid, your booby traps are working great."

Peter's Sten gun ran out of ammunition. He picked up his M1 instead, but targets were appearing as fast as he could shoot them, and he soon emptied that clip too. He looked for more ammunition, but the box closest to him was depleted. Nelson came back into the trench then, carrying several ammo boxes. Peter hadn't noticed Nelson leave, but he ran along the back of the trench and reached for one of the boxes. The weight felt correct, but as Peter pulled it along the bottom of the trench, the weight shifted in a way he wouldn't expect from a fully packed ammunition box. Peter opened the box and found rocks instead of bullets.

"Nelson, what's in the other box?" Peter shouted above the battle noise.

Nelson ripped the second box open. It contained more rocks, packaged with bits of blanket to keep them from shuffling their weight as the other box had. Nelson looked down at the box in confusion then at the box Peter had opened. "I suppose that would explain Constantin's laughter when I retrieved these."

Peter looked down the trench. Sherlock's body was still lying at the far end. Baker and Luke were wounded, Luke seriously. Fisher, Moretti, Nelson, Zielinski, and Peter were still capable of fighting, but they wouldn't be very effective without bullets.

Peter met Baker's eyes and knew he'd come to the same conclusion. "Jamie, go check our other supplies; see if any of them are useable," Baker ordered.

Nelson ran for the blockhouse. Peter took Nelson's rifle, which had a full clip, and concentrated on buying the team more time. Moretti and Fisher still had a supply of bullets near them, but after they shared them with Zielinski, Baker, and Peter, there weren't many left.

"There's some ammo at the other safe house, the one Logan and I set up," Moretti said.

"May as well be on the moon, all the good it'll do us," Fisher replied.

Nelson returned with depressing but expected news: there was no additional ammunition in the blockhouse. Condreanu had compromised all of their remaining supplies. A dozen grenades were the sum total of their remaining arms. They split up the grenades and quickly put them to use.

"Time to fix bayonets?" Moretti asked after shooting the last round from his pistol.

Baker looked at each of the men in turn. "How is Quill?"

"Conscious. Unable to fight," Nelson said. "Wesley, I hate to say this, but it might be time to ask for terms."

Baker pulled at his chin. "That could be complicated since our presence is supposed to be secret."

"Condreanu already told them all about us. I am sorry I let him get away, Wesley."

Baker reached into his pocket and pulled out a white handkerchief. He handed it to Nelson. "You speak the language, Jamie."

The men in the trench stopped firing. Nelson tied the handkerchief to a stick and raised it into the evening light. And gradually, the incoming fire diminished until it halted altogether.

Chapter Thirty-Three

Defection

THEY WERE SURROUNDED IN A matter of seconds and soon had three or four rifles pointed at each of them. Peter stared up at his captors. They were calm and disciplined, but he could also detect a hint of anger in their eyes. He attributed that to the normal aftermath of a difficult battle and did his best to remain perfectly still.

A Romanian maior joined his men after a few minutes. He gave them orders, and half the men moved into the trench, two of them pulling Peter's arms behind his back and forcing him and the rest of the team out onto the ground in front of the blockhouse. They allowed Moretti to move Luke into the post as they began restraining the rest of the team. Peter felt the Romanians place handcuffs on his wrists and tie his legs. Then they pushed him to the ground. Since his hands were behind him, his face hit the dirt. Nelson fell beside him, equally immobilized.

Peter looked toward the blockhouse. He and Nelson were only a few yards from its entrance. Moretti, Fisher, Zielinski, and Baker were tied up, sitting with their backs against the outside wall. Baker's injury was starting to wear him down—he looked barely conscious. Six men guarded them, and four men guarded Peter and Nelson. As Peter watched, the Romanian troops helped Condreanu out of the blockhouse basement. They dragged Mrs. Ionescu out after that and, at Condreanu's directions, tied her hands and left her inside with Luke and Quill. Condreanu looked at his former teammates with satisfaction as he spoke to the Romanian maior. Then the maior walked down the hill, leaving Condreanu as the senior officer.

"I should have killed him before we surrendered," Nelson said. "What was it like to be tortured?"

Peter looked at Condreanu and remembered the techniques he'd suggested during their interrogation class at Dravot Manor—most of them involving knives and fire. Peter was suddenly terrified as he realized what would happen.

Condreanu would be just as vindictive as the Gestapo had been—maybe worse. Peter didn't know any information that would be useful to the Romanians. If he broke, he wouldn't be betraying friends or strategic plans, but that wouldn't make the pain any less severe. He looked back at Nelson and answered honestly. "I don't know if I can go through it again."

Nelson was silent for a while, watching Condreanu kick Zielinski in the gut and shove his rifle butt into his face. Then he pulled Moretti to his feet and began working on him. "Look, Peter, Condreanu doesn't like any of the men on the team, but he has a special loathing for you and for me. I have a feeling we won't get off as easy as Zielinski. Can you reach into my pocket?"

Peter shifted himself along the ground, slowly, so he wouldn't alert the troops standing over him. It was dark now, and the guards' attention focused on Condreanu pummeling Moretti, but it would take only one downward glance and they'd stop him. Peter eased one of his shackled hands into Nelson's pocket and felt what he guessed Nelson had sent him for: two capsules. Peter pressed one into Nelson's hand and kept one for himself.

"Potassium cyanide," Nelson explained. "I stole it from Condreanu last night. It's the rest of what he used on me, but I only took a sip of what had been mixed into a cup of tea, and I vomited it up within minutes. If you don't think you can take the torture again, that pill will do the job more completely and much more swiftly than the tea did. You can hide it in your mouth if you need to then crush it with your teeth if you decide it is time."

Peter nodded, not sure what he would do. Condreanu still wasn't finished with Moretti, but it looked like the tough American paratrooper, fallen to the ground, was no longer conscious.

"Two choices," Nelson continued. "There is the pill. 'The way to dusty death. Out, out, brief candle.' Or you can try enduring it again. 'Stiffen the sinews, summon up the blood, disguise fair nature with hard-favored rage.'"

"What will you do?"

Nelson shrugged. "I haven't decided yet, but I am loath to endure the full measure of Constantin's wrath. He is insecure, sadistic, and wielding complete power for the first time in his life. A rather frightening combination. But I don't have a pretty French tart waiting for me back in England. I imagine she will want you back, even if you are in pieces." Condreanu strutted over to them. "Now that he is warmed up, I suppose we shall see which of us he despises the most."

Condreanu pointed at Peter, and two of the guards forced him to his feet. "I am sorry, old boy. I thought it would be me," Nelson said. "I should have warned you when Wesley went off to destroy that train."

Peter gripped the pill as they dragged him away. If he was to be executed anyway, he thought it the easier course of action. He would rather a quick end now than weeks of torture and then death anyway.

The Romanian troops followed Condreanu's directions, unlocking Peter's handcuffs, looping them over a tree branch, and then fastening them to Peter's wrists again. Peter tried to remember what Nelson had said. Something about blood and sinews. Peter was sure there would be blood and possibly exposed sinews—but that wasn't what Nelson had meant. Peter had the capsule in his hand. His arms were stretched above him, the branch high enough that Peter's toes barely touched the ground. Still, if he positioned his head just right, he might be able to drop the capsule into his mouth. He tried to remember the quote, but it was no good. Shakespeare couldn't provide him with the right motivation. But he did remember Genevieve. Her laugh, her voice, her smile—his reason to live. Her face in his mind, he let the capsule fall to the dirt. He would make it through the torture for Genevieve, for his sisters, for his parents. Whatever the future held, he would do his best to survive.

Condreanu stood before him and prodded Peter with the end of a rifle. Peter's balance on his toes was so incomplete that the nudge sent him swaying from the tree branch. When he regained his footing, Condreanu leaned closer, right next to Peter's ear. "Are you scared, Eddy?" Then he plunged his rifle stock into Peter's gut. Peter clenched his jaw, trying to control a grunt of pain that wanted to escape. He was angry and frightened and wanted to know what idiot in Cairo had stopped the team from getting rid of Condreanu when they'd had the chance.

"Praying for deliverance yet, prayer boy?" Condreanu smiled and shoved the rifle butt into Peter's face. It hurt, and Peter felt blood trickling from his nose and broken lips. "The interesting thing, Eddy, is that I don't have any questions for you. There's nothing you know that I care about. So I guess that means you won't be able to talk your way out of this interrogation." Then he swung the rifle into the side of Peter's head.

Peter heard himself groan. His head ached, and he could barely keep his eyes open. Squinting through the pain, he saw Condreanu pace in front of him.

"You know, we never got to finish our baseball game, did we? Maybe you can help me with my technique. You swing the bat like this, right?" Condreanu stepped behind Peter and swung the rifle into his kidneys. He repeated the motion a few more times, all along Peter's back, each blow building on the pain of the previous strike. "I don't suppose you could see any of those—but I think my swing is coming along nicely." Condreanu finished circling Peter and pulled the rifle back, preparing for another strike.

"Leave 'im alone, you blighter!" Peter recognized Fisher's voice.

Condreanu looked away briefly then turned back to Peter. He took out his knife and let the blade rest against Peter's neck. "You see, Eddy, that's one of the things I don't like about you. You inspire such loyalty in the men you lead. It's sickening. But I wonder how Fisher will react when I do the same thing to him."

Peter forced his eyes to meet Condreanu's, forced himself to find his voice and his last bit of courage. "Fish isn't the one you hate. Leave him alone, and take it out on me. That's what you want, isn't it?"

Condreanu shrugged then swung the rifle again, hitting Peter's head. The resulting burst of pain ended in darkness.

* * *

Krzysztof watched Eddy's head slump forward and thought unconsciousness was probably a blessing. Condreanu frowned, disappointed that Eddy was temporarily unable to feel further pain, but after chewing on his lip for a few seconds, Condreanu called out more orders, and the Romanian troops strung Nelson and Fisher up under a tree next to Eddy.

Krzysztof's face and abdomen ached from Condreanu's earlier attack, but he knew he'd been lucky—for the moment at least. Moretti was unconscious, lying a few feet away. He could see Moretti's torso rising and falling rhythmically, so he was alive, but Krzysztof wondered how long that would be the case for any of them. He hadn't seen or heard Iuliana since the surrender, and he was worried about what Condreanu might have done to her and about what he might do to Fisher and Nelson.

Fisher was swearing nonstop, using a few words Krzysztof had never heard before, and between curses, he managed to kick Condreanu as he walked past. That only earned Fisher a particularly vicious strike from Condreanu's rifle butt. Krzysztof kept fingering the chain on his handcuffs, but the weak link he hoped to find wasn't there.

The Romanian maior returned, listening to Fisher's British curses and looking unhappy. He spoke with Condreanu, who immediately started arguing in rapid Romanian. As the discussion continued, Krzysztof watched the reactions of the Romanian troops: surprise, pleasure, embarrassment. Then he caught sight of Nelson's face, a broad grin spreading across it as the maior made tense hand motions. Nelson didn't seem surprised when the maior motioned to some of his men and they released the three men handcuffed to the tree branches. The maior pointed toward Krzysztof, and he and Baker were freed as well. Another Romanian untied the ropes around Moretti.

"What's going on, Jamie?" Baker asked.

Nelson rubbed his wrists, still smiling. "The maior says we are allies now. A few hours ago, there was a coup. The Romanians have switched sides."

"Are you sure?" Krzysztof asked, skeptical.

"I think so." Nelson got as many details as he could and translated for the rest of the team. "Colonel Eliade told him we were Russian commandos and that there were fifty of us. The maior apologizes. He said he wouldn't have given Condreanu free rein if he had known we were mostly British."

The maior didn't know all the details of the coup. He simply knew King Michael had arrested Marshal Antonescu, the military dictator of Romania, and told the German Army to leave. Then the king gave the Red Army permission to enter the country. A fighting force of over one million had switched from fighting with Hitler to fighting against him.

As Krzysztof helped Baker carry Moretti into the blockhouse, he felt a mix of emotions. He looked at the Romanian troops, the men who'd tried to wipe out his team—now their newest allies. He'd known Romania's position during the war had been more a result of anti-Soviet feelings than pro-German ones. Romania's enthusiasm for Hitler's war had been on the wane since their defeat on the Russian steppes outside Stalingrad when two Romanian armies had disappeared, Iuliana's father along with them. But this latest change still seemed sudden and surprising. Krzysztof shook his head but couldn't completely dislodge the last remnants of anger or the lingering disbelief.

Iuliana was inside. She listened to the news with surprise as Krzysztof untied her. "Where is Condreanu?" she asked. "I didn't have a chance to shoot him—I wasn't sure what was happening outside. But he promised he'd deal with me later." He felt her tremble and studied her face. She was still frightened by whatever Condreanu had threatened her with.

Nelson and Fisher brought Eddy, still unconscious, into the blockhouse.

"Does anyone know where Condreanu went?" Krzysztof asked.

Nelson immediately began looking, but Condreanu had disappeared. Nelson questioned the Romanian maior, but he didn't know where the locotenent had gone either. The maior was missing several of his men; not everyone could switch sides in an instant.

With Nelson as translator, the Romanian maior apologized for the misunderstanding about their nationality then sent up a medic and a radio. The medic treated Quill, Luke, and Baker. Moretti and Eddy regained consciousness, but there wasn't much the medic could do for either of their bruises. Then the battered team listened to the BBC's eleven o'clock broadcast, confirming the news of the coup.

"Congratulations, Mrs. Ionescu. Your country now has a democracy," Baker said.

Iuliana nodded, but the small smile she managed soon faded.

"What's wrong?" Krzysztof was sitting next to her, and he reached for her hand. It felt cold.

"I'm not sure I trust the Soviet Union to keep their end of the deal. I'm happy—and I'm proud of the king. By all accounts, Antonescu practically had him under house arrest. That he managed to pull this off—it's wonderful."

Krzysztof nodded then turned to Baker. The major's arm was wrapped tightly, and though he still looked exhausted, he seemed to have partially recovered. "Sir, what are our plans?"

"Get your radio and call Cairo. We'll probably leave at dawn. I have a feeling the Romanian Army will come through here soon on their way to retaking Transylvania. If Gibson wants us out by air, we'll need to move quickly."

"Wesley . . ." Nelson interrupted.

Baker sighed. "I know, Jamie. But can I get a few hours of sleep before I worry about that?"

"I think it would be wise to decide before we contact Cairo." Nelson was persistent.

"Would you mind explaining what you two are talking about?" Moretti asked, one side of his face red and swollen.

Baker motioned for Nelson to proceed. "Our mission in Romania was two-fold. First, we were to do whatever Colonel Gibson ordered. Thus far, that has consisted of a great deal of watching and one train sabotage. Second, and unknown to Gibson or the people in Cairo, we were to set up a few information sources. Back in the summer of 1941, all our networks in Romania fell apart. We were completely blind, and we still haven't recovered. We do not want that to happen again, especially since, like Iuliana, we expect the Soviet Union to be rather influential in postwar Romania. But before Wesley and I could start our part of the mission, we had to find out who we mustn't trust."

"And that's where Condreanu came in, right?" Moretti leaned forward.

"Indeed. Now that we know about Eliade and the others, we can start building our sources. But I fear we won't have time to get very far."

Iuliana reached into her pocket and pulled out the envelope she had tried to give Tiberiu Ionescu the day before. "This may help you." She handed it to Nelson.

He took it and read it out loud. "*Tiberiu, If you need help, seek out those on this list. They can be trusted. The key, like Romania, will ever be in my heart, despite the heartache both have caused me. The rest is in code.*" Nelson handed the paper to Krzysztof.

The penmanship was small and neat, written with black ink. Krzysztof read through the introduction. *The key, like Romania, will ever be in my heart.* As Krzysztof pondered the meaning of Vasile's message, the Romanian medic finished packing his gear and stood, ready to leave.

Nelson translated what the medic said. "He will come again in the morning. In the meantime, he is leaving morphine and bandages."

"It's time for me to leave too." Iuliana stood, and Krzysztof stood up with her, but she shook her head. "You look exhausted. And the side of your face is swollen." She brought her hand toward his face but didn't touch it. She met his eyes for a moment then looked away and let her hand drop. "Stay here—I'll go back with the medic. Their barracks aren't far from Cosmina's home. But thank you, Krzysztof."

Krzysztof thought he saw the gleam of a tear on her cheek as she turned abruptly and left the building ahead of the medic. As Krzysztof watched her go, a dull ache filled his chest—worse even than the pain from Condreanu's blows. Something told him this new wound would take longer to heal than the others. He longed to have a private good-bye and wondered if that was exactly what Iuliana wanted to avoid.

* * *

When Iuliana returned to Cosmina's estate, she was exhausted, and she had a headache from the tears she'd cried as she and the medic climbed down the mountain. She liked Krzysztof, but he was leaving. *Perhaps if things were different we could see where it would lead,* she thought. The last two days had been trying. Krzysztof had been a bright spot amid the fear, threats, and near-death events. He was someone she could trust, and he had saved her life, but he would soon be gone. She shook her head. She hadn't had good luck with heroes anyway, not in the long term, be they knights in shining armor or modern military men.

She'd left most of the Carpathian bellflower Krzysztof had picked for her in the blockhouse, but she fingered one of the blossoms she'd placed in her pocket. She hoped her new feelings would fade soon, just as the little flower with delicate petals would.

She walked down the hallway toward her room, suddenly missing her son. She longed to hold him again, to play with his hair and feel his chubby arms wrapped around her neck. She'd left him only that morning, but she'd never been apart from him for so long. She opened the door to Sabina's room, managing to enter without waking her. But Anatolie wasn't with Sabina. She went to her room next, expecting to find him sleeping there. Instead, the room was empty. The mattress was still there, but none of Anatolie's toys remained, none of his clothes. All of her belongings were gone as well. *Perhaps Cosmina is angry. We'll have to go back to Bucharest . . . The Americans won't be bombing us any longer, although the Germans might. Anatolie must have just slipped under Sabina's blanket.* Her son had a bad habit of burrowing under blankets while he slept.

Iuliana went back to Sabina's room. Anatolie had to be there—she just hadn't looked closely enough because she hadn't wanted to wake Sabina. But she still didn't see him. She gently shook Sabina's shoulder to wake her. "Sabina, where's Anatolie?"

Sabina looked surprised. "Didn't you send for him hours ago?"

Iuliana felt panic tightening her chest. "Who told you that?"

"Colonel Eliade. He said you moved in with him, so he picked up your things and took Anatolie."

Iuliana could barely breathe. She should have told Sabina her real feelings about Eliade, should have taken his threats more seriously. Fighting the horror that filled her chest, she managed to get a few words out. "Where did he take him?"

CHAPTER THIRTY-FOUR
VASILE'S CODE

Thursday, August 24

PETER YAWNED AND RUBBED HIS wrists. They'd supported most of his weight while he was suspended from the tree, and the metal had bit into his skin. He tried to ignore the stinging in his wrists, the throbbing from his head and back, and the aching in his neck and stomach. Things could have been worse—they *had* been worse on previous occasions. Peter was grateful he hadn't taken that cyanide capsule and murmured a quick prayer thanking the Lord for the coup, and for Genevieve.

A team of thirteen, Peter thought. *Two traitors—one dead, one vanished. Three good men dead, two seriously wounded, and six remaining. Mission only half completed.* Even with all of their sacrifices, it didn't seem they'd accomplished much. They'd destroyed an 88 and blown up a train. Nelson had figured out who they couldn't trust, but they still hadn't determined who they could. He tried to analyze what had happened, thinking through his decisions and wondering if he should have done something differently when he was in command, but his brain was too exhausted to form any conclusions.

Most of the team was asleep. Peter wanted to join them, but the bruises from his beating made it difficult. Nelson was on patrol, because even with the change in Romania's loyalties, no one was willing to trust them completely. And Condreanu was still around, somewhere. Nelson thought he'd probably left to join with German forces, but no one was really sure. Peter sighed.

"How are you feeling, sir?"

Peter glanced over at Zielinski, who was still trying to break Vasile Ionescu's code.

Peter forced a smile, despite the steady anguish he was feeling. "If King Michael walked into the room, I might break into a rousing chorus of 'God Save the King,' and being an American, I normally don't fawn over royalty. Although I might ask him why he didn't pull off the coup an hour earlier."

Zielinski nodded his agreement then paused, looking at the paper and tilting his head to the side. He stared at it, his face expressionless for a few seconds. Then a smile formed, starting right under the bruise Condreanu had given him and spreading across his face.

"What are you smiling about?" Peter asked.

"I think I know the key to the code."

* * *

A few hours later, Krzysztof woke when Nelson returned to the blockhouse. He handed him a paper listing thirteen names with addresses. "Here are your contacts." Now that he knew the key, Krzysztof wondered why it had taken him so long to figure it out. *The key, like Romania, will ever be in my heart.* Krzysztof had read the words several times before they'd suddenly seemed obvious. Vasile wasn't so different from him.

Nelson's blue eyes studied the list, and his smile caused laugh lines to form around his mouth. "Well done, Kapral."

Krzysztof went back to sleep for a few hours before Baker woke him. "I think we've postponed our contact with Cairo long enough."

No longer worried about anyone triangulating their signal—the local authorities already knew exactly where they were—Krzysztof transmitted his previously encoded message about the battle of the day before and waited until Cairo replied. Krzysztof finished decoding the message on a piece of paper. "They want us to report to these coordinates in two days' time." He handed the paper to Baker.

"Two days?" Nelson frowned. "That does not give us much time for anything else."

Baker looked up from the map he was studying, his finger marking the coordinates from Cairo. "Near Ploieşti. Have they mentioned anything about the government official we were asked to evacuate?"

"No, sir," Krzysztof said.

"Ask them. And request more time . . . on behalf of the wounded." Baker winked at Nelson.

Krzysztof followed his orders, coding, sending, receiving, and decoding. "They'll get back to us in forty-eight hours."

"Which means they can't expect us to be at those coordinates until Sunday— Saturday evening at the earliest." Nelson drummed his fingers on the map.

The sound of someone outside made the three men reach for their weapons. Nelson ran to the door then returned his pistol to its holster. "It's Mrs. Ionescu."

Krzysztof peered over Nelson's shoulder. He thought Iuliana a beautiful woman, but that morning her hair was tangled and she had dark circles under red eyes. She wore the same clothes she'd worn the day before, and after the battle, they were dirty and wrinkled.

Nelson stepped aside, letting Krzysztof be the one to greet her. She fell into his arms and started to sob.

"I'm sorry . . . I didn't know where else to go. He's taken Anatolie."

"What? Who?" Krzysztof could feel her tears soaking through his shirt.

"Colonel Eliade—he kidnapped Anatolie while I was gone."

Baker walked over to them. "Mrs. Ionescu, we owe you our lives. Do you know where Eliade took your son?"

"Bucharest."

"Most of Vasile's contacts are in Bucharest. So is the official we were ordered to evacuate," Nelson said.

Several of the other men had woken when Iuliana arrived. Moretti tilted his head toward Nelson. "I thought that official was in Scorţeni?"

Nelson smiled. "No, that's just what we wanted Condreanu to think. He's in Bucharest, and so, it seems, is Anatolie Ionescu. Wesley?"

"We have only two, maybe three days." Baker studied the map. "In normal times, that would be enough, but if the German Army leaves willingly, they'll be coming through the Prahova Valley. And if the German Army doesn't leave willingly, they'll target the Prahova oil fields and Bucharest. Either way, that means our route and our destination. And we have two severely wounded men. The rest of us aren't exactly in top form either."

"The German Army won't leave without a fight," Nelson predicted. "But what if we didn't haul Quill and Luke with us all the way to Bucharest? We can split up."

"And how would we meet again?" Baker asked.

Nelson glanced around the room, looking over each man. "Quill can use a radio. You stay with Luke and him. I can take the rest of the team and Mrs. Ionescu to Bucharest. Zielinski and Quill can talk every night if they need to."

"And when we evacuate, you would have one wounded major evacuating two nonambulatory men?" Baker crossed his arms. A small spot of blood had seeped through his bandages.

Nelson looked around the room again. His eyes stopped on the team's most muscular member. "I would wager Sergeant Moretti is up to the task."

"Leaving you with Eddy, Zielinski, and Fisher." Baker put one hand on his chin, massaging it. "Lieutenant Eddy will be in charge, not you."

Nelson nodded. "Fine."

Baker had one final question. "Are you sure you wouldn't rather just go home?"

"Abandon Anatolie and leave our mission only half accomplished?" Nelson shook his head. "I think we had better carry on, Wesley."

CHAPTER THIRTY-FIVE

A DARK PRISON

Marseilles, France

GENEVIEVE STIFLED A YAWN. THE sun had set hours ago, and she hadn't been getting much sleep the last week. She and Browning had spent most of their days observing the German engineers and most of their nights trying to undo their work. They couldn't undo everything; that was impossible. They hadn't been able to do much about the ships the German engineers sank to block the harbor's entrance or about the mines they'd laid. But if they managed to save a pier here, a crane there, it could make a difference in how well supplied the Allied Armies would be as they moved toward Germany.

French troops had surrounded Marseilles several days before, and they'd already liberated part of the city. The battle for the rest of Marseilles continued. The sound of artillery and small arms was constant, the smell of spent munitions competing with the scent of the waterfront. Genevieve balanced on a small peg sticking out from one of the posts supporting a pier they were trying to save. She snipped a few wires leading from it to one of the remaining German strongholds. The pier was in the narrow channel between Fort Saint-Nicholas and Fort Saint-Jean. A scuttled ship already blocked the mouth of the channel, but Browning wanted to salvage the pier. She'd learned to trust his judgment but sensed that he too was growing less enthusiastic with their orders, received almost daily from SOE. The Allied generals were obsessed with ports—and Genevieve knew they were vital. Yet, knowing freedom was less than a mile away, Genevieve wondered if it was perhaps time to end their efforts.

Genevieve handed the wire clippers to Browning, who was waiting at the top of the pier. This would be their last task for the night. Both of them were so sleep deprived that they were approaching sloppiness, and then they'd be easy targets for German sentries.

"I see a patrol—wait." Browning's words were almost inaudible, but Genevieve heard the footsteps. In the water, she shivered, hoping their luck wasn't about to run out.

She couldn't see anything other than the post and the water, but she heard boots hitting the pavement—several people were running. When she heard the gunshot, she decided to take a swim. She slipped out of one shoe, but just as she pulled off the other, she heard the tramp of boots on the pier. Before she could lower herself into the water, she was blinded by a flashlight. She couldn't see anything behind the glow, but she knew it was a German military light; the German models had hand-cranked generators and distinctive hums.

"Hello, Genevieve. Don't move, or you'll be shot. Although we might shoot you anyway." The sneer behind the words sounded vaguely familiar, but she couldn't pinpoint the voice. It wasn't until after she'd been hauled to the top of the pier that she recognized her captor as Gestapo agent Weiss.

He marched Genevieve barefoot to the German-held Fort Saint-Nicolas. She looked for signs of Browning, or of his body, but saw nothing. *Maybe he escaped.* The fortress was dark on the outside, but there were lights when they entered. Weiss tied her hands behind her back and dismissed the rest of his associates.

"To think that you almost escaped." Weiss shoved her ahead of him, down a hallway, up a flight of stairs, and into another hallway. He knocked her against the wall a few times and made her stub her toes and shins on the stairs. Then Weiss pushed her into a doorframe midway down the second hallway and finally into an office. The room, like most of the fortress, was lined with thick tan bricks. "The one that got away," Weiss announced.

Schroeder looked up from a table covered with maps. "Ah, Mademoiselle Olivier. Welcome back."

"We found her in the water, balanced on a post, clipping wires from a pier. We also found an accomplice. He's not dead yet, but he's injured. I had him sent to the prison."

"Then I assume the accomplice wasn't who you expected it to be?"

"No," Weiss said, disappointment strong in his voice.

Schroeder stared at Weiss. "Thank you. You may return to your post, Rottenführer."

"So you can let her escape again?"

Genevieve looked at Weiss with surprise. He'd always shown complete deference to Tschirner, but these words were insubordinate.

Schroeder ignored the remark. "You may return to your post, *Rottenführer.*"

Weiss glared at the two of them but obeyed his orders, slamming the door behind him.

"Have a seat, mademoiselle. Your new hairstyle does not at all suit you."

Genevieve's shins ached, as did her feet, so she found a stool to sit on.

Schroeder continued his work for some time before speaking again. "Did you know I had three of my best men watching you? By the time they connected an old woman's exit to your disappearance, she too had disappeared. Weiss forgot to tell us your family has a knack for disguises."

Genevieve remained silent. Schroeder's office was quiet—none of the battle sounds carried through the thick walls this deep into the fortress. Weiss was Schroeder's source. That explained everything: the physical description down to the birthmark, her relationship with Peter, her previous alias. She thought back to the glimpse of the SS man she'd seen at the restaurant when she'd slipped away from the drunk naval officer. It must have been Weiss.

"What was it you were doing out on the pier?"

Genevieve still said nothing. Schroeder was looking at his maps, not at her. Then he glanced up.

"Trying to save it?" Schroeder held her gaze. "Seems a silly thing to do. In another week, perhaps less, the Allies will have the whole of Marseilles. They have engineers to fix anything we destroy."

Genevieve was surprised by his calm acceptance of impending defeat.

"Genevieve, if you insist on being mute, I cannot help you."

She met his eyes then looked at the floor. "Why would you help me?"

Schroeder limped around the table until he was only a few feet from her. "Because I don't like Rottenführer Weiss." Genevieve looked up in surprise. She studied Schroeder's face: he was serious. "I have an entire city to defend with a limited number of troops. Of those, half are from the Kriegsmarine or Luftwaffe—they aren't completely useless, but they certainly aren't trained in urban warfare. Morale is low, casualties are high, and yet Weiss insists on using my resources to hunt down the girlfriend of an American agent he has a grudge against."

"Has he been using many of your resources?"

Schroeder chuckled. "Twenty men the night you left a brokenhearted naval officer at the restaurant and between thirty and forty every day thereafter. Do you know what I could do with thirty to forty well-trained men?"

Genevieve looked away.

"I'll release you if you tell me where Lieutenant Eddy is. Then I can send Rottenführer Weiss away with the information he obsesses over and I can concentrate on holding the south end of Marseilles for a few extra days."

"You're Weiss's superior officer. You can send him away regardless of where Peter is."

"You're forgetting something," Schroeder said.

"Am I?"

"Yes, Weiss is a member of the Gestapo. The Gestapo is independent of the army, especially after the botched attempt to kill Hitler last month. My Führer has little trust for the army at present."

Genevieve flexed her shoulders, trying to ease the strain caused by Weiss's binding. "Perhaps it's time you stopped obeying his orders."

Schroeder clicked his tongue. "I always obey my orders. It seems you and I are not so different. Surely you realized the futility of trying to dismantle our explosives? Yet you continued to clip your wires. Destroying Marseilles may be the only part of my assignment I'm successful in, but the destruction of its harbor will be complete. On the other hand, I see no reason to destroy a charming young French girl with so much life ahead of her. Help me help you."

Genevieve stared at a spot on the wall behind Schroeder.

"Where is your Peter?"

"I don't know where he went."

"But he is out on assignment?"

Genevieve bit her lip. She hadn't meant to give that much information away. Wherever he was, Genevieve was sure Peter wouldn't be able to rescue her, not this time.

"Very well, mademoiselle. I can waste no more time trying to assist you." Schroeder walked past her, opened the door, and called out to a passing guard. He gave the instructions in German, but Genevieve understood them. She was being put with the rest of the prisoners.

* * *

The jail was underground. It was cold, with a ceiling and walls of concrete and a floor of hard-packed dirt. The guard pulled his light away, and it was dark. Genevieve shivered in her bare feet and wet skirt, pausing just inside the doorway the guard had pushed her through and waiting for her eyes to adjust to the lack of light. Gradually, she could make out about a dozen shapes: the other prisoners.

"Gerard?" she whispered. She couldn't see faces, but Weiss's earlier remarks made her think Browning was there.

A muffled sound drew her toward one of the corners. "Genevieve?" Browning's voice sounded strained.

She knelt by the figure. "How are you?"

"Shot in the shoulder. I think the bleeding is under control. They didn't let me see a doctor."

She felt the front and back of his shoulder, trying to judge how fresh the blood was. "I worked in a hospital long enough to know how to clean a wound. But in the dark, I don't think I can do much." She wiped her hands on her skirt and sat on the cold dirt floor.

"I'm sorry, Genevieve," Browning said. "I helped you out of one mess and into another. I was selfish to want your assistance."

Genevieve shook her head then realized Browning wouldn't be able to see the movement in the darkness. "No, I was foolish to think I could be as good a spy as my brother or my father."

"Your brother would have shot me for not getting you to safety when I could have."

Genevieve could hear the guilt in Browning's voice, but she didn't think it was his fault. He'd asked for her help, but she could have turned him down. "Jacques used to say you can't change the past; you can only learn from it and shape the future accordingly."

"That's not the Jacques I remember."

Genevieve thought of her brother. Browning had known the hardened spy who never made mistakes and rarely showed emotion. But there had been more to her brother before the war changed him and then again during the last days of his life. Jacques probably would have whisked her off to safety and taken her place as Browning's assistant, but he wouldn't have shot the Englishman. "What do you think will happen to us? Schroeder questioned me before I was sent here. He doesn't think his forces will hold out more than a week."

Browning forced a weak laugh. "We are in a unique situation, Genevieve, and we may end up lucky. There are no trains running from Marseilles to Germany, so they can't send us off to a concentration camp. They might shoot us before they're overrun, but that too might be more merciful than the alternative."

Genevieve pulled her knees toward her chest and leaned her head on them, forcing herself to breathe evenly, trying to ignore the overwhelming fear she felt. Whatever the future held, there was little she could do about it other than pray.

CHAPTER THIRTY-SIX

HESCHEL'S REPORT

Friday, August 25
Near Bucharest, Romania

PETER SAT BEHIND THE WHEEL of a 1936 German Maybach SW38. It was the nicest car he'd ever driven, but he wasn't surprised that James Nelson had convinced one of Scorţeni's wealthy residents to sell it to them for almost nothing. With the sudden shift in Romania's alliance, most of Scorţeni's residents were suddenly hospitable. Cosmina Ionescu, overcome with guilt for Anatolie's abduction, was hosting Baker, Moretti, Luke, and Quill.

After securing an extra radio to leave with Moretti and the wounded, Peter's part of the team had headed south, through the Prahova Valley. They'd made it through Ploieşti, despite the massing of the newly defected Romanian Army that was there protecting the oil fields. Near Baneasa, just north of Bucharest, the team found themselves unable to advance farther.

Nelson, the only male in the group without bruises on his face, returned from his reconnaissance trip and bent down to the driver's side window. He was wearing civilian clothing, as was everyone in the car. "No one is getting across that bridge. Not without connections."

Peter looked behind him, where Zielinski, Iuliana, and Fisher were sitting. Iuliana was convinced Eliade had taken her son to Bucharest. Now they were close—but not close enough. "Should we try to go on foot?"

Nelson shrugged. "Perhaps. Let me see Vasile's list again." Zielinski handed it to him. "One of our contacts lives not far from here, or at least he did when Vasile wrote the list. A Jewish căpitan by the name—probably at the front or dead. Worth a look anyhow."

* * *

They found Căpitan Heschel's flat without a problem. Eddy and Fisher provided security for the team, while Iuliana went inside with Krzysztof and Nelson. There was no answer when they knocked, but they let themselves in. A telegram addressed to M. Heschel lay on a table near the door. It was dated the day before, suggesting Heschel had been home as recently as Thursday.

They waited a half hour before four taps on the door—made by one of their lookouts—signaled someone was coming. The three visitors stood. Heschel walked into his apartment and looked less surprised to see the three people waiting for him than Iuliana would have expected. He was a muscular man, with salt-and-pepper hair and one arm in a sling. He pulled his lips to the side as he studied them, but he didn't speak as he removed his hat, turned it upside down, and placed his keys and a set of folded papers from his pocket inside it.

"Let me guess, members of the Iron Guard . . . and you would like me to detail Sanatescu's security arrangements so you can plan a countercoup? Or an advance party of the NKVD here for a similar purpose? In either case, you're going to be disappointed. Things have been happening so rapidly that I know little of our new prime minister's plans. I don't even know where the king has gone other than he's not in the palace." He put his hat on the table by the telegram. "Come to think of it, I doubt anyone's in the palace. I imagine General Gerstenberg's reduced it to rubble by now."

Nelson was the group's spokesperson. "We are neither Fascists nor Communists, but we do come seeking information. To be honest, we were surprised to find you. Your last name is Jewish, is it not?"

Heschel nodded. "That is why I am fifty-five years old and still only a căpitan. My father and grandfather served honorably in the Romanian Army, and my ancestors have lived in Romania for hundreds of years. My family has proven our loyalty, so we have escaped the worst of the pogroms." Heschel walked closer to the rest of them. "The Romanian government did its part to help Hitler eradicate the Jews from Europe, but economic necessity tempered their enthusiasm. I trust you haven't come to deport me to a more unfriendly territory?"

"No, sir. Your name appeared on a list written by Căpitan Vasile Ionescu. He seemed to think you were more sympathetic to Great Britain than to Germany or the Soviet Union."

Heschel sat in an old armchair and studied his guests. "Yes, I remember Căpitan Ionescu. What is your connection to him?"

"He was my husband," Iuliana said.

"Well then, Mrs. Ionescu, please sit down. The rest of you as well." Iuliana complied, sitting on a sofa between Nelson and Krzysztof. "Did you receive any letters from your husband after he was arrested?"

"None."

"Then I have something to tell you about his final days, something I heard from Locotenent-Colonel Dorin Eliade. I see Colonel Eliade's name is familiar to you. How do you know him?"

Iuliana hesitated, but Nelson encouraged her with a small nod. "We suspect he has lingering Nazi sympathies. He's probably in contact with members of the Iron Guard."

"And is that all you know of him?"

"No . . . He came to our house once, while Vasile wasn't home. He offered to ensure Vasile's promotion in exchange for a favor, but his price was too high. I sent him away, and Vasile never advanced beyond căpitan."

"What was his price?" Heschel asked. Iuliana felt her face grow hot. "I think I already know. He tried to seduce you?"

She nodded.

"And when you refused, he blocked your husband's promotion."

She nodded again.

"I'm afraid that's not the end of Eliade's wrongs against your family. I had the misfortune of working with Colonel Eliade. He's a clever military strategist. He received an award for his efforts in the Crimea. He not only denied his enemy their goal, but he also surrounded them and annihilated them. That technique carried over into his personal life, and when he was drunk, he told me the story of a talented young officer with a beautiful wife. The officer was up for promotion. Colonel Eliade, locotenent-colonel at the time, lusted after the woman and offered to ensure the young man's promotion if she would give in to his desires. She spurned him, and he blocked the promotion.

"But that's not where he stopped. He told the young man his wife had been unfaithful to him. Coming from his commanding officer, the young man believed the lie. The marriage was destroyed by the lie just as it would have been through actual infidelity. Colonel Eliade thought his revenge was complete.

"But then an opportunity for greater retribution appeared. The officer was arrested, accused of assisting saboteurs near Ploieşti. At the same time, a German liaison officer complained that the Romanian authorities weren't granting adequate access to Romanian prisoners. Knowing of Hitler's sensitivity for Ploieşti oil, Eliade offered the German officer a prisoner—one who had dared threaten the Nazi oil supply. The prisoner could be transferred to Germany and interrogated at will. From there, a return to Romania would be unlikely. Colonel Eliade's destruction of Căpitan Vasile Ionescu would be complete."

Heschel looked at Iuliana, who could feel tears flowing freely down her cheeks. "I saw your husband the morning he was to be transferred. The night before, flush with impending success, Eliade celebrated in the officer's club. I learned the details of his scheme over his fifth glass of pálinka. I told Căpitan Ionescu what I learned, and he cried."

"But my husband never cried. Not at our wedding, nor the birth of our son. Not when his mother died or when the army crossed the Dniester River," Iuliana said.

"He cried that morning, Iuliana, when he found out he'd alienated the woman he loved, the mother of his child, and doubted her without cause. More than anything, I think that's why he tried to escape. He wanted to return to you and beg your forgiveness." Heschel leaned forward and put his hand on her knee. "Since Vasile's death, has Eliade left you alone?"

Iuliana shook her head, barely able to speak. She felt Krzysztof's hand on her shoulder, offering her his support. "He kidnapped my son."

Through her tears, she saw the look of concern on Heschel's face. "Did he leave demands?"

"No, but I suspect he's returned to Bucharest. That's where we're going—if we can get there."

Nelson entered the conversation again. "We have several favors to ask of you, Căpitan. First, can you get us across the bridge and into Bucharest?"

Heschel nodded. "Yes, I would be happy to get the necessary paperwork for you."

"Do you know where Colonel Eliade is?"

"No, I requested reassignment after Căpitan Ionescu's death, and I haven't seen him since. But if you're tracking him, take care. He does not give up easily, and his fellow Legionnaires will assist him. Are those your only requests?"

"No," Nelson said. "Unofficially, one of my assignments is to prepare for the postwar world. Should the Communists end up with a dominating role in Romania, could we count on you to keep us informed?"

Heschel smiled. "Do you know how many times the leaders of the democratic parties in Romania tried to set up arrangements with the British since the war started? It's about time someone from Britain asked me that question."

* * *

It took awhile for Nelson and Heschel to work out all of the details. When they were finished, Heschel gave them the necessary passes for entry past the Romanian barricade into Bucharest. The four members of Baker's team and Iuliana reconvened in the Maybach.

Krzysztof waited until Nelson had finished filling everyone in. Like Eddy and Fisher, Krzysztof was hearing it for the first time because the conversation with Heschel had been in Romanian.

As Eddy drove the car toward the bridge, now with permission in hand to cross it, Krzysztof leaned toward Iuliana.

"I forgot to tell you earlier, Iuliana. Your name was the key to breaking Vasile's code. Even when he doubted you, he loved you."

CHAPTER THIRTY-SEVEN

MERCY

Sunday, August 27
Marseilles, France

GENEVIEVE WAS GLAD WHEN THE sun rose and added a bit of light to the basement prison. She examined Browning's shoulder again. It was infected and getting worse. He was so weak that he hadn't spoken since Friday. She realized she still didn't know his first name—he was known as Gerard in Marseilles, but that wasn't his real name. She didn't even know if Browning was his real surname. She'd done the best she could for his shoulder, but with no soap and only rags for bandages, it wouldn't be enough, especially if they stayed in the fort much longer. She stood to ask the guard for some water to clean it. The guard yesterday had given her some; perhaps the man on duty today would be equally merciful.

As she stood, she felt a rush of dizziness. She put her hand on the wall and leaned over until the room stopped spinning. She'd had nothing but a single piece of bread to eat and only a little water since she was arrested Thursday night.

The room was small, and the fourteen prisoners had no privacy and little fresh air. Many of her fellow prisoners had been languishing there for several weeks, and the smell of their unwashed bodies and the buckets of raw sewage grew to a nauseating stench each afternoon, even though the temperature rarely climbed above twenty-seven degrees Celsius. Worse than the smells were the rats. She hated rodents, and the prison was home to at least a dozen of them.

Genevieve stepped around the other prisoners and made her way to the door. Beside the door sat Jean-Luc, Arnaud's driver. Jean-Luc had been in prison for a week, arrested with another man he'd been passing Arnaud's assignments to. Genevieve called out to the guard, but no one answered. Her voice was scratchy, and she wondered if it was inaudible as well. Standing on her toes, she could just peek over the bottom lip of the small window in the door. There had always been a guard before, but now she could see no one.

Genevieve felt her dirty tresses until she found two of the three hairpins she remembered using the last time she did her hair.

She removed the hairpins, bent them, and slipped her arms through the bars in the window. If she stood on her tiptoes, she could barely touch the top of the lock that secured the door. She tried to get a better position, but her arms weren't long enough.

"Jean-Luc?"

"Hmm?" Like most of the prisoners, Jean-Luc spent the majority of the day half asleep.

"Can you find me something to stand on?"

"Why?"

Genevieve pulled her arm back into the room and showed him one of her hairpins. "If I can reach the lock, I might be able to pick it."

* * *

Schroeder listened to the exploding artillery shells. They were getting closer. He looked out the window, taking in the port he'd helped destroy so it couldn't be used by his enemy. He turned away, not proud of his thorough work. He limped down the hallway, glanced at his watch, and began limping more quickly. He had reports from patrols to listen to. Then would come the planning. He wasn't sure the fort would hold out another day, but it was his duty to try.

Schroeder heard the footsteps behind him and looked over his shoulder, annoyed to see Weiss approaching him.

"Heil Hitler!" Weiss saluted.

Schroeder responded with a standard military salute, despite the month-old order requiring the army to adopt the Nazi salute. He noted Weiss's narrowed eyes, but Schroeder knew Weiss could do nothing. The two of them were doomed to surrender or death. "What is it, Rottenführer?"

"The prisoners, sir."

"What about the prisoners?" Schroeder continued walking, motioning for Weiss to join him.

"I think it unwise for them to fall into our opponents' hands. Several of them have killed German soldiers, and most of them have skills that could hurt the Reich should they be released and later infiltrate our lines."

Schroeder stopped. "What are you suggesting?"

Weiss's response was immediate. "Execution. Now."

"How?"

"I'll take care of it." Weiss displayed the submachine gun he was carrying.

Schroeder shook his head and walked away. "We're running out of ammunition, and you wish to waste it on our prisoners?"

"A knife, then."

"I'll consider it. Right now I need you to probe the Allied line. I think they've moved closer overnight. Take a squad and report back to me."

Weiss looked like he was about to protest. His assignment was dangerous, and Weiss had little experience with reconnaissance. Weiss had little experience with anything other than repressing civilians. The Gestapo man opened his mouth, but just then, a large shell hit, temporarily deafening them both. Schroeder motioned for him to get on his way, but something in the way Weiss set his face made Schroeder suspect that if Weiss returned, he would find a different officer to ask about the prisoners or act on his own volition.

Schroeder tried to pay attention to the reports. Most of the news was bad, most of the estimates spotty. He hurried through his orders to the units still fighting to hold the area around the fort, but his mind was on other things. Schroeder hated Weiss. He hated his arrogance, hated how he was sidetracked by things of secondary importance, hated his obsession with vengeance. Most of all, Schroeder hated that Weiss's obsession was distracting him too from his duty. That wasn't the end of it though. Schroeder had developed a soft spot for Agent Olivier. She was young, clever, loyal, and talented. It seemed a pity to let Weiss destroy her, especially when saving her would infuriate Weiss like little else would.

* * *

Standing on the emptied latrine bucket, Genevieve could reach the lock, barely. She'd almost succeeded in opening the lock twice now, but then her hands or her arms would shake with the strain of holding them in their precise position, and she would lose ground. She rested her arms for a minute before making her third attempt.

Genevieve was sure the padlock would open this time and forced her arms to be steady. She used the pin in her left hand, bent at a ninety-degree angle, to apply gentle pressure on the lock, and the pin in her right hand, bent at a much shallower angle, to carefully push each pin up to the shearline. Her previous attempts had given her a feel for the lock, and she pushed the first three pins into position within seconds. She felt the fourth slide into place then pushed the final pin up and felt the lock opening. "I've got it," she whispered to Jean-Luc. But before she could remove the lock, she heard the footsteps of a guard as he descended the stairs outside their jail.

Crushed, Genevieve sat on the floor next to Jean-Luc. She heard the man outside their cell fiddle with the lock before removing it from the door and opening the dungeon.

"All female prisoners are to come with me," the guard said.

Genevieve stared at the German soldier for a few seconds before realizing that meant her. Of the fourteen prisoners, she was the only woman.

"You'd better go," Jean-Luc said. His voice was dry and weak, defeated.

"Look after Gerard for me?"

Jean-Luc nodded.

Genevieve slipped her hairpins to Jean-Luc, hoping he would know how to use them, and forced herself to her feet. She was dizzy again. When she reached the door, the guard grabbed her arm and yanked her from the cell. He locked the door behind him and pulled her up several flights of stairs and down several hallways.

Her escort slowed and knocked on a door. It wasn't until the door opened that she realized she'd been in the room before. Schroeder was there with his table of maps.

"Thank you; you may return to your post," Schroeder said, dismissing the guard.

Genevieve looked down at her skirt and noticed the bloodstains from where she'd wiped her hands after treating Browning's wound. She was sure her hair was a mess, and she knew her skin was filthy, but she tried to keep an impassive face as she met Schroeder's gaze.

"Prison does not agree with you, mademoiselle."

"No."

"I have a different prison for you. Someday, you may thank me." Schroeder opened the office door and looked into the hallway. Then he grasped her arm and led her from the room, stopping midway through the corridor and unlocking a small closet. "Inside, mademoiselle."

She opened her mouth to question him, but he shook his head. She found a spot on the floor of the closet and waited. She wasn't sure what was going on, and her head hurt too much for her to care. She heard Schroeder locking the closet then felt the key when he slid it under the door toward her.

Genevieve's mind wandered as she waited in the closet, then the sound of an exploding shell would bring her back to her current situation. She thought she'd been waiting two or three hours when she heard the sound of running boots striking the ground in the hallway, accompanied by shouts in German. Not long after, she heard two voices she recognized.

"Schroeder!" Weiss's voice boomed down the hallway, full of rage, devoid of deference.

She heard the tell-tail limp of Schroeder's footsteps as he walked past the closet.

"Schroeder, where is she?" Weiss yelled again.

Schroeder's footsteps paused. "Your Führer has demanded we hold Marseilles as long as we can. Will you disregard the fort's defenses and your orders so you can take revenge on your enemy's girlfriend?"

"I won't let her escape again."

"Get back to your post. Now!" Schroeder ordered.

"No," Weiss said. "I'm sick of obeying your orders. You are a traitor to the Third Reich—"

"And you are a disgrace to the German military tradition," Schroeder cut him off.

There was silence for a few seconds, then Genevieve heard a gunshot. She gasped in astonishment and put her hand over her mouth. She had no idea who had shot whom.

It was hours before she heard anything else. The noise was faint at first then grew louder as what sounded like a small army ran past the closet. She couldn't make out any of the words they spoke. It wasn't until the third time she heard dozens of boots tromping down the hallway that she recognized a few words and that they were French.

She tried to speak, but her voice was too weak to carry over the sounds of the fort. She hammered on the door, and after a few seconds, she received a response.

"Hello?"

Genevieve slid the key under the door. "Please let me out."

When the door opened, she gazed past the rifle aimed at her and up to the face of the soldier cautiously studying her, then to the emblems on his uniform. He was a member of the Régiment de tirailleurs Algériens. French Algerian Troops were liberating the fort.

"I was a prisoner." She tried explaining, but her voice wouldn't cooperate. The Algerian lowered his weapon and offered her his canteen. She made sure it contained water then gulped at least half of it. "Thank you. Have they surrendered?"

"Mostly."

When she handed the canteen back, the soldier helped her to her feet.

"Come with me, mademoiselle." He offered her his arm and led her to the fort's courtyard.

"Have you found the other prisoners?"

She was concerned about Browning; he needed medical attention at once.

The soldier pointed to an officer. "I haven't seen any, but he may have information for you." The man nodded politely and returned to his duties.

Genevieve headed toward the officer, but as she walked past a wall and her view of the courtyard opened up, she halted and counted. Thirteen. It should have been fourteen. Her vision blurred as tears filled her eyes, and she lost what little strength the Algerian's water had given her, sliding to the ground. Her thirteen prison mates, the men whose fate she had almost shared, were lying in the courtyard dead, including Jean-Luc and Browning. Each had his hands tied behind him and a bullet hole in the back of his head.

* * *

Genevieve spoke with an Algerian tirailleurs officer, a leader in the FFI, and an American OSS agent. Her information given and her identity verified, she was told she could leave Fort Saint-Nicolas. Physically, she left. Emotionally, she didn't know if she would ever really leave it behind. On the way past the destroyed Vieux Port, she passed a group of German troops who'd been rounded up with the fort's surrender. They were being disarmed and processed prior to being sent to POW camps. Schroeder was among them. She watched him for a while, and then he noticed her and met her eyes. She nodded her thanks and mouthed "*merci.*" He smiled at her. His war had come to an end, and he seemed relieved.

That evening, Genevieve went back to Browning's apartment. It was closer than her old apartment, and there was food there. She ate without tasting the food, bathed without feeling the water. Marseilles was free, but Genevieve was numb.

CHAPTER THIRTY-EIGHT

WEISS

Monday, August 28

GENEVIEVE WOKE TO THE SOUND of a revolver being cocked. When her eyes flew open, she saw the gray metal inches from her face.

Weiss took a step back and sat in an armchair a few feet from the sofa Genevieve was lying on. She'd fallen asleep on her stomach and remained as she was, as if frozen, while she gazed at her Gestapo nemesis. He was wearing civilian clothing. His right arm was in a sling; his left arm held his weapon, aimed at her. "You should know by now, Genevieve, that I don't give up easily."

"How did you find me?"

"I followed you. It was easy to escape from the medics." Weiss sneered at her. "I did a better job than Schroeder's tails, but you weren't being very careful, were you?"

Genevieve had been too weary to watch for tails. After all, Marseilles was liberated, and she'd thought Weiss was dead. "Did Schroeder shoot you?"

"Not fatally."

Genevieve looked at the revolver, wondering why Weiss hadn't shot her in her sleep. "What do you want?"

"I want Lieutenant Eddy."

"I don't know where he is. I haven't seen him in more than a month."

Weiss smiled. Genevieve had seen that smile before. He was about to inflict pain on someone, and he was going to enjoy it. "Then even without the use of my right arm, I shall take my revenge on you."

Genevieve forced her mouth to move. "Why do you hate Peter so much?"

Weiss stood. His eyes never left her face; his weapon never moved from her body. "Because he outsmarted us in Calais, and then he outsmarted us in Basseneville. Several of my associates are dead because of him, and I've been taken prisoner not once but twice now, although the latter time was more your fault." Weiss turned his head sideways and looked at her, his evil grin returning.

"He could have killed you in Normandy."

"Yes, and I'm sure he'll wish he had if he ever finds out what happened to you. But I doubt he will. No one will recognize your corpse, not after I'm finished with you." Weiss gestured in the direction of the fort. "I owe Schroeder my thanks. Killing you here will be much more satisfying than executing you with all the other prisoners would have been."

"How did you find us in Basseneville?" Genevieve was doing her best to stall him, and he took the bait.

"We scoured Calais. We eventually discovered the work your brother was involved in. None of the descriptions we had of him were very detailed, but we gathered enough clues that Tschirner recognized him when we saw his picture." As Weiss elaborated, he lowered his weapon a few inches, too busy gloating to keep it pointed at Genevieve. "Then we received a tip from the neighbor of the couple who hid you in Rouen. Once we arrived and Tschirner questioned your benefactors—oh yes, they're dead now—it was a simple matter to track you down. Tschirner was deeply disappointed that he wasn't able to question your brother himself, just as I am going to be very put out that I have only you and not Lieutenant Eddy."

"Did you learn much about my brother?"

Weiss nodded. "Enough."

"Then you shouldn't be surprised that he always slept with a pistol under his pillow." Genevieve gripped Browning's spare handgun underneath her pillow and pulled the trigger. The bullet struck Weiss in the forehead. "And his sister learned to follow his example," she said to the corpse.

Genevieve sat up, leaving her weapon under the pillow, but she didn't have the strength to stand. The tremors started in her hands then moved up her arms and into her chest, where they became sobs. She covered her face with her hands and let the tears come. She hadn't wanted to kill anyone, not even a man who'd once tortured Peter and then executed unarmed prisoners at the fort.

"Father in Heaven, forgive me," she whispered into her hands.

* * *

Later that morning, after reporting Weiss's visit and death to the FFI, Genevieve went to number 3, rue Gabrielle. The US Army had set up its intelligence headquarters there, and she had an appointment with an OSS colonel, arranged the day before at Fort Saint-Nicolas. She walked up the long flight of marble stairs to the second floor and asked a guard for directions.

"Excuse me, an agent at Fort Saint-Nicolas told me to report to Colonel Knudson today. Where is his office?"

The guard directed her down the hall, and she knocked on the door when she arrived.

"Come in," a distinctly American voice answered.

It looked as if the office was just being set up. A few suitcases—Genevieve suspected they were radios—sat in one corner. Cardboard boxes were stacked along one of the walls, and miscellaneous articles of clothing and a few weapons were scattered about the rest of the room.

"Colonel Knudson?"

His head appeared from behind a pile of boxes, and he grinned when he saw her, causing several wrinkles to form around the edges of his eyes. "I hope you'll excuse my mess, mademoiselle. I only arrived a few hours ago." He stood. His uniform, in contrast to his office, was immaculate. "Please make yourself at home." He moved an open box of files from a chair and gestured for her to be seated. "And give me your name."

"Would you like my real name or my alias?"

"Both."

"Colette Bertrand, born Genevieve Olivier."

"Ah, sent over from the fort?" Knudson turned toward his boxes, looking at the numbers written on their sides.

"That's correct, sir."

Knudson located the box he was searching for and shifted the boxes on top of it to other piles. He opened it and thumbed through a stack of files until he found the one he wanted. "Colonel McDougall sends his regrets that he can't be here personally. Marseilles was liberated a month earlier than expected."

"I'm glad. I don't think I would have survived another month." *I barely survived another night.*

Knudson sat behind his desk and flipped through the file. "Yes, we had an office pool as to whether the Germans would shoot all their prisoners if they couldn't send them off to concentration camps. I'm happy to report that with your survival, I've lost a week's wages, and I've never been happier to lose." Knudson looked up and smiled again. "McDougall filled me in on the circumstances of your mission." Knudson slid a paper across the desk so she could see it. None of the dates had been filled in, but there, in front of her, was her US visa.

"Thank you, sir," Genevieve said, hoping he could hear her sincere gratitude.

"Now you just need your lieutenant back in one piece, and you can both live happily ever after."

She felt a blush warm her cheeks. "I didn't know OSS colonels were such romantics."

"Most aren't. I'm an exception. I truly hope everything works out for you."

"Do you have any news of Peter?" she asked, eager to hear anything about him but worried there might be bad news.

"Nothing recent. There's a letter for you. McDougall asked me to pass it along." Knudson took an envelope from the file and handed it to her. "Eddy's not under my jurisdiction right now—like Colonel McDougall, I just work in France. An SOE major wanted some Americans for his team, and we loaned him Lieutenant Eddy and everyone else he requested. I don't know how long he'll be in the field, but I can guess where his team will end up when they're finished. I'm authorized to give you leave for as long as you'd like. Or I can set you up as a nurse's aide in Bari."

"Bari?"

"Italy. There's an OSS headquarters there, and I think that's where your Lieutenant Eddy will end up." Knudson smiled, his grin slightly mischievous, reminding her of Peter.

"Thank you, sir. I'd like to go to Bari."

* * *

While Genevieve waited for the car that would take her to the airfield, she opened her letter from Peter.

Wednesday, August 2, 1944

Dearest Genevieve,

We'll be leaving soon, so this letter will have to be short. And it will probably be read by about twenty censors, but I don't want to pass up what could be my last chance to tell you I love you. I love everything about you. I love your smile. I love the way you laugh and the way you sing. I love that you're beautiful but don't seem to know it. I love your kindness, and I love your goodness. Most of all, I love the way you make me feel: more alive, more content.

Your inner strength is a wonder. I'm in awe of your ability to be pushed beyond the point where most mortals would give up and yet you keep going. And you keep me going too.

No matter how long this war lasts, I'm going to find you when peace comes, even if I have to walk all the way across mainland Europe and then swim the English Channel. I don't care how long it takes or how many suitors you have by then☐I'm going to come back for you and convince you to marry me. And then I'm going to spend the rest of my life making you happy.

I'll be praying every day that I can hold you again soon.

All my love, Peter

Genevieve reread the letter a few times, wondering what Peter would think of her now that she had Weiss's blood on her hands. It took her a few minutes to realize that Peter too had killed in self-defense and in battle. She squeezed her eyes shut, feeling warm tears creep from the corners of her eyes. She didn't think she'd been wrong to kill Weiss, and deep down, she knew Peter would love her anyway. Still, she hoped she would never have to do anything like it ever again.

CHAPTER THIRTY-NINE

KIDNAPPERS AND WIRETAPPERS

Friday, September 1
Bucharest, Romania

PETER WASHED THE LAST PLATE from breakfast and handed it to Fisher so he could dry it. They'd been in Bucharest for nearly a week, staying in Iuliana's small home. She'd started calling everyone by their first name, and for the most part, it had worn off on the men. But with Fisher, it had gone the other way around, and Iuliana was now calling him Fish.

During their stay, they'd found a dozen men and women from Vasile's list, and ten of them had agreed to keep in touch with the British. Most of them would eventually recruit others to assist them, so Jamie's spy ring was well on its way to success. The wounded back in Scorțeni were stable or improving, and the other members of the team had mostly recovered from the roughing up Condreanu had given them.

But not everything was going so well. The German Army hadn't left at the Romanian king's request. Instead, they'd brought in Generalleutnant Rainer Stahel, fresh from his efforts to smash the Warsaw uprising. Reports were rampant of Romanian and German troops fighting each other north of Ploiești. The team had managed to avoid death in the Nazi carpet bombing of Bucharest, but they knew staying in Romania much longer was a bad idea.

Anatolie had been gone for more than a week. Despite their best efforts, no one had been able to track down Eliade. They'd found clues, followed up on leads, and questioned every source they could find, but Eliade, it seemed, had disappeared, and Anatolie Ionescu along with him. Krzysztof had worked with Cairo to postpone their extraction until September second, but that was tomorrow. They were running out of time.

"He might have fled to Germany." Iuliana sat at the kitchen table, her arms folded on the tabletop, her chin resting on her forearm. "The way the

Communists have been acting, Germany would be the safest place for him."
Three days after the coup, the Romanian Communists had suddenly taken
credit for it. The Red Army, disregarding its earlier promises to leave Bucharest
unoccupied, had marched through the city two days before, behaving like
conquerors and forcing the team to keep a very low profile.

Krzysztof put his hand on Iuliana's shoulder. He'd spent most of the last
week heading the search for Anatolie. Privately, Peter had heard Krzysztof
confess frustration at the search's failure, but around Iuliana, he remained
optimistic. "We'll find him."

Peter heard iron-shod heels strike the cobblestone street outside the Ionescu
townhome. He looked out the window and saw a young locotenent approach
the door. "Incoming. Romanian junior officer."

Jamie answered the door when the officer knocked, spoke a few words with
him, then let the young man leave. He closed the door and turned around with
an envelope in his hand. "He had a letter for you, Iuliana. A colonel he has never
seen before ordered him to bring it to this address."

Iuliana's hands trembled as she reached for the letter, her face drawn.
Everyone hoped this would be the lead they needed to find Anatolie. Today
was the last day they could spend in Bucharest. If the letter was a false alarm,
the men would be faced with the difficult decision of leaving without rescuing
Anatolie or of staying without official permission, which would be viewed
as desertion. Peter didn't want to make that choice. If Iuliana hadn't warned
them about the howitzer, he didn't think any of them would be alive. But by
going into the mountains to alert them, Iuliana had unintentionally left her
son open to Eliade's scheme. They all felt a responsibility to find Anatolie.

Iuliana looked up from the paper. "It's from him." No one needed to ask who
she meant. "I'm to meet him at sunset—an address here in Bucharest. He says
he knows I'm being assisted by several men. I'm to come alone—or never see
my son again."

* * *

It was a warm summer evening, but Iuliana felt cold. She reached up to knock on
the door of the Bucharest home, but before her fingers could grip the iron knocker,
the door opened. A Romanian junior officer stood there, and he motioned her
inside. He led her to an upstairs room and knocked on the door for her.

"Send her in." It was Eliade's voice.

Iuliana opened the door, and her escort disappeared down the staircase.

Eliade sat behind a thick hardwood desk. He looked as he usually did:
handsome and conceited, but he also looked on edge, as if he didn't feel completely safe. "You're alone?"

"Yes. Where is my son?"

Eliade motioned her to sit in a chair across from the desk. "First we make a deal. Then you shall have your son."

"I want to see Anatolie first." Iuliana remained standing. She had Krzysztof's handgun tucked into the waistband of her skirt, hidden under her blouse. Sitting would make it less accessible.

"He's not here. And since I hold all the cards, I will dictate the terms of our negotiations. I could have you arrested for treason."

Iuliana flinched. "I'm not a traitor. I just switched sides a little early."

"Romanian troops died because you warned a foreign commando team of their presence."

Iuliana glared at Eliade. "No, Romanian troops died in Scorțeni because you told them they were fighting a detachment of Soviet soldiers. Had they known the truth, men on both sides could have been spared." Iuliana placed her hands on Eliade's desk and leaned toward him. "I want my son back. Where is he?"

Eliade's eyes narrowed. "I had to take him to protect him."

"Protect him? From what?"

Eliade stood and walked around the desk until he was standing next to Iuliana. "From his mother. Major Baker's team is using you, Iuliana. You're going down a destructive path. It will lead you and your son to harm if you're not stopped."

Iuliana spun toward him. "Tell me where my son is!"

Eliade began pacing across the room, staying between her and the door. "You must understand, Iuliana, I'm doing all of this for your own good. Come with me to Vienna. I'll have Anatolie brought to you there."

While his back was turned, Iuliana brought her weapon out and pointed it at him. "I want my son back, now."

Eliade turned. If he was concerned, he hid it well. "If you shoot me, you'll never see Anatolie again. Trust me, the men I left him with will kill him without hesitation should I disappear." He walked toward her slowly. She held her arms steady, but Eliade was right. She couldn't shoot him—not before he told her where Anatolie was. "Iuliana, your only option is to come with me. I plan to leave tomorrow morning. If you agree now, I can have your son brought to the airfield and he can fly to Vienna with us. If you persist in delaying, he'll have to join us later, and with the political and military situation being what it is, later could be a very long time." As he spoke, he took the pistol from her hands. She didn't resist.

Iuliana sat in the chair Eliade had offered her earlier. "Make the call, Dorin." She'd never before called him by his first name. "I'll go to Vienna with you."

She didn't meet Eliade's eyes, looking at the floor instead. He was silent. After awhile, she looked up. His face exuded satisfaction. He was staring at her in a way that made her want to put on several additional layers of clothing, and she quickly looked away. "Please arrange for my son to meet us at the airfield."

Eliade picked up his phone, made the connections, and spoke the request Iuliana was waiting for. "Have the boy at the airfield tomorrow at dawn."

* * *

A few blocks away, Krzysztof spliced together the telephone wires he'd cut earlier that afternoon. "Was the connection adequate?"

Jamie nodded. "He put a call through to Ploieşti and ordered someone to bring Anatolie to the airfield at dawn."

"Did he say which airfield?" There were several in the area. They could split the team up and monitor multiple locations, but that would reduce their chances for success.

"No." Jamie picked up a phone connected to a different line.

* * *

Iuliana told Eliade she'd like to pack some things from her home, and he insisted on escorting her. She stared out the window as one of Eliade's assistants drove, and she hoped the team's plan would work. Fisher was monitoring Eliade's home from the roof of one of the neighboring buildings. Peter was monitoring her home, but Iuliana still felt uneasy. After being mistrusted by so many—Vasile among them—she found it difficult to trust others. What if Eliade tricked them again?

Of two things she was certain: she didn't want to go to Vienna, not with Eliade. And she liked Krzysztof Zielinski more than she thought she could after knowing him only a week and a half. Without his calm, gentle concern and faithful persistence in the search for Anatolie, she didn't think she could have managed the past week.

When they arrived, Eliade had his assistant wait in the kitchen. Eliade followed her through her front room, up the stairs, and into Anatolie's room. The furniture had been rearranged so the four men could sleep there, but she found a few of Anatolie's cold-weather clothes and did her best to ignore Eliade's presence. Then she went into her room, the room she'd shared with Vasile. "Do you have my things from Scorţeni?"

Eliade didn't answer her. When she turned to look at him, his gaze shifted from her to the bed.

Iuliana felt her temper flaring. "I may have agreed to go with you to Vienna, but do not for a moment think my heart holds anything but loathing for you."

"Iuliana, that isn't fair. Everything I've done has been for your own good."

Iuliana stepped back as Eliade stepped toward her. "You've done everything in your power to ruin my life. You destroyed my husband's trust in me and then sent him to his death. You've taken my son from me, and now you're forcing me to Vienna. If I didn't need you to bring Anatolie to me, I would kill you with my bare hands."

Eliade hit her with the back of his hand. It was a hard blow, but it wouldn't have knocked her down if the bed hadn't tripped her. She fell onto the bed, wishing she still had her weapon.

Eliade wasn't finished. "You may not love me, but you will respect me. And you will obey me, or I'll kill your son."

"I think that's enough." Iuliana looked past Eliade to where Peter stood in the doorway, his pistol pointed at Eliade. She'd known he was near but hadn't expected him to appear without a sound.

Eliade's surprise was visible on his face. "Where's my assistant?" Peter had spoken in English, and Eliade had answered in the same language.

"Downstairs, attached to one of the kitchen chairs." Peter pointed to a similar chair in the corner of the bedroom. "Please have a seat, Colonel Eliade." Peter handed Iuliana his pistol, and she pointed it at Eliade as Peter tied him to the chair.

"You won't get away with this." Eliade was back to his usual, confident self. "No matter what the current political climate, I am a Romanian war hero, and—"

"And a kidnapper," Peter cut him off. "And a man responsible for the deaths of several dozen of your own mountain troops. I suggest you save your threats for someone who cares. The only thing I'm interested in hearing from you is where Anatolie Ionescu will be brought for your dawn flight to Vienna."

Eliade's face was more cautious. "How did you know that?"

Peter took his pistol back from Iuliana. "We listened to your telephone call. Your assistant asked the operator to put him through to Ploieşti. Glad you got through; I understand the phones have been a bit off-and-on this week." Iuliana was amazed at how casual Peter sounded, as if it was the most normal thing in the world to tap a telephone on a few hours' notice.

Eliade studied Peter, and his worried expression turned into a sneer. "I know who you are. You're that guilt-ridden, God-fearing American farmer. Condreanu told me all about you. You can't kill me—not if you want the safe return of the Ionescu brat. And you're too squeamish to get the information you need from me yourself."

Peter remained calm. "I think Condreanu made an error in his description of me. It's not his first. He's right; I don't enjoy violence. I remember most of the men I've killed, including the soldiers from Scorțeni. I expect their faces to haunt me for years. They were only following orders, after all; they didn't really deserve to die. You, however, are more of a free agent. If you'd been honest, I wouldn't have had to kill them. So I may not enjoy torturing you, but be assured that your pain will be a comparatively small burden for my conscience to bear."

Eliade was quiet, thinking.

"Name the airfield," Peter ordered.

"I think you're lying."

Peter's eyes were determined. Iuliana had come to think of Peter as a good man, but she didn't think he was bluffing.

"Name the airfield," he repeated.

Eliade sneered as he shook his head in refusal.

Peter hesitated an instant before he took his pistol in both hands, aimed, and shot Eliade in the leg.

Eliade screamed in pain. "You maniac!"

"That was a warning shot. It went through the muscle on the back of your calf. If you keep the wound clean you'll be good as new in a month. The next shot will be in your kneecap, so if you ever want to walk again, I suggest you name the airfield."

Iuliana looked past Peter to the hallway outside her room. Krzysztof and Jamie had just arrived. Eliade looked at Peter, then at the two men in the hall, and knew he'd been beaten. "It's a private airstrip just outside Bucharest. The coordinates are in my left front pocket."

Iuliana took the paper from Eliade's pocket and handed it to the American lieutenant. Peter put his weapon on the bed, and as he reached for the paper, Iuliana noticed the tremor in his hand and the tense set of his jaw.

* * *

Krzysztof finished decoding the radio transmission he'd just received and sat back, unhappy.

"Something bad?" Iuliana asked.

He looked up, surprised she could read his mood so easily. "Do you want the good news or the bad news?"

"Both," Jamie said. "Start with the good."

"I convinced them to use the same airfield as Eliade. Anatolie shows up at dawn, Baker shows up sometime during the day, and we leave tomorrow night."

"And the bad news?" Jamie was pacing along the trail of blood Eliade had left behind when they took him and his assistant down to Iuliana's root cellar.

"You remember that official we were supposed to evacuate? Cairo could never give us a firm yes or no? It's officially a go. We have ten hours to find him and get to the airfield."

While Jamie and Peter began thinking of ways to find their target, Krzysztof tried to contact Baker's portion of the team. The distance wasn't bad, but they were going to have to sneak through the remnants of the German Army and stay invisible to the Soviets. Krzysztof wanted to give them every possible minute.

CHAPTER FORTY

SHOW NO FEAR

THE ROMANIAN OFFICIAL THEY WERE to evacuate, Ioan Davidescu, was not at his primary residence, a large home a few blocks from the palace. Since she spoke the language and knew the city, Iuliana questioned the neighbors and was given two addresses: one belonged to the man's brother, the second to his parents.

Iuliana walked with Krzysztof toward the brother's home. The rest of the team went to the parents' home, Davidescu's most likely location according to the neighbors. She'd expected the home to be deserted, but when they arrived, there was a crack of light in a second-story room. A tall, middle-aged man answered the door not long after they knocked.

"Mr. Davidescu?" Iuliana asked.

"Who's asking?" The man was jumpy, his brown eyes darting from Iuliana to Krzysztof to the long garden path that lay between his front door and the main road.

"We represent the British government. We're here to evacuate you."

"You represent the British government?" His eyes narrowed, and he was clearly not convinced.

"He does." Iuliana nodded toward Krzysztof. "I'm acting as translator. There are others, but they went to your parents' home, thinking you might be there."

Davidescu nodded and led them into his brother's home. They'd been told Davidescu's brother was a civil servant. Judging by the quality of the furniture, he was a senior civil servant. A lean gray cat sat on one of the elegant chairs.

"Do you have any family that will be coming with you?" Iuliana asked.

"No, just me."

"Are you ready? We have limited time."

"I have a bag packed upstairs. We can leave as soon as I fetch it."

Iuliana nodded, relieved. They still had to meet up with the other men and smuggle Davidescu out to the airfield. They had sufficient time but little extra. Davidescu went upstairs to get his bag. Iuliana glanced at Krzysztof. He was looking at her. He smiled when their eyes met then returned to keeping watch out the window. She studied him for a moment, certain he had been flirting with her, and that thought brought a smile to her face.

Davidescu returned, interrupting her thoughts. "I wasn't expecting someone to come so soon. I only confirmed my intention to defect this morning. Tried to earlier, but the phones were down."

"We were already in Bucharest."

Davidescu offered her a seat. "Doing what?"

"Preparing for the inevitable. We've contacted a few people who can provide information without drawing suspicion should the Communists give us trouble."

"Someone's coming!" Krzysztof said from the window. "Red Army troops." He grabbed his rifle and positioned himself between the door and Iuliana.

"You led them to me." The accusation in Davidescu's voice was clear.

"I promise we have nothing to do with the Communists. We took every precaution to ensure we weren't followed." She didn't have time to say anything else. Two Soviet soldiers kicked in the door and rushed inside.

They stared at Krzysztof's rifle but didn't lower their own weapons. Everyone in the room was tense. Then a third man, an officer, kicked open the kitchen door. Iuliana and Krzysztof looked in the direction of the noise, and the second Krzysztof was distracted, one of the enlisted men lunged at him. Krzysztof pulled the trigger, but his shot didn't hit anyone. The other soldier, a muscular man with blond hair and a beard, swung the butt of his rifle into Krzysztof's head and shoved him against a wall. Krzysztof looked groggy as the Russian pulled his rifle from his hands and frisked him.

The guard didn't find anything of interest, so he tied Krzysztof's hands behind his back and moved on to Iuliana, tying her hands in front of her and pushing her into the same wall a few feet from Krzysztof. He was rough, joking with his comrade in Russian as he held her fast. She tried to twist away, but the guard grabbed her more firmly and laughed with the other enlisted man. The officer was indifferent to his men's bad behavior.

"Stop that now." Krzysztof took a step toward her, and though he spoke in English, it was impossible not to know what he was saying. The rage in his narrowed blue eyes and the growl in his voice cowed the soldier, who backed away, turning from Iuliana to Davidescu.

Before the Soviet soldier reached him, Davidescu pulled a pistol from his pocket and aimed it at the officer. In less than a second, the third soldier used the butt of his rifle to knock the gun from Davidescu's hand. The pistol fell to the floor, landing on the rug. Iuliana brought her hands to her mouth to stop a scream. The motion made the man bring his rifle around, but he didn't shoot.

The Soviet officer stepped toward Davidescu. He was about the same height as the Romanian, with brown hair and a visored cap. "Why did you attempt to shoot me?"

Davidescu cradled his injured hand in his other arm. His face had paled, and his voice shook as he spoke, whether from rage or pain, Iuliana couldn't detect. "I was defending my home and my guests. I should be the one questioning you. What is the meaning of this intrusion? Your government promised there would be no Soviet troops in Bucharest. We are your allies now, not your subjects."

"Why are my allies trying to shoot my men and me?" The officer stared at Davidescu with one eyebrow raised. "Take him into the other room," he ordered the man who'd held Iuliana. "Ally to ally, we can discuss your mistrust further. Speransky, watch Mr. Davidescu's guests. They need to remain until I've had a chance to chat with them."

"Yes, Politruk Tokarev."

The officer followed Davidescu and his man into the kitchen, kicking Davidescu's cat along in front of him and closing the door behind him.

"What did they say?" Krzysztof's lips barely moved.

Iuliana had forgotten Krzysztof knew almost no Romanian. He was watching Speransky, who'd sat down and was staring at his two charges. "Davidescu told them we're allies now, but he didn't seem to care," Iuliana whispered. "He knew Davidescu's name without an introduction. I don't know who Davidescu is, but he must be important if the Soviets are looking for him this quickly."

Speransky ordered them to remain silent. In the absolute stillness of the house, it was easy for Iuliana and Krzysztof to hear exactly what type of conversation the two *allies* were having. Few words were used. Instead, thuds, cracks, and cries of pain filled the air.

* * *

They listened to Davidescu's cries for a half hour, with Speransky's rifle pointed at them and their backs against the wall. Krzysztof watched Iuliana's face grow paler with each cry of anguish coming from the other room. Krzysztof suspected he'd be next, and the sneer on the bearded guard's face when he came through the door confirmed his fears. Krzysztof knew he'd been lucky on the mountain when Condreanu had been battering other members of the team. He didn't think he'd get off so lightly this time. The Fascists and the Communists—they both knew a thing or two about inflicting pain.

He leaned toward Iuliana's ear. "Don't lose hope, Iuliana."

She looked from him to the guard now at Krzysztof's side then back again. He looked into her eyes, and hope was not one of the emotions he found.

Straining against the guard tasked with bringing him to the other room, Krzysztof leaned toward her again, and this time he kissed her. He felt the curve of her lips, the warmth of her mouth, felt her tears spilling from her eyes onto both of their cheeks. He felt her kissing him back and the guard pulling them apart. He fought against the Russian soldier, struggling for each second as a drowning man struggled for air. He heard all three Russians yelling at him, and still he lingered in his kiss. The last thing he felt was a rifle butt crashing into the back of his head. The last thing he heard was Iuliana's cry as he fell to the floor. Then everything went black.

He wasn't unconscious for long. He could feel the scratch of the rug's bristles against his forehead and the massive pain originating in the back of his skull. Iuliana called to him, but he couldn't find his voice to reply. Tokarev barked out orders, and the two enlisted men grabbed his arms, still tied behind his back. They pulled him toward the kitchen, where he was sure he'd be tortured. Davidescu would have told the Russians he wasn't Romanian, so he had some explaining to do. It was probably too late to divert all bad feelings between the Western Allies and the Soviet Union, but perhaps he could convince them to spare Iuliana.

Davidescu was tied to one of the kitchen chairs, his head slumped forward, unconscious. Blood trickled from his nose and from gashes along his forehead and cheeks. As they dragged Krzysztof to another of the high-backed chairs, his boot stepped on what felt like a small pebble. Looking back after he'd been forced into the chair, he recognized the small object as a piece of a tooth.

Once Krzysztof was tied to the chair, Speransky went back to guarding Iuliana, and Tokarev strutted into the room. He stared down at Krzysztof, who looked away. *Don't show them your fear*, he told himself.

Tokarev addressed him, but it was in a language Krzysztof didn't know. He thought it was Russian. A second question seemed to be in Romanian. The next time he spoke, it was German. "What languages do you speak?"

"I speak a little German. We can communicate in that language." Krzysztof kept his eyes on the floor.

"Davidescu said you were British. Are you?" Tokarev asked in English.

Krzysztof glanced at the unconscious Romanian then down at the floor again, wondering how much Davidescu had told the Soviets.

Krzysztof felt something on his chin, and his head was forced back. Tokarev had placed a baton under his jaw to force eye contact. "I am only asking a simple question. You do speak English, don't you?"

"Yes."

"And are you British?"

"England is my home now." Krzysztof wondered if the man would catch the distinction. His eyes wandered over to the door.

"She's very beautiful. I have the power to spare her."

Krzysztof looked into the man's face. He didn't trust him, but he didn't have many options. "What are you proposing?"

Tokarev paced the floor, always staying within Krzysztof's eyesight. "Mr. Davidescu informed me that you're setting up a chain of spies to work against the Communist Party. Imagine that. Our own allies working against us."

"Perhaps Mr. Davidescu is lying."

Tokarev stopped pacing, considering it for a moment. "I think the possibility of him lying to me is small. For the sake of our conversation, let's assume he's telling the truth. I would want the names of your other contacts."

"And *if* Mr. Davidescu was telling the truth, and *if* I have other contacts, what would you offer in exchange?"

"In exchange, you would be released. The woman too. All as soon as we confirm the veracity of your list." Tokarev began pacing again.

"And Mr. Davidescu, what will become of him?" Krzysztof asked.

Tokarev glanced at the unconscious Romanian. "He is to remain the guest of my superiors. His fate is not part of our bargain."

Krzysztof watched the man walk back and forth. "What assurance do I have that you'll release us after I give you the list?"

"You shall have my word."

Krzysztof considered the offer. Given time, he was sure the man could drag the same information out of him anyway, and they'd have time. The rest of his team was on the other side of Bucharest, and they were supposed to meet back at Iuliana's home. Peter, Jamie, and Fisher wouldn't suspect anything was amiss for some time yet, and in the meantime, Tokarev could put him on a train to Moscow. Eventually, they'd discover he was Polish, and then they could keep him as long as they wanted and do anything they wished to him. And Iuliana—he didn't want to see or hear her being tortured. She had to be at the airfield by dawn.

Krzysztof didn't want to give the contacts away but thought he might be able to take a lesson from Peter and make up a few names, perhaps accuse Condreanu and Eliade. They were, after all, no allies of the Communists. That they equally disliked democracy was a detail he planned to temporarily forget. "Let her go, and then I'll give you the names."

Tokarev tilted his head to the side, considering the bargain. "I can get the information I want anyway."

"That may be true, but if I were to hold out for a few days, some of my contacts might go into hiding and you'd miss them."

Tokarev considered it. "All right, I'll agree to your changes." He shouted to Speransky, who brought Iuliana to the doorway. "You're being released. Go home."

"But what about Krzysztof?"

"He'll be staying with me awhile longer." Tokarev stood in front of her, his hands clasped behind his back.

"I'd prefer not to leave without my friend. I'll stay until he's released."

"Go, Iuliana, please," Krzysztof said.

"Krzysztof, I can't leave you—look what they did to Mr. Davidescu." Her voice shook, and her cheeks were wet with tears.

"Think of your son. You have to go." Krzysztof wasn't sure how strong her feelings for him were, but he knew Anatolie had to come first. Slowly, she nodded her agreement.

Tokarev smiled. "Good. Karpovich will escort you to the train station."

"No." Krzysztof remembered the bearded man's earlier treatment of Iuliana and knew she'd be safer alone.

"Fine, Speransky will escort her."

"I don't think she needs an escort. Just let her go," Krzysztof said.

Tokarev's eyes narrowed, and he slapped his baton into his left hand. "I have compromised with you enough."

"It's all right; I'll go." Iuliana reached out and brushed her fingers along Krzysztof's cheek. He smiled at her caress, doing his best to hide his fear. She turned and nodded at Speransky. "Just take me to the main road."

The two left.

As soon as the door closed, a smile crept onto Tokarev's face. He grabbed the collar of Krzysztof's shirt and yanked, sending the top button to the floor. Then he dug a finger under Krzysztof's shirt until he found the chain with his military identification tag. "Krzysztof Zielinski? That's not a very English name, is it? I'd hesitate to torture a citizen of the British Empire, but I have no such scruples when it comes to interrogating Poles. You will give me the names now."

"I'll give you the names when Speransky returns, and not before." Krzysztof set his jaw.

Tokarev's eyes narrowed. He brought his baton up again, weighing it in his hand, carefully considering its use.

CHAPTER FORTY-ONE

OUT OF THE SHADOWS

SPERANSKY GRIPPED IULIANA'S UPPER ARM, pulling her down the road, opposite the way she and Krzysztof had come. "This isn't the way to the train station," she said.

Speransky pursed his lips. "It's a short cut." But the road terminated at a dead end. A brick wall blocked their progress, and thick hedges lined the street on either side.

Iuliana sighed with irritation. She was in a hurry. If she could find Peter or Jamie or Fisher, perhaps they could do something for Krzysztof while she went to the airfield, but she had a sinking feeling in her stomach that with every minute she delayed, another of Krzysztof's bones would be broken before he was freed. "I can find my way from here. I lived in Bucharest for almost four years."

"Then you should know that no one lives at the end of this road. No one will be able to hear you scream."

She shrieked anyway as Speransky pulled a knife from his side and brought it toward her. She screamed again when a dark figure stepped out from the shadows with a knife of his own and placed his left hand over Speransky's face, pulling it back to expose a larger target for the blade in the figure's right hand. She felt the spray of blood and screamed again as Speransky's body dropped to the ground.

Iuliana backed away, her hands shaking and her breath coming in gasps. She turned to run but felt a firm hand on her arm, stopping her. "Please let me go!" she sobbed.

* * *

Krzysztof tested the cords that tied him to the chair. They had not magically loosened in the last five minutes. Tokarev sat in another chair, his legs crossed, one ankle swinging impatiently. Krzysztof thought of a few more Romanian-sounding names and tried the ropes again. They were still snug. He looked around Davidescu's kitchen, noting, not for the first time, the unwashed plate on the table and the small pile of papers in the corner. There was no sign of Davidescu's cat.

Davidescu moaned, and though his eyelids fluttered, they remained closed.

"Can't you let him loose? He's still bleeding—he needs to lie down," Krzysztof said.

Tokarev yawned, shifted his baton from one hand to the other, and looked at his watch. "What will you offer in exchange? Will you give me your names now?"

Krzysztof shook his head. "I'll give you the names when Speransky returns and I'm confident he's treated Iuliana honorably."

"Then Davidescu remains in his chair."

A firm knock on the door brought Tokarev to his feet. Karpovich looked at his officer for instructions. Tokarev said something in Russian, and Karpovich left the kitchen.

Krzysztof couldn't see the front door from where he was tied in the kitchen, but he thought it was too late for an innocuous visitor. *Who else is walking into a trap tonight?* He heard Karpovich question Tokarev from the other room. Tokarev swung his ankle a few times before replying.

Karpovich didn't answer. Instead, he flew into the kitchen as if he'd been chucked in from the other room. When Peter walked into the kitchen, his pistol pointed at Tokarev and a streak of blood across his right sleeve, Krzysztof thought perhaps Karpovich had been thrown.

Jamie entered immediately after Peter and gave Karpovich an order in Russian, and Karpovich stayed on the floor and placed his hands on his head. Jamie untied Krzysztof and used the rope to immobilize Karpovich. Krzysztof stood and rubbed his wrists where they'd been bound, working the blood back into his hands.

"What is the meaning of this?" Tokarev was pale.

"NKVD." Jamie fingered the emblems on Tokarev's uniform and studied his red and blue cap. "I would not have expected you to arrive so quickly."

"My reinforcements will also arrive quickly. You'll find yourself surrounded within minutes. I suggest you surrender to me before you're killed in the firefight."

Jamie's lips pulled into an amused smile. "If by reinforcements you are referring to Speransky, you should reevaluate your position. He won't be joining you again."

"Is he dead?" Tokarev didn't seem concerned.

Jamie nodded.

"And the woman?"

"Rescued," Jamie said.

"Where is Iuliana? Is she all right?" Krzysztof asked.

Peter smiled at him. "A little shaken up and worried about you but otherwise fine. Speransky was ordered to kill her, but he didn't notice me tailing him. She's with Fish now."

"Speransky was not my only reinforcement," Tokarev said, regaining some of his earlier composure.

"Then we will make our visit a quick one." Jamie untied Davidescu.

"Oh, a bullet through our heads and then you'll be gone? Is that your plan?" Jamie smiled and shook his head. "Nonsense; we are allies, remember?"

"Then what?" Tokarev asked.

Davidescu regained consciousness, and Jamie helped him lean on the table, still seated. "A trade. Stalin is an expert negotiator. I suggest we follow your leader's example."

Tokarev hadn't relaxed, despite Jamie's hint that he would live. "What would our trade consist of?"

Jamie straightened. "You will promise us your silence. And we will exchange prisoners. We are holding a member of the Legion of the Archangel Michael. He commanded Romanian troops in the Crimea and is responsible for a vast number of Soviet casualties. I am confident he will be much more valuable to you than Mr. Davidescu."

"And when will this trade take place?"

"Tomorrow. You and Comrade Karpovich will be our prisoners until then." Tokarev nodded, but he didn't look pleased.

* * *

Peter placed Davidescu's bag in the trunk of the Soviet vehicle, a Ford. Peter smiled at the irony. The car had no doubt been shipped to the USSR as part of the US Lend-Lease Act and then had almost been used to kill members of an Allied team that included several Americans. Now an American driver was commandeering it back.

"How did you get here so fast?" Krzysztof asked.

Jamie finished helping the bound Tokarev into the backseat of the car. "About fifteen minutes after we parted, Peter changed his mind and decided we should follow you. I told him he was being ridiculous—we didn't have time to follow you, not if we were going to make it to the airfield by dawn. He insisted. And I suppose he was right."

Krzysztof turned as if to ask for more details, but Peter just shrugged. Jamie had explained it well enough. "What I'm wondering is why you kissed Mrs. Ionescu in front of Tokarev. You handed him a lever."

Krzysztof was thoughtful, a small smile on his face. "The last man who loved her passed up countless opportunities to show her how he felt. I didn't want to repeat his mistake, not when I might never have another chance."

Iuliana and Fisher had joined them. Peter hadn't meant to ask Krzysztof such a personal question in front of Iuliana, but when he saw the look that passed between them, he doubted he'd harmed their budding romance.

Iuliana turned to Peter. "I would have thought we were on a first-name basis by now, Lieutenant. You've helped save my life at least twice."

Peter smiled. "Do you know where the airfield is, Iuliana?"

"Yes, Peter."

He threw a key to her, and she caught it. "Fish knows where the Maybach's parked. Get Davidescu loaded and head to the airfield. Take Krzysztof too. Jamie and I will round up our prisoners and join you before dawn."

CHAPTER FORTY-TWO

THE AIRFIELD

Saturday, September 2

PETER SQUINTED INTO THE DARKNESS. He was driving the Soviet Ford without headlights because he didn't want to attract any attention. As they approached the airfield, Peter said another prayer. *He's just a little boy, Lord. Please help us get him back to his mother.*

He recognized the Maybach parked under a row of trees and pulled up next to it. Fisher was gone, Peter assumed on reconnaissance. "Everything all right?" he asked.

Krzysztof nodded and helped Iuliana out of the car. "Fish is scouting the area."

"Where shall we leave our Soviet allies?" Jamie asked. "In the boot?"

"In the trunk?" Peter asked. "Yeah, why not, it's only for an hour or two. Then they can have their prize."

Jamie pulled Karpovich from the backseat of the Ford and put him in the trunk. "A trunk is something you put at the end of your bed and pack clothes into."

"A boot is something you wear on your foot." Peter escorted Tokarev to the back of the Maybach and assisted him into its trunk.

They'd left Eliade's assistant in Iuliana's cellar with the promise that they'd call his base before they flew to Bari. Eliade would get no such deal. Krzysztof pulled the Romanian colonel out of the car. Eliade winced as he put weight on his injured leg, but there was no sympathy in Krzysztof's eyes. "Where are they bringing Anatolie?"

Eliade glanced at the multiple firearms pointed at him. "By the hangar."

Fisher returned and motioned toward the airfield. "There's a small 'angar with an even smaller office attached. No one around."

"Good. Stay with the cars and Mr. Davidescu." Peter glanced at the backseat of the Maybach, where Davidescu was awake but making little movement. "The Commies are in the trunks."

"He means the boots." Jamie clapped Fisher on the shoulder and pointed Eliade toward the hangar with a firm push. "Remember, Colonel, things for you can still get much worse than they are now. If you fail to cooperate fully, you will regret it."

* * *

The sun had just inched over the horizon when the car appeared. Iuliana waited with Krzysztof near the hangar. She'd been pacing the last thirty minutes, waiting for the sun to rise. As the car drove closer, she didn't feel any more at ease.

"It's okay." Krzysztof was behind her. He placed one hand on her shoulder and leaned next to her ear. "Try to stay calm."

She nodded and stopped pacing, confining her nervous energy to hand wringing. She couldn't stop thinking about Eliade. She detested him but couldn't deny he was bold and clever. He would have some plan, some trick.

The car stopped ten meters from the hangar. Krzysztof stayed with Iuliana in the building's shadows while Eliade walked out to meet the car. Two men exited, both in civilian clothing. They greeted Eliade with a Fascist salute, making Iuliana think they were members of the Iron Guard. Then Peter and Jamie emerged from the shadows; Peter walked to Eliade's left and Jamie to Eliade's right.

The driver spoke. "I thought the only passengers were the boy and his mother?"

"There has been a slight change of plan," Jamie said. Then he and Peter revealed their pistols and pointed them at the two men, who had no chance to draw their own weapons. "Kneel on the ground and place your hands on your heads." The two men obeyed. "You as well." Jamie gestured at Eliade.

When the three Guardists were disarmed, Krzysztof led Iuliana to the car, and she opened the back driver's side door. Anatolie was there, lying across the backseat, completely still. The car was in the hangar's shadow, so she couldn't see his details. Nor did she initially see the third man, crouched on the floor of the car with a Mauser pointed at her.

When she saw him—and recognized him—she screamed. Krzysztof pushed her to the ground, and a second later, Condreanu's pistol went off. Krzysztof cried out and fell to the dirt. Condreanu dove over the seat of the car and started the engine, driving away with Anatolie still inside.

Peter and Jamie both turned their weapons to the car, aiming for the tires, but the second they pulled their weapons away, Eliade and the other Iron Guard members sprang from the ground and tackled them. Jamie managed to escape from one of them only to find himself in the path of Condreanu's car. With damaged tires, the vehicle had slowed some, but it still hit Jamie's body with a sickening thud. Iuliana watched in horror as Jamie's body lifted off the ground and flew to the other side of the car. Eliade and one of his friends pulled Peter to the ground and tried to wrestle his pistol from him. Krzysztof reached for his weapon with one hand and tried to staunch the blood flowing from his shoulder with the other. And Condreanu drove farther and farther away with her son.

Iuliana stood to run after the car. "Not yet; stay down," Krzysztof said. He shot one of the men attacking Peter. Then Peter managed to break away from Eliade by ramming his elbow into the colonel's face. He shot the third Guardist, who was heading toward Jamie, and the Nazi fell dead.

"Krzysztof, how bad is it?" Peter got to his feet and pointed his weapon at Eliade and the Guardist Krzysztof had wounded.

"Manageable," Krzysztof said, breathing heavily. Iuliana looked at the blood covering his left shoulder; she wasn't sure she agreed.

"Jamie, are you all right?"

Jamie pushed himself to his feet. "I was just hit by a car, so, no, I am most certainly not all right. But I can handle Eliade. Don't let Condreanu get away again."

Peter ran after the car. One of the tires had come off completely, so he gradually closed the distance. When Peter was within ten meters, Condreanu jumped from the car and ran toward the nearby woods. Peter stopped and pulled the screaming Anatolie from the backseat and used a pocketknife to cut the ropes around his wrists. As soon as Iuliana saw her son, she ran toward him.

"Be careful, Iuliana," Krzysztof said.

Iuliana knew it was wise counsel, but her son needed her.

* * *

Peter slammed another clip into his Colt pistol and slowed as he approached the trees. He couldn't see Condreanu anymore and didn't want to run into an ambush. He wiped the sweat from his forehead and tried to control his heavy breathing. He glanced back and saw Anatolie clinging to Iuliana's neck. Krzysztof, Jamie, and the Iron Guard were in the distant shadows; he couldn't make them out.

Peter inched around a tree, keeping his weapon up and his eyes moving, searching for signs of Condreanu. A burst of shots aimed at Iuliana and Anatolie sounded, and Peter caught sight of his quarry and sent two shots toward Condreanu, forcing him to put his head down and stop firing.

Peter glanced at the Ionescus. "Get behind the car, Iuliana!" Condreanu had missed, but he might try again.

He moved toward Condreanu's last location, darting from one tree to the next. He heard footsteps behind him, coming fast. It was Fisher. Peter caught his eye and motioned for him to swing around in the opposite direction, but when they reached their destination, Condreanu had moved on. Like everyone on the team, Condreanu had practiced stealthy exits. Peter thought about ending the chase but doubted Condreanu would leave them alone. He had to be stopped.

Peter and Fisher continued the search, coordinating their movements but not finding Condreanu anywhere. They were a quarter mile from the airstrip when Peter looked at Fisher and saw Karpovich sneaking up behind him, about to hit Fisher over the head with the stock of a rifle. Peter shot the NKVD man an instant before he felt a rush of air and something pummel him in the back of his head.

The blow knocked him to the ground, and Peter fought to stay conscious. Tokarev appeared from behind a tree and pivoted his rifle toward Fisher, shooting him in the torso before Fisher could get a shot off.

"Tsk, tsk." Davidescu reached down and picked up Peter's pistol. "There was no need to shoot poor Karpovich. He wasn't going to permanently harm Fisher, but now the poor private will probably bleed to death."

Peter stayed on the ground—Tokarev's rifle suggested any movement would be quickly punished—and watched Davidescu wash the blood from his face. There were no cuts, no gashes, no bruises. Davidescu met Peter's eyes. "A little makeup, courtesy of the stray cat I took in yesterday morning. Comrade Tokarev did a good job of applying it, did he not? And you did an excellent job carrying my weapons out to the car for me."

"I thought you were working against the Communists," Peter said.

Davidescu laughed. "What better cover could I have? I've been secretly working with Moscow for decades."

Peter's head pounded—a combination of Tokarev's whack and confusion at the sudden turn of events. "Did you really intend to come to England with us?"

"No, but I assumed if your team was still in Romania more than a week after the coup, you were up to something worth my interest. Thus far, I haven't been disappointed."

"And your plans now?" Peter asked.

Tokarev answered. "If you cooperate and provide us a list of your anti-Communist contacts, you may eventually be released. If not, you'll simply disappear."

Peter gritted his teeth to keep from swearing. He glanced at Fisher but detected no movement.

"Come along with us, back to the airstrip," Tokarev said. "I want it to appear that I'm your prisoner rather than the other way around. Your fellow commandos will also be my guests."

Peter walked to Fisher, and neither of his captors stopped him. Fisher's face was twisted in pain, his eyes screwed shut and his hands pressing into a red stain spreading across his stomach. "Keep some pressure on it, Fish."

"We'll leave him be for now, see if he survives the hour." Tokarev used the end of his rifle to prod Peter forward.

Peter felt his jaw clenching. "Will you let me bring him along?"

Davidescu shook his head. "No, he's expendable."

Tokarev led, and Davidescu brought up the rear. Peter marched between them, waiting for something, anything, that would give him an opportunity. As Davidescu wandered closer to his side, Peter slowed his pace. He waited until Davidescu was a yard away then rushed him. Peter's hands found the pistol Davidescu had stolen, and he ripped it way, firing two rounds into Tokarev's body. Then Peter felt Davidescu's muscular arm slip around his neck and felt the blade of a knife press against his larynx. Peter had aimed for Tokarev first, assuming Davidescu had little, if any, military training. Peter had underestimated the Romanian Communist.

"Drop your pistol."

Peter obeyed, but the second he felt the pressure on his neck ease, he brought his hands up, gripped Davidescu's forearms, and pulled the man over his head, throwing him to his back. Davidescu rolled away before Peter could exploit the situation, heading for Tokarev's rifle. Peter found his pistol and fired, missing as Davidescu dove into the lower branches of an evergreen.

Peter ducked behind a large sycamore. His head pounded. He had only one shot left and no spare clips. "Maybe we can compromise. Surrender, and we'll let you go when we fly out."

Davidescu didn't answer. Peter inched his head away from the tree to see what Davidescu was doing and heard a bullet whiz past his ear. Before Davidescu could pull the trigger a second time, Peter shot him in the forehead.

Peter sighed with relief and wiped perspiration from his forehead. He glanced at the dead bodies in front of him and wished it hadn't been necessary to kill so many Communists. Then he turned his thoughts to Fisher. He headed back to his now-unconscious friend and knelt down to bandage the wound for the trip back to the runway.

Peter's hands froze when a twig snapped nearby.

"I was counting, and I believe that was your last shot, wasn't it, Eddy? Stand up and turn around slowly. I want to see the fear in your eyes before I put a hole through your miserable brain."

Peter turned to face Condreanu and death, but he felt strangely calm. The Romanian was about ten feet away—too close to miss, too distant to rush. Peter looked back at Fisher, noticing for the first time that Fisher's rifle was missing, as was Karpovich's. Peter met Condreanu's eyes and tried to keep his face impassive, waiting for the shot.

Condreanu frowned. "If your own death doesn't scare you, perhaps what I'm going to do afterward will. First I'll finish off Fisher. Then I'll pick off Jamie and Zielinski and the little boy. Eliade wants Iuliana, so I can't kill her, but her new life will be miserable."

Fisher's red hair blew in the wind; his face was pale. With stabbing clarity, Peter realized Fisher would have been better off captured in Normandy and sent to a German POW camp.

Condreanu smiled. "Yes, his death will be your fault." He raised his weapon. "That's a fitting thought for you to die with."

Peter heard the crack of a pistol but felt nothing. It was only after Condreanu slumped to the ground that Peter saw Jamie behind him, his own pistol still pointing at the dead locotenent.

"'Then trip him, that his heels may kick at heaven, and that his soul may be as damned and black as hell, whereto it goes.'"

CHAPTER FORTY-THREE

A GOOD MAN

IULIANA WATCHED PETER AND JAMIE bring Fisher to the airfield's office. Soon after, the doctor Iuliana had called arrived and spoke with the men.

"Iuliana, the doctor doesn't have any sedatives, so you might want to take Anatolie outside." Peter was covered in sweat—and blood.

"You should have him look at your neck when he's done digging out bullets," Iuliana said.

Peter felt his neck and looked surprised to see blood on his hand when he pulled it away. "I'm sure it's just a scratch."

Iuliana squeezed Krzysztof's hand before lifting Anatolie and walking past the two Iron Guard prisoners out into the open air. Anatolie buried his head near her collarbone. She hadn't expected to cry again, but she did as Anatolie's arms circled her neck and his hands wrapped themselves in her hair. His tangled hair looked as if no one had brushed it since he was kidnapped, and as she studied his face, it looked like he hadn't been bathed either. He also felt thinner than she remembered, as if he hadn't been getting regular meals. "My poor little boy."

She wandered back to the Ford and dug through Davidescu's luggage until she found a handkerchief and comb; then she used the items and water from a canteen to make Anatolie more presentable. He was clingy and didn't want her to put him down, but even with his lack of cooperation, she finished untangling his hair and scrubbing off the dirt long before Peter came to tell her she could see Krzysztof.

She found him in the hangar, sitting on a blanket between the two single-engine planes the building housed. Peter tried to get Anatolie to join him with a chocolate bar as bribe, but Anatolie shook his head and reached for Iuliana, pressing his face into her neck when she picked him up, as if he was afraid his mother would vanish again. Peter left the chocolate and disappeared.

Iuliana shifted Anatolie's weight and sat down next to Krzysztof. His shoulder was wrapped in fresh white bandages. His face was pale, his hair was damp from sweat, and the soft creases around his blue eyes told her he was in pain. "I'm sorry, Krzysztof."

"It's only temporary. If I keep it clean, it should heal up fine." He reached for her hand with his uninjured arm, and she gladly gave it to him.

She watched Krzysztof. He controlled his breathing by inhaling through his nose and exhaling through his mouth. Exhaustion was written all across his face, but it was a face she had grown to love. She felt a few more tears fall onto her cheeks as she thought about the sacrifices Krzysztof had made for her and for her sweet little son, whose warm breath she could feel on her neck. She put one arm around her son and grasped Krzysztof's hand more firmly—it had been a trying week and a horrifying morning, but now, holding those two people, everything seemed right.

* * *

Peter spent part of the afternoon sitting next to Fisher.

"How do you feel?" Peter asked when Fisher's eyes opened.

Fisher groaned and closed his eyes again. "Rotten. What 'appened?"

"Davidescu was a Communist, so he released the NKVD, and they set up an ambush. I'm sorry, Fish—one of them was about to knock you unconscious and cart us off to Moscow, so I shot him. Then Tokarev shot you—you'd have been better off with a lump on your head."

Fisher opened his eyes again. "I would 'ave done the same thing. And I don't much want to visit Moscow, not with the NKVD. Condreanu?"

"Jamie shot him."

"Good. And Eliade?"

Peter glanced over at the Romanian colonel. "He's tied up. One of his assistants too—the other one's dead. I think we'll leave them for the Red Army."

Fisher chuckled then grimaced.

"Take it easy. That bullet came close to killing you. Maybe Baker will have some morphine from the mountain troops when he gets here."

It took him awhile, but eventually Fisher fell back asleep. Peter was glad the Englishman would make it home again to his mum.

Peter had been second-guessing himself ever since he'd assumed command of Fisher and the other paratroopers in Normandy. As he looked at his friend, he felt sorrow that Fisher was wounded, but the guilt was slipping away. Peter had done the best he could with the information he'd had. And that was all an officer could do, wasn't it? But it also worried him that he didn't feel guilt, as if he'd misplaced part of his conscience. He'd done that before, and finding it again hadn't been pleasant. He spent the rest of the afternoon wondering how he was supposed to feel when he issued orders and the consequences weren't what he planned for.

Baker, Moretti, Luke, and Quill arrived that evening. The team would travel back to Bari in two modified British Mosquitoes. When the first one landed, they loaded the seriously wounded first: Fisher, Luke, and Quill. Baker took the last spot on the plane, because although Krzysztof's shoulder wound was more serious and more recent than Baker's arm wound, having a radio operator on the ground would help the second plane land on the small runway to pick up Jamie, Krzysztof, Moretti, and Peter.

"Wesley, I expect a fresh cup of tea to be waiting for me when we arrive," Jamie said before Baker stepped into the plane.

"I'll do my best, Jamie. Remember Lieutenant Eddy will be in charge for the next few hours. I intend to recommend him for promotion."

"Certainly, Wesley," Jamie said. "I will obey Captain Eddy as faithfully as I have obeyed you."

Baker laughed. "Keep an eye on him, Peter. He's never been very good at obeying orders."

Peter smiled. If someone had pulled him aside before the battle of Scorțeni and told Peter how much he would come to trust Jamie, he wouldn't have believed it. The Shakespeare-quoting Englishman was a good man to work with now that he wasn't pretending to be Condreanu's sidekick. And he'd saved Peter's life.

The first plane moved to the end of the runway, turned, and accelerated into the air. With the wounded safely away, Peter let his thoughts turn toward the future. He couldn't wait to see Genevieve again. When he wasn't near her, he felt like a part of him was missing. It was a part he hadn't known existed until he'd met her, but now that he knew about it, he ached for its return.

Krzysztof finalized the landing of the second plane then put his radio away. "Lieutenant Eddy, sir?"

"Yes?" Peter wondered what was going on. No one on his half of the team had used formal military titles for at least a week.

"I have a favor to ask you, sir." Krzysztof began. Peter noticed Jamie smiling like he already knew what Krzysztof wanted.

Peter looked back and forth between the two of them then saw the feminine silhouette stepping out from the trees, a smaller figure holding the first one's hand.

"I thought you were going back to Bucharest, Iuliana." Peter looked from the two Romanians to Krzysztof, who was smiling hopefully. "I could get into a lot of trouble evacuating civilians without permission."

"You did it in France, sir." Moretti grinned as he lit a cigarette, leaving Peter to think he was the only one who hadn't been in on the plan.

"Genevieve was being hunted by the Gestapo. Her life was in danger," Peter said.

"All we want is freedom, Peter," Iuliana pleaded.

Freedom and a certain Polish paratrooper, Peter thought, feeling a smile pull at his lips. "What's the weight limit on a Mosquito making a trip of this range?"

"How much do your bags weigh?" Krzysztof asked Iuliana.

"Ten kilograms, total," she answered.

"Sir, if the crew is average weight, we'll still be a few kilograms below the limit."

"And if the pilot or navigator is heavier than average? Or if they left without a full fuel load?" Peter asked, not surprised Krzysztof had thought of all of the details.

"If the pilot is overweight, sir, I will gladly leave behind my boots, my equipment, and my left leg if necessary," Krzysztof said.

Peter laughed. He had never planned to turn them down. "All right, you can come."

Their plane landed, and they loaded the equipment. Anatolie tried to play with most of it until Krzysztof put his helmet on the little boy's head. After that, he played with the chin strap. Peter spoke with the pilot and navigator to make sure there was enough fuel to carry them all to Italy before wedging himself into the back of the plane.

As the plane reached altitude, Peter watched Jamie and Moretti, both to his right, fall asleep. For some reason, he couldn't do the same.

"Is something troubling you, Peter?" Iuliana asked. She was sitting on the left side of the plane with Krzysztof and Anatolie.

Peter ran his hand through his hair and sighed. "A little. It was easy to kill Speransky. I don't know if that's because I've changed or if it's because he was about to kill you. And I feel like I should regret shooting Eliade's assistant and killing the Communists, but I don't."

"Maybe that's because it was the right thing to do given your situation."

"Maybe. Or maybe I'm slowly killing my conscience."

Iuliana looked at him closely. "No, I can tell you're still a good man, Peter." Anatolie's head was resting in her lap, and he shifted in his sleep.

"Sorry," Peter whispered. "Didn't mean to wake him."

"Oh, Anatolie will sleep through anything, but I don't want to wake Krzysztof."

The Polish kapral's head rested on Iuliana's shoulder. Peter stifled a laugh and turned away.

"What?" Iuliana sounded puzzled.

"He's not asleep."

"Yes, I am," Krzysztof mumbled. "And I'm having a lovely dream, so don't spoil it."

Iuliana laughed. It was the laugh of a woman in love, and it sounded like music. "Tell me about your dream, Krzysztof."

He sighed sleepily. "I'm in Krakow. The war's over. There are no German troops left in the entire country and no Soviet soldiers either. I'm with my family, and I'm introducing you to all three of my sisters."

"It does sound nice," Iuliana said, leaning her head onto his.

"Mm, but it's just a dream. I don't think the Communists will leave us alone. And I don't know if my older sisters are alive." His voice was raspy.

Iuliana played with Krzysztof's fingers. "What about a different setting? Somewhere without any Nazis or Communists? England, perhaps?"

"It's not quite as good, but it might work." His eyes were still closed. "I do love Poland."

Iuliana's hand moved to touch Krzysztof's lips.

Peter leaned back and tilted his helmet over his face to give them their privacy, and then he drifted off to sleep.

CHAPTER FORTY-FOUR

JUST A SCAB

Sunday, September 3
Bari, Italy

GENEVIEVE WOKE FROM ANOTHER NIGHTMARE, her breathing ragged and her face covered in sweat. She reached for Peter's Purple Heart on the trunk next to her cot and grasped it, trying to replace Weiss's image with Peter's. She missed Peter, ached to see him again, and longed to have him tell her everything was going to be okay. She said a prayer, pleading for assistance to get through another day. Prayer and Peter's Purple Heart were the two things helping her survive the aftermath of Marseilles.

She got ready for work and walked to the hospital, still trying to shake the image of Weiss's face and the hole she'd left in his forehead. She arrived a few minutes before her shift was set to begin and hoped her work would help take her mind off the past.

"I told you it didn't need stitches."

Startled, Genevieve looked along the row of hospital beds, certain she recognized that voice. She saw Peter sitting on a hospital bed, scowling at a nurse as she cleaned an ugly cut on his neck. Genevieve stared. Colonel Knudson had predicted Peter's team would fly into Bari, but she hadn't expected him to show up in her hospital. She walked toward him, passing a few other patients, wanting to get a better view and needing to touch him to make sure he was real. She finally found her tongue. "I thought I told you not to collect any more scars."

Peter jerked his head around. His face showed shock, then he laughed and broke into a grin. "It's not a scar. It's just a scab."

"Hmm, I think this scab is going to turn into a scar," the nurse said, putting a hand on his shoulder to keep him from standing up. "Hold still so I can finish."

Peter frowned at the nurse then turned back to Genevieve. He reached for her hand, and when she drew near enough, he threaded his fingers through hers. He looked at her hair then at her with questioning eyes. "What are you doing here?"

"It's a long story," she said.

"Jamie, what time's the debriefing?" Peter asked.

Genevieve recognized Corporal Nelson and raised an eyebrow at Peter. *Jamie?*

"Oh nine hundred hours. Wesley wants to wait until Luke is out of surgery." Nelson noticed Genevieve and smiled. "So feel free to disappear for a few hours."

Peter glanced at the nurse. She threw her hands up in frustration and halted her work on his neck. Genevieve looked around. The head nurse was probably in surgery, so she couldn't ask for the morning off—but she intended to take it off anyway.

"If skipping out for a few hours will remove this patient from my hospital, by all means, go, Genevieve." The nurse winked at her and moved to another patient.

Peter grinned. "Maybe she's not so horrible after all." He pulled Genevieve into an embrace. "I can't believe you're here."

Genevieve leaned her head on his chest, listening to his heartbeat and feeling his breath on her cheek. Between the excitement and shock of seeing him again and the firm way his arms were holding her, she was having trouble breathing but decided breathing was highly overrated. She took his arm and led him to a nearby supply depot, where they could be alone.

"Don't get me wrong, seeing you in that hospital is the best surprise I've ever had. But how did you end up in Bari?" He used one hand to caress her cheek and ran the other through her hair. "And what did you do to your hair?"

Genevieve wasn't sure where to start. She needed to tell him about her baptism, about her parents, about Marseilles, and about killing Weiss, but none of the words came. She just stared at him and felt tears stinging her eyes.

Peter noticed the tears and wrapped his arms around her. She tried to hold back a sob without success. Peter held her tightly as she fought to gain control of her emotions. She was relieved Peter was safe but still overwhelmed by what had happened in Marseilles.

"That bad, huh?" Peter planted a gentle kiss on her forehead.

She nodded against his chest.

He relaxed his grip on her and leaned back so he could see her face and wipe away her tears. "I'm sorry; I shouldn't have said anything about your hair. You're still gorgeous, *mon beau canari*."

She shook her head. "It's not the hair. I . . . I did an assignment for OSS." She squeezed her eyes shut, afraid she'd start crying again if she said anything else. She couldn't see Peter, but she felt him tense.

"That means I did a poor job protecting you," he said.

"No, Peter, it wasn't your fault. McDougall knew my parents during the last war. They were both spies, and so was my brother. I couldn't just sit by when I was needed, could I?"

Peter put a hand on her shoulder. "Genevieve, one of the biggest reasons I'm fighting is so people like you won't have to. The thought that you were waiting for me, safe and whole, was what kept me going on my last mission."

She snuggled closer to him and looked up into his face, seeing concern in the tense muscles along his jaw. "You aren't angry at me, are you?"

His face softened. "No, I'm just terrified of what could have happened to you."

"A few good things happened to me while you were gone."

"Yeah, we're both still alive. That's something." Peter's fingers played with her hair. "And we're both in Bari."

"Not just that. I was baptized, Peter."

She watched his face break into a smile.

"When?" he asked.

"Just after you left. I wrote you a letter about it, but I don't suppose it's caught up to you yet."

Peter's fingers found her face again, and she felt herself smiling as he said, "That's wonderful news because if I ever convince you to marry me, I'll want you for forever, not just for the rest of your life, especially since spies aren't exactly known for longevity. What would I have to do to convince you to stop spying?"

The last thing Genevieve wanted was another OSS assignment—Peter wouldn't need to convince her to quit; he'd just need to convince someone to discharge her. She slipped her arms around his neck. "Maybe you could start with a kiss."

Peter grinned mischievously as he traced her lips with his finger. Then he slipped his hand through her hair, leaving his fingers on the back of her neck as he gently met her lips. She trembled, and he pulled her closer and kissed her more firmly, leaving her absolutely breathless. It was soothing and exciting, intimate and overpowering, familiar and surprising. She felt the tension and horror of the last few weeks fade, replaced by love and hope and the feeling that somehow everything would be all right again.

"Peter?"

"Yeah?"

"You're very persuasive, but I'd like a little more convincing."

Peter brushed his lips across her cheek next to her ear. "Which part did you need more persuasion on? Marrying me or retiring from OSS?"

"I think I'm ready to agree to both your requests, but first I want another kiss."

Peter glanced at her. "Well, if that's what it takes." Then his mouth found hers again.

She hadn't thought anything could top his previous kiss, but she was wrong. "Peter?" she asked once she'd caught her breath.

"Yeah?"

"I love you."

He answered with another kiss.

AUTHOR'S NOTES

ALL ACROSS THE NORMANDY FRONT, paratroopers like the fictional Fisher, Sherlock, and Grey were scattered behind German lines on D-day, many of them dropped in the wrong locations. I had Peter and Genevieve run into British paratroopers based on geography: the easternmost beaches and drop zones were assigned to the British. Ranville was headquarters for the British 6th Airborne division for a time after D-day, and an artificial harbor at Arromanches became a hub for men and machinery crossing the English Channel, thus a likely port of departure for refugees leaving France for England.

During WWII, it was not uncommon for military groups to use estates like the fictional Dravot Manor in England. London was frequently filled with rowdy foreign troops, and while most Londoners treated their allies with respect, there were some exceptions, represented by Genevieve's landlady. The USO hosted many events for soldiers stationed overseas, but the dance Peter and Genevieve attend is fictional. "O, Canada" was not the official national anthem of Canada until 1980, but it was a popular patriotic song at the time of this novel, often sung in schools and at public events—it would have been a good choice for a seemingly stuck-up English corporal wishing to celebrate an American loss. Hammersmith Hospital, where Genevieve briefly worked, is still in operation today.

In the 1930s, Polish code breakers successfully decrypted German codes. As war approached in 1939, they gave copies of the German Enigma encoding machine to the British and French, thus jump-starting the Ultra project. Ultra, the long-classified British program that broke German codes throughout the war, is credited with shortening the war by several years. The Polish contribution is often overlooked, so I thought it appropriate to have Krzysztof's father work at Bletchley Park, home of the British decryption project. Though the Government Code and Cypher School's name was changed to the Government Communications Headquarters in 1942, most code breakers still referred to it as the GC&CS.

As late as August 7, 1944, Winston Churchill was encouraging General Eisenhower to move the Operation Dragoon target away from the French Riviera. But the Allies did invade southern France and reached Marseilles ahead of schedule, as has been described in this book. Genevieve's work is fictional, but her techniques, the destruction of the harbor, occasional Allied use of shady characters for intelligence sources, and fighting between various Resistance groups are real. Details of German forces in southern France, including naval leadership, *ost* troops, and naval-personnel-turned-infantry, are factual, as is the tension between the Gestapo and the German Army. There were many instances during the war when prisoners were executed shortly before liberation. The execution at Fort Saint-Nicolas is fictional but is based on events that occurred elsewhere.

General information about Romania's leaders and its involvement in WWII is historically accurate. During the evacuation of Bessarabia, Jewish Communists were among those credited with persecuting the fleeing Romanian majority. In the anti-Semitic climate of the time, the newspapers laid most of the blame on the Jews, with significant consequences for how they would be treated when Romania retook the province the next year.

The Dniester River was the prewar border between Romania and the Soviet Union. Most Romanians were happy to join forces with the Germans to take back their previously owned territories, but when the Romanians crossed the Dniester into Transnistria, the war became less about reclaiming stolen property and more about supporting Hitler's regime. Antonescu was loyal to Adolf Hitler until the end, but many Romanians began to sour toward Germany after the huge defeat at Stalingrad. All refineries mentioned in the novel did indeed operate during WWII, and there was an air raid using B-24s (and some B-17s) on the Romano Americana refinery on August 18, 1944, though naturally, Peter, Fish, and Ionescu weren't really there to observe it. It was the second-to-last raid before the refineries were put out of commission. With the loss of the Ploieşti oil fields, the Nazi war machine didn't grind to a halt, but it was severely hampered—so much so that the German Army launched a campaign to take the oil fields back the following spring. They were supposed to retake the oil fields as a birthday present for their Führer, but they were unsuccessful.

Details about the Iron Guard and the Legion of the Archangel Michael are factual, including information about initiation into assassin nests. Romanian Mountain Troops were among the best trained in the Romanian Army, though the battle of Scorţeni that they are involved in during this book is fictional.

King Michael and the democratic political parties he worked with after the August twenty-third coup succeeded in establishing a representative government in Romania, but it was short-lived. Despite agreements made during negotiations, the Soviet Army did not stay out of Bucharest, and Romania was treated more like a conquered nation than an ally. In 1947, King Michael was forced to abdicate by a group of armed Soviet-trained Communists who threatened mass arrests and civil war. Romania and most of Eastern Europe would have to wait until the fall of the Soviet Union to experience freedom once again.

I have tried to describe weapons, airplanes, artillery, and other items as they would have existed at the time of the story. Leaders of nations and any generals or admirals who are mentioned throughout the novel are historical characters. Those with the rank of colonel or below are fictional.

The scripture quoted in chapter twenty-two is 2 Nephi 10:25. Jamie's Shakespearean quotes are from the following plays: *As You Like It*, 3.3.253; *Richard Duke of York*, 2.1.86; *2 Henry IV*, 3.1.5–8; *Troilus and Cressida*, 3.3.144–145,149; *Henry V*, 4.3.61–62; *Julius Caesar*, 3.1.276; *Henry V*, 4.1.286–289; *MacBeth*, 5.5.22; *Henry V* 3.1.7–8; and *Hamlet*, 3.3.93–95.

ABOUT THE AUTHOR

A. L. SOWARDS GREW UP in Moses Lake, Washington, then came to Utah to attend BYU and ended up staying. She wrote most of *Sworn Enemy* while her twin toddlers were sleeping and did most of the revisions while they were supposed to be sleeping but were really using their crib mattresses as trampolines.

You can find more information about the author, pronunciation guides, and social networking links online at ALSowards.com.